GODS'
GOLD

Author acknowledgments:

The author would like to express deep appreciation to **Robert Dean**, **Neil Freer**, **Laurence Gardner**, **Zecharia Stitchen** for their collective inspiration, courage and dedication to alternative truths. **Steve Filmore** who helped with logistics in Iraq. **Ted Funston** who helped the original manuscript beyond its wounds. And especially to **Donna Prete.** Her help with the manuscript was immeasurable. Moreover, through her generosity, uncompromising effort and unfailing support, she gave so much more. So much so, that it is impossible for me to adequately express my gratitude. Nonetheless, I am eternally grateful.

Much thanks to all!

First published by AuthorHouse 4/18/2011

ISBN: 978-1-4567-6076-2 (e)
ISBN: 978-1-4567-6077-9 (sc)

Library of Congress Control Number: 2011905382

Printed in the United States of America

This book is printed on acid-free paper.

AuthorHouse™
1663 Liberty Drive
Bloomington, IN 47403
www.authorhouse.com
Phone: 1-800-839-8640

For Donna, Forever

Also by Frank Prete:

GORDIAN WEAVE
SECRETS TO NO ONE

GODS' GOLD

A Mystery

BY FRANK PRETE

authorHOUSE®

"The name of the first is the Pishon; it is the one that winds through the whole land of Havilah, where there is gold. And the gold of that land is good…"
-- Genesis 2, 11:12

"…science is an enemy of religion."
--Nicola Bounetti

"…finding the truth is never a foolish search."
--Morgana Barnes

"…as is often the case (with an archaeological find)
the unexpected results even exceed in value those for which we had hoped…"
--Flinders Petrie

"This is all about how we choose to deal with the things we discover. We can either accept the truth of those discoveries, or we can deny those truths."
--Analisa Scotti

IRAQ

OUTSIDE a small village on the outskirts of Mosul, Army Staff Sergeant Mitchell Harrington, II removed his helmet and tossed it on the front seat of his Humvee. There was just a hint of distain staying below the comprehensive interpretation of his movement. The practical gnawing of self pity he refused to display, were greedily devoured by Harrington's own sense of honor and commitment. His pride did not permit him to yield or acknowledge the alternate reality that struggled for recognition.

Since his deployment to Iraq, Harrington learned to command his inner turmoil, as well as his four-man squad, with a balanced sense of detachment and concern. Being responsible for the safety and lives of others, while managing his internal ravages, was something Harrington took seriously. It weighed heavily on him. His rank offered a faith he needed to embrace, as he tried to deny the opposing forces of doubt and peril.

Harrington's muscular frame bore the cumbersome weight of the Army protective gear with relative ease. Protective, yet choking, the gear caused sweat to trail down his face. He disregarded the heat of the desert, but the glare of the sun was beyond his discipline. Harrington unfolded a pair of dark sunglasses and slid them over his eyes. They protected his eyes from the solar assault, concealing any prying inquiry into the true nature of his consciousness that lurked in every prolonged stare.

Private, Hector Solis, along with Ed Dobson and Ed Heywood, were members of Harrington's squad. Harrington assessed his soldiers and categorized them through some remote law of physics. Heywood was an observer with the quick reflexes of a prize fighter. Consequently, Harrington chose him as the driver of the squad's Humvee. Dobson, the tallest of the soldiers, at six feet five inches with broad and sturdy shoulders like a defensive lineman, defaulted to the backup position. The presence of Dobson's mass assured the best kind of reliable support.

Hector Solis was taunt, aggressive and quick. His jabbing attitude was best served as a gunner, manning the M-19 .50 caliber machine gun. Solis and Harrington were just an inch above six feet. Harrington was broader and more muscular to Solis' thinner, wiry frame. Normally fair of complexion, the desert sun had darkened Harrington's complexion matching Solis' natural tone. Beyond their physical appearances, there was a level of necessity Solis provided in the context of war. He represented a galvanizing force running parallel to the true definition of comradeship. It was a brash reality Harrington counted on. Solis had a swaggering rhythm that was defiant of intimidation, yet somehow agreeable to the currents of war. The four men combined to create a single force which was the capstone of guardianship, ensuring a level of security in a hostile environment.

Harrington walked from the Humvee to where the squad leaders were planning a reconnaissance mission. Harrington's physical language displayed a comprehensive philosophy of the impending mission and the military rational.

The area where the four Humvees were parked had been recently occupied by a small US Army force. Harrington and his squad were part of this small force, and used it as a field base command post. The squads were commanded by officers ranging in rank from staff sergeant, two lieutenants and Captain, Eli Hicks. The captain had full command of the four squads.

At six feet, five inches, Captain Hicks was well suited to play point guard for the University of Virginia. After losing a bid to his school's round of the NCAA, Hicks joined the military. His first tour was a four year stint in Afghanistan. Then two years in Iraq. With an extensive background in the military, Hicks was hardened to the ways of war. The long pull of conflict had not worn Hicks down. Conflict, duty and the lure of authority and command, were his first love. His look, rounded by a constantly clenched jaw and stern eyes, was of a man who understood the true nature of his work. He was one with it, propelling his desperate nature.

Groups of towns' people mingled among the soldiers who were part of the larger contingent belonging to Alpha Company, Fifth Army Division. The towns' people appeared weary and not at liberty to display their intolerance of the soldiers' presence. Only through deep restraint did they conceal their true feelings. The mistrust and anger in the peoples' eyes was deep rooted in every passing glance. Fear and displacement resided in the downturn scowl of their lips and rounded shoulders. Some of the men sat hunkered, smoking Turkish cigarettes. The language of their resentment was clearly conveyed in the slightest flick of an ash. Their only motivation was a true liberation, ideal for their manner and culture.

A woman knelt on the hard, dry ground and removed a cloth covering a clay pot. In the pot was a dome of yellowish dough. The women's hands were rough and dry. Her face was leathery and cracked. The absence of her burka was a minor victory in an otherwise desolate struggle.

The woman tore clumps of the dough from the clay pot and stretched them into thin, crude circles. Her hands worked quickly and proficiently. She had been taught the art of baking as a child, and she was convinced it was her purpose by birth. The woman stuck the dough to the inside walls of an ash oven that resembled a hollowed-out tree trunk. The constantly repetitive task kept her occupied and distracted, while keeping a distrustful eye on her surroundings. The strangers in uniforms posed threats to her heritage and culture. More importantly, they threatened the tradition of her bread making.

After a brief time, the woman removed the breads as they became toasted, and placed them on a tattered cloth. The six pieces of bread were her family's meal for the week. Life for her had always been hard. With the presence of an invading force, it had become unreasonable. She still continued her daily routines, trying to keep a semblance of rule and order.

The soldiers also appeared displaced. They were away from home in a place where death was only a whisper away. To combat the constant presence of death, some kicked a ball; a false safety in the illusion of sports. Nonetheless, they were always mindful of the reality that being a soldier was not a sporting event.

"Okay, listen up," Captain Hicks shouted to Harrington and Lieutenants Michael Hart and Donald Farley. His booming voice was filled with command and authority, and did not take into account the noise of the Humvees or any of the silent suspicion around him.

Hicks spread a cloth map on the hood of his Humvee flattening it out. There was something apparitional about the way he touched the map.

"Here's our reconnaissance for today," Hicks said. "We've gotten reports about some yellow and black vehicles. They are the colors of the taxi cabs. Intel has reported the enemy is using yellow and black vehicles for weapons transportation. Sergeant Harrington, you are to go northeast toward Kanisah, but not beyond Tall ash Shawr. Here," Hicks continued, pointing to the towns depicted in red circles.

"Lieutenant Hart, drive around the city proper. You're on a course northwest toward Tahrawah not beyond Darato. Here," Hicks commanded, pointing once more to another spot on the map.

"Now, we need penetration into the southeast. Lieutenant Farley, that's you. Your destination is Khidr Lyas. I'm headed to Dibashah and Arbid. Okay, you all know your destination and operation. Let's get to it," Hicks concluded.

"Captain Hicks, what are our rules of engagement?" Farley asked.

"You are on a reconnaissance mission. That's your main objective. Stop and detain all vehicles painted yellow and black. If you are engaged, then engage with extreme and total force. That means fire on anything. Kill whatever moves or whatever you deem a threat. If it's not a threat, kill it anyway. Okay. Squads move out," Hicks concluded.

Each squad climbed into their respective Humvees and drove out into four directions. Dust clouds from the vehicles, and the roar of their engines, combined to create an aggression common to the country and to the soldiers. There was a severe lack of benevolence exuding from the four vehicles, and the weapons mounted on them. The rolling machinery had come to life with menace and foreboding. The threat was a modern day expression of the mythical Four Horsemen. The forceful cadence of Captain Hicks, the sound of ordinance being clicked into weapons, had also infused the soldiers with cumulative bravado; a blind loyalty to orders and duty. Reconnaissance was the objective, but force was the means and destruction, the only true purpose.

Private Ed Heywood drove the Humvee over the bumpy, unpaved roadway. A layer of dust covered the windshield and seeped inside the vehicle. The bright sun rising behind them was becoming brilliant and scorching. The heat rose up from the road in a wavy texture, blending with the mountains, creating an appearance of melting liquid.

"Hey, Deuce," Solis shouted over the roar of the Humvee's engine. "See out there, I bet there's a lot of bones your archaeology self would love ta dig up."

"Anthropology, Solis. I'm a student of anthropology, not archaeology. I believe I've already explained the difference," Harrington shouted.

"You did. But like I said, same shit. So, you think there's dinosaur bones out here, Deuce?"

"Yes. Some believe Mesopotamia was the cradle of humanity."

"I thought it was Africa where people were startin' ta be born from. Black Eddie here knows that shit."

"Hey, Solis, why do you call Heywood, Black Eddie?" Dobson asked.

"Because you're Eddie too, and you're white. I can't call either of you just Eddie. There's gotta be a different way ta call you."

"So why call him Black Eddie?"

"Cause he's a minority like me, and he won't take it personal. We understand that shit. How would you feel if I called you, honkie Eddie?"

"I'd probably get upset."

"That's why I call him Black Eddie. He's cool. He don't get upset."

The vehicle struggled through the rough terrain, jolting the soldiers. Solis' helmet became dislodged from his head. He let it fall over his eyes as he grabbed for the back of the sergeant's seat.

"Shit, Black Eddie, watch the fuckin' pot holes. They're worse than the ones we got in New York. Damn!"

"Sorry, sergeant," Heywood said.

"Why you sayin' sorry ta the sergeant? Shit, I'm the one almost lost my helmet. Shit! I don't believe this guy. Hey, Deuce, let's get back ta what you said about people being born here in Mesopotamia," Solis continued. "I thought this was Iraq."

"Damn, Solis," Dobson responded. "I thought you had to have at least a high school education to get into the army. How'd you get by, Solis?"

"Don't take much brains ta know how ta kill, does it, Dobson? Seems that's all the education the army wanted me ta have."

Heywood suddenly locked his attention on a vehicle in the distance. Its movement and speed was hardly discernible in the landscape.

"What's that, sergeant?" Heywood said, pointing toward the vehicle in the distance.

"I see it. Stop the vehicle," Harrington ordered.

Heywood applied the brakes, and the Humvee came to a complete stop in a cloud of sand. The soldiers watched the vehicle coming toward them, and reached for their weapons. The sergeant retrieved a pair of binoculars and focused on the vehicle.

"Two vehicles," He observed. "They're coming this way. Moving fast. Solis, man the automatic weapon."

Solis climbed to the top of the Humvee and made ready the Squad's Automatic MK-19 machine gun.

"Hold fire until I give the order," Harrington shouted.

A bright glare reflected off the windshields of both vehicles as they appeared out of the undulating heat. A contrail of sand sprayed from the rear of both vehicles. From a distance, there was no sound to be heard from the vehicles, yet Harrington could sense an anger and danger about them.

"Two vans. Both white," Harrington said. "Not yellow and black. They appear hostile, nonetheless. Dobson, Heywood, deploy from the vehicle," Harrington commanded. "Solis stand ready and open fire on my command."

Only Solis remained with the vehicle, poised with the MK-19. The soldiers had their weapons loaded and positioned to fire. The small combat force understood the true nature of their weapons. They represented a hallowed triumvirate: part golden lyre, part patron statuary, and a metaphysical link to their divinity. Mostly, it was a military-designed scapular bearing a tentative promise of safety and protection.

In the distance, Harrington heard the muffled report of gunfire. The front vehicle began to sway erratically. It was obvious to Harrington it was under attack and performing evasive maneuvers. The gunfire became more rapid and louder as the vehicles drew closer. Harrington knew the hostile skirmish being played out before him was not aimed at him or his squad. Nevertheless, he would retaliate when the approaching vans came to a marker he had visually chosen in the desert.

"Get ready to open fire on my command," Harrington shouted.

The soldiers stood poised. Being combat ready was part of their action, but instinct and survival became their primary impulse.

The vehicles drew closer to the marker Harrington had chosen. The perimeter had not been breached, but it was rapidly being threatened. The sergeant knew the target spot was well within range of the .50-caliber machine gun. He wanted to be certain the M-16s would also have maximum effectiveness.

Harrington became focused on the approaching hostility. Nothing distracted him. The heat was no longer an issue. The sand was non existent; no longer a disturbance. The engine roar from the Humvee was an indistinguishable purr. His mind remained still, focusing only on the distance between the approaching vehicles and the spot he chose for his attack.

"Get ready," he said, measuring each word, stretching them into a portion of the space that was the equation between the speed of the vans and the time it would take to give the command.

The vehicles appeared animated, reluctant to break the visual mark in the sand. Time and distance no longer seemed to be a valid gauge. Suddenly, they became suspended in the landscape. Everything went into an absurd free fall, stretching into surreal movement. Then, in an instant, the vehicles regained their identity and resumed their speed.

The first vehicle made a broad turn off the road and bounced in the rough terrain, moving away from the spot in the desert Harrington had designated. Dust and rocks flew up behind the speeding vehicle. The second vehicle followed, relentless and challenging, as the sound of gunfire became more audible to Harrington.

Making another swift turn, the first vehicle headed back on the road toward the Humvee.

"Steady. Steady." Harrington shouted.

Just as the first van approached the spot Harrington had chosen, it disengaged from all purpose, flipped over and slid, kicking up a thick cloud of dust creating a new reality. The second van came to a screeching halt. Four men jumped from the vehicle and continued shooting at the flipped over van. Three men scrambled out of the disabled van and fired back. One by one, the three men were struck and crumbled to the ground. A misplaced gunshot struck a man from the second vehicle. His arms flailed outward as he crashed to the desert floor. The surviving three men from the second vehicle moved forward and continued shooting. Their position and aggression had breached Harrington's chosen marker igniting his sense of combat.

"Commence firing," Harrington shouted.

Solis engaged the fury and force of the MK-19. Dust obliterated his targets as he fired into the general area. Discharged bullets burst forward at an immeasurable rate. Ejected shells kept pace with his heart rate, as the sound of the weapon muffled his scream. A stream of .50 caliber bullets ripped into one of the men. The bludgeoning force knocked him to the ground, gouging large, bloody chunks of flesh.

Harrington, Dobson and Heywood joined in. The dull ping of their bullets indicated some struck the vehicles. Others sent puffs of sand exploding near the fallen bodies. The surviving two men quickly jumped into their vehicle and drove away. The cloud of dust kicked up by the van obscured it until it totally disappeared into the distant landscape.

"Cease fire!" Harrington commanded. "Cease fire!"

The chase and shooting ended as quickly as it had started. A veil of settling dust began to conceal the vehicle and fallen bodies as if the incident had not occurred. The sounds of exploding ordinance and primal screams faded into the desert.

Dobson looked at Harrington and Heywood, adamant that he had provided the proper backup and support. Solis could not find the strength to open his fists and remove his hands from the weapon's handles. His forearms vibrated from the gun's fury and his own adrenalin. His jaw and teeth ached from being clenched so tightly. The echo in his ears was indistinguishable between the sound of the MK-19 and his own screams.

Harrington gripped his weapon with a delicate force. He squinted over the heated barrel, assessing the carnage that seemed to come from his most wicked dreams. Slowly, he tried to fit the incident into a specific time frame as a reference to reality. But the conditions made the sequence elusive and erratic. He looked up at the sun to chart its movement in the sky from when he first noticed the vehicles. If he could graph the movement, no matter how slight, he could then determine how much time had elapsed. With that as an affirmation, it would prove the incident did take place. But the bright sun remained still and silent, content in its own conspiracy. The only remaining confirmation of the incident was the sounds.

Harrington was sure when the men were struck by bullets or at the instant of their deaths; they must have moaned or cried out. Their cries were the natural laws of human frailty. He knew those sounds had to exist. They were the span from life to death, representing the only positive scale and measure for time. That was the one true reference point that sufficed for Harrington.

Harrington gave the command for the squad to board the Humvee and drive toward the overturned vehicle. As they approached, they heard steam hiss from its engine. Two of the wheels were burning creating a cloud of black smoke and fine, gray dust.

"Heywood, drive around slowly. Get us behind the van for cover and stop," Harrington commanded. "Solis, you remain alert. Assume the vehicle and its inhabitants to be hostile. At the sight of movement, continue aggression."

As Heywood stopped the Humvee behind the van, the squad proceeded slowly and cautiously. Harrington had become acutely familiar with death and recognized it quickly in all the victims. They had each been shot multiple times. Their blood had seeped into the dry sand. He looked into the overturned van and saw the driver slumped over, blood pouring from his head and chest.

"All Arabs," Dobson observed.

"Are they all dead?" Heywood asked as he approached.

"They are," Harrington said.

Solis climbed down from the Humvee and approached the squad. He carried the M-16 and continued aiming at the van.

"What do you think this was all about, Deuce?" Solis asked in a low whisper.

"I don't know, but I want to see what's inside that van."

Harrington walked to the back of the van. The rear door had been torn open and the glass panel window shattered. Heywood and Harrington moved forward shifting rapidly from one side of the van to the other. There was no movement from within the van. It was quiet and still. The only noise came from the steam hissing from the engine. The dark cloud from the burning tires fell slowly but steadily onto the van.

"All clear," Harrington announced.

In spite of the silence, Harrington remained distrustful and stayed alert. The presence of his meager squad maintained a force and exercised a meaningful power. He knew it could all change in an instant. At a quick glance Harrington determined the toppled cargo to be hundreds of gallon-sized sacks. Several sacks were torn open and a white powder spilled from them creating a fine, billowing cloud. Harrington reached in and withdrew one of the torn sacks. He shook some of the white powder from the sack, and then threw the sack to the ground to get a closer look.

"I'll be a lucky son born of a worthy momma," Solis said in dismay. "That shit looks like heroin."

"Do you know what heroin looks like, Solis?" Harrington asked.

"Shit yeah."

"And you believe that to be heroin?"

"Once again, Deuce, shit yeah."

"Dobson, Heywood do you concur with Solis?"

"Not sure, sergeant," Heywood responded. "I've never seen heroin."

"Same holds for me, sergeant," Dobson said.

"Shit, Black Eddie, boy like you from Detroit don't know what heroin looks like?"

"I'm from Chicago, Solis. And yes, I don't know what heroin looks like."

"I think the van is filled with it," Harrington said. "Solis, confirm the cargo of the van is consistent with the contents of this sack. On the double."

Solis handed his weapon to Dobson then jumped into the back of the van. He worked feverishly choosing sacks from different sections of the van. He crawled about oblivious to the heat and the dead body slumped just inches away. One by one, he threw out twelve sacks, and crawled out carrying two more.

"Heywood, open those sacks," Harrington ordered.

Private Heywood withdrew his bayonet and slashed open each sack. The contents of each sack appeared to be the same white powder as the original sacks.

"These too," Harrington said, referring to the sacks Solis was holding.

Solis dropped the sacks that Heywood slashed open.

"Told you, Deuce, that shit's heroin. I bet these dudes were rippin' off those guys that got away."

"They all didn't get away," Dobson observed.

"It's no secret the Taliban is growing and smuggling heroin from Afghanistan, through Turkey, and into all parts of the world," Harrington said.

"Well, even if these guys were ripping off the Taliban, they're way off course," Heywood said.

"Who gives a shit if they're off course. It fell right inta our laps," Solis said. "Ask me, that's right on course."

"Solis, check those men," Harrington ordered, pointing to the dead bodies. "Search them for any intel or identification."

"Shit, Deuce, why me? If those guys are Taliban, they ain't gonna have ID sayin' they are."

"Do it, Solis! Do it now!" Harrington shouted, with more than a hint of authority and rank. "Do it before the sun beats on them a moment longer and you won't be able to get through the stench."

"Yeeees Siiiir," Solis said and walked toward the bodies.

"What are we going to do if this is heroin, sergeant?" Heywood asked.

"I tend to agree with Solis' assessment," Harrington confirmed. "It certainly looks like this group tried to hijack heroin. Or at the very least, it's a drug deal that went bad."

"Is it possible this heroin is the Afghanistan-Turkey connection?" Heywood said

"No way of knowing," Dobson offered.

"If it is, the logistics seem a bit out of place," Heywood said.

"The logistics are very out of place," Harrington commented. "But we have no way of really knowing. You can be certain of one thing; the people in this country are very desperate. They'll do anything for just the necessities of life. Stealing heroin from the Taliban is certainly understandable and worth the risk to them."

"So what are we going to do, sergeant?" Dobson asked.

"What we gonna do?" Solis said from behind Dobson. "We gonna make a nice score. That's what we gonna do."

"Did you uncover anything on those dead men, Solis?" Harrington said.

"Yeah, I uncovered their bodies. They're naked now."

"Solis, I want a straight answer."

"Yeah, I searched them real good, sergeant. Sun didn't need ta beat down on them. They already stunk. Like goat herders. Or just goats."

"Did they have any identification on them?"

"No. Nothin'. That one guy there, the one from the van that drove away. He's sportin' a Russian-made Kalashnikov AK-17. Coulda got it in Afghanistan when the Russians were there."

"Good observation, Solis. Okay. Let's assume for the moment they were Taliban that drove away. And the men in this van did rip them off for the heroin. It's a safe bet those men will regroup, probably get more support and will be coming back here very soon," Harrington observed.

"Okay, then. Let's hurry," Solis said. "We can pack up the heroin and make a fortune off it."

"We're going to do no such thing, Solis," Harrington said angrily.

"Sergeant, you have any idea what this shit's worth? I mean really, this shit's valuable, man. You can't just leave it here."

"I'm not going to leave it here. Heywood, get a can of gas and drench the contents of the van and light it on fire," Harrington ordered.

"Sergeant, you're kiddin'. That shit's valuable," Solis protested.

"Not to me it's not. It's getting destroyed."

"Oh man, I don't believe this shit. No mercenary soldier would be burnin' this shit up."

"Probably not. But we're not mercenary soldiers. And, I expect more from you, Solis. You're not back on the streets of your neighborhood. You're a soldier, and you're in my command. So knock it off. Keep looking toward those mountains. The Taliban, if that's what they were, won't take this loss lightly."

Heywood and Dobson poured gasoline on the contents of the van and the opened sacks lying on the ground. Then Dobson doused the outside of the van.

"All done, sir," Dobson said.

"Okay, torch it," Harrington commanded.

Dobson took pieces of cloth from the van and saturated them with gasoline. He handed one cloth to Heywood and lit it with a cigarette lighter. Heywood dropped his cloth onto the sacks lying outside the van, as Dobson threw his burning cloth into the van. Immediately, fire spread onto the desert floor. The van became angrily engulfed in flames.

The heat of the desert became exaggerated by the burning of the van. Harrington watched the flames bursting out of the broken windows as black billowing smoke rose up. Harrington knew it sent a signal to the men who fled. He knew they would be angered over the loss of their cherished white powder. Resentment would fuel their already enraged hatred. But, Harrington did not concern himself with that possibility. Six men lie dead in the desert; their blood already evaporated into the dry heat and swallowed up by the parched sand. Their blood, an identity as to who they were, no longer existed. It was gone; a universal edict that had become an overabundant commodity in the godforsaken desert.

Harrington remained transfixed on the fire and the death around him. The heat from the scorching sun did not bother him. He didn't feel the sweat gathering under his uniform nor did he feel the need for water. He became aware of the pungent smell of burning heroin and the van's tires. But most of all, he smelled death. It wafted compellingly from the lifeless bodies. For Harrington, the day had become just another crude and remorseless reminder of the true sweep of cruelty. The combined odors intoxicated Harrington. The rancidness surpassed those of the raw sand and the dry beds of the distant Khabur River. The sight of death distorted the backdrop of the beautiful Maqloub Mountains.

"Let's go, Deuce," Solis said quietly over Harrington shoulder. "Let's get out of here before the Taliban come back."

Harrington was immobilized. The sights and smells made him catatonic. He blotted all knowledge from his mind hoping it would be therapeutic. But, there was danger in his trance. If left unchecked, it was an unconditional invitation to the forces of death.

"Come on, Deuce. Let's get outta here," Solis repeated.

Harrington gathered himself, but still could not turn away from the fire and the dead bodies. He saw no nobility in dying for the unholy profit that came from heroin. Consequently, the lifeless men represented a desecration of sorts to him, and the fire was no surrogate as a redeeming baptism.

Finally, Harrington looked off into the distance. There, he saw a lone F-16 fighter jet flying above the distant mountain range. The craft moved effortlessly with deceptive grace. He watched until the jet disappeared into the distance. Harrington continued looking up at the bright blue sky until he saw the sun. Its glaring brightness burned his eyes. Shutting them, the glaring brilliance obliterated the fire and the dead bodies. They were no longer a part of his vision, but somehow, Harrington knew they would always be a part of his memory.

BACK at the base camp, Harrington and his squad set down wearily in the abandoned house they now occupied. The field base on the outskirts of Mosul, in the northern region of Iraq, was nothing more than a mud-plastered box once owned by an Arab family. The current occupants were a band of unwanted American soldiers forcefully exercising their unlawful right of eminent domain.

Inside the house were only the meager remnants of the former owners. A tin table, marred and dented lay on its side. Next to it was a wooden chair, missing one leg. Dangling from the seat of the chair was a shredded, burned cushion. A broken empty drawer, once part of a cabinet, probably held the barest necessity of clothing or the family's prayer books. On the far side of the room, was a large gash in the wall where plumbing might have been torn out by marauders. There was a rusted pail with a missing handle with two large bullet holes in it. Under the pail was a child's worn sneaker. It was pink with no shoe lace. The front of the sneaker was charred and split open revealing a dried spot of blood. A sharp shard stuck up from its soft inside. The shard did not belong to the battered table or wooden chair. It was not glass or tin. The small shard was bone perhaps from the foot of the child who once wore the sneaker. A layer of sand that no amount of sweeping could remove covered the floor. Wind blew from the east, past the distant Mt. Maqloub and across the acrid desert keeping the ocean of dry sand coming like an incessant wave.

A collective strain and fierce silence took hold of the soldiers as they sat with their backs against the walls. The ragged soldiers were tired, wrapped in their own confusing thoughts, largely devoted to the plague of guilt and senselessness that ravaged their humanity. Only Dobson felt at ease knowing his primary function of protecting his fellow soldiers had been his true mission.

Heywood remained guarded and silent, keeping the incident of the day folded close. In a way, he didn't want his actions to be known to anyone outside the small, dry and dusty hut. He acknowledged an alternate sense of reality, which differed from what the army or the world wanted from him. So it all came down to just what he wanted--he wanted his own inner peace.

Solis could no longer feel the vibration in his arms. His jaw and teeth no longer ached but there remained a slight echo in his ears. His legs were folded up and his head hung between his knees. He gathered a hand full of sand and held it in his fist. Slowly, he let the sand fall in a thin strand as if passing through an hour glass.

He kept his eyes on the tiny mound of sand he created. Solis could not evade the struggle between those things that were in his hands to control and those that were not. He saw himself as a temporary instrument, with the potential for right and wrong until the mechanics of his body come to a sudden stop. Whether measured in Roman numerals or shifting sand, the events of the day were a potent reminder all things had their own eventuality. He decided to extricate himself from the involvement in the slaughter of the unidentified men as it would serve him best if the things he attempted in the future were for his higher good.

Harrington felt removed from his squad and the field hut. He began calling into question the archaic tradition of physical combat. He knew it was hard wired into the human experience and fighting didn't have to be taught. War, with all its contrived laws, was written by an industry whose true commodity and commerce was blood. The sounds of the recent skirmish merged with a ghastly confusion creating a sense of absurd authority that resonated through Harrington. It was like the coddled memory of a perverse addiction that consumed him. Harrington didn't take the time to consider if his destiny was chosen for him. He didn't care. He just assimilated to it and adjusted to the hot desert conflict with the legacy of his tortured soul. A sense of ancient mastery, crowned by the bullying of indisputable might made its presence known by defying all hope of fairness.

Harrington became aware he was a bastard-child of the recent skirmish as well as many ancient battles of the area. The sounds of his modern weapons mingled with the ancient battles that echoed in his mind, claiming him for eternity. Cries from the dying bodies his squad left in the desert and those from two thousand years ago were still audible and took turns haunting his memory. He could feel the ghosts of the battle of Carrhae between Crassus, the bully of the Roman Empire, and General Surenas of the Parthian Empire swirling around him. The struggle was played out on the very sand where he left several dead men, a burning van and a poisonous white powder.

Within the uncertainty of time the warriors remained there waiting for him. Through the wind and the sand Harrington could hear Surenas tell him how the warriors of Parthian defeated seven Roman legions with archers on horseback. The defeat, the worst since Hannibal's two hundred years earlier, set the scene for the rise of Islam seven hundred years later. But for General Surenas, the biggest prize was to have Crassus' head cut off. Then his skull filled with gold and put on display in the Parthian Court.

For Harrington, history occurred on many levels. Those he was taught and that which he lived. The history he recalled went back to his grandfather, Lucas Harrington, a small soy bean farmer in Arizona. Harrington remembered spending summers on his grandfather's ranch. It was a quiet life with an undercurrent of discipline and toil. Waking early to plow, tilling and harvesting was endured with measured struggle and silent complaint. Harrington recalled seeing the old man not as a farmer, but more as a soldier; locked all his life in tiring combat with the elements and the earth. It was a constantly shifting battle. His grandfather attacked the earth and the earth yielded only what it wanted. In the end it all came full circle. His grandfather claimed the earth for an eternity, and the earth allowed him to lay claim to a portion of it--six feet.

It was a soldier's effort fortified by discipline, but the only violence was the occasional slaughter of a chicken, Cornish hen or spring lamb. In fact, it was Harrington's grandmother, Lucille LaToit, who slaughtered the animals. Her lineage was traced back to the Huguenots. She was a descendent from French Protestants, whose quiet stillness was the reference point for everything that happened on the farm. Harrington could recall how she would approach a passive lamb and slit the animal's throat, using a large knife with an ebony handle. She would hold the animal still against the ground until it bled out. There was no emotion to her actions, nothing that could be traced to a vile nature. It was just firm stillness that caused everything to submit to her will. Perhaps imprinted into her DNA was the unacceptable slaughter of her Huguenot forebears that caused her to equate necessity with retribution.

His grandmother was constantly aware of the reformist clan to which she was part. It was also the ingrained knowledge of the clan's punishment for the righteous opposition to the Catholic doctrine that fermented within her. Perhaps it was the centuries-old brutality that echoed in her cells and gave rise to her dogged consciousness. But there was no revolutionary banner under which his grandmother rallied. She was a woman of immediate necessity and insisted on her family's survival. But Harrington was convinced, if his grandmother would have been alive the day of the St. Bartholomew's Massacre, all those unfortunate Huguenots would not have been killed. Harrington could envision a young Lucille LaToit defeating the Vatican-sponsored forces that day. Moreover, he could see the young LaToit entering Vatican City slicing the throat of Pope Gregory XIII, the instigator of the slaughter, in the same manner she applied to the gentle spring lambs.

His father, Mitchell Harrington, Sr. was an accountant; a man who dealt with numbers and balance sheets. But more to the point, he was a man who gave up before the end. If all that could be measured in one's life were the amount of finances amassed, then this was the stature the son assessed of his father. No gallant struggles or movements of reform were ever attributed to him. The elder Harrington's heritage seemed to come from a line of church goers who lived by a set of stifling laws designed for the sole purpose of emasculation.

Consequently, Harrington knew his gene pool was from the Huguenots, and perhaps from the Parthian general. He believed his tribal bloodline to be so fierce; the only compensation for gallantry was crowned victory.

Harrington allowed the recent skirmish and the ancient battle of Carrhae to fade from him. He turned to Solis who appeared to be bearing his personal sense of dejection with a resilient defiance. The relaxed swagger of Solis was so entrenched in him that all the hours of standing at attention could not erase it from his muscle memory. There was reliability in the language of his movements that expressed itself when he rested. It was a specific dialect, germane to the nuances of his authority and insolence. Solis' brashness was not just under his skin, it infiltrated the air around him. Perhaps it was the byproduct of his youthful impoverishment that molded his attitude, or more likely, a shared ancient ancestry with Harrington's. But Harrington knew there were unexplained mysteries in life. Solis was one such mystery. The more Harrington got to know Solis, the more he began to realize the Bronx youth needed to legitimize his own need for aggression and assuage his street-born rancor.

Solis was a product of his environment. Of his own admission, it was a blend of the tough streets and the constant violence between his mother and father that gave him his edginess. He lived in a small apartment with his parents and three siblings. The walls of the Bronx project dwelling closed in on him. The closeness was caused by something insurmount-able, something other than his family living in the three small rooms. It was faceless, but with form that Solis knew to be alive, fire-breathing, flesh eating and spirit-breaking. The lack of space carried weight that was suffocating to Solis. Compounding the attack of claustrophobia were the small, narrow hallways of the project, putrid with the thick smells of foods fried in rancid oils. The molecular structure of the air mutated to a viscous mass clogging the pathway and stairwells and inhibited Solis' ability to breath. A yellow cloud constantly shrouded overhead lights confirming the air was being overtaken by pollutants.

Solis knew he had to escape the confines of the apartment complex. Prison was the next logical progression, but not an option he wanted to encounter. Through a strange churning of events, the army seemed to be the perfect venue for his predicament and inclination. The army offered a sense of freedom and space through worldwide travel. The world was a big enough place for Solis to stretch out in. A vastness where every sound ever made could go and their echoes repeat forever. A world with a horizon that was not visible from any other vantage point on earth.

In spite of the vast differences in backgrounds and culture, Harrington recognized the commonality between himself and Solis. He cautiously entertained a level of trust and understanding for the streetwise Solis.

The blistering sun and constant dry heat of the desert made Solis' crav-ing for water greater than that of any drug addict he remembered from his Gun Hill Road neighborhood. There were no apologies to be found in the dense air or the dry heat. Solis held a mouth full of water before swallowing. He looked around the field base house. It was square, not much larger than a good sized Gaylord Box. The windows on either side of the house had been blown out. The outside walls were pockmarked with bullet holes.

The house was much smaller than Solis' three room apartment. Yet somehow it appeared larger. Perhaps it was because it was one open room, unlike the apartment's compartmentalized rooms. Or perhaps Solis was taken in by the illusion of scale. When he stood by the door and looked to the north, he could see Turkey.

No matter what the size, Solis had co-ownership of the house. The former tenants were gone, forcibly evicted without regard for the disruption to their lives. No matter how small and confining his three-room apartment on Gun Hill Road in the Bronx had been, Solis knew if anyone attempted to forcibly take it over he would die defending it. Perhaps the former owners tried valiantly to defend their meager property. But it didn't matter because Solis knew, just by looking around, they failed miserably.

The house ultimately had been deserted before the soldiers had arrived.

But Solis knew better. He knew the house was not deserted. It was dead, killed by the bullets that left the awful holes in its mud packed walls.

Before Solis finished the bottle of water, he poured some into his hand, and then splashed it on his face. In spite of the minor flush, the grit remained embedded in his pores, and the wrinkled skin of his forehead. His eyelashes and brows remained gray from the sand. His whole body was hot and sticky; chafed in every joint and fold. Sand had gotten into his boots and was grinding between his toes. He removed his boots and the thick cotton socks.

"Fuckin' sand," he said shaking it from his socks.

"Here," Harrington said, handing Solis another bottle of water.

Solis took the bottle of water and dumped it on his feet.

"My feet are so damn hot, the water's sizzlin'."

Harrington unscrewed his own bottle of water and took a long, deep swallow.

"Hey, Deuce" Solis said. "Why couldn't we get based in the middle of the city where they got those nice palaces? Can't deal with this shit out here in the country."

"They've got sand in the palaces too, Private Solis. And just in case you didn't know it, the sun is just as hot there as it is here. Besides, away from the city is safer. Who knows what danger is lurking in the alleys there. Just be glad you have plenty of water. That's most important."

"Tell you, Deuce," Solis says. "I wish sand was worth somethin'. I'd package this shit and sell it for a good profit. Bet on that shit."

"Forget it, Solis. If sand was valuable, your government, and those no bid corporations wouldn't allow you anywhere near it," Dobson said.

"That's fine with me. If I live five more life times I ain't never want ta see sand again. The heat too. Damn! When I get outta here I'm gonna live in Alaska. Sleep in my shorts. No blanket, with the windows all open and shit. I never wanna feel heat like this again."

"Tell me, Solis, have you ever visited the Bahamas, or any Caribbean island?" Harrington asked.

"No. Why"?

"I have. I've visited the Caribbean many times. They have sand there, too. The sun is also very hot. You walk in the sun, let the sand ground into your feet and guess what? It's fine. It's okay. It's even fun. The sun doesn't bother you there. The sand is no problem."

"Yeah, so what you tryin' to say?"

"I'm saying it's all a matter of perspective."

"You tryin' ta make me feel better, Deuce? Because I gotta tell you, your shit ain't workin'. It's makin' me feel worse."

"I'm just trying to give you perspective."

"What, like I'm supposta think this desert is the garden spot of Eden? Fuck that shit. In the Caribbean, you get ta wear shorts all day. You get hot, you jump inta whatever blue ocean water they got there. You dry and thirsty, you need somethin' ta drink, some poor native boy brings you somethin' cold ta drink. The glass is filled with ice and got a tiny umbrella on it. Even the fat, plump cherry in the drink sits in the shade under that little umbrella. It ain't the same, Deuce. It ain't the same."

"No. No, it's not. I'm just trying to fortify a positive visualization for you. That's all."

"Positive visualization? What's that supposta be a sergeant's job? That what they teach you in military school?"

"If you want to see it in those terms."

"You know Deuce, you been in the army too long. Either that or the army bought your soul."

"We're in the army, and we're in Iraq, Solis, remember? Here we don't have souls," Dobson said.

Dobson tapped his helmet on the floor to shake loose the sand lodged inside it. He proceeded to pour water into the helmet and on the red and black bandana that had been tied around his head. He unfolded the bandana and wiped his face and neck. The remainder of water he used to saturate the back of his head.

"You okay, Private Dobson?" Harrington asked.

"Yes sir. Just tired," Dobson responded breathing heavily.

"You ain't hot?" Solis asks.

"That too," Dobson responded.

"What do you think about what the staff sergeant here trying' ta tell me? He says it's hot in the Caribbean too. Like that's supposta not make it hot here. I don't get it."

"It's called perspective through diversion."

"I don't care what you call it. It all says the same shit. It's hot here."

"Perspective, Solis. Perspective."

"So what now? You tryin' ta tell me this heat's like a three card Monty hustle? The sucker may not find the card he's bettin' on, but sure as shit, that card is still there; one of the three."

"Well, okay if you want to make that analogy. It's still all about diversion. You're focused on trying to find the card you bet on, so you don't think about the other two. It's a trick of the mind. You think about the Caribbean, which is the one card, the betting card. Consequently, you forget Iraq, the other two cards. The diversion cards. Get it?"

"Only thing I get is if you start believin' this place is the Caribbean, you let up, you lose your edge. When you let up around here, you die. Simple as that. That's the right perspective. The only perspective with no diversion. So if it's all the same ta your sorry ass, I'll keep my eye on the one card I'm bettin' on."

The roar of Humvees shook the house making the sand on the floor jump. The guttural and primal sound was ominous and intimidating, like hate and sin. The soulless sound of the vehicles was a reminder to Harrington of the carnage his squad had recently inflicted.

"Does any of this make sense to you, Solis?" Harrington shouted trying to dismiss the sounds of the Humvees and the memory they jarred.

"The only thing that makes sense ta me, Deuce, is just two more months of this shit and I'm outta here. Goin' home. Sit my glad ass on Gun Hill Road and not move for a year."

"I thought you were going to Alaska," Dobson said.

"Yeah, that's where I'm goin'. Hey, Deuce, you getting' outta here soon too. Goin' back ta your civvy life. Goin' back to your archaeology."

"I was studying to be an anthropologist, Hector," Harrington responded.

"Well, you still dig up dinosaur bones and shit, whatever you do."

"No."

"No? What you mean, 'no'?" I see that shit on television. That's why you like this desert. You can dig up bones."

"I'll make it simple for you, Solis, because I know you're really interested. The excavation and study of fossil bones and artifacts is archeology. Anthropology is the study of man and his relation to his origin, his environment and his culture. Anthropology, get it?"

"Same shit. You gotta dig up bones anyway, right?"

"Let's go Solis. Focus. As you said, this isn't the Caribbean."

"I know this ain't the Caribbean," Solis said, as he poured more water on his feet. "Thing is, I haven't figured out what this place really is. The only thing I know is that this place ain't got what ta eat."

"What does that mean, 'aint't got what to eat'?" Dobson asked.

"It's a sayin'. It comes from my neighborhood."

"Your neighborhood, the Bronx, New York, Gun Hill Road, right?

"That's it Dobson. You heard me say it before, Gun Hill Road. Gun Hill Road takes care of business."

"I bet it does. I also bet Gun Hill Road doesn't have a family named Dobson living there."

"What you tryin' ta say? It's a neighborhood filled with poor, minority people. Run down and shit?"

"No, I'm not trying to say anything of the sort."

"Then what? You never saw a Hispanic family in your home town in Utah? How 'bout blacks then? You musta seen Hispanics, or a token black family. You know, one of us was probably cleaning your house or tendin' ta your horses."

"It's not what I meant, Solis. I was just saying that you seem to come from a tough neighborhood."

"There you go again. Now you're sayin' everybody in my neighborhood carried a gun or a knife. You probably think we killed people for a pastime sport."

"Come on, Solis, get off it. That's not what I'm saying at all and you know it."

"Well, you're right anyway. White boy like you in my neighborhood, we'd womanize you."

"And what does that mean?"

"Means just what it says."

"Well, then in that case, Solis, you're right. White boy like me knows that everybody in your neighborhood carries a gun or a knife and kills innocent people for sport. So, I'll just stay in my Utah neighborhood. There they kill people with Bible spewing, plain ordinary brimstone preaching, God fearing tel-Evangelism."

"See, Dobson, I always knew we had somthin' in common. Your kind kills in a different way. I guess your Evangelists like killin'. It's just the sight of blood they don't like. So, I guess you might say we're brothers of a sort. Except your papa's got more money than mine."

"Perhaps so, but you have the better looking sister."

"That ain't no lie. But trust me brother Dobson, she'd slice you up real good if she had ta."

"If that's the case, then let's just forget it, Solis. I don't want to be part of your family if your sister is going to treat me so poorly."

"So tell me, Solis, I'm curious, what does 'ain't got what to eat' mean?" Harrington asked.

"I'll tell you what it means because I really know you're interested, sergeant. Let's say you got ta fight a guy for somthin', your homies will say 'that guy ain't got what ta eat'. Shit means the guy can't punch, or he don't have balls. Nothin'. Or if you make it with a girl. Guys would say she 'ain't got what to eat'. Means she ain't got what ta eat. Not good lookin', no tits, no ass, nothin'."

"So, it's a weakness, if a guy ain't got what to eat?" Dobson said.

"Yeah, if you want ta put it like that. It's a weakness, a handicap. But it goes beyond that. A guy ain't got what ta eat if he can't figure things out in my neighborhood. Knowin' shit is the best chance a guy's got ta survive on the streets. And that comes from readin' the streets. Streets got a text all their own. A guy's got it or he don't. He survives or he ain't got what ta eat."

"So where did it come from. Who came up with that saying?" the sergeant asked.

"There was this homeless guy in the neighborhood. Jesus was his name. That's pronounced 'HAY SUSE' to you, Dobson..."

"I get it, Solis."

"He lived around in hallways of the housin' projects. Sometimes the priests of the church there, Mt. Carmel, would let him sleep in the rectory or the school. Not the high school, not Evander Childs. That place was all barbed wired up and shit. It was like maximum security. Mt. Carmel had a school there on Gun Hill Road. They'd let poor Jesus sleep there sometimes. I think they gave him clothes, too. But, I was a kid and always remember the poor bastard walking around, dirty, mumblin', and dribblin'. But, I'll say one thing; the poor bastard never bothered nobody..."

"Sounds like no one helped him either," Dobson interrupted.

"Get over yourself, Dobson. My mama would always give the poor guy somthin' ta eat. Drop off some change ta him when she would see him panhandlin' at the IRT station when she went ta work. Believe me, Dobson, that change my mother gave him was her lunch."

"Sounds like a nice woman. On second thought, Solis, with a nice mother like that I'll be your brother. I'll be part of your family and make sure your sister never has a knife in her hands when she's near me."

"My mother will treat you good and shit as long as you don't fuck with her. If you do, she'll hurt you quicker than my sister. Anyway, she came home from work one night. It was cold, windy, snowin'; she brought Jesus home ta sleep in my house. Poor bastard stayed washin' in the tub for two hours but still didn't get clean..."

"Solis, stay on point," Mitchell interrupted. "Are you going to tell us where that saying came from?"

"How smart you gotta be ta figure it out, Deuce? It came from Jesus. The homies would always see him in the street and shit and ask him what he had ta eat that day. Not that they cared. Jesus had nothin'. But, trust me, if he came inta some change they'd take it from him just because they could. Anyway, when they asked him what he had ta eat for the day, he'd always say, 'I ain't got what ta eat'. It went around the neighborhood. You know, like a joke gets around. I always remember somebody sayin' it as a kid. It became part of the urban folk lore."

"The grand colloquial philosophy of a hungry, homeless Jesus Christ," Harrington said.

"Yeah, if you wanna make it out ta be that."

"Do they still use that saying in your neighborhood?" Dobson inquired.

"I don't know. I haven't been home in a while."

"So, it seems to me, Solis," Dobson continued, "you've made Jesus famous by keeping alive his saying and passing it along to us."

"Dobson, you been livin' in white America too long. Ain't nothin' famous about a hungry, homeless Latino. They found Jesus dead on the street one Christmas Day morning. Jesus was supposta be born on Christmas, not die on it. The police came, took him away. Nobody came ta see him, nobody cried for him. My mother was the only one missed him. So, you can fuck the idea of famous."

"You seem melancholy talking about him now, Solis," Harrington observed.

"Bullshit, Deuce. All I'm melancholy about is the life I traded on Gun Hill Road for this sand filled hell. And yeah, Jesus, somehow he was part of what was good on Gun Hill Road. Don't matter what you white guys think about my tough, poor neighborhood, there was some good shit went down there. Good people lived there. Not famous people, just good people. So Deuce, what do you say, let's do what we gotta do here. Let's get this shit *all* over with, whatever it is we gotta get over with, so maybe the poor screwed over people of this country can have their fuckin' neighborhoods back."

The soldiers fell quiet and introspective once again. Harrington knew Solis' rant was prophetic. Webbed in the sensibility was a world that could not provide enough reason for the absurdity that war creates peace. In the end, war creates orphans and regret. Ultimately, it creates stillness and dust. Harrington noticed Heywood had remained silent, agonizing over his own disillusionments. He knew the skirmish, and the war in general had claimed his optimism. Heywood could not keep that a secret. Harrington picked up his head and looked toward Mt. Maqloub and the space in between where the battle of Carrhae had been fought. Nothing had changed. It seemed to Harrington nothing was going to change. The amplified voices from every battle that had ever been fought there, absorbed into every grain of sand. It all became an endless inspiration to the gods of catastrophe.

He looked at the small, bloody sneaker that once belonged to a little girl. All that was left of her was a shard of bone, and probably her crying voice that was still swirling out there. Harrington could not allow himself to listen for the unknown girl's voice. Nor could he listen to the cries of six recently killed Arabs or even General Surenas. It was all too much for him to bear. He knew at another time he would hear the anguish in their voices again. They were sure to cry out for mercy and justice within his evilest dreams.

"You're right about one thing, Hector," Harrington finally said softly still looking forlornly at the tiny sneaker.

"Yeah? What's that, Deuce?"

"This place," Harrington said.

"What about this place?" Solis questioned.

"This place ain't got what to eat."

COPENHAGEN

THE morning sun burned away the last remnants of dawn mist that shrouded the ocher roof tops of the Niels Bohr Institute. The row of tan buildings absorbed the emerging sunlight as soft shadows formed from the many aligned dormers. There was nothing unusual about the start of the day. A steady flow of cars drove past the Institute at a moderate pace, as a cyclist pedaled easily, keeping pace with the cars. A long French baguette bread stuck out of the nap sack strapped to the cyclist's back. A street sweeping truck sprayed water along the curb as the two large bristle sweepers gathered the debris and liter.

There was a balanced lull to the morning that the passing cars and the street cleaning machine could not disturb. A soft breeze blew in from the Baltic Sea giving the air a salty freshness. The sky, a brilliant blue, held a promise that judgment had been postponed indefinitely.

The Institute, founded in 1921, was named after theoretical physicist, Niels Bohr. Bohr had made fundamental contributions to understanding atomic structure and quantum mechanics. For his efforts, he received the Nobel Prize in physics. During the German occupation of Denmark, Bohr narrowly escaped arrest by the German police by traveling to Sweden. He then traveled to London, finally winding up in New Mexico at the top secret Los Alamos Laboratory. There he worked on the Manhattan Project. Because of his controversial ideas regarding the sharing of nuclear research with the Russians, he drew the wrath of Franklin Roosevelt and Winston Churchill. After the war, Bohr returned to Copenhagen spending the rest of his life advocating the peaceful use of nuclear energy.

The Niels Bohr Institute continued to be the center of developing disciplines for atomic physics, quantum physics and other sciences. Over the years, the Institute took great strides in understanding and exploring the core nature of these sciences. To enhance that goal, the Niels Bohr Institute had partnered with Brookhaven National Laboratory in the United States. The laboratory, at Brookhaven, was basically the research arm of the Bohr Institute specializing in nuclear physics research.

Unlike the contributing laboratories at Brookhaven, the Bohr Institute did not boast of its own police station, fire department and postal zip code. The Niels Bohr Institute was much smaller in scope, but not overshadowed in prestige.

A bright blue Honda Hybrid was parked in front of one of the Niels Bohr Institute buildings. Thomas Swenson unbuckled the seat belt pulling it away from his rumbled jacket. Adjusting his plastic framed glasses and patting down his long unruly hair, he drew an exacerbated grin from his wife, Michele, who sat next to him. Swenson absently returned a smile as he felt his shirt pocket for a pen.

Originally born in the United States, Swenson attended Cubberly High School in Palo Alto, where he played first board on the chess team. At the National Science Fair in Albuquerque, New Mexico, Swenson, just in his teens, won the Hertz Engineering Scholarship. He went on to receive a Bachelor of Science, Summa Cum Laude from Harvard University placing within the top five of his physics class. It was at Berkeley Radiation Laboratory at the University of California, where he received a Ph.D. While at Berkeley, Swenson met Michele Livingstone, who was studying theoretical physics. Her main interest was the study of gravity and electromagnetism. When Michele met Swenson, she began to understand magnetism and the effects of gravity on completely different levels. Their courtship was brief. After only three weeks, Swenson proposed to Michele. One year later, they were married. The newlyweds continued their scientific endeavors sharing insights. They gained greater knowledge and deeper concerns regarding the anthropogenic cause of global warming. They found it easier to deal with their concerns as they had hopes of contributing positively in finding solutions to the problems affecting mankind's future.

As the years passed, they became concerned over the launch in the Autumn of 1997, of the Cassini-Huygens space probe. During an interview on a local television news station, Michele called attention to the probe, explaining it carried plutonium for use by its radioisotope thermoelectric generator. Her concern was, if fuel should somehow be dispersed into the environment, the results would be catastrophic to all of mankind. In spite of the opposition, which included numerous letters sent to NASA, the probe launched.

Two days after the interview, Michele became dizzy. She visited her doctor who confirmed she was two months pregnant. Michele was stunned over the news. Swenson was so excited; he went out and purchased a small telescope for his child's introduction to astronomy. The pregnancy was difficult for Michele. She was constantly ill, and in the final trimester, she would need complete bed rest. Three weeks prior to her due date, Michele began to hemorrhage. Swenson rushed her to the hospital. After several tense hours, Swenson was told by the attending physician, Michele had lost the baby.

Swenson was disturbed to see Michele frail and vulnerable. She was exhausted from the ordeal and her complexion was pale, accentuating the redness of her eyes. Her gentle, beautiful features were distorted by the physical pain and emotional anguish. He put his arms around her and hugged her gently. There was an uncontrollable trembling through her body.

"I lost the baby," she said between sobs. "I lost the baby."

Swenson wiped the tears from her eyes. He gently brushed her hair away from her forehead and kissed her.

"Is that what the doctor said?" Swenson asked.

Michele was momentarily confused by the question.

"What do you mean?" she asked

"Is that what the doctor said, 'you lost the baby'?" Swenson whispered.

"Yes. Yes. I believe I heard him say that."

"No. You didn't lose the baby, Michelle. You had nothing to do with it. The doctor's terminology was poor and insensitive. You did not lose the baby. We'll try to find another explanation. One that will make sense. But, I will not hear it was of your doing."

Swenson remembered holding Michele the entire night. They remained silent, her hopelessness too new and too deep to be approached with words. Not long after Michele left the hospital, she regained some of her strength. A memorial service was held for their son, Zachary Michael Swenson. Michele didn't analyze the loss, nor did she try to find a reasonable explanation. She tried to hold it within a scientific context. She reasoned, with global warming and the possible threats of more Cassini-Huygens-like probes, the world and its climate may not hold much future for humanity. Michele felt optimistic by nature, but it was that pessimistic logic that helped heal her grief.

After its launch, there was no more attention they could bring to the Cassinni-Huygens probe. They remained outspoken regarding the threat of global warming and became advocates of alternative fuel sources and ways to conserve energy. This became their focus and passion. Having another child was not in their plans.

Five years after their marriage, Swenson's parents returned to their homeland of Denmark. Within three days of their arrival, they were in a serious car accident. Swenson's father sustained permanent damage to both legs and was confined to a wheelchair. His mother lost her right arm, and the sight in one eye.

Upon hearing the news, Swenson boarded a plane and flew to be with his parents. Before leaving, he told Michele he did not know when he would return. The next day Michele listed their home with a real estate agent. She told the agent she would be in contact from their new address in Denmark.

When Michele arrived in Denmark, she advised her husband of her decision to sell the house and take up residence in Denmark. She explained to Swenson her decision was a matter of physics. She described how electrons travel in discrete orbits around the atom's nucleus, which became the metaphor for her reality. As she explained it to Swenson, he understood her reasoning

Michele handed Swenson his eyeglass case and brushed the hair away from his eyes.

"Thank you," Swenson said, as he took the case from Michele.

"Now you should have everything," she said.

"Yes," he said looking in his briefcase. "I have more than I need. I don't know how paper accumulates. Paper has a reproductive system all its own."

"Why don't you have your secretary transcribe all the paperwork to your laptop?"

"I have almost everything in my laptop or my computer at work. It's just that I had printed out a report that I needed to go over last night. I really need that report for my meeting today."

"Which report?"

"The one we've been working on for…ah, this one…here it is" he said removing a folder marked 'Au' at the top. Beneath, in smaller type: 'A.K. Barnes, U.S.A.' I need these reports."

"What are they?" Michele asked.

"Findings from testing that Nicola Bounetti and I have been working on. Actually there are two. One I worked with Nicola, the second I've done on my own. A miner from Arizona sent us a sample of the material he mined."

"What did he send? What was the material?"

"I want to discuss it with Nicola first."

"Okay, can you tell me why the miner sent you this material?"

"His name is Alex Barnes. According to his correspondence, he sent the material to laboratories in the US but was not satisfied with their conclusions. He obviously knows of our advanced testing methods and trusts our findings will be conclusive."

"You're vague, Thomas. Is the material dangerous?"

"No. Of course not. Why do you ask?"

"Because you appear to be afraid of it," Michele suggested.

"Nonsense," Swenson responded with forced conviction.

"You're not convincing," Michele observed.

"I'm sorry. I don't mean to be vague. I'll talk to you about it tonight."

Swenson opened the door of the Honda and stepped out into the sunlight. He carried his briefcase in one hand with the report tucked securely under his other arm. He walked briskly, his jacket hanging in disarray over his shoulders.

SWENSON stood by the window of his office, in the Geophysics Building, looking out at the Elysian green grass. Edging the grass was a double row of yellow daffodils and red chrysanthemum that surrounded two recently planted silver firs. The groundskeeper stood watering the plants and trees. The colors were brilliant, with an order to their opposing shades and textures. Swenson watched as two common starlings landed on one of the fir trees. He liked the song of the starling, and opened the window to hear them more clearly. Suddenly, a common chiffchaff flew into the same tree causing the starlings to fly away.

Turning from the window, he sat at his desk and ran his fingers along the edges of the report. He knew the empirical findings of the report were potentially explosive. It cautioned his scientific mind to proceed with analytical assurance.

There was a soft knock at the door diverting his attention from the small interactions outside his window, and the random thoughts in his head. He turned as Nicola Bounetti entered.

"Good morning, Thomas," Bounetti said. "Sorry I'm late."

"That's alright, Nicola. Actually I was going to call you last night to discuss the report instead of meeting this morning. But it was very late."

Bounetti looked outside Swenson' office before closing the door. A hint of suspicion carved into his dark eyes. Two inches taller than Swenson, with a stocky frame, his appearance was neater, his clothes expensive.

Bounetti removed his jacket and placed it neatly on the coat rack. He joined his colleague at the desk where the two scientists were seemingly bound by science, and the world of discoveries.

"I saw Michele driving away," Bounetti said. "How is she feeling?"

"She's doing well, thank you. How is Lucia?"

"She's well. We're planning a trip to Italy. We're visiting our families. Lucia's mother's health is failing. My mother is not doing so well herself. They are both getting on in years. There are many cousins still there. Every time we go back home, we make it a point to see all the relatives. Family is the only constant one can be sure of. Science has not yet discovered a better model, theoretical or otherwise. Italian families are legendary for that. Someday I hope to show it's a genetic trait among my clan," Bounetti said.

Bounetti had been born in Calabria, Italy. Before joining the staff at the Niels Bohr Institute, he worked at the State University in New York at Stony Brook and at Padua and Bologna Universities. The Italian scientist's main scientific field was population genetics and evolutionism. As a population geneticist, Bounetti had been working on several aspects of human genetic variation. His focus led him to a theory that statistical comparison of patterns of genetic and linguistic variations showed language differences may have contributed to reproductive isolation, and hence, promote genetic divergence between ancient populations.

Bounetti's studies suggested the amount of DNA differentiation among human populations failed to account for most of the existing patterns of genetic variation. His DNA studies focused on genetic characterization of ancient human populations, such as Paleolithic, Cro-Magnoid and the Neolithic. The more Bounetti studied, the more he knew there was a great deal more to learn about the origins of mankind. A recent archaeological model termed demic diffusion for early migration also fascinated him. It suggested civilizations of antiquity either displaced or intermixed with a pre-existing population for the spread of agriculture across Neolithic Europe. But, Bounetti felt it was something more than intermixing or displacement that assisted in the spread of ancient agriculture.

It was because of Bounetti's work, and the major implications resulting from it, that Swenson thought he would make the perfect research partner for the A.K. Barnes study. It was also because Swenson had complete trust in his colleague.

The Italian scientist opened his briefcase and removed the report. The identification on his report was the same as the one on Swenson's: "Au" followed by "A.K. Barnes, U.S.A." He placed the report on the table.

"Okay. Now for the report," Swenson said opening his folder. "The sample provided by Mister Alex Kenneth Barnes from Arizona, USA. I will go through my findings. If yours differ from mine, we can discuss it point by point."

The screen on Swenson's computer flashed to a row of tiny icons. He brought the cursor to one icon titled "BARNES." He double clicked on the icon and waited for the screen to display the spreadsheet. The spreadsheet depicted a graph with multiple colored headings. The first heading was marked "Cumming Micro." The second was labeled "Diffraction Micro." The third, "Fluorescent Micro," and the last heading "Spectroscopy."

Swenson drew the cursor highlighting the first three headings. He double clicked and another screen opened.

"Now this is the first sample submitted by Barnes. In total weight, the sample was slightly more than fifty-six grams."

"Not a great deal of matter," Bounetti commented. "Barnes did not mention in his correspondence if he had more."

"I suspect he's being extremely protective of the material. Or, he just doesn't know what the material is."

"He must suspect something about the material. Why else go through all the trouble of reaching out to us and sending the sample?"

Swenson flipped open the folder on his desk and used it as a reference.

"As you are aware, before spectroscopy testing, three other tests were performed," Swenson said. "Note the three tests I've highlighted on the screen. Let's coordinate them to the report. I prefer to take all three and refer to them as one group. The first was Cumming microscopy, then diffraction microscopy and finally, fluorescent microscopy. The three sets of testing showed the sample was iron, silicon and aluminum. Proceeding to emission spectroscopy, the findings are much different."

Swenson clicked on another icon. The screen with the three headings brushed across the screen as though being blown by wind. The computer gave off a wind sound to correspond to the data being closed out as an electronic voice said "goodbye". He placed the cursor on the heading marked, "spectroscopy", and double clicked the section. Instantly another graph of yellow, red and blue bars appeared. Each colored bar corresponded to a legend in the lower right corner of the screen. The bars were stepped in varying heights extending to the end of the graph. Text and formulas were prominent, along with the colored bars and crowded each column of the graph.

"This is where it gets very interesting," Swenson continued. "The material was placed on a tray. A single carbon electrode sheathed in argon gas was placed into the Barnes sample. A second carbon electrode, it too sheathed in argon gas, was placed above it. The argon gas was used obviously to keep oxygen away. Once the carbon electrodes were in place, a DC arc was struck. The elements ionized giving specific light frequencies…"

"As indicated on the graph labeled fifteen seconds," Bounetti said, pointing to a blue column on the computer screen.

"Yes. The printout is not as clear as the representation on the screen."

"It's fine."

"Okay. So, after fifteen seconds the only reading that showed on the scope was electronic gas. Clearly that criterion was not enough time to produce any significant finding. Keeping the DC arc in place for more time was the answer. By doing so, eighty-five percent of the reading came after ninety seconds. That is the critical time frame. So after the ninety seconds, fractional vaporization began to develop. When the elements began to burn off, all the colors were correct as were all the oxidation potentials."

"Yes. Yes. Then at one point the color spectrum turned to forest green as indicated here," Bounetti said, pointing to the computer screen.

"Yes...and alas.....Forest green...monoatomic gold," Swenson whispered as though astonished by an ancient secret discovery.

Both men paused. There was a stunned silence to their collective gaze that was commanded by the screen. A sacred oracle pulsated in the color fields of information that laid claim to their respect and awe.

"Now," Swenson finally said. "I did something else. I went a step further," Swenson found his excitement difficult to conceal.

As Swenson closed down the screen, the visually designed wind blew the graph away with a whooshing sound. Once more the electronic voice said "goodbye". He returned to the desktop icons and clicked on another icon marked 'BARNES TWO" The screen went to another graph displaying one heading: "Thermo-Grav". Swenson handed a second folder to Bounetti.

"Here, I think you will find this extremely interesting. First, I want to apologize for conducting these experiments without you present. I was uncertain of the outcome. Clearly, if you disagree with my findings, please feel free to conduct your own experiments. In fact, I encourage it. Please feel free to double check my work."

Bounetti took the folder from Swenson and began reading it.

"Maybe it's because I'm insecure of my own findings. Or perhaps, I'm afraid of them," Swenson continued.

"Why should you be either?"

"You'll see at the conclusion of my presentation."

Swenson aligned the papers in his folder and synchronized them with the information on the screen. He was so engrossed in the highly refined work, at times he felt lost or consumed by it. The language of the report was opaque and complex. Yet, he was glad he didn't have to explain or unravel it for his colleague.

"Okay, Nicola. Now, let's look at the thermo-gravometric analysis. With the separated sample the thermo-gravometric produced hydrogen auride…"

"So, the forest green then changed to what, gray?" Bounetti questioned.

"Actually dark gray. More like a gray-black. Now at that stage, this is where the testing became interesting and exciting. When the sample was heated and the proton was annealed away…look what happened."

"I see it. It went to pure white."

"Yes. Pure white."

"And what's this?" Bounetti asked pointing to a segment of the screen.

"That is the continuation of the annealing process. I kept annealing it and look what happened."

"I see it. Amazing. Absolutely amazing," Bounetti whispered in astonishment.

"It lost four-ninths of its weight. The more I kept annealing…well look," Swenson said pointing to another portion of the screen.

"It levitated," the Italian scientist said, in disbelief.

"Yes it did. And furthermore, it took the host pan with it."

"Incredible."

"Yes. I kept going with this procedure, and look," Swenson said. "At different cooling temperatures it would sometimes go to two or three hundred percent of its weight."

"And in heating it goes to nothing?"

"Yes. Nothing. But notice the mass is never compromised."

"I see that," Bounetti said, his astonishment never wavering.

"So, in the cooling process, the material formed a single wave length, a single vibration and frequency…"

"A laser," Bounetti interrupted.

"Yes. But even more so, losing weight during the cooling, I was able to get it to absolute zero."

"At absolute zero you have a superconductor," Bounetti said, his breathing becoming deeper.

"Yes. A superconductor. Zero electrical resistance and perfect diamagnetism. The current does not experience heat. It can flow indefinitely… forever," Swenson said.

"So, does the perfect diamagnetism extend to the Miessner Field?" Bounetti asked rhetorically.

"Yes. The Miessner Field, void of north and south polarity. The Meissner Field forces all other magnetic fields to circumvent the superconductor. It's totally unaffected."

"So, by extension, once superconductivity is achieved, levitation is possible in earth's magnetic field."

"Precisely," Swenson said with a hint of pride in his conclusion.

"Astounding.….Astounding." Bounetti whispered. "A superconductor. But, in reality it's monoatomic gold".

"Yes. It is monoatomic gold."

"I wonder if Barnes knows what he has here with monoatomic gold."

"Well, he's about to find out."

"So, the question is how did Mister Barnes come to have this monoatomic gold?"

"The real question should be does he know what he has and how potentially useful it is."

"Or, how potentially dangerous it is. Especially for him."

Swenson rose from the chair and walked to the window. The grounds keeper was still watering the two newly planted silver firs. He noticed a band of common chiffchaffs dominating one of the firs. They sat perched on a branch with a sense of dominance and entitlement.

"You know," Bounetti said, standing beside him looking out the window. "The fact that your report even hints at superconductivity means it must automatically be sent to the Defense Department in the United States."

"That really only applies to laboratories in the U.S."

"But we are associated with Brookhaven. There is a connection that warrants compliance. We wouldn't want to offend anyone in the Defense Department and run the risk of having our grants and funds become an issue."

"I see your point. I can send the reports to Horace Gardner at Brookhaven. It would then be incumbent upon him to forward them to the Defense Department. This way, we will be in compliance."

"It is the best procedure. But, that does not address the deeper implications. The least of which is the U.S. Defense Department. I'm sure you are aware of the implications our testing has uncovered?"

"Yes, I am. Now can you understand my fear?" Swenson said.

"Yes."

"If this miner, Barnes, has discovered a substantial amount of monoatomic gold, his finding could have enormous potential."

"Yes. A large discovery could support the theories of many archaeologists, anthropologists, Egyptologists and linguists. Their research and scholarship needs this find for their confirmations and conclusions," Bounetti commented.

"If a few grams can levitate, and take a pan weighing fifty times its weight, imagine what a substantial amount can do?"

"Yes, finally definitive answers to ancient questions. Imagine the mystery of the pyramids at Giza explained."

"Or the Baalbek Temples. Finally, we can understand how the trilithon monoliths of the temples were moved into place."

"Are we getting ahead of ourselves?" Bounetti asked.

"It's hard not to," Swenson said, his enthusiasm elevated.

Their enthusiastic logic fought against the temptations of a runaway fantasy. They let the moment draw itself out, allowing pretense to run its course so reason could be restored. They leaned back in an attempt to distance themselves from whimsy and regain their collective sense of impartiality.

"Thomas," Bounetti finally said. "While this preliminary testing is extremely promising, it could be far-reaching. There's much to consider. The biggest questions are where did Barnes get this material, and how much does he have. Once the Department of Defense learns of this, we may never get answers."

"The Department of Defense is not the only interference to be concerned with. There are other forces that would be served well if this report was destroyed. They would do anything to make that happen and ultimately undermine this discovery."

"I am very aware of the implications and dangers. On the one hand, this could be extremely beneficial for every aspect of humanity, especially for the military. But, on the other hand, science is an enemy of religion."

"And it is that enemy that will be the most dangerous."

"Yes, it will."

There was a sightless clamor rising about them; a prelude to an ominous threat. A mirthless frown permeated them to the core with real peril that could not be dismissed. The scientists knew the report must be filed. Their only hope was not to be held accountable for the actions of others.

"I will send the findings to Horace Gardner in Brookhaven," Swenson finally said. "He will have to forward it to the Department of Defense. At that point, it's out of our hands."

"Please send me the complete report as well. I'd like to have it."

"I will. Thank you for your time, Nicola."

Bounetti gathered the folders. He shook Swenson's hand and left the office.

Swenson sat, staring at the computer. The morning sun was still low in the sky and the glare on the screen was not disturbing. He went into his e-mails and addressed a message to Horace Gardner at the Brookhaven National Laboratory in New York. Swenson drafted a detailed cover letter and attached the complete scientific findings and conclusions of Alex Kenneth Barnes' material. In the letter, Swenson included Barnes' home address, his telephone and e-mail address. It was still only 4 a.m. in New York. He was certain when Gardner read the e-mail it would set into motion an unknown chain of events having the potential for catastrophe.

It was impossible for Swenson to measure the impact of the scientific study. It all came down to a simple touch on the "enter" key. A simple key stroke would ultimately communicate an astounding assortment of information whose results may not be altogether harmless. For reasons not of his doing, he was apprehensive to send the e-mail. Finally, Swenson realized he could not allow himself to succumb to his general distrust and suspicion. He could no longer maintain a level of negative speculation. It was a scientific study, like the numerous studies he had conducted in the past. It was his job to analyze data, and be freed from forming judgments.

He rose from the chair and looked out the window. The grounds keeper was no longer watering the trees and the beds of flowers. There were no birds in the trees. The courtyard outside his window was still and quiet. Now, all he thought about, was what would take precedent over sending the results of the testing to Horace Gardner at Brookhaven; science or fate.

ITALY

NICOLA Bounetti sat with his wife, Lucia on the balcony of the Hotel Zilema in Cosenza, province of Calabria, mesmerized by the soft, pastel blue water of the Tyrrhenian Sea. He took a sip from a cold bottle of Pellegrino water and kicked off his shoes. He unbuttoned his shirt to let the soft breeze blow against his skin. Bounetti was tired and hot from the overcrowded plane, which also experienced a three-hour delay. To remove himself from the unpleasant trip, Bounetti sat still becoming aware of the melodic whistle caused by the breeze passing through the lattice work of the balcony's railing. Lucia had put on a tape of Rossini's *Giunone* cantata that Bounetti found relaxing and appeasing.

Lucia had already unbuttoned her blouse. The breeze blew it slightly exposing her full breasts. She stood and faced the sea feeling the invigorating breeze over her entire body. With her open blouse and long sandy brown hair blowing in the breeze, the suggestion of her sensuality seemed at odds with the sedate vision of Lucia's profession as a concert violinist. Bounetti was always impressed by the dichotomy between her profession and her womanhood. He reasoned Lucia's passion for music was the same as her passion for life. To reflect that connection, the music Lucia favored were classical pieces which were bold and passionate, full of bold movements, thoughtfully paced allegros, moderate adagios and long, deep crescendos. Lucia dipped a wash cloth into the ice bucket containing the Pellegrino water and wrung it out. She folded the cloth and placed it on her husband's forehead.

"Ah, that feels very good," he said.

"Sorry the trip was exhausting for you," Lucia said.

"You had nothing to do with it. It could have been worse."

Lucia removed the cloth from Bounetti's forehead and wiped the perspiration from his neck and chest. Bounetti enjoyed Lucia's gentle, sensual touch. Her skin was smooth and silky with the exception of her fingertips. They were callous from the many years of sliding up and down the strings and fretless neck of her violin. There was also a permanent purple bruise on her left shoulder, just above her breast. A smaller discoloration on her chin caused by the way she held her violin. To Bounetti, the bruises were not the result of an ongoing professional irritation. They were the romantic blush of her artistic passion.

"Are you glad we made the trip?" Bounetti asked.

"Yes, I wanted to see my mother. I know you wanted to see yours. I'm glad our schedules allowed it."

"I am too. We both needed this holiday. It's hard. Your work and your travel are very demanding."

"I know. Sometimes the demands are exhausting. Before we realize it, so much time has past. It's terrible to think about it, but who knows how much longer they'll be with us."

"I'm glad our mothers decided to live together. They've become sisters. They need each other more now than ever," Bounetti observed.

"Speaking of sisters, I should call or e-mail my sister, Analisa. I haven't spoken to her in a while."

"Is she back in Arizona?" Bounetti asked.

"Yes. She recently finished research work in Africa. She was in Chad and Niger working on several archaeological digs there."

"I find it fascinating, in some ways, you and your sister have chosen similar careers."

"How could they be similar? I'm a concert violinist, and she's an anthropologist. She studies old bones, and I make music."

"She studies ancient civilizations, and you play an ancient instrument. There's a love of antiquity you both share."

"I suppose so, but I have to stretch a bit to see the connection. Should I tell her of the research work you and Thomas have done with the powder?"

"No. Absolutely not," Bounetti said quickly.

"She would be interested in it."

"Yes, I know she would. I think it's better if you don't say anything just yet. This could be tricky. It could have a negative outcome."

"You mean it could be dangerous?"

"Let's just say, at this point, I think it better if Analisa doesn't know about the results."

"Is the work dangerous for you?"

"No, not at all. We did routine testing within the framework of our jobs."

"Then why would it be dangerous for Analisa?"

"I'm not saying it would be. It would be better if you don't tell her. Perhaps when I see her, we'll have a discussion about it."

"Who knows when we'll get to see her?"

"Well if she's going to be staying in Arizona and working at the university, we should plan to go see her."

"That would be nice."

Lucia rested her head on the back of the chair. She listened to the melody of the sea as it splashed on to the shore. The resonance had an inner pulse and a rhythmic backbeat to the Rossini cantata. The combining sounds instigated a dull melancholy that gnawed at her. She felt an acute loneliness brought on by the distance from her younger sister. She also could not ignore the nipping gloom she felt thinking about not having her mother in her life one day.

"My mother always wanted me to give her grandchildren," Lucia said, as melancholy framed the contours of her face.

"You did, Lucia. You gave her your violin….Your Guarneri."

"I don't think that's how she sees it."

"That's exactly how she sees it. She knew what was in your heart your whole life."

"Well even if it's not true, thank you for saying it, Nicola."

"I say it because it's true, Lucia…It is absolutely true."

Lucia turned to her husband making sure there was no hint of deception in his eyes. He acknowledged her glance, nodded to her and whispered. "It's true."

Lucia dipped the cloth into the bucket again, and wrung it out. After wiping her face with it, she placed it on her feet. She looked out at the pastel blue sea and tried to connect with a deeper meaning to Bounetti's observation. In a sense, he was correct. Her career was born from her soul's desire. It was instinctive to her passion and was fostered by her hard work. The music beat through her entire body. It required a lifetime of nurturing and dedication. Hers was a life that pulsated with the rhythms and meters of music. For the first time, Lucia realized the technique required holding the instrument so close to her breast had another meaning. The music she played required caressing, at times gently, with deep reverence. Other times, it was prudent to play ardently with full vitality. Each gentle stroke of the bow across the strings, the knowing, the loving touch of her fingers, combined to represent the perfect maternal metaphor.

Suddenly, her Guarneri was no longer just a child born to concerts. Due to Bounetti's observation, the instrument had been born to a new, loving family and baptized in their deep personal yearning.

"After I unpack and shower, I'd like to go to my mother's house," Lucia said.

"Yes. My mother invited all our relatives. They'll all be there."

"I'm looking forward to it. Will your cousin be there?"

"Which one?"

"Pietro…Segretti."

"Yes."

Lucia moved her hand pretending to conduct an orchestra to the tempo of the cantata wafting out to the balcony.

"Nicola?" Lucia said bringing her hands back to her lap. "I've never asked you this before. But is it true Pietro Segretti once killed a man?"

"Why do you ask?"

"I guess there's always a fascination about someone like that."

"Someone, like whom?"

"You know what I mean. If it's true he did kill someone….The act of taking a life requires a certain cold detachment."

"What's your point?"

"Clearly, I've known him since I was a child. I could remember him visiting and always paying attention to Analisa and me. He was much older than us, and he was always considered family. We were never told how he earned a living. Whenever the older relatives spoke of him, it was always in whispers and half sentences. Analisa and I always referred to him as 'Uncle' Pietro. But we always felt he was mysterious, and suspected he had a checkered past. I'm not casting judgment. It's just people seem to be afraid of him and cautious not to say too much around him."

"Some people had good reason to fear him?"

"So the stories about him are true?" Lucia questioned.

"And what if they were?"

"Well, if they were, it just seems odd this man, who may have killed someone and people fear, hires two full time nurses for our mothers. That act is neither cold nor detached. He pays for all the medicine. He even pays a staff of gardeners and contractors for the upkeep of the house. The complexity of his nature is just that…complex."

"He provides nursing care for our mothers because it reflects his true nature. It's what he does," Bounetti assured.

"But it's so difficult to accept."

"It's simple. Just accept his help. Accept all he does," Bounetti was adamant but gentle. "To refuse or object to Pietro's help would be an insult of the highest order. His gesture is to be accepted graciously. There is no other way around it."

"But, what if your mother and mine live another twenty-five years? The financial burden would be devastating."

"If your mother and mine live another twenty-five years, that's exactly what he will continue to do. That's why he's hired the nurses. The money is insignificant to him. He's a man who feels honor is a fading human trait.

That's why he remains so close to his old friends, Alberto LaTesta and Gino Mafaldi. They share his sense of honor and loyalty. They trust each other explicitly. His fiancée, Gabriella DeCeasere, fits well into that group. In a sense, she rounds out the dynamic of trust."

Lucia dipped the cloth into the ice bucket once more, wiping away the perspiration from her neck and under her breast.

"Okay…then what of the man he killed?" she asked.

"My cousin is not a man to be trifled with. He has his own moral code that can't be rebuked. His own law makes perfect sense to him. He has the strength of conviction to enforce it. A long time ago, someone tried to defile his sister. He responded to the assault. My cousin is the type of man who will defend the weak…especially, if they are family. That's what concerns him."

"Nicola, I'm not passing judgment. I'm curious, that's all."

"There's always a certain fascination with men like Pietro. The world tends to view men like him in a mystical way. We grew up in this province. He's no mystery to me. I just know what he's capable of. We have a bond that transcends judgments. Pietro used to say it's a comfort to be able to stand next to a lion."

Lucia turned her head toward her husband, holding up her hand to shield her eyes from the sun.

"What did he mean by that?"

"It's all about trust and honor for Pietro. It's not the complexity of his nature. It's the simplicity of it."

"But what about the business he's in? He's an international arms dealer."

"He was, not any more."

"But was he not arrested in Monte Carlo recently?"

"Not arrested, no. He did have some difficulty there resulting from his attempt to sell beam technology."

"What's that?"

"Beam weapons are the most advanced weapons today. They create an electromagnetic beam," Bounetti said, his scientific sensibilities becoming evident.

"Beam weapons can disable any electrical devise; a missile, a bomber, satellite stations," Bounetti continued. "No weapon of aggression can escape their speed and accuracy. They are a defensive weapon; a super laser beam is the best way to describe them. Selling them was in keeping with the simplicity of his nature; the desire to protect the weak from the abusive strong. He tried selling the weapons to the Iraqi military."

"How do you know all this?" Lucia asked astonished.

"Because Pietro trusted me with the information. I would like to think if he had sold the weapons to Iraq, then perhaps the Iraqi people would not be in the turmoil they find themselves in today."

"Is that how you think he sees himself, as a protector of those people?"

"I really can't know for sure. I believe Pietro tried to sell the weapons for the purposes of protection," Bounetti answered. "And now that I think about it, yes. He tried to protect them."

"Somehow the mere concept of weapons is a contradiction to defense or neutrality," Lucia observed.

"That's a noble theory. But, the real issue is governments are made up of people with frail motivations. At times, we need to look beyond their threatening rhetoric and focus on the truth they rarely address. Perhaps, trying to protect the Iraqi people was an attempt at truth by my cousin."

Lucia turned away from Bounetti, seemingly untouched by sentiment or contradiction. She knew there was an irrefutable truth in arranging for the safety and protection of others. It required a commitment so vast, in the end, the only legacy was the laurel to stand next to a lion. Being born to the challenge was a way of being cursed by it. It was a test from the world that could only be responded to with truth. In no unmistakable terms, it was the same truth Segretti clearly aspired to and achieved.

"So, your cousin, Pietro Segretti, will he be there tonight?" Lucia asked.

Bounetti sipped the remaining Pellegrino water. He placed the empty bottle on the tile floor beside his chair. Rising up, he stood in front of Lucia, blocking the sun. He leaned forward and gently touched the purple bruise on her shoulder. Rossini's *Giunone* cantata was coming to a conclusion. He wondered how many times Lucia had played a Rossini cantata or opera that contributed to the bruise. In the end, it didn't matter. It was that simple bruise, a testament of valor that allowed Lucia to figuratively stand next to the lions of classical music; Rossini, Schubert, Verdi. She did them all justice by honoring their works and breathing passionate life into their collective creations. In a sense, he saw a distinct connection between her and Pietro Segretti.

"Yes," Bounetti responded. "He will be there."

THE stucco on Rosa Scotti's century-old house had been recently repaired. The cobblestone steps leading to the house had been realigned and secured. Rust from the wrought iron gate, as old as the house, had been repainted and oiled so it would not squeak. Pietro Segretti insisted on the quiet gate and all the masonry improvements.

A crowd of family and friends had gathered in the backyard of Rosa Scotti's home. The atmosphere was joyous, filled with the low roar of family contentment and familiarity. Rosa Scotti, Lucia's mother, sat at the head of the table with her lifelong friend, Melia Bounetti. The two women were granted a matriarchal status, ordained through the law of order and rule, after the deaths of their respective husbands. Their stature was total. They were unceremoniously crowned through the unspoken language of seniority. In spite of their frailty, they were allowed authority over the clan. But their rule was a gentle one. While their husbands were alive, they lived in a sort of idolized subservience. Becoming heir to their husbands' authority, they were somewhat out of place. All their lives, they were at the service of their families. Now, they were elevated to an almost mythical rank from which they seemed mildly out of place. The irony was not lost on either of them. Nor was the sardonic humor of it. Their advanced age and failing health made it all seem insignificant. However, the purpose of the gathering temporarily cancelled out the ravages of age and ill health. The women patiently awaited the arrival of their children. Their longing would soon be overturned through the embrace of a reunion.

The elderly women gravitated to each other by a natural tenant. Rosa sat in her wheelchair, while Melia sat beside her in a wooden, straight back chair. They doted over each other in the only way they knew how. They made sure each had something to eat and drink. Rosa would adjust a shawl over Melia's shoulders to ensure protection from the sea breeze. When Rosa coughed, Melia patted her back and reached for a glass of water. Their protection for each other came naturally. They had become masters at it. But for an instant, they turned away from each other and looked out at the family and friends. There was a weary contentment in their eyes. They could not escape the fatalistic wisdom that took hold of them. But for this night, all negative intuitions were bound in delight, and tucked neatly out of sight.

The collective laughter of the group was hardy and filled the spacious backyard. A lush, green lawn spread to a stone wall edging the high cliff overlooking the Tyrrhenian Sea. A line of torches stretched across the top of the stone wall. On one side of the lawn stood a vine of garden tomatoes surrounding a statue of The Holy Mother. In the center of the lawn was a long wooden table covered with a white table cloth. An abundance of fresh vegetables, focaccio bread, and large round serving bowls filled with pasta were placed on the table. Bottles of homemade wine were strategically placed along the entire table. Candles burned in clear glass vases, giving a warm glow to the equally warm evening. Over the table stood a wooden arbor covered with a white cloth, gracefully undulating in the breeze.

Bounetti helped his wife out of the taxi. As Lucia stood looking at the house, she reflected on how long it had been since she had last seen it. For an instant, she was brought back to her childhood. The house suddenly seemed surreal, vague, yet familiar. The house exuded a quiet majesty she had never recognized before. It was alive with a heartbeat and breath. Silently, but surely, the house smugly kept all its memories stored in every cell of its structure. Lucia felt a strange pull from the house, inviting her back, but on terms she knew it could not offer. The house could not give her back time and restore her youth. It could not make her mother young and well, or her father vibrant, strong and waiting in his favorite chair.

"Ready?" Bounetti said over Lucia's shoulder.

Lucia nodded and held her Guarneri in her arms.

Entering the backyard, Rosa and Melia were the first to see them. Rosa had heard the taxi door slam. The old woman knew it was her daughter returning home. Several cousins gathered around Bounetti and Lucia, hugging and kissing them. Lucia was glad to embrace the well wishers. One of the nurses took hold of Rosa's wheelchair and started to push her toward her daughter. Melia quickly stopped the nurse and advised she would wheel her.

As Rosa and Melia approached, Lucia laid down the Guarneri. Kneeling on the soft, lush grass, she knelt down and hugged her mother. The frail woman still displayed remarkable strength in her embrace. She hugged her daughter tightly. For an instant, Lucia felt she had been granted her desire making her mother well and young. She felt happy, yet she knew it was too much to ask to also see her father sitting under the arbor, well and alive. It had been almost a year since she saw her mother. She wanted the hug to bridge the lost time.

Bounetti hugged his mother. He could feel her small frame in his arms. Yet, there was a force about her that transcended her size. Melia had reclaimed her unique stature. The old woman had displayed her durability, as if she had been storing it up for this moment. With a reaffirming hug, all Bounetti's identities suddenly vanished. With a simple hug, he became recognizable to himself becoming what he had always been…a son.

"Ciao, mama," he said. It was the first spoken greeting he trusted himself to say.

Lucia stood and hugged and kissed Melia. It was a homecoming reconfirming her sense of belonging. She had felt the adulation from applauding audiences. That was a feeling of acceptance and approval on a grand scale. Being in the most prodigious, opulent opera houses in the entire world, filled with adoring fans, could not compete with this…her homecoming.

"Let's eat!" One of the cousins shouted.

"Not until Pietro arrives," Rosa responded.

Lucia wheeled her mother back to the table as Bounetti walked with his mother.

There was a gentle tap on Lucia's back. As she turned, she saw Segretti's younger sister, Julia Segretti-Tomba. They greeted each with a joyous cry, hugs and kisses. Julia's husband, Jacomo hugged Lucia and Bounetti. It was a whirlwind of fond greetings from relatives and friends. Fredrico Monti, one of Lucia's cousins, approached with two glasses of wine.

"Welcome home," he said. "Salute," he continued raising the glasses toward them.

Lucia and Bounetti took the wine and raised it above their heads.

"Thank you all for coming. It is wonderful to see you," Lucia shouted above the noise of the family.

"I saw your last performance at Teatro Communale di Bologna!" cousin Luigi Bosca shouted. "You were fantastic. I cut out the news clipping. I'll show you. I'll show you."

"Don't bother, Luigi. I cut them out myself," Lucia confessed with a Cheshire smile and sense of embarrassment.

From the corner of her eye, Lucia spotted Segretti and Gabriella standing at the entrance to the backyard. Segretti appeared quietly poised and elegant. He sported a white linen, collarless shirt and tan linen pants. Modest gold cufflinks adorned the French cuffs of the shirt. His gold watch reflected the setting sun. Segretti expressed a refinement that was not overstated. In one hand, he held a white fedora by the brim. In the other, a decorative bag obviously containing gifts. Gabriella matched his elegance and poise. She wore a yellow, cotton dress with a large brimmed hat. Carrying two large bouquets of flowers, Segretti led Gabriella to the middle of the gathering, adhering to a familial protocol of greeting and respect. He put the gift bag on the grass and set the fedora on it. He embraced Rosa and Melia with doting respect.

"Rosa te volio bene assi…assi," he whispered.

"And I do you, Pietro. You're like my own son." she responded.

Next Segretti greeted Bounetti. The cousins embraced with a bonding firmness.

Gabriella handed the flowers to one of the nurses, then hugged and kissed Rosa and Melia.

The family watched as the greetings unfolded. It was a ritual that had its roots in an ancient formality; a pecking order that owned its etiquette to blood status. Segretti acknowledged his sister with an embrace. He gently patted her on the top of her head.

"Cara Julia," he whispered.

After all the greetings were completed, the nurses took the flowers and placed them in vases. Segretti encouraged Rosa and Melia to open their gifts. With the packages unwrapped, they discovered a set of hand crafted bowls made of blue Azulejo tile.

"They're beautiful," Rosa said running her fingers along the inside of the bowl. "I love them. But, Pietro you do too much for us already. This is not necessary."

"I saw them on my trip to Portugal. I just had to get them for you."

"We appreciate it. I'll only use them when you and Gabriella come. Only you will eat from them."

"Yes, of course. I've also brought some Bucaco wine made by the Carmelite monks of Portugal."

Everyone sat at the table and started passing the food to each other. Gabriella took a piece of fish from the bowl and placed it into Segretti's dish. She gave some to Rosa and Melia.

The party was festive. After drinking four glasses of the Bucaco wine, Luigi Bosca started to dance. Consuming three more glasses, he sat in a chair, and in less than one minute, was sound asleep. His son, Raphael, along with three of his young cousins, went to the front of the house. They sat on the stoop and were captivated by Segretti's new Bentley.

Segretti and Gabriella conversed with Bounetti, Lucia and Rosa and Melia. At one point during the conversation, Segretti rose from the table and approached the nurses.

"So tell me," he asked. "How are Rosa and Melia feeling?"

"Mister Segretti, they're doing just fine," one nurse responded. "They have their issues, but all things considered, they are as well as can be expected."

"What exactly does that mean? Segretti asked.

One of the nurses hesitated before speaking.

"Well, their doctor will know better," she finally said.

"And what would he say?"

"Pretty much the same thing."

"Then, is there anything they need?"

"I'd say they already have what they need."

THE sun had gone down behind the La Sila Mountains. A soft three-quarter moon was shining a bright line across the sea. The food had been cleared from the table. A display of pastry, cake, cappuccino, demitasse and bottles of Anisette and Amaretto were served.

Lucia rose from the table and retrieved the Guarneri. She opened the case and lifted the violin. Removing the bow, she applied rosin and delicately drew it across the strings to ensure it was properly tuned. The first note rose from the strings, embracing the night. The entire crowd suddenly went silent. Everyone looked at Lucia, but none as fondly as Rosa.

Lucia closed her eyes and began to feel the music within her. She knew the open backyard, with the constant breeze, did not provide the best acoustics. But, it didn't matter. With the first stroke across the strings, Lucia knew the violin was in perfect tune with the setting.

Filling the night, the sweet, sacred sounds of Ava Maria rose from the violin. A deep reverence took hold of the family. They became joined in a holy union, forgiving their minor bickering and individual flaws. There was hope and emotion only the Ava Maria could evoke. In a strange way the prayerful strains of the strings beckoned their individual longings and appeased their personal sorrows. Rosa could not explain the tears rolling down her face or the ache in her heart. All she knew was the strange delight and joy edged with sorrow. Melia touched Rosa's shoulder. It was a confirmation of their connection.

Lucia was coming to the end, but trying to hold each note for an eternity. When she finally finished, sobs and sniffles replaced applause. No one could move or speak. Shouts of "Bravo" became impossible to utter. Lucia lowered the violin pressing it to her breasts.

Segretti was the first to react. Rising from his chair, he approached Lucia and hugged her tightly.

"That was beautiful," he said. "Absolutely, beautiful."

He took the violin from Lucia, allowing her at kneel by her mother's side. It was a touching, private moment. Segretti stepped back allowing all the spontaneity and privacy it required. He observed the purity and truth that anointed them.

IT had become late. Relatives and friends began to leave the party. Segretti remained with Gabriella, as did Bounetti and Lucia. Rosa and Melia had grown tired and beckoned their nurses. After kissing their children goodnight, Rosa and Melia retreated to the house.

"Pietro, I want to thank you for all you do for Nicola's mother and mine," Lucia said. "I want you to know how grateful we both are. I know it hardly seems enough but…"

"Lucia, it's my honor. I'm privileged to do it," Segretti interrupted.

"I understand, but how can I thank you for all you do?"

"I think you may be misjudging all this. How can I thank you for what you did tonight?"

"But what I did was nothing. Playing is what I do. I do it for a living."

"Lucia, why don't you ask your mother and Melia if what you did tonight was nothing?"

Lucia studied Segretti's face. She noticed a natural gentleness combined with a strong, immovable conviction. There was no judgment in his stare, only a broad wisdom which she was helpless to oppose. A great deal had been revealed to Lucia. She permitted the lessons to take hold of her, and reconfigure her insights and perceptions. Segretti's observations had redirected her convictions, and she was grateful for it.

"I think a walk along the beach would be just the right thing now," Gabriella suggested. "Let's go before the sun comes up."

THE beach was rocky and the moon hung low on the dark horizon. It cut a path of light across the sea. The breeze was gentle as it swirled around the high cliffs, creating a continuous whistle. It was an ancient ritual that produced the night's song. The air maintained its unique texture and was filled with the aroma of salt and fish. On top of the cliffs, lighted homes offered another context that was relevant to the night.

Walking behind Segretti and Bounetti, Gabriella and Lucia held each other's arm. They huddled close, giggling like two young school girls exchanging innocent gossip. They were both amazed how quickly they divested themselves of the demanding world, and their relationship to it. This, for them was a reprieve, a timely shift allowing for frivolity and gullibility.

Occasionally their laughter caused Segretti to turn. He marveled at their innocent ease with each other.

"They get along well," Bounetti observed.

"They seem like good friends."

"Speaking of friends, how are Gino and Alberto?"

"They're doing well. Now that we're out of the arms business, they're glad yet bored."

"Bored because they need the excitement of the deal?"

"Yes."

"Do you feel the same way?"

"I don't give it much thought. I'm content with my life now, as it is."

"There's a lot to be said for contentment."

"There is. Sometimes, we need to examine the reason we chase after things."

"Tell me, Pietro, did you ever hear of monoatomic gold?"

"Gods' gold? Yes, I have. I do have several rich, industrialist friends who would pay handsomely for it. Why do you ask?"

"At the Institute, I received a sample from a man in the United States. I tested it with a colleague of mine. Sure enough it was monoatomic gold."

"I always wondered what's so unique about this substance. Why would people pay a great deal of money for it?"

"I can tell you it's not called Gods' gold for nothing. In the ancient Hebrew tradition, it was referred to as the manna. Manna means 'what is it'? The phrase 'what is it' is found repeatedly in *The Egyptian Book of the Dead,* as well. Manna refers to white powder of gold. Clearly, the ancient people didn't know what it was, but they knew, applied properly, it could be used for anything."

"Can this manna be applied for weapons?"

"I haven't thought of it in those terms, but I'm sure any nation's military would like to have it."

"Well, why don't they have it?"

"It's really not that simple. The basic knowledge of alchemy turning medal, yellow gold to monoatomic gold was apparently lost in the destruction of the First Temple...the temple of Solomon."

"Can it be mined?"

"Yes. It's in the bowels of the earth. In volcanoes. Nature produces monoatomic gold. But, it doesn't surrender it easily. Quantities would be very limited."

"But it is available?"

"It's not that simple. One would need to drill down half a mile or more to get one third of one ounce per each ton of metal. The problem then becomes the other elements, such as palladium, platinum, osmium, ruthenium, that are in the ore. Scientists can boil away these elements to get to the gold. However, boiling gold, requires temperatures of two thousand six hundred degrees Celsius, and that will still not produce monoatomic gold. Mining is the solution. But, you can see the ratio between the effort and yield presents a problem."

"Can it be smelted?

"No, smelting does not produce monoatomic gold. It only leaves a dense black slag."

"What's so special about the gold? Segretti asked.

Before responding, Bounetti took a deep breath. He ran his fingers through his hair.

"Pietro, I need you to humor me for just a bit," he said, guardedly.

"Go on."

"The testing, I helped conduct, was just a small amount of monoatomic gold. It revealed something very anomalous under certain conditions. The gold became weightless. In so doing, it transferred its weightless property to the host pan it was in and raised the pan. It literally raised the pan. So if just a small amount can make a pan weightless, who knows what an indeterminate amount can lift. The ancients knew all about monoatomic gold. I believe they used it for many things. Even to build the great pyramids of Giza."

"Is that so?"

"The old belief, as to how they were built, is absolutely ridiculous. Consider this…to raise the heavy stones to the top of the pyramids; the builders would have to construct an inclined plane to the top of the pyramids, conforming to its slant. This would require a ramp forty-eight hundred feet high. The ramp would need to have the volume three times greater than that of the pyramid itself. Conventional explanation about their construction was it took twenty-two years to build. There are about two and half million stones in the pyramids. Do the math. That explanation is impossible. I suggest, without the use of monoatomic gold, and its weightless property, it is impossible for the Egyptians to build the pyramids. Furthermore, it has been discovered rainfall has caused erosion to the pyramids. The rains could only have come some ten thousand years before the Giza Plateau became a desert. This leads one to believe the pyramids predate the ancient Egyptians."

"I never heard this explanation," Segretti said, amazement circling his words.

"You are now. But I caution this is my opinion as a scientist. Consider the Baalbek Temples where much larger stones were used. There, one can find the trilithon, a row of three stones each weighing in excess of one thousand tons. Nothing can lift that volume"

"So what does this really mean?"

"It means gravity determines space-time. The monoatomic gold, in lifting these large stones, essentially is defying gravity, and literally bends space-time."

"That's a bit too scientific for me."

"I understand. It's very scientific indeed. But I tell you all this to give you an idea of what this material can do. Its properties are mysterious and miraculous."

"Does it have other uses?"

"It's known to affect the pineal and pituitary glands. It increases melatonin, which heightens energy and stamina. It has physical anti-aging properties. With a heightened pineal and pituitary function, it is said one's intelligence, awareness and aptitude is increased to extraordinary levels. It can also bring about the ability to read another's thoughts. Literally."

Segretti contemplated what Bounetti was saying. It was a challenge to his complacency and understanding. He thought sometimes the biggest secrets were those spread out in plain sight, and some day all secrets would be exposed.

"I don't understand the connection to the pineal gland," Segretti said.

"The pineal gland looks like a small pinecone. That's why it's called pineal. Ancient civilizations throughout the world were obsessed with the pineal gland. Its image is abundantly depicted in their drawings, statues and stone carvings. They knew the importance of this small gland in the center of the brain. The gland has the highest amount of energy than any other part of the body. Once the gland is shielded from the effects of electromagnetic fields and radio waves, the micro clusters in the gland allow it to see into space-time. The Vatican honors this pine-looking gland. You're familiar with the monument of the pinecone in Cortile Della Pigna in Vatican City?"

"Yes, I am."

"Then you also know of the open sarcophagus beside it. Where you ever curious about those monuments?"

"Not until now. What of the open sarcophagus?"

"The open sarcophagus is symbolic of enlightenment…eternal life. They're linked with the pineal gland. Also, look closely at the Papal Staff. On the top of the shaft is a carved pinecone. The pineal gland has always been referred to as the third eye; the source of all enlightenment….The single eye full of light, as Jesus referred to it."

Segretti felt the weight of new discoveries pressing down on him. He turned and watched Gabriella bend down to pick up a stone.

"Enlightenment, the ability to read one's thoughts," Segretti whispered. "And the pineal gland is capable of that?"

"That and more."

"That's a lot to consider."

"It is. One needs to be open minded about this. As a scientist, I've learned nothing is impossible."

"When you say monoatomic gold is capable of anti-aging, what does that mean?"

"Again, I refer to the ancients. With me, the past is an addiction. Consider Enoch. He lived to be three hundred sixty-five years of age. Methuselah died at nine hundred sixty-nine. How do you suppose they lived that long? Once more, there seems to be no record that Enoch did die."

"This is not all just a myth?"

"I suspect not. Aging is directly related to the cells of the body that divide many times during one's lifetime. However, the process of division and replication is finite. When a non-dividing state is reached, that is the crucial factor of aging. When monoatomic gold is placed at the end of double-helix DNA, it becomes ten thousand times more conductive. In effect, a superconductor. Consequently, the division and replication process continues, and aging does not become a factor."

"Interesting," Segretti said thoughtfully. "What about someone who's sick, can monoatomic gold reverse any disease?"

Bounetti turned to look at Segretti. He could see the contemplative strain on his face, begging for the proper answer to his question.

"Again, when a DNA state is altered it will resonate with the deformed or diseased cell. This causes the DNA to relax and become corrected which reverses disease."

"So in theory, one's disease can be eliminated."

"Not in theory, in actuality."

Segretti grew silent. He no longer heard the laughter of Gabriella, nor did he hear the whistling of the breeze or the water lapping on the shore. He was engulfed by the information and jarred by the possibilities. It intrigued him more than the newest technology of any weapon he had ever sold.

"Pietro, consider this," Bounetti continued. "In the book of *Exodus,* Moses took the Golden Calf which the Israelites had made. He burnt it in the fire and ground it to a powder. There was a reason for that. Also, in the same book, there is a man named Bezaleel. He was a skilled goldsmith and craftsman placed in charge of building the Ark of the Covenant. In the Ark, he was to place among other things something called 'shewbread'. Legend tells us how extraordinary and mystifying the Ark of the Covenant was. In *Genesis,* shewbread is mentioned there as well. The term shewbread shows up in many books. And shewbread is generally reserved for priests. And what was shewbread? It was a white powder...derived from gold... Monoatomic gold." Bounetti said answering his own question.

Segretti had not reacquainted himself with the lush night and the sights and sounds within it. In a way, he felt removed from them. He felt out of place, transported to a different place and time. Perhaps beyond any time in antiquity that even predated the surrounding La Sila Mountains; he knew were there but hidden by the night. Segretti had once been told by a priest, all the answers to the mysteries of life are within our souls. Segretti liked to believe the priest. He would like to have faith in the priest's council and wisdom. But, there was little his soul knew. The answers to strange puzzles eluded him. Perhaps the night, the sand he walked on, or the silent mountains knew all the answers. If they did, then perhaps they were selfishly hording them because they believed humanity could not deal with its own past.

Bounetti noticed Segretti's uncertainty. He sensed the level of hesitation in his demeanor. His middle ground had shifted to a vague, more unfamiliar course. Skepticism had taken root and, suddenly, his way of seeing things had been challenged and altered. Bounetti felt Segretti wanted to say something,. But Segretti remained silent and turned away.

"The Bible is not the only book littered with references to monoatomic gold and the production of it," Bounetti continued in a slight whisper. "In *Revelations,* it says the Lord provides white stone to eat. In the *Book of the Dead,* the Pharaohs taking the white manna, shewbread, white gold, it's all the same. The book of *Exodus* mentions Mount Sinai saying the Lord descended upon it in fire, and smoke ascended. It goes on to speak of the burning bush. A story we all know. The burning bush was on fire, but not consumed. *Genesis* cross references this smoke. It mentions the smoke from a burning furnace and a burning lamp...Pietro, monoatomic gold is not legend. It's not fable. It's not myth. It's very real. Its properties go way beyond any substance known to man."

Segretti now understood why tahe rich industrialists would pay anything for monoatomic gold. He suddenly saw the implications the substance would have on every military in the world, and all the popular religions. Pharmaceutical companies would have the biggest interest. In the case of religions, he suspected they would want it destroyed. Ironies and paradoxes ran around in Segretti's mind. As an arms dealer, he was very familiar with the extreme dangers, and gross contradictions in brokering destructive weapons. As an agent of monoatomic gold, he understood there would be no difference. Segretti needed Bounetti to tell him something that made sense. He needed something familiar that the proverbial sea, or the softly lit homes built into the cliffs, could not supply. An exaggerated dignity that held the right balance of common sense and reason would suffice.

"Pietro," Bounetti said. "Are you alright?"

The question had a strange tone. It was the language that recognized uncertainty Segretti yielded to a force outside of himself. The force was neither menacing nor shielding. It was just there, like the breeze he began to feel again coming off the Tyrrhenian Sea. Segretti stopped and turned to Bounetti. Whatever light there was in the night, it shown on Segretti's face. The tentative compliance that registered in his eyes was plain for Bounetti to see. Segretti relinquished all struggle concerning the information of the powdered gold. He reminded himself of the first lesson he learned selling arms; always trust yourself.

"What about the sample you received at the Institute?" Segretti conceded. "How much was there, and how did you get it?"

"From a man named Alex Kenneth Barnes. He lives in Arizona."

"How much did he send you?"

"Very little."

"Did Barnes indicate he had more?"

"No, but I tend to think he has a lot more in his mine."

"Is there anything legally or ethically that would prevent you from giving me his address?"

"None."

Segretti nodded his head and put his hand on Bounetti's shoulder. "Good," he responded.

As Gabriella and Lucia approached, they were still engrossed in their playful conversation. But, Gabriella could not see the pensive look in Segretti's eyes.

"Are you alright, Pietro," Gabriella asked, stopping at Segretti's side.

"Yes I'm fine."

Gabriella put her hand under Segretti's arm. She trusted him and did not want to question him any further. Instead, she showed him the stone she had picked up on the shore. It had been flattened and smoothed by years of tides and winds. Segretti took the stone from Gabriella. He rubbed his fingers on it. He could feel it was warmed and dried by Gabriella's hand. After years of being exposed to the elements, Segretti recognized the stone had been worn down to a new texture. But in the end, all the elements and time could not change its true composition. Segretti handed the stone back to Gabriella. He looked into her eyes, and put his arm around her shoulders. Her arm felt chilled and sticky from the salty air. Her hair was blowing on his face.

"Tell me, Gabriella," Segretti said. "How would you like to take a trip?"

"You know I enjoy taking trips. To where?" she asked.

"The United States," he replied.

"The United States? For what?"

"Some business."

"Business? What kind of business?" she said, fear framing her words.

"This is not my usual business. This is different."

Gabriella looked at Segretti. Her playfulness had yielded to a veil of unease. She started to tell him something, but realized she didn't have to. Segretti saw all her concerns.

"What is it you want to say?" Segretti asked.

"Nothing. Nothing, really."

"Gabriella, this is family. What you say will not go beyond the night."

It was more than a superficial state Gabriella felt part of. Beyond her relative safety was a potential predicament threatening the personal shelter that existed for her. She wanted to burrow into a hiding place and appease her paranoia.

"It's not the family that concerns me," she said softly. "I trust that. What I don't trust are those people…those security agencies that will take notice of your movements. You have to know if you travel, especially to the United States, you will be followed every step of the way. Everything you do will be monitored and observed. Who knows what else? There's a deep rooted obsession in the world that allows for vengeance and penalties. Do you really need to bring that upon yourself?"

"Your concerns are well founded. I don't take exception to what you say. There was a time when my trade was a bit simpler. I was able to move about with less visibility. That's all changed. Just because of that, I can't allow myself to live in fear of surveillance."

"No one is asking you to live in fear. Just be cautious. That's all."

"This is something I have to do. It has less to do with arms dealing, and more with trying to buy something that may be helpful for Rosa and Melia."

"But there's danger involved. Yes?"

Segretti looked directly into Gabriella's eyes. He did not try to avoid her concerns or the weight of her gaze. Instead, he focused on the deep attachment between them. He tried to remain open to everything inside her. Segretti totally understood the equation between her will and his needs. They were not necessarily poles of opposition or contention. Instead, he believed they had a core root of commonality.

"Yes," he said as he lightly stroked her cheek.

Gabriella suddenly found herself immersed in the past. A past that constantly repeated itself. She fully realized the notion of moving forward was really synonymous with the history of misgivings. A sense of accord with Segretti's simmering dynamic fused with her own sturdy but compliant nature. It was a compelling unity, and one which she could not escape. In the midst of complexity and doubt, the conclusion was simple for Gabriella. It all came down to acceptance.

"Where in the United States?" she questioned.

Segretti smiled at her and kissed her forehead.

"Arizona," Segretti responded softly.

NEW YORK

HORACE Gardner was a chemical engineer at the Brookhaven National Laboratory in the town of Upton, on New York's Long Island. Brookhaven, with its own postal code, was operated for the United States Department of Energy. The facility was spread out over five thousand acres and staffed by more than three thousand scientists, engineers and technicians. Discoveries made at the laboratory won six Nobel Prizes and a handful of Priestley Medals and Davy Medals. The Priestley Medal was conferred by the American Chemical Society and the Davy Medal by A-Side Medals and Awards Committee. Horace Gardner had received the Davy Medal when he was just four months short of his thirty-fifth birthday. The ten professor members of the committee cited Gardner for his work in chemical evolution of life.

Gardner, six feet, three inches tall and slender, with graying hair and a neatly trimmed beard, was slightly imposing. He stood with hunched shoulders and appeared a bit gangly when he walked. Mostly introspective, with a shy, soft-spoken voice, Gardner avoided personal attention and notoriety. In a room full of strangers, he felt awkward and out of place. Only with his work did he feel completely comfortable and in control. Although a modest man, he was proud of the Davy Award. The only vanity he allowed himself was to keep the round bronze medal, encased in clear Lucite, prominently displayed on his desk.

On the corner of his desk, stood a framed picture of Clara, his wife of twenty-one years. The picture of Clara had been taken a few years earlier, outside St. Peter's Basilica in Rome, on a pilgrimage they made to Vatican City with their church group. Clara's smile was soft and pleasant. She wore a black beret on her head, a modest black two-piece cotton suit and matching gloves. Under her suit jacket, she wore a beige turtle neck sweater. Around her neck, and hanging off the collar of the sweater was a plain gold crucifix.

Standing next to Clara was an old friend, Monsignor Joseph Clementi. Gardner had met the Monsignor, a member of the Apostolic Nunciature, six months after he won the Davy Medal. They were introduced by Gardner's mentor and fellow scientist, Alan Richardson, on a visit to Rome.

Richardson was a member of Gardner's church group and instrumental in arranging the trip. On the flight, Richardson confided in Gardner the annual trips were wearing on him and becoming strenuous. He further admitted he didn't know how many more trips he would be able to make. Richardson's predictions became prophetic. Two weeks after their return, he died suddenly of a massive heart attack. Gardner and Clementi shared a sense of grief over the loss of their close, mutual friend and remained friends ever since.

The second framed picture on the desk was of their daughter, Gloria, dressed in cap and gown at her graduation from Loyola College in Maryland. Gloria resembled Clara, so much so, that on many occasions they were mistaken for sisters.

On the opposite side of the desk, was a small glass dome covering another one of Gardner's few prized possessions: a five-pound gold nugget resting on a small purple velvet pillow. Gardner found the nugget while hiking in Logan Canyon, Utah. The nugget was lying in a dry gulch reflecting the sun. Gardner could not explain, with any scientific certainty, how the nugget came to be deposited there. In the absence of reasonable scientific explanations, Gardner envisioned a simple scenario that over time became an exaggerated narrative involving a sad old-time prospector who lost it while traveling from Arizona or the Badlands of Wyoming or, the vast Yukon Territory. One evening at home, Gardner spewed his convoluted tale to Clara with dramatic flair. He imagined the nugget and the prospector made an arduous journey, filled with the peril of bandits and highwaymen. Enduring treacherous elements, the nugget simply fell from the prospector's torn pocket, fatefully waiting for Gardner's arrival.

Clara listened politely to the fabricated details of his tale and replied *"For a man who deals in the facts of science, Horace, your fanciful tale of the nugget is somewhat overstated and out of character"*.

What Gardner did not confess to Clara was his detailed visualization of the prospector. He imagined the man as tall, a bit hunched with a partially gray, grubby beard. He wore thick baggy pants, puffed and worn at the knees and held up by a crude rope. He also wore a rough, woolen sweater with holes at both elbows. On his feet were worn out, dusty boots. The old man traveled with a pack mule. Hanging from the mule's side were two dented panning tins. With each plodding step of the mule, the pans clanged their melody echoing through mountains or across the flat, desolate Yukon tundra.

Gardner knew Clara was correct in her observation. The entire fantasy was out of character. But he didn't mind her conclusion. It was a scientific fact that prospectors did discover gold. Some made fortunes from their claims, while perhaps, one old lonely prospector, beaten by the mountains, lost the large, five-pound nugget that could have made him a folk hero.

On Clara's 60th birthday, Gardner presented her with a fine gold chain necklace. Hanging from the chain was a gold crucifix Gardner had made from a portion of the nugget. The sun had shone on the nugget when he found it, making it a religious experience for him. He wanted to honor Clara with the reverence he felt. In keeping with his belief, he brought the crucifix to his parish church, Our Lady of Grace, and had it blessed by his longtime friend, Father Michael Keating. Father Keating had officiated the vows of marriage between Horace and Clara. A few years later, he had performed Gloria's Baptism rite. Gardner had always admired the approach Father Keating took toward his clerical life. He found it to be sound and deeply rooted in pragmatism.

During his teen years, Gardner felt his life's calling to be in religion. He contemplated entering the seminary after high school. However, science had an equal tug on him. In the end, and after strong encouragement from his father, he embarked on the path of science. Nevertheless, over the years, Gardner had made an effort to maintain an equal balance between his religious beliefs, and his endeavors in science.

Gardner earned a Bachelor of Science from the Michigan College of Mining and Technology. His Master's Degree was in Mineral Engineering from the University of Utah. His Ph.D. was in chemistry from the University of Minnesota. After acquiring his Ph.D., he spent four years performing post-doctoral work at the University of Manchester, England. While at Manchester, he wrote a book about technology and its impact on mining. Although scientific in nature, his conclusions were miners still had to use picks, drills and shovels to break mountains apart.

For the next two and a half decades, Gardner worked in Montreal at the Chalk River Laboratories. Finally, he become a research associate at the Massachusetts Institute of Technology. He slowly began to return to his first interest in molecular biology. During a sabbatical break in 1997; an accidental leak of tritium into the groundwater in Upton at Brookhaven National Laboratory, forced management to make changes. Due to the managerial changes, Gardner was contacted by his friend, Alan Richardson. Richardson asked Gardner to end his sabbatical and join the staff at Brookhaven. Gardner accepted the offer, and after the tritium problem was resolved, Gardner enjoyed the relatively quiet working environment at Brookhaven. The tranquility lasted for several years. When the public learned that Brookhaven was the site of a Relativistic Heavy Ion Collider, they arrived with placards protesting loudly. Some placards read, "RHIC the Doomsday Machine". Others protestors demanded an immediate halt to the experiment by repeatedly shouting, "Stop RHIC now".

By interlocking arms, a group of protestors made a human fence blocking some of the roadways leading to the facility. The laboratory's own police force quickly removed the human barricade through the use of moderate force. The angry public knew the collider allowed ions to collide traveling at relativistic speeds. They understood the result would be the creation of primordial form of matter that existed in the universe shortly after the Big Bang. They feared the extremely high energy, created by the collider, could produce a black hole and swallow the earth. Their further concerns were the experiment could create a strain of strange matter that could be more unstable than ordinary matter. The protestors wanted the physicists spearheading the project to show an exact zero probability for such a catastrophic scenario of not occurring.

Gardner trusted the physicists and was not concerned with the outcome of the collider experiment. As a scientist, he knew the moon had been bombarded with cosmic particles of significantly higher energies for billions of years. After the collider experiment, the world remained intact. It had not been swallowed by a black hole. The earth remained spinning on its axis just as it had done since the beginning. Consequently, the well meaning protestors with their fears and misgivings assuaged finally disbanded. Once again Gardner and the staff at Brookhaven were not impeded by the protestors and enjoyed the relative quiet at the laboratory.

Turning on his computer, he drummed his fingers on the desk as the machine booted up. His quick glance shifted from the photos of his wife and daughter, to the gold nugget. For no apparent reason, Gardner moved the glass case with the nugget, repositioning it between the two family photos. As he reached for the briefcase key, the phone on his desk rang.

"Yes," he said.

"Mister Gardner, this is the receptionist," a voice said. "I have Mister Erik Dawson and Mister Timothy Finley from the Department of Defense here to see you."

Gardner looked at his watch and became somewhat annoyed. Apparently, the two agents had taken the liberty and were forty minutes early for their meeting.

"Our meeting is at ten o'clock," Gardner said into the phone.

"They did say they were early. Should I have them wait?"

Gardner took a deep breath, and looked at his watch again.

"Okay, have security show them to my office," he said and hung up the phone.

Gardner quickly retrieved the briefcase key and put it in his jacket pocket. He removed his jacket and placed it on a hanger on the back of his door. Upon returning to his desk, he confirmed his briefcase was well concealed beneath it.

Shortly, Dawson and Finley entered the office. Each man had a red and white visitor label affixed to their jackets. Both agents wore identical dark, conservative suits and stripped ties. As they entered the office both agents declared themselves with a sense of entitlement.

"Good morning, Mister Gardner. I'm Agent, Erik Dawson," one agent said pointing to the visitor label. "And this is Agent, Timothy Finley. As you know, we are from the Department of Defense."

Dawson was somewhat older with closely cropped white hair. Although shorter than Finley, he looked like a recent retiree from the world of professional wrestling. His neck was thick. His jaw line chiseled and strong. His motions and movements were snappy and pronounced, suggesting he had extensive military training. Finley was leaner, his hair darker and his eyes the color of slate.

"Good morning," Gardner responded, deciding not to correct the "Mister" with "Doctor."

"Thank you for taking the time to see us. I know we're a bit early," Dawson said.

Gardner nodded his head trying to conceal his annoyance.

"We want to thank you for forwarding the report from Professor Thomas Swenson of the Niels Bohr Institute. Quite an interesting report," Dawson continued.

"How can I help you, gentlemen? Your phone call was vague," Gardner said.

"Well, quite frankly, we would like information that is not part of the Niels Bohr report."

"What kind of information?"

"We understood the information in the report. That was straight forward," Finley said. "What we'd like to know more about is Alex Barnes. He's the man who sent the material to the laboratory for testing."

"Yes, I know who he is. I assume the correspondence from Mister Barnes went directly to Thomas Swenson. I was not privy to any of the correspondence between them. Consequently, I know nothing of Mister Barnes."

"Then would you know how Barnes gained possession of the material he presented for testing?" Finley asked.

"I have no idea. I'm sure you will be visiting Mister Barnes. Surely, you can question him personally."

"Of course, we will be visiting him," Dawson said. "We just wanted to know all we could in the event he would not be completely forthcoming with information."

"I understand."

"It appears Barnes is not a scientist, nor is he a physicist," Finley said. "So, how do you suppose he came into the possession of material Doctor Swenson's test results confirm is a superconductor?"

"Barnes is a miner. I believe it's safe to assume he mined the material," Gardner said. "I would also go so far as to say, Barnes does not know his material is a superconductor."

"What makes you speculate that?" Dawson asked.

"It's just that, speculation. I also suspect he doesn't know what other properties the material contains."

"He will when he receives the report," Dawson said.

"Yes he will," Gardner responded.

"Do you think the 'other properties,' as you call them, are a bit unusual?" Finley asked.

Gardner looked at Finley and then Dawson. He sensed their probing with concealed mistrust.

"I believe you both work in DARPA, the Defense Advance Research Projects Agency. Is that correct?"

"It is."

"Then I believe you should certainly understand the unusual nature of the material," Gardner said.

"We do. We also read the report carefully," Dawson said. "We both understand the implications of the material."

"There was limited information about Barnes," Finley added. "And just to repeat, that's our focus at this point. Anyone with the ability to produce or mine material, that is a superconductor, becomes a concern to us."

"Superconductors are serious business." Gardner said. "But, unfortunately, there's little I can tell you about Barnes. Other than his name and address that was supplied to your agency, I have nothing. I'm sorry. Doctor Swenson at Niels Bohr may be able to supply you with the information you are looking for."

"We will contact him," Finley said.

Dawson studied Gardner and sensed a slight reluctance. There was a faint trace of arrogance, but he did not appear dishonest or uncooperative.

"We were anxious to meet with you, Mister Gardner. We know of your education and experience in mining technology and mineral engineering. That is the background we need to give us an insight into Barnes' discovery," Dawson said.

"We also read your book about the technology of mining," Finley added. "You're quite knowledgeable about mining. Your expertise is something we would appreciate."

"My book has been out of print for several years," Gardner advised.

"We have our ways," Finley said.

Gardner felt there was something fundamentally improper about the scope of their investigation. He also realized, with a sense of futility, whoever controlled and manipulated information controlled and manipulated the world. He knew the DOD had access to a great deal of information and the capacity for extensive manipulation.

"I'm sure you do," Gardner said. "But, unlike you, I know nothing of the extent of Barnes' mining operation. I don't know what type of drilling equipment he's using or how deep he's drilling. In spite of the lack of information, I can't believe he mined a lot of the material."

"Can you be certain?" Dawson asked.

"Not certain, but almost. It's not like mining for yellow gold…gold nuggets and such. A miner could come across a healthy vein and have a substantial yield. Mucking out coarse ore is much different than mining powdered gold. In fact, it's extremely difficult to mine powdered gold. Geologically speaking, volcanic process is required to produce the material in question. That occurs deep in the earth. When it does, it mixes with the earth and becomes slag. There's nothing definable about it in that state. Quite frankly, I suspect Barnes came across the slag quite by accident. That's what I meant when I said he doesn't know what he has."

"But could Barnes have tapped into a substantial vein of this material?"

"I would highly doubt it."

"Why?" Finley asked.

"In the absence of a full geological study of the area, I can't be certain. I do believe there is not the type of subterranean volcanic activity that would produce much of the material. Even if there was, it would be so far into the earth, it would be extremely difficult to reach. You will learn all that when you speak directly with Barnes."

"We certainly will contact him," Dawson said. "Thank you for your time," he continued and rose to shake hands with Gardner. Gardner felt a sense of dread in the handshake. There seemed to be nothing official in the meeting. Instead, it was more a resemblance to an impromptu inquisition.

Gardner sat quietly welcoming his self-imposed state of isolation. He embraced the feeling as a form of foreboding for forwarding the Niels Bohr Laboratory report to the Department of Defense. It was within the framework of his responsibility, but he also understood the potential ramifications for Alex Barnes. Gardner dealt with the DOD, many times before, on experiments conducted within the context of fulfilling government contracts. But this was different. Laboratories functioned within the sphere of compliance with governmental agencies. Those were the treaties and bargains each made for the purpose of secrecy and control. Barnes worked outside the alliances. He was an unknown rogue and his discovery was a potential threat. Gardner knew the findings invited a severe risk to Barnes because of the threat it presented to secrets centuries old. It also spawned a disruption to Gardner's own consciousness, as he was instrumental in exposing Barnes.

Unlike Gardner's fantasy of the old prospector, he could not allow himself to envision features, or the humanity of Barnes. Any perceived image would further bind their connection, and ultimately haunt Gardner. Barnes must remain a faceless phantom; only a name printed on a form. Within that context, Gardner could see himself as a scientist following protocol and not become recognizable as a potential executioner. Because of his discovery of monoatomic gold, Barnes became important to people he had never met. To them, he was neither loved nor respected. To them, he had become the worst thing of all…feared. By forwarding the analysis to the DOD, Gardner became an unwilling pawn in the struggle between their fear and reaction. He also found himself stuck in the middle of a volatile contradiction. More importantly, he knew he became a contradiction to himself.

Gardner retrieved the briefcase from the floor and placed it on his desk. He removed the key from his pocket and unlocked both clasps. Reaching into the briefcase, he withdrew a large blank envelope which he quickly stuffed into a larger FedEx envelope. Turning to the picture of Clara, he focused on Monsignor Clementi standing beside her. He recalled the picture was taken on the last day of their trip. It was a bright sunny day at the Cafe Bernini situated in the Piazza Navona. Gardner and Clara were ambivalent about the day. They were sad to leave Rome, but anxious to get home. Gardner remembered the Monsignor saying: *"Do good things and let me hear from you. We need to keep in touch. You know that."*

"Yes, I know. I'll keep in touch," he had replied.

Gardner was true to his word and kept in touch. They had many communications and some were not social in nature. They maintained a strange alliance; the scientist and the clergyman. Somehow, they were able to strike an understanding that circumvented the intrinsically opposing philosophies. Gardner reached for the phone and tapped in the code for Rome. He suddenly replaced the phone and turned toward his computer. Clicking on the Instant Message icon, he entered the address for Monsignor Joseph Clementi.

"*Hello, Monsignor,*" he typed. "*r u there?*"

The screen remained still for a moment, then a reply appeared.

"*Yes. Good evening, Horace. Although, I suspect its afternoon where u r. I had just finishing a text conversation with a colleague. I was about to sign off. You caught me in time. How r u?*"

Gardner began typing again.

"*I'm glad my timing was good. It appears to be the work of divine intervention. I'm well. And u, Monsignor?*"

"*Doing well. Busy. Pope Benedict is in the process of making appointments to the Holy Church's Supreme Court. He's also choosing a representative for the International Eucharistic Congress being held in Canada. Needless to say, there's much work to do. Clara and Gloria r well?*" came the typed reply.

"*Both r well. Thank you.*"

"*And things at Brookhaven?*"

Gardner hesitated before typing. He suspected any events at the Institute were the Monsignor's main concern.

"*Interesting,*" he typed slowly and hesitantly.

"*How so?*"

"*I'm sending u via FedEx a report from a laboratory in Copenhagen. A report prepared by Thomas Swenson. Read it carefully. If u have any questions, please don't hesitate to call.*"

"*Should I ask what's in the report?*"

"*When u receive the package, I suggest u give it your highest attention.*"

"*Thank u. Then I will.*"

"*There is also a name and address of a man in the United States...*"

Gardner stopped typing. He put his face in his hands and closed his eyes. Instinctively, he wanted to delete the entire text message and tear up the envelope containing the report.

"*What of him?*"

Gardner removed his hands from his face and opened his eyes. He read the terse reply and sensed it was laces with anger. He paused unable to continue; consumed by a strange anxiousness and doubt.

"*Horace?????*" Clementi's typed message appeared. The multiple question marks confirmed Gardner's suspicion of Clementi's impatience and anger.

"Just his name and address" Gardner typed. *"Alex Kenneth Barnes. You'll understand when u read the report."*

Gardner deleted the entire text message giving the illusion it was never sent. However, Gardner's conscience knew otherwise. Sitting back in his chair, he looked at the picture of Clara and Clementi. This time he focused on Clementi. The clergyman appeared benign and friendly, at ease with redemption. In his black shirt and white priestly collar, he projected an image of clarity and reverence. Gardner looked closer and distrusted Clementi's self-ordained notion of salvation. He sensed Clementi had learned the nuance of salvation was best when used to manipulate and as a barrier for disillusionment.

For the first time, Gardner took notice of the Monsignor's smile. It was bright and welcoming yet somehow sinister and deceiving. Clementi was part of a centuries old society that made an art of keeping its worst secrets protected and hidden. Gardner knew the Monsignor was just one more in a long line of clerics and crusaders struggling to prevent true enlightenment. Gardner leaned forward in his chair and picked up the phone. He tapped in a number and waited.

"Our Lady of Grace Rectory," a voice answered.

"Father Keating, please," Gardner whispered.

There was a click then a slight pause.

"Hello, this is Father Keating. How can I help you?" The priest's voice sounded trusting and familiar. Yet it could not penetrate Gardner's distress.

"Father Michael, its Horace Gardner."

"Hello, Horace. How are you?"

Gardner could not conceal his angst. A wayward flutter of menace had taken hold of him with command and authority.

"Father, I was wondering if you'll be at the rectory tonight."

"Yes, I will. Why do you ask, Horace?"

"I'd like to come by later. After work."

"Certainly. What is it you want? What can I help you with?"

"I would like you to hear my confession."

"Horace is everything alright?" the priest asked.

"I'm not sure. I just want you to hear my confession tonight?"

"Of course I will. You sound a bit distressed. Is there anything you need to tell me now?"

Gardner looked at the photo of Monsignor Joseph Clementi once again. It revealed a deeper truth with each viewing. It captivated him in a way that was ominous. The deceptive smile revealed a mercilessness that stepped beyond the bounds of consciousness. Seeing beyond the smile was a way for

Gardner to unveil Clementi's dubious mission. It suddenly became clear to Gardner; Clementi's personal crusade was to preserve the orthodoxy and chosen fundamentalism without reverence or morality.

Gardner printed Alex Barnes' name on a piece of paper and drew a double line under it. After rubbing his eyes, he looked at the lines, which blurred and seemed to reconfigure, converging into a cross-hair.

"Yes, Father. There is." Gardner replied. "I think I just condemned a man to death."

ITALY

MONSIGNOR Joseph Clementi knelt in a pew in the long portico of Maderno's nave in St. Peter's Basilica. The nave was a long barrel vault and decorated with ornate stucco and gilt. It was illuminated by the sunlight pouring in from the small windows between the pendentives. The nave was quiet and occupied by only a handful of tourists. An occasional flash from a camera, mixed with the light reflected in from the piazza and onto the ornate marble floor. A woman, wearing a white bandana, sat on the floor sketching the equestrian column of Charlemagne. Everyone in the nave seemed isolated and engrossed in their own personal reverence.

Clementi positioned himself between the ionic columns by Cornacchini and Bernini. He made the sign of the Cross on his forehead, lips and chest with his thumb and looked at the mosaic reproduction of Raphael's "Sistine Madonna." Clementi bowed his head, cupping his face in his hands. He placed a blank envelope on the floor by his knees. The envelope contained the report from Horace Gardner. The Monsignor's shoulders were hunched. His head bowed. He was locked humbly in the secret mystery of prayer. The mystery was absolute and universal; laid down for a child or a Pope. It was not always that Clementi accepted the mystery and trusted in its laws of blessings and forgiveness. Prayer became a deeper mystery, especially in times of trouble and doubt. He could never clearly decipher the manner in which they were answered.

The burden of Clementi's doubt, caused by the contents of the envelope, became a burnt offering for which he sought guidance and intervention. Clementi knelt quietly trying to will his way into the sphere of mystery. There were no doors to unlock, no chambers to navigate. Just a mystical presence he hoped to penetrate. Trusting he was in that place, he needed his prayer to be honest and simple, void of judgments and guilt.

"Dear Jesus," Clementi whispered. "Know my intentions and guide my actions. All done in your name. I know judgment is yours. I trust in your mercy...Amen."

Clementi knew there was nothing more to say. He retraced the Sign of the Cross on himself and rose from the pew. Gathering up the envelope, he walked to the four cherubs against the first piers of the nave. He dipped his fingers into the basin of Holy Water and blessed himself. Then he left the Basilica.

The morning sun shone brightly in St. Peter's Square. The breeze that often swirled within the walled enclave was non existent. The area was now thick and overrun with worldwide tourists. A group of German school children, led by two teachers, passed by Clementi as they entered the Basilica. A tour group posed for a photo taken by their guide. People with cameras dangling from their necks milled about, occasionally referring to guide books and maps searching for directions to exhibits. Clementi overheard the fragments of their conversations spoken in many different languages. Two members of the Vatican Police Corps casually walked the square, attentive to the people and their movements. Noticing Clementi, they acknowledged the Monsignor, bowing their heads respectfully. Flocks of pigeons strutted among the tourists, pecking at the ground for discard crumbs, morsels of nuts and seeds.

Clementi walked through the crowd until he approached the Vatican obelisk. Brought to Rome by Caligula, it was the only obelisk in Rome that remained intact since the Roman Empire. He stepped on the circular shadow of the top of the structure and was quickly reminded of the original gilt ball that had been removed. It was claimed to contain the ashes of Julius Caesar. Clementi could not concern himself with the history of the obelisk or the ashes of Caesar. He believed history could become cumbersome, and a distraction and should never be confused with tradition.

Standing among the crowd at the foot of the obelisk, was Monsignor Carlo Benotti. The old Monsignor looked frail; worn down by years and the things that prayer had not yet resolved. From a distance, Clementi could see the old Monsignor was uncomfortable, bothered by the warm sun. Benotti removed a white handkerchief from his back pocket and wiped the perspiration from his forehead and upper lip.

Clementi was just a priest when he first met the Monsignor. They were chosen to serve under the General Secretary of Conferences of Catholic Bishops. Benotti was younger then, but displayed early signs of contrition to the onslaught the world placed on his faith. A fierce duality raged within the core of the old Monsignor. His belief in fundamentalism ran contrary to his sense for the romantic. As a young boy, Bonetti was deeply influenced by the romantic poetry of Giacomo Leopardi and the Iranian poet, Hafez.

The poet, Leopardi, a child candidate for the priesthood, loved what was not directly given in life. After years of disillusionment, Leopardi clung to his poetry but came to despise the consolations of religion.

Hafez, a quiet teacher of the Koran, seemed to never surrender his romantic slant nor relinquish his religious belief. The works of both poets still lined the book shelves in his library. He still read them in his later years and still assessed their influence and impact. However, Benotti found his sensibilities and disillusionments more aligned with those of Leopardi.

In later years, using a pen name, Benotti became a novelist. His stories were gothic and grand. The settings were always medieval Europe. The stories always pitted the nobility, who included bishops of the church, against the lower class serfs. The members of nobility were traditionally bound by service and loyalty, while the serfs were confronted with suppression and survival. A local book critic once described Benotti's novels as inconclusive in that the author exposed the struggles of each class, but ultimately never declared which became victor or vanquished. Clementi suspected Benotti's novels were an extension of his own inner duality that still remained unresolved. In some cases, the novels were a replacement for his personal prayers.

"Sorry to keep you waiting Monsignor," Clementi said as he approached Benotti.

"It's rather warm today," Benotti observed.

"Yes it is. Have you been here long?"

"No, just long enough to observe the tourists. Tell me, Joseph, do you travel?"

"It's not one of my priorities, Monsignor."

"Pity. You should make it so. Take it from an old man."

"You're far from old, Monsignor."

"Ha. Says you."

There was a slight hint of melancholy in the old Monsignor's voice. It cracked slightly like the scratchy sounds of the old records Benotti would play. Clementi looked closely at the Monsignor trying to gauge what traits of his he was manifesting, and those he was trying to avoid.

"Tell me, Monsignor, what do you think attracts so many tourists to Rome, especially the non-Catholics?"

"Not a simple question, Joseph. But, I'll tell you what I think. Non-Asians travel to the Great Wall. Caucasians travel to Africa...Jews to Germany and vise versa. I had an old friend of mine, a Sicilian farmer. As unlikely a traveler as you're apt to find. He once climbed the pyramids of Giza and trekked across Tasmania. On the day I administered the sacrament of Extreme Unction to him, he admitted to me he regretted not flying in one of the U.S. Apollo missions. I suspect the reason people travel is to fulfill their need to experience history. They need to embed their spirit into something greater than themselves. Being a part of history means one will be eternal."

"Is that why you suggest I travel more?"

"No. You see that's the tourists' illusion. All that travel succeeds in creating is personal memories. No matter how much they travel to any ancient place, they will never be a part of that place's history. I don't want you to suffer their illusion, Joseph. I don't want you to create personal memories. I want you to create history."

Clementi felt a sudden weight of responsibility and expectation he had never felt before. It was unexpectedly thrust upon him by the old man, who passed off a mantle that was much too burdensome for him to carry. On this ordinary sunny day, in an enclave filled with people, the old Monsignor bequeathed to his protégée a directive and a curse. Clementi was suddenly reminded of the envelope he carried. It was like a haunting presence that caused his sweaty palm and fingers to make moist impressions into the brown velum paper.

"So tell me, Joseph," the old Monsignor continued. "Does that envelope you're carrying have anything to do with your phone call and this meeting?"

"It does. Let's walk, Monsignor."

The young Monsignor slipped his hand under Benotti's arm as they walked away from the obelisk.

"The envelope contains a report sent to me by Horace Gardner..."

"Horace Gardner, your doctor friend from Brookhaven in the United States?"

"Yes. Actually the report originated in Copenhagen....The Niels Bohr Institute. They're affiliated with Brookhaven..."

"Go on," Benotti said impatiently.

"Because they're affiliated, certain discoveries made by the Copenhagen Institute must be sent to Brookhaven. Especially, if those discoveries contain information the U.S. Department of Defense is interested in."

"Why would the Department of Defense be interested in the report?"

"Because the material tested in the Copenhagen laboratory showed to have properties conducive to a superconductor."

"And what's so unusual about that?"

"The material is manna."

Monsignor Benotti stopped and turned to face Clementi. The old man's frailty suddenly vanished, replaced by a vitality of anger and surprise.

"Manna?" Benotti whispered.

Clementi looked into the old Monsignor's wide, fiery eyes and nodded.

"Are you sure? Is the report conclusive?" Benotti continued.

"Yes. It's conclusive."

Benotti took a deep breath. The signs of his age crept back into the graying color of his skin.

"Tell me more about the material," Benotti said softly. "The manna…I want to know about its origin."

"Apparently, it was submitted by a miner from Arizona."

"How did this miner come to have possession of this material?"

"The assumption is he mined it."

"Not likely."

"Why?"

"Not likely, I say. Possible, but not likely. How would this miner even suspect what the material is?"

"It's speculated he has no idea what the material is."

Benotti became quiet and sullen. He felt his mind sorting through a maze of old memories and new situations. He suddenly encountered a bold epic that could make a great novel, if he was truthful and brave enough to approach the subject. Benotti allowed his inner turmoil to fester, but did not permit it to disrupt his process of logic.

"Tell me, Joseph, how much manna was sent to the Institute for testing?"

"As I understand it, very little."

"But, did the miner give anyone at the Copenhagen Institute any indication how much manna he has in his possession?"

"No."

"You don't suppose the Flinders Petrie find has resurfaced?"

"No, Monsignor. Petrie's manna find was lost over one hundred years ago. His find was in Iraq."

"Egypt. His find was in Egypt, not Iraq."

"It was lost, nonetheless."

"Perhaps it was. But, who can be certain? I've seen things happen in this world, Joseph, that were totally improbable. But, yet…"

"Surely, after one hundred years, the laws of probability have been accounted for," Clementi interrupted.

"Joseph, never take too much for granted. In this case, the law of improbability is not a history I envisioned you to be a part of."

"History or not, Monsignor, I sense a strange fate drawing me into a role I can't quite understand."

"It will all be revealed. Just be careful how you proceed and be patient."

There was a subliminal blessing in the way Benotti spoke. It revealed a pact that had been instigated by his earlier prayer. Clementi felt a trust emanating from the old Monsignor and tried to test his theory further.

"Monsignor, I was thinking of contacting Mario Orisi and Umberto Nunarro. I was thinking of utilizing their services to have them intervene in this situation. Have them deal with the miner, and his mine as well."

"So, that's what you wanted to ask me from the beginning?" the old man said.

"Yes."

"I see…What causes your doubt?"

"I guess my doubt is Mario and Umberto. Their methods can be alarming…I believe they're Godless men."

"Joseph, it's not your doubt that troubles you. It's your guilt."

The brutal honesty of Benotti cut Clementi to his consciousness exposing the root of his failure. The old Monsignor's implication was clear to Clementi. He was unable to convince Orisi and Nunarro of God and salvation.

"Don't concern yourself with their methods," Benotti continued. "Mario and Umberto are trustworthy men. Their honor is God given. They're not as godless as you suspect. You should rely on them…You should rely on them immediately."

MARIO Orisi sat next to Umberto Nunarro at an umbrella covered table outside a cafe on the Piazza della Rotonda. Behind the café was the Pantheon, an ancient structure older than Jesus Christ. The sound of water pouring from the Fontana del Pantheon was overcome by the conversation of the patrons at the cafe. A blur of golden, candescent lights softened the warm night air that hung over the piazza. An old man, clutching his cap, stood in the center of the piazza singing an Italian love song. It was clear his baritone voice had been professionally trained but was showing signs of wear. The baritone was accompanied by a violinist who looked to be the baritone's twin. The two old troubadours attracted a small group of admirers. A little girl of five, encouraged by her mother, broke from the circle and shyly handed the baritone a flower. The clopping sounds of horse hooves striking the ancient cobblestone blended like the percussion section of an orchestra. A horse pulled carriage, filled with a tourist family of four, were eating gelato from plastic cups. A man, with a small red ball on his nose, walked around the baritone's audience, juggling three colorful circus clubs.

Orisi and Nunarro heard the horse hooves on the cobblestone. They heard the violin, the baritone, the applause of the small circular audience and saw the juggler, but acknowledged none of them. They remained stoic among the lively chatter of the tourists at the café. The centuries old Pantheon, accented in the golden light, with its sacred history, did not command their slightest attention. Orisi and Nunarro remained tucked in their insulated world of detachment and indifference.

Orisi peered out over the rim of the demitasse cup. His suspicious nature made him a slave to his distrust. He watched the crowd as though somewhere within it a threat was lurking. As a former member of the Esercito Italiano army, Orisi was part of the 2nd Alpini Regiment serving in Afghanistan. As part of the 1,700 NATO force, serving in a peace keeping capacity, his missions were usually considered low risk as compared to the United States and other coalition combat troops. Nonetheless, danger was everywhere in the mountainous terrain. Orisi had a natural command of war. His instincts were cunning. His reactions to combat were swift and fearless. During a single skirmish with Taliban forces, Orisi disabled two enemy tanks with a rocket launcher, killing five of their fighters. Approaching the disabled tanks, one of the wounded soldiers attacked Orisi. During the struggle, Orisi managed to subdue the fighter. Then he proceeded to strangle the fighter with his own unraveled turban.

Upon his discharge from the service, Orisi was awarded the Military Order of Italy in the Knight Class. The commendation sited his bravery and actions specific to the skirmish. On his bookcase, Orisi proudly displayed the badge made of a golden Matuna cross, enameled in white with a wreath of green enameled laurel and oak leaves between the arms of the cross. Prominently displayed next to the award was a Damascus steel knife the wounded Taliban soldier used to attack him.

After his tour of duty in Afghanistan, Orisi joined the Carabinieri, the official police of Italy. According to the Sea Island Conference of the G8 in 2004, the Carabinieri were given mandate to establish a Center of Excellence for Stability Police. Orisi was spearheading a conference in Vicenza on the doctrines of development and training for civilian police units. It was during this time, everything changed for him.

On a cool evening, Orisi strolled through the narrow streets of Vicenza when he heard muffled struggles coming from the hallway of a home. He burst into the hallway to see five men attacking a young girl. Without saying a word, Orisi struck one man in the head with a baton. The man fell to his knees, blood spraying onto the floor. In one swift motion, Orisi spun and quickly struck a second man in the throat. The man grabbed his throat gasping for air. The remaining men turned and attacked Orisi. In the ensuing scuffle, Orisi was able to swing his baton again crashing it against the nose of another man. Blood sprayed onto Orisi face and neck. One of the attackers punched Orisi, while the other grabbed the baton. The men were young and strong, disciplined in the way of combat. The struggle was fierce, and in the end, Orisi had all five attackers down and bleeding.

It wasn't until after the fight did Orisi realize he had been slashed across the face by a knife.

When the civilian police arrived, it was discovered the five men were all drunk and part of the 173rd Airborne Brigade stationed at Caserma Ederle in Vicenza. They were part of a bilateral agreement with NATO membership, allowing them to be stationed in the host city. The five soldiers were departmentally charged with assault, but were ultimately given minimal military reprimand. The army felt the beating by Orisi was enough of a reprimand. Fortunately, the girl, the daughter of a textile worker, was not harmed. Thanks to Orisi, her honor remained intact.

Unfortunately, the damage to Orisi's face left permanent nerve damage. At times, his mouth would twitch involuntarily. The scar traced a crimson line from the edge of his mouth to his jaw giving Orisi a clownish frown. Shortly after the incident, Orisi developed alopecia. Attacking his immune system, the disease caused all his hair to fall out. With no hair on his head and face, the crimson scar became more pronounced. Because of the nerve damage to his face and compromised immune system, Orisi was discharged from the Carabinieri.

Umberto Nunarro did not acknowledge the waiter, who made his way through the narrow spaces and approached the table.

"Yes, sir?" the waiter asked.

"Bring us a bottle of Sambuca," Nunarro said still not looking at the waiter. "Also, a full pot of demitasse and a third cup," he continued.

"Yes sir," the waiter said. "Would you also like…"

"Just what I ordered," Nunarro interrupted. "Just bring it."

"Yes sir," the waiter said a bit frightened and walked away.

Nunarro took a cigarette from the package on the table, and lit it with a solid gold lighter. He offered Orisi a cigarette, pushing the package toward him. Orisi looked at the package, then turned his attention to the patrons in the café. Taking a long drag from the cigarette, Nunarro blew a stream of smoke into the night air. He looked at the expensive lighter and rubbed it fondly. The lighter, along with a gold watch, diamond bracelet, and gold cuff links had been gifts from an Arab emir. The lavish show of gratitude from the emir was for the professional bodyguard services provided his daughter.

Nunarro had been a demolition engineer working on the construction of the Dubai Central Library. It was a humid afternoon, and Nunarro had just set dynamite charges into the shelf bedrock. The dust from the explosion had settled, and Nunarro was scheduling demolition at another location on the site. He walked by a deep crater he had recently detonated. It was being backfilled to support the deeply struck pilings. It was hard for

Nunarro to imagine his demolition and destruction would give way to a building designed to look like a Turkish lectern.

On the opposite side of the deep crater, Nunarro spotted a long, dark limousine. Emerging from the vehicle was the emir, four of his associates and the emir's daughter. The emir and his associates were greeted by several Arab engineers. They were quickly escorted to a staging area, where they could overlook the entire construction site. The emir's daughter remained by the limousine. While she held a cell phone to her ear, she struggled with the wind to hold her loose fitting dress close to her body. Her gaze passed over the construction site to the Al Mamzar Lagoon in the background. A flatbed truck carrying piles of galvanized piping drove past the limousine. The truck struggled to navigate the rugged, hilly terrain. Turning into a bad angle, the truck listed to one side. Just as Nunarro approached the limousine, the top-heavy load caused the flatbed truck to topple over. The straps holding the pipes gave way and avalanched in the direction of the limousine. The emir's daughter heard the crash behind her. Turning to see the pipes rolling toward her, she had become terrified and unable to move. Nunarro grabbed the young woman and jumped into the crater. An instant later, the pipes slammed into the limousine crushing it.

The emir had witnessed the entire incident. He was helpless to save his daughter. He ran from the staging area past the fallen pipes and the crushed limousine to the crater where Nunarro and his daughter had jumped. Several of the pipes had fallen into the crater, but they had bounced away and did not harm Nunarro or the emir's daughter.

Climbing out of the crater, the associates pushed Nunarro aside and attended to the emir's daughter. Finally, the emir approached Nunarro who was coughing and spitting out dirt. Before the emir could say anything, Nunarro apologized in Arabic to the emir for grabbing his daughter and jumping with her into the crater. The emir looked at the crushed limousine, and realized if Nunarro had not reacted the way he did, his daughter would have been killed.

That evening, as Nunarro sat in his hotel room applying a bag of ice to his swollen hand, there was a knock at the door. A tall man, wearing a dark suit, asked Nunarro to come with him. Nunarro's sense of caution was overcome by his curiosity. He followed the man to a black Mercedes Benz parked at the curb. There was another man holding the door open, allowing Nunarro to enter. They drove a moderate distance, finally stopping before an elaborately scrolled gate that completely surrounded an elegant palace. The gate opened, and the car continued into a lavish courtyard where Nunarro saw the emir standing under a lighted portico. There was no entourage or servants with the emir. The man seemed perfectly at ease not being surrounded and waited on by associates, secretaries or servants. More importantly, he felt comfortable being alone with the foreign construction worker. As the escort left the courtyard, the emir approached Nunarro and embraced him.

"Greetings, Mister Nunarro," the emir said. "Thank you for accepting my invitation to come to my home."

Nunarro knew, in the short time since the incident, the emir had him thoroughly investigated. If Nunarro had a dubious past or questionable reputation he would not have been shown this courtesy and hospitality, even if he saved his daughter's life.

"I'm honored to be asked to you home," Nunarro responded.

"I am grateful beyond words for the bravery you displayed today."

"With all due respect, I just reacted. I truly didn't see my actions as a show of bravery."

"You don't seem to understand, Mister Nunarro. Fate put you between my daughter and the danger she faced. You saved her life. Someone else in that same position may not have acted in the manner you did. You don't see that as bravery? That's modest of you. But, allow me to present this another way. Because of what you did, brave or otherwise, you and I are forever linked."

"I am honored by that bond between us," Nunarro said. "I also accept the fate that drove me to act the way I did today."

"Good. We understand each other. Now, follow me. I would like to properly introduce you to my daughter and her mother."

Nunarro remembered the extravagance of the palace. Gold was everywhere; inlaid in the Italian marble columns and floors, in the rims and stems of glassware, and elaborate designs in the windows. Ornate vases with pure gold handles lined every hallway and sitting room. Ibrahim Marzouk paintings adorned several walls. Sculptures by Youssef Ghossoub were placed around the grounds, as if created exclusively for the setting. The palace was a total dedication to the virtues of opulence and indulgence. They walked through a large sitting room. Damascus cotton drapes billowed as the breeze blew in from the garden. A woman stood just outside the room facing the garden. The smell of jasmine filled the air capturing her attention.

"This is my wife," the emir announced. "Aaminah."

The woman turned from the garden and smiled. Nunarro approached the woman and shook her hand. She seemed awkward and uneasy. Aaminah made a slight movement toward Nunarro with the thought of hugging him. The instant she did, the emir shot her a disapproving glance, stopping her abruptly. Aaminah was permitted to keep her gratitude only within the distance of her out stretched hand, and forced to keep her thankfulness silent, neatly placed within all the other silences of which she was accustomed. The moment was awkward, as she expressed herself with only a slight nod of her head.

"Aaminah," Nunarro said deflecting the uncomfortable silence. "I am honored. Please forgive my familiarity, but does not Aaminah mean lady of peace and harmony?"

The emir's eyes widened and a slight smile of admiration crossed his face.

"You know our language well," the emir said.

"I've been working in your country for several years. I'm trying to learn as much as possible. Not just your language but your culture."

Then Nunarro looked past Aaminah seeing the daughter of the emir walking toward them. With each step, she exuded a deep rooted grace and self-assurance. He noticed the scrapes and bruises on her cheek and forehead, remnants from the fall. Her skin was raw, and covered with salve. Nunarro did not focus on the bruises; only her beauty. Her eyes were dark, bright and alert. The luster of her bronze colored skin was accentuated by the setting sun flooding in from the garden. When she smiled, there was a radiance of truth and honesty. She did not look down or away but right into Nunarro's eyes. Every detail and feature of the emir's daughter, Nunarro recalled with exact clarity.

"My daughter, Adilah," the emir said with pride.

"Hello, Adilah. I'm sorry for the bruises to your face," Nunarro said.

"Nonsense. I'm sure my father has told you how indebted he is to you. Speaking for myself, I too am indebted beyond words."

Adilah seemed more assertive than her mother. She was not encumbered by traditions that governed gender. Nunarro learned later Adilah had attended schools and universities in Paris, Zurich and the United States. He suspected some of her independence had been molded by the experience.

Nunarro was treated to a lavish dinner. Adilah sat on opposite him at the table. Their glances toward each other were more than casual or accidental. After dinner, the emir walked with Nunarro through the courtyard to a waiting car. There he offered Nunarro a job as bodyguard to Adilah. Refusing would have been an insult, as the emir was certain a spiritual connection had formed. Rejection, on Nunarro's behalf, would further demonstrate a callous disregard for the emir's beliefs and disavow the possibility of a divine bond. As Nunarro had become dissatisfied with his position as a demolition engineer, he accepted the emir's offer.

For two years, he traveled the world with the emir's daughter. It was a remarkable experience. The pay was beyond anything he could have earned by blowing holes in the earth. During the two years, Nunarro had fallen in love with Adilah. However, marrying her would not have been accepted by the emir. Having an affair with her would not have been accepted by Nunarro. On a trip to Monte Carlo, Nunarro stood with Adilah on the deck of the emir's yacht. They looked at the city aglow with lights. Nunarro held Adilah's hand and kissed it igniting her intuitiveness.

"What does that kiss mean?" she asked.

"It means I have to leave," he said reluctantly.

"Why?" she asked.

"We both know why, Adilah. I will not be permitted to marry you…"

"I decide who I will marry, and who I will not."

"Yes, I'm sure you will, but there are traditions and beliefs you should not try to oppose. Your father would be hurt if you decided to marry me."

"My father loves you like a son."

"Yes, but not like a son-in-law."

"That's absurd…"

"No, it's not. It's something he will never allow. I cannot betray him by dishonoring you. That is something I can never allow."

"What of things I can never allow? Such as letting you go."

"Adilah…"

"No. No." She interrupted. "I won't hear of it. The old traditions were meant in my mother's time. Let them stay there, buried. I'm of a new generation…a new philosophy."

"Adilah, your name means one who deals justly…"

"I know what my name means."

"So does your father…Adilah, we both must do what's right. There is no other way."

They shared a final dinner at Le Louis XV in the Hotel de Paris in Monte Carlo. Adilah struggled with the night and with the fear of it ending. She was hurt and angry. Her eyes showed only sadness. Nunarro could never forget the look of pain in her eyes, and time had not diminished the haunting effect it had on him.

As they left the hotel, Nunarro placed a silk shawl over her shoulders. Adilah ran down the stairs of the hotel into a waiting car. It was only when she was in the back seat of the car, did she cry. Nunarro watched as the car drove away. He stood on the stairs of the hotel struggling to deal with his own pain, and to find a clue to his future. The emir knew exactly why Nunarro decided to leave. He had great respect for Nunarro's decision and had offered him gifts of a gold watch, cigarette lighter, cuff links and bracelet.

Nunarro finally put the gold lighter into his shirt pocket as the waiter brought the pot of demitasse and a bottle of Sambuca. Orisi spotted Monsignor Clementi walking through the crowd, maneuvering past the closely spaced café tables.

"Good evening, Monsignor," Nunarro said, as the Monsignor sat down at the table.

"Hello my friends," Clementi responded. "The tourist crowds grow larger each year."

"It seems that way, yes."

"I was speaking with Monsignor Benotti earlier today. He believes people travel because they feel the need to be part of history."

"But, I believe people travel because it gives them one less regret in their lives," Orisi responded.

"Well, whatever the reason, I thank you for coming here on such short notice."

"Your message sounded urgent," Nunarro said

"It was. I hope you both have some time."

"How much time?" Orisi asked.

"About a week."

"When?"

Clementi reached for the pot of demitasse and poured it into the cups of Nunarro and Orisi; then his own. Orisi removed the cork from the bottle of Sambuca. He gestured to pour into the Monsignor's cup. The Monsignor nodded.

"Immediately," the Monsignor responded.

Clementi stirred his demitasse and sipped it slowly. He looked at Orisi and Nunarro and realized the years did not affect their physical appearance as much as their spirit. He noticed they both had become more distant, more indifferent and expressed a deep passion of abandonment.

Clementi met Orisi and Nunarro when they were part of a small, secretly funded group established to infiltrate Propaganda Due. Propaganda Due was a Masonic lodge once operating under the jurisdiction of The Grand Orient of Italy. Among P2's early history were crimes and mysteries, including the nationwide bribery scandal that caused the collapse of the Vatican affiliated Banco Ambrosiano. It was also alleged, P2 was involved in the assassination of Prime Minister Aldo Moro. There were concerns in the earlier part of P2's charter, certain members had plotted the assassination of the Pope. When two known members of P2 were found shot to death, Clementi suspected Orisi and Nunarro, and asked if they wished to make a confession. They both refused. The clandestine relationship with Orisi and Nunarro worked well. What became more important for Clementi, than learning any covert information of the workings of P2 was to trust the methods and loyalty of Orisi and Nunarro.

"So tell us, Monsignor, what is so urgent?" Orisi said.

The Monsignor finished stirring his demitasse. Then pushed the cup aside. Leaning in, his eyes shifted to the nearby tables.

"I need you to take a trip to Arizona," Clementi whispered. "Butler, Arizona. It's in New Kingman."

"What's in New Kingman," Nunarro asked.

"A mine," the Monsignor responded.

"What kind of mine?" Orisi asked.

"It's a mine in the Cerbat Mountains. A mine that may contain secrets. The owner of the mine has filed an unpatented claim in Mohave County. I checked it. The claim is public record."

Orisi and Nunarro immediately recognized the Monsignor's vagueness and avoidance.

"Is it the mine or the owner of the mine that's significant?" Orisi asked.

Clementi sat back in his chair and nervously rubbed his hands together. He looked at the café crowd to avoid the reality proposed by Orisi. But mostly it was the stern demonic look in Orisi's eyes that attested to his capacity and penchant for a means to a resolution Clementi struggled with.

"Well, which is it?" Nunarro asked.

"The Mine. Mostly, the mine," Clementi finally responded. "However…"

"We understand," Orisi responded. "Don't say anything else."

"Good…So, will your schedules permit you to accommodate my timetable."

Orisi reached for the Sambuca and poured some into Nunarro's cup. Nunarro stirred the demitasse with the liquor and gently tapped the rim of the cup with the small spoon. The gesture was a proclamation, a stamped conclusion like the sentencing of one's fate. Clementi understood the verdict. He reached into his jacket pocket and produced two envelopes. Clementi placed them on the table.

"The envelopes contain first class airline tickets. There is also cash for expenses and fees. If more is required, please advise me. There will be no questions asked."

"What about the miner?" Nunarro asked.

"In the envelope, there's a map of where the claim is located. There is also an address in Butler, where the miner lives."

"What's the miner's name?" Nunarro asked.

"His name is Barnes…Alex Kenneth Barnes.

IRAQ

TWO Air Force Falcon F16CGs screamed over the Azmir Mountains, flying in close formation past the Ifraz Water Project. They banked northeast, and for a brief instant, sun reflected off their wings. In a gradual descent, they came in low and loud over the desert on the outskirts of Mosul. The deafening sounds of the engines reverberated on the desert floor with anger and aggression. Their unison flight was designed to convey the utmost of malice and hostility. They flew with a blind authority that was aggressive and beyond challenge.

The technology of the Falcons was honed for the sole purpose of massive violence, capable of delivering ordinance that controlled the apocalypse. They contained a power, claimed through self-serving righteousness. The only competition for total annihilation was God.

Approaching the pre-selected target, three air-to-surface missiles flew from each jet's external stations strafing the desert floor. A group of mud-packed homes, newly suspected enemy hiding places, were blown apart and disintegrated. In an instant, the jets flew beyond the village, coming upon a vehicle driving from it. The vehicle drove at a frantic pace, but was shattered to tiny pieces by the jet's M-61 A1 20-mm weapon, precluding its escape with ultimate judgment. The ground shook from the barrage of exploding ordinance. A stack of black acrid smoke, mixed with plumes of sand, rose up like a genetically engineered mass. A mingling profusion of plotted devastation peeled open the earth exposing gaping wounds.

The jets were unforgiving. They gave no quarter to the mud homes, the truck or the desert. Their swift flight and heavy arsenal patronized their own solemn power and massive effect. There was a smug bullishness to the Falcons' attack, and an unsighted victory to their mission. The smoke and sand were the only visualizations. They conspired in concealing all possible harm making the strike seem like an impersonal video game.

The mechanical strike, delivered with authority and precision, forged a demolition complete with maximum rule. The simple homes were gone forever; never to conceal suspected enemy or harbor an innocent family. The truck and its inhabitants existed only in smoldering shards and bloody pieces soon to be buried by the shifting sand. All that remained was the disfigured desert. Eventually, it would recover from the vicious attack. The natural cycle of the desert would fill in and heal the fresh signs of injury and abuse.

The two F16CGs flew away as quickly as they arrived; co-conspirators in an act of state-run terror. The pilots did not stay to revel in the meager triumph. In an instant, they were beyond retaliation. In their wake remained rubble and non-assessable damage permitted by the protocols of engagement and power. The once peaceful landscape was now a vision of damage and chaos.

The jets climbed high into the blue sky, maneuvering in unison away from the fires they created. Streaks of white exhaust trailed from their engines. They were at ease with the sky and made a complete full circle rotation in the expanse of its safety and openness. Their aerial spin was a collaborative expression of jubilation and mocking celebration of a mission well performed.

FROM a distance, a caravan of four Army Humvees drove toward the decimated site. The vehicles approached from the undulating horizon. They sped across the desert harboring their own intent and level of destruction. There was nothing merciful or benevolent about their approach. The concept of rescue and aid was truly divergent to the orders of the soldiers and melded with the power and philosophy of the weapons they manned. Each Humvee was occupied by four American soldiers. Captain Eli Hicks sat in the first Humvee and commanded the entire squad. He held on tightly as the vehicle bounced on the unpaved road.

As the caravan drew closer to the demolished village, they remained in formation, driving in a wide circle around the rubble. With each pass, they slowed and made smaller concentric circles until they neared the crumbled foundations of the former village. The gunners of each Humvee stood manning the MK-19s.

Hector Solis steadied himself concentrating on the destruction and for any potential movement. He did not allow the swirling sand, the roar of the engines or the acrid smoke to break his concentration. His focus was keen and absolute. Solis understood the mission. Field base was advised the bombed location may be a newly formed center of enemy activity. He took the intelligence seriously. With only weeks remaining to his tour of duty, he became more cautious, more frightened. Somehow, he aligned his upcoming discharge with the convention of chance. His mind gave in to the rationalization the longer he stayed in combat, the greater his chances of harm. Consequently, he saw a fatalistic race unfolding between his discharge and impending doom. To Solis, it became a matter of numbers; an equation of statistics and likelihood. A grand formula he believed was always fate based. Through superstition, or the earnest sense of his mortality, Solis mastered a new standard to his caution. He did not want to tempt the humbling features of fate.

Captain Hicks stood up in the lead vehicle and ordered his driver to stop. As he jumped from the vehicle, the remaining Humvees halted behind him. Hicks walked backed to the vehicle commanded by Sergeant Harrington, never diverting his attention from the rubble.

"Sergeant Harrington," Hicks shouted over the sound of the engines. "Continue around to the northern point of the village. Establish a position there and maintain surveillance and radio communication. Above all, remember this is a combat zone considered highly volatile. Act in full offensive mode with total malice."

Hicks turned as a jeep approached rapidly. He stood astride from the Humvee and aimed his weapon as the oncoming vehicle drew near. Solis also responded. He pivoted and swung the .50 caliber machine gun around, aiming it at the vehicle. Harrington jumped from the Humvee and braced to fire.

"What the hell is this?" Hicks shouted angrily.

The jeep came to a stop. An Arabic man stood up. He was wearing a light blue long sleeve shirt, dark blue utility pants and dark blue baseball cap with the word POLICE embroidered above the bill. Beneath the word police were Arabic symbols also spelling "police". On the left sleeve of the policeman's shirt was an insignia of a blunted obelisk with a single embroidered line under it. The emblem indicated the rank of the patrolman.

"Don't shoot," the Arab man shouted. "Don't shoot. I'm Haddad bin Nasab of the Iraqi Police Service. Me and my driver are Iraqi police," bin Nasab said, pointing to the man driving the jeep.

"I don't care who you are," Hicks shouted. "Turn that vehicle around and leave this area, immediately."

"We're here to help. We're the I.P.S...."

"I said I don't care who you are," Hicks continued shouting, the veins in his neck protruding. "Vacate this area, immediately. We don't need your help. This is our mission."

"Captain, give me the order, and I'll neutralize this situation," Lieutenant Farley shouted from the gunner position on his Humvee.

"I got it from here, captain," Solis shouted, as he aimed his weapon at the occupants of the jeep.

The sound of bolted live rounds into the chamber from Farley's weapon shrieked above the combined sounds of the Humvees. The scene became angry and surreal for Hicks. The sounds of engines, weapons, overlapping shouts from his soldiers, and the Iraqi policeman concentrated into a ball of urgent confusion. The tension grew thick as it crackled in Hicks' eardrums and in his nerves. He tried to infuse the flashpoint with his own authority which he was becoming unsure of.

"Lieutenant, stand down," Hicks shouted to Farley in an attempt to take control of the situation. "Solis, you too! Shut up," Hicks shouted.

Turning back to the jeep, Hicks continued. "Now, for the last time, Haddad bin Nasab, this is my mission. Leave this area, immediately."

"Yes, it is your mission," bin Nasab responded. "We are not here to interfere. We will support your effort."

"You can support my efforts by standing down and leaving."

"We were trained by U.S. military. Trained by your military at Marez Base."

"This is no time to have this discussion. I will give the command to shoot if you don't stand down."

Policeman bin Nasab saw the two .50 caliber machine guns aimed at him. Through the dust he saw the anxiousness in the eyes of Farley and Solis. But, what became more of a threat was the sight of Harrington moving closer until he was standing directly beside him. The barrel of his weapon just inches from his head. The intensity of the two men manning the machine guns did not intimate bin Nasab as much as Harrington. He conveyed a silent menace that was immediate, and apparently not controlled by rank or command. Harrington appeared to be unfazed by the sounds and confusion of the moment. He was focused, purposeful and intent on controlling the standoff. There was an assuredness about his intentions that were measured and commensurate to the provocation.

"Sergeant Harrington, stand down," Hicks shouted.

Policeman bin Nasab turned slightly toward Harrington and nodded his head slowly.

"Allah, be with you, Sergeant Harrington," bin Nasab whispered to Harrington. "Peace," he continued, a coldness framing his words.

Then turning his attention to Hicks he shouted: "Very well, captain. Very well, sir. Your orders to stand down will be obeyed. We will back away," bin Nasab said.

"Good," Hicks shouted, relief in his voice. "Sergeant Harrington, get back in your vehicle and proceed to the northern point."

Harrington slowly lowered his weapon and leaned toward Haddad bin Nasab.

"You should really give thanks to Allah," he whispered to bin Nasab as he got into the jeep.

"Allah knows we shall meet again, Sergeant Harrington. It's a prophecy," bin Nasab said, as the jeep drove away.

Climbing into his Humvee, Harrington tapped Private Ed Heywood's leg and pointed to the north. Hicks approached the third vehicle as a fresh layer of sand poured over him as Heywood drove away.

The third vehicle was commanded by Lieutenant Michael Hart. Captain Hicks jumped up on Hart's vehicle and peered through his binoculars at the smoldering vehicle in the distance.

"Lieutenant," Hicks said. "Take your squad and investigate that vehicle. It appears to be totally compromised. Confirm that. Return and maintain presence on the east flank."

Hicks raised his tunic to protect his nose and mouth from the coarse sand. He pointed to the fourth Humvee commanded by Sergeant Farley, raised his two fingers to his own eyes; then moved his arm in a circular rotation. Farley understood the silent directive, and immediately started to drive in a tight circle around the zone. Three soldiers from Hicks' squad jumped off the vehicle. The meager force spread out and waded toward the rubble. On the north side of the village, Harrington's squad advanced toward the destruction.

The piles and mounds of dried mud were no longer recognizable as hideouts or homes. There was nothing that could be acknowledged as backyards, alleyways or gardens. Only three walls of a small house remained standing. Occasionally, protruding from the rubble, were pieces of damaged wood, remnants of a fence, or the framing of a wall, a cabinet, or pieces of a basket hand woven by the former inhabitants.

Harrington stepped on shards of pottery avoiding a crumbled book. He stopped and opened the flap of the book with the barrel of his M-16. He determined it to be a copy of the Koran. Next to the slightly burned holy book, was a piece of sheep skin, with a hand drawn map. The edges of sheep skin were charred. Looking at the map, Harrington recognized the Arabic writing but could not discern anything about the terrain or locations depicted. Continuing to move around the rubble, Harrington noticed three spade shovels and two long handle pick axes. Next to the pick axes were several bundles of canvas sacks tied with hemp and dozens of plastic pails. He noticed two crudely made wooden ladders. One had several broken rungs. The other was intact. Harrington drew his bayonet and cut the hemp binding of the sacks. Stabbing into the layers, he flipped them off and confirmed they were empty sacks. The pick axes were damaged and worn. The handle of one of the shovels was bound with a cloth.

The sound of the engine from Farley's Humvee diverted his attention from the sacks and tools. Turning, he noticed Solis carrying his M-16 in firing position. He had it pressed to his shoulder aiming at any phantom threats. Solis appeared stiff and tense beyond alert. The wide-eyed fright in Solis' eyes was apparent and disturbing with each step he took. Harrington looked at Heywood and Dobson. They appeared more at ease with the environment and seemed more assured by the lack of threat.

"Sergeant Harrington!" Hicks' voice blared through his field communication ear pieces. "You are within my visual contact, sergeant," Hicks informed.

Harrington looked up to see Hicks standing on top of a partially destroyed stone wall.

"Yes sir, I see you."

"Bring your squad to my position, sergeant. On the double."

Harrington waved to his men and pointed to the command position held by Hicks. Harrington's squad moved forward, traversing the newly ruined village. When they approached Hicks' position, the other squads were all present. Some of the soldiers were drinking water from plastic bottles while others poured the water over their heads and faces.

"This area appears to be secured," Hicks said to the squad leaders. "If this was an enemy position, I see no signs of weapons or communication equipment.

"I see no sign the area was inhabited," Harrington reported. "Perhaps, the intelligence was faulty or purposely misleading."

"Well, the vehicle we investigated seemed to be running from something," Lieutenant Hart reported.

"What's your assessment of the destroyed vehicle, lieutenant?" Hicks asked.

"Captain, the destroyed vehicle appears to be civilian in nature," Lieutenant Hart said.

"How many occupants were in the vehicle?" Hicks asked.

"As near as we can report, sir, there were eight," Hart said. "The vehicle was destroyed with total casualties."

"Was the vehicle equipped with weapons or communication equipment?"

"Negative, sir."

"Nothing to report here either," Lieutenant Farley commented. "There was no activity around the perimeter."

"Perhaps, the people may have been warned about our mission and cleared the area," Hicks said.

"All except those eight," Hart said pointing to the destroyed vehicle.

"Affirmative. Let's move out. Sergeant Harrington, give this place one more sweep and meet us back at field base."

"Yes sir."

The three Humvees with their squads left the area. As the vehicles drove away, the sun reflected brightly off the windshields. For an instant, the desert was quiet and still from the tempest of roaring engines and explosions.

"I'm glad this mission didn't turn out bad," Heywood said.

"I never trust a mission that could be the sight of enemy activity. But, it was a relief to see the F16s," Dobson commented.

"Let's go, Deuce," Solis said. "I just want to get outta here."

"Solis, you need to tell me why you're so on edge," Harrington said.

"What do you mean?"

"You know exactly what I mean. What's going on in your head, private?"

"What's goin' on in my head? I'll tell you what's goin' on in my head. My head is sayin' I just wanna get the fuck outta here. Two weeks and I'm done with this shit."

"Listen up, Hector. Whatever has brought you to the edge, you need to suck it up. Two weeks is not a lifetime."

"It could be."

"Get that fatalism out of your head right now, Solis. I told you once before, stay focused. Don't project. Your actions don't only affect you. Do you understand?"

Solis did not respond. He just turned his head and bit hard on a grain of sand in his mouth.

"I said do you understand?" Harrington said forcefully.

"Yeah. Yeah. I understand, sergeant."

"Good. Our orders are to make a final sweep and head back to the field base. Take the same positions going out as we did coming in. I no longer consider this a combat zone, but don't sleep walk. Move out."

"Hey, Solis," Heywood said, as he stepped over debris. "Why get so uptight. Living should scare you more than dying."

"That's real clever, Black Eddie. Real clever. Livin' here is like dyin'. That's why they call it hell. But, you're too stupid to know that."

Solis kicked at a plastic pail. He pulled on a splintered piece of plywood that was in his way. Under the plywood was a stone post. He climbed on it and raised his arms above his head.

"Two weeks and then fuck this desert," he shouted to the mountains and sky

Solis jumped down from the post and forced himself to sling the M-16 over his shoulder. It was his attempt to take command of his fears. The act was a meek try at freedom from his self inflicted paranoia. In the process of distancing himself from the weapon, he hoped his action would not invite the attention of a callous and vengeful fate.

There was no clear path for the squad to walk. They avoided mounds of sharp protruding pieces of wood and medal. Harrington saw the pick axes, shovels and the cut open bundles of sacks and wondered about their purpose. He tried to imagine them being used to build the small village.

"Hey, Dobson, we're almost home," Heywood shouted, pointing to the Humvee.

"You've been in this desert too long, Heywood," Dobson responded.

"Yeah? Why's that?"

"You refer to field base as home. This place will never be home."

Harrington stopped to search the ground for the sheep skin map and the battered copy of the Koran he had seen earlier.

"Hey, Deuce, what' you lookin' for?" Solis asked.

"A book. I saw it when we moved in."

"What kind of book?"

"A book that may tell me who was living here."

"There was nobody livin' here, Deuce."

"How do you know for sure?"

"How do I know? Because I don't smell blood. That's how. I got good at smellin' blood. Too good. That smell don't ever leave me. I got it all in my nose, and I can't get rid of it."

"Can you smell the difference between American blood and Arab blood?"

"No. All blood smells the same, Deuce. It's scary, blood smells sweet. There are times the smell is so strong, I can taste it too. It drives me crazy. I smell blood in my sleep. I wish I could get rid of that smell. Sometimes, I wish ta smell a strong, healthy fart."

Harrington looked up and saw Dobson standing beside the Humvee. Heywood had climbed into the driver's seat and started the engine.

"Solis, go on ahead. I want to look for the book."

"Don't stay long, Deuce. I wanna get outta here."

Solis climbed up on to a mound of rubble, then jumped on a piece of plywood that was once a door. Landing on the door, one end pitched violently upward, causing Solis to slide down into a pit below.

"Oh fuck!" Solis screamed as he fell.

Harrington gripped his M-16 and ran to where Solis had fallen. Heywood shut the engine of the Humvee and jumped down, joining Dobson who had already ran toward Solis.

Solis scrambled on the floor of the pit trying frantically to retrieve his weapon.

"Holy shit!" Solis shouted. "Holy shit!"

Harrington picked up the door and threw it aside, exposing a neatly dug out rectangle in the earth. He looked down and saw Solis standing in the stream of sunlight. Suddenly, the image of the shovels and pick axes came to his mind.

"Private Solis, are you alright?" Harrington's voice echoed in the pit.

"Yeah. I'm okay," Solis responded.

"What happened, sergeant?" Heywood asked as he reached the pit.

"Solis fell into a pit."

Heywood and Dobson looked into the pit to see Solis pivoting in a tight circle with his weapon ready.

"What's down there, Solis?" Harrington asked.

Solis concentrated on the contents of the pit. Assured there was no threat, he finally responded.

"Nothing, just a hole."

"Any weapons or communication equipment?"

"None that I can see."

"What else can you see?"

"Flat walls."

Harrington studied the carefully cut mouth of the pit. He spotted another piece of plywood that may have covered the opening.

"Are you sure? Something must be down there."

"How's about you get down here and take a look around with me, sir."

Harrington laid his weapon on the ground and ran out in the rubble to where he first saw the two ladders. Retrieving the unbroken ladder, he ran back to the pit.

"Grab this," Harrington said as he lowered the ladder to Solis.

Solis stabilized the ladder as Harrington climbed down. Reaching the bottom of the pit, Harrington felt the air cool but dusty. He estimated the depth of the pit to be almost eight feet, yet there was a closeness making breathing difficult.

"What is this place?" Solis said.

Looking around, Harrington noticed it was dug out in a perfect square. The farthest point was about twelve feet from the opening above. Three of the four walls were smooth and empty. On the fourth wall, Harrington noticed eight large round clay jugs. Each jug was slightly more than half the height of the walls. Clay lids covered each jug and were crudely bound with cloth.

"What are those things, Deuce?" Solis continued referring to the jugs.

Harrington approached one of the jugs and began unraveling the cloth. When the cloth had been removed, he opened the lid. Solis moved closer and looked inside the opened jug.

"Holy shit, Deuce. Heroin," Solis observed. "This place wasn't an enemy hideout. It was a stash for drug dealers. I'll be a son of a bitch."

Harrington became wide-eyed, transfixed by the white powder in the jug. In the defused light, the whiteness of the power was luminous. It captivated Harrington. His mouth remained agape. An unknown euphoria took hold of him. He retrieved the cloth and held it up to the light. Then he examined the lid and the exterior of the jug.

"Deuce, what the fuck you doin'?" Solis observed. "That shit's heroin and you're lookin' at the jugs like you just dug up ancient bones. Stop bein' an archaeologist."

Harrington moved quickly to the second jug and began examining it. Solis started to open the third jug.

"Leave that alone!" Harrington ordered abruptly. "Don't touch anything. That's an order."

"Damn, Deuce, what's up with you? You're actin' like this shit's gonna' explode. Heroin kills, but it takes time."

"Hey, what's going on down there?" Dobson shouted.

"Looks like we found ourselves a big stash of heroin," Solis replied.

Harrington began removing the bound cloth from the second jug, examining it carefully and deliberately. There was a wild delight in Harrington's face. He appeared childlike and delirious. The sight and touch of the cloth and jugs excited him.

"Deuce, you're startin' ta worry me. Why are you actin' crazy over rags?"

Upon completely unraveling the cloth, Harrington removed the lid of the second jug. It too was filled with white powder.

"Shit, more heroin," Solis observed.

Harrington stood and observed the jugs for a brief moment. He backed up and stood directly under the opening of the pit.

"Heywood," he finally said.

"Yes, sir?"

"There are three shovels about thirty feet west of where you're standing. Get them. You'll also see canvas sacks by the shovels, bring them too. Heywood, one other thing," Harrington said. "There are plastic pails there, too. Bring me some of them."

Harrington quickly returned to the unopened jugs. He knelt down and gently ran his hands along the round shape of one of the jugs. He put his face close to the jug and remained perfectly still as though listening for a heart beat. Continuing to unravel the cloth of the next jug, he examined the frayed threads and edges. He then rolled a section up in his hand and let it fall to the ground.

"Okay," he whispered to himself and continued to unravel the cloth without examining it.

Lifting the lid of the jug he discovered more white powder.

"More of the same," Solis observed. "Deuce, my guess they're all filled with heroin."

"Help me open the rest of the jugs," Harrington said.

"What, now I can touch them?" Solis said.

"Come on, open them."

Of the eight jugs, six were filled with the white powder. The last two were empty. As they opened the last jug, Heywood appeared at the opening of the pit.

"I have the shovels, sir. And, the sacks and pails," Heywood said.

"Good. Drop them down."

"Hey, Deuce, what you doin'?"

"We're going to empty those jugs."

"What? What for? You had us burn the last load of heroin. Now this load you want? What happen ta you between then and now?"

"Solis, take a good look at those jugs. Are you certain that's heroin?"

Solis looked at Harrington and became suspicious.

"Come on, look at it," Harrington commanded.

Solis approached the first jug and looked at its contents. He studied it from different angles and touched it with his finger. He moved to the second and then to all the jugs that contained the powder, examining them carefully.

"I'll be damn, Deuce…it's not heroin. It feels like talcum powder or corn starch. But, not really. It doesn't bunch up like talcum or corn starch when I press it together with my fingers. It's dry, but not like sand. But yet it feels oily," Solis whispered, a veil of mystery engulfing him. "I know this ain't heroin," he concluded.

"I didn't think it was," Harrington said.

"Then what do you think it is?" Solis asked, shaking his head.

"You're positive it's not heroin?" Harrington asked a sense of pleading edging his words.

"Deuce, why you second guessin' me? I told ya it ain't heroin. I'm positive."

Harrington remained still, struggling with a strange force that encouraged him to cry out and perform the ritual dances of aboriginal Bushmen around a camp fire. There was a turbulent clashing of astonishment and disbelief raging in the core of his being. Random thoughts transported Harrington to a place very far from the open pit to the middle of history. He tried to control and modulate the rapid beat of his heart and pulse, a rate higher than the conflict of battle.

"Deuce? Deuce?" Solis said interrupting Harrington's thoughts. "What is this stuff, if it ain't heroin?"

"How much do you think is there, Solis?"

"Fuck do I know."

"I bet there's a ton. Probably a lot more than a ton."

"Yeah, so?"

"So, we have to get it out of here."

"What? You're crazy."

"I am, but we're going to get it out of here anyway."

"How? How are we goin' ta lift these jugs up?"

"We're going to fill the sacks and carry them out."

"All of that stuff?"

"Yes."

"Listen, Deuce, I left the Bronx and joined the army mostly ta stay out of jail. Somethin' tells me if we get busted, that's just where I'm gonna wind up."

"If this is what I think it is, you'll wind up with more money than you can count."

"I won't be able ta bring all the money I can count inta jail."

"You're not going to jail."

"No, why?"

"Because."

"Because ain't a good enough answer. If this ain't heroin then tell me what is it? Deuce, you gotta know what this is or you wouldn't be actin' crazy and takin' it out."

"Get Heywood and Dobson down here," Harrington ordered.

"Shit…"

"Get them!" Harrington ordered forcefully.

"Black Eddie, Dobson, get your asses down here," Solis shouted.

When Dobson and Heywood descended the ladder they looked at the opened jugs.

"Is that heroin, sergeant?" Dobson asked.

"Ain't heroin," Solis responded.

"What is it?" Dobson asked.

"That's what I've been askin' since we fell inta this hole."

"So what is it, sergeant?" Heywood asked.

"I don't know for sure, but I'll let you know when I find out."

"When is that gonna' be?" Solis asked.

"Listen, we all need to be in on this," Harrington said. "All of us or none of us."

"Sergeant, we should know what we're getting into here," Heywood said. "I understand you don't really know what this stuff is. But, I know you have a strong suspicion as to what it is."

"Hey, Black Eddie, that's smart. Sorry, I said you was stupid up there."

"You're right, Heywood. I do have a strong suspicion as to what this stuff is," Harrington confirmed.

"Is it an illegal substance? Something that can land us in jail?"

"That's what I asked," Solis interrupted.

"If it's what I think it is, it's not illegal."

"Is it dangerous?" Dobson asked.

"Define dangerous," Harrington said.

"Is it an explosive or a component to an explosive?"

"No."

"Well then how is it dangerous?"

"Dangerous through competition."

"You mean somebody else would want this?"

"Yes."

"How bad?"

"Dangerous bad."

"Now, for the last time. What is it?" Solis shouted.

"When I'm certain, I'll let you all know. So, are we all in?" Harrington asked.

"What's the risk factor versus the reward?" Dobson asked.

"You people from Utah got a real nice down home way of askin' a question," Solis said.

"Fair question. I think I can minimize the risk and maximize the reward," Harrington responded.

"How much is maximize?" Solis asked.

"Pick a number."

"One million, cash," Solis said.

"You dream too small, Hector," Dobson responded.

"Why? Do you know what its worth? We don't even know what the shit is," Solis responded.

"Listen, we can calculate numbers later. Right now, we need to move this stuff," Harrington said.

"Sergeant, unless I'm missing something, once we get this stuff out of this pit, then what?" Heywood asked.

"I have a plan for that. Actually, I have one or two plans."

"Sergeant, that's all well and good, but I haven't heard how you're going to minimize the risk," Dobson said.

"I'll explain all that later. Before anything, I need to know we're all in…Dobson?"

"Yes. I'm in."

"Solis?"

"I better not wind up in jail."

"You won't…Heywood?"

"I'm in."

"Good. Okay, let's fill those sacks. Put them into the Humvee. Once we get back to field base, I'll tell you what I plan to do."

FILLING each sack carefully, Harrington estimated the weight about one hundred pounds per sack. The men filled twenty sacks. After each sack was filled, Harrington tied them with the drawstring, and the arduous task of bringing them out from the pit began. Solis handed the sacks to Dobson who stood on the ladder. He passed them to Heywood who loaded them into the Humvee which he had backed to the pit. Once the final sack was carried out, Harrington retrieved one of the cloth wrappings and stuffed it into the pocket of his flap jacket. He unraveled the cloth from the shovel handle and put it into another pocket. Returning to the jugs, he looked at them for a final time. Taking a shovel, he smashed one of the jugs. He picked up a piece of broken clay and put it into his pocket.

After all the sacks were in the Humvee, Harrington covered them with a tarpaulin and stacked containers of ammunition on top. Confident the sacks were concealed, Harrington finally took a drink of water. As he drank the water, he noticed how much he had been sweating. The pants of his uniform showed a ring of perspiration above his knees. He opened his flap jacket and felt the wetness of his T-shirt. He felt slightly dizzy and faint from his efforts. He had become dehydrated. Perspiration no longer exuded from his face. It was dry, encrusted with a thin layer of sand.

Harrington's hands and arms began to tremble from the shoveling. His legs felt weak. His back strained. He slouched, placing his head on the back of the seat. He took a deep breath but had barely enough strength to exhale. Solis bent over and buried his head between his legs. He too drew in deep breaths and closed his eyes. The movement of the Humvee rocked him, and for a moment, he felt as though he was riding on the IRT as it pulled away from the Gun Hill Road station.

Private Heywood maneuvered the Humvee back to the desert road. The glare from the setting sun gave the sand a golden hue. He slid his sunglasses from the top of his helmet over his eyes to see more clearly. Looking up, he adjusted the rearview mirror. In it, he thought he saw the jeep of policeman bin Nasab jutting out from a partially destroyed wall. He was too tired to mention it. As he drove, the jeep appeared to grow smaller, until it faded into the rubble of the house they had just left.

The soldiers felt drained and fatigued as they drove back to field base. A universal silence of exhaustion permeated the soldiers. Their collective weariness precipitated a longing that was not adequate for words. A conspiracy of isolation created the solemn mood that could only be transformed by long, undisturbed rest.

Upon arrival at the field base, Sergeant Harrington reported to Captain Hicks. He confirmed with the captain there was no activity in the village. The mission was routine, with the exception of the incident with policeman Haddad bin Nasab. There was no enemy engagement, discovery of weapons, or communication equipment at the site.

Harrington walked back to their field base position and entered the mud clad house. Private Solis sat on the floor with his knees up and his back against the wall. He had his head bent down between his legs. His arms rested on his knees. An empty bottle of water stood on the floor between his legs. Solis breathed slowly and deeply, on the verge of sleep. Heywood was lying on a thin blanket, his flap jacket rolled up and tucked under his head. His boots were off. His belt was unbuckled hanging from his waist. Dobson sat sprawled in a chair pouring water over his head and face.

Harrington observed the weary soldiers and became fearful the war had become a second endeavor to the white powder they now possessed. He was acutely aware of how tired they became from lifting the sacks out of the pit. He hoped it would be the only toll that would be placed on them.

"Listen men, I know you're all tired, but clean up and let's get together after chow. There's a lot we need to discuss."

SERGEANT Harrington stood alone outside the field base house. He had showered all the sand from his hair and body. He had put on freshly washed clothing. His boots were newly polished. The evening desert air had become cool and dry. Harrington felt it gently pass over his body. He felt refreshed, but a nagging fatigue remained in his muscles and joints. He looked out at the rooftops of Mosul; outlined in dark charcoal gray against the red and black fading sunset. The rounded dome of a nearby mosque stood in the center of the city. It appeared bold, proclaiming its own solemn rite of worship. The city around the mosque seemed to be struggling for its own end of day quest for peace and quiet. The fighting was relentless in Mosul, living up to the region's history of struggle and combat. War and death was sold to the people of Mosul as a way of life. Throughout the years, invading nations kept the legacy alive with improved and modern ways to perpetuate the combative philosophy. But this night seemed to be different. From the distance, Harrington could be convinced war didn't exist in the streets. He remained extremely still, observing the outline of the city through a momentary absence of war.

Leaning into the evening, he heard the chanting of sacred Muslin prayers coming from the mosque. He listened for a while, but the memory of the sounds of war long accumulated in his mind and drowned out the chanting. After a while, he gave up straining to hear the praying. He realized the echoes of thuds and screams not only existed in his memory, but traveled on the wind circling the earth, never coming to rest.

Harrington turned from the city and looked at the pieces of cloth he took from the pit. He compared the piece from the jug to the one wrapped around the handle of the shovel. Looking at them closely, he was convinced they were identical. By their texture and feel, he knew they were cotton, cut in strips from a shumgg. He examined the broken piece of jug, focusing on its outer glaze and organic clay. In both materials, he was specifically looking for antiquity. However, both showed signs of being recently loomed and fired.

Throwing the material on the desert sand, he walked into the field base house. Upon entering, he notice Heywood was sitting against the wall cleaning his M-16. Solis had a set of ear plugs stuck into his ears, listening to a CD of violin music Harrington had given him. Dobson sat motionless reading a battered version of *Johnny Got His Gun*.

Harrington grabbed a chair and placed it in the middle of the room. "Good evening, men," Harrington said, abruptly, and sat. "Now, let's talk."

Dobson folded a corner of the page he was reading and closed the book. Solis listened to the final strains of the violin, then removed the ear plugs and shut off the CD player. Heywood completed cleaning his weapon and rested it on his lap.

"Okay, you're on, Deuce," Solis said. "Let's hear what you got."

"First things first," Harrington said. "I would never engage in anything illegal. I would never smuggle illegal or dangerous substances. And, I would never permit members of my squad to engage in such an activity. I want that perfectly understood from the get go."

"We understand," Dobson said.

"Good....Heywood, you said I had strong suspicion as to what the substance was in the jugs. Well in the pit, my imagination was running away with itself. Now that I've had some time to consider, I'm not as certain..."

"Be up front with us, sergeant," Heywood said. "What do you suspect was in the jugs?"

"Listen, I really need you guys to trust me here. Without getting the substance tested, I really can't say for sure. All I can say, and I repeat; the substance is not illegal. It's not anything that's going to land any one of us in jail…"

"You said it was dangerous," Dobson said.

"Yes. I explained that."

"You said it was competition dangerous. That's not explaining anything. Who would be coming after us if this stuff is what you suspect it is?" Dobson pushed.

"Fair enough. If the tests confirm my suspicions, and as long as we control the substance, we'll be okay no matter who comes for it. But, trust me; there will be people and organizations coming to us with blank checks, too."

"But somebody will be comin' ta take it too, right?" Solis said.

"If that somebody knew we have the powder, then I would say that's a safe bet."

"Sergeant, this may not mean anything," Heywood said. "But as we drove away, I saw a jeep go to the pit. It looked like the same jeep the Iraqi Policeman bin Nasab was driving."

"Yeah, I couldn't figure why that guy was there," Solis said. "He was really pissed off that we chased him away. Man, he looked like he wanted to kill us."

"Do you think he owned the powder or was selling it?" Dobson asked.

"I don't know," Harrington said. "He could have something to do with it."

"Well if he was, he was willin' to get shot for the stuff. The mystery is getting' thick, Deuce."

"So is bin Nasab the type of guy that could make the powder competitive dangerous? Heywood asked.

"Yes," Harrington said. "Solis is right, bin Nasab was willing to kill or die for it."

"Sergeant, I notice you took some pieces of cloth from the jugs. You broke one of the jugs and took a piece of it. Why? What were you looking for?" Dobson asked.

"I was examining for dating purposes."

"You wanted ta see if it was old, antiquity shit, right?"

"Yes."

"Well?"

"The cloth was modern cotton. So were the jugs."

"So then that tells me you believe the powder is old, antiquity right?"

"Now you're asking the right questions?"

"Yeah, but if I ask, I bet you're gonna say you don't know how old the powder is, right?"

"Right."

"Can't that archaeological testing shit tell ya?"

"I really don't know."

"But you're an archaeologist. You know how that all works."

"Once again, Solis, I'm an anthropologist."

"Whatever. We're going round and round here about what this stuff may or may not be," Dobson said. "Let's move away from that for now. Let's focus on logistics. Sergeant, what's your plan to move the stuff out of here?"

"I have two plans, one of which I think is the best. First, we can each package some up and mail it home through the field Post Office. That I believe is not the way to go. We would each have to mail only a small amount. Solis and I are looking at discharge in two weeks. Dobson when is your discharge?"

"I've got a little over three months."

"Heywood?"

"Five months and three days."

"That means the Post Office is out. We can't mail that much at a time. We'll have to declare everything we mail. Logistically, that won't work."

"So what's your other plan?" Solis asked.

"I have a college buddy of mine. He's Air Force. A staff sergeant, load master here in Mosul. He's assigned to a C-5 Galaxy that flies out of Luke Air Force Base in Arizona…"

"Your home state," Heywood observed.

"Exactly. As a load master, he's responsible for everything that gets loaded and off loaded. If we can get him to take the load, he can fly it into Luke. Once it's there, he can probably off load it and drive it to wherever I say. That plan might work."

"But what if your buddy doesn't go along with the plan?" Dobson said.

"Then we're stuck with the material, and quite frankly, I'd hate to give it up."

"You think he'll go for it?" Heywood asked.

"I won't know until I speak with him. But if he says yes, this becomes a five way split. Even if one of us doesn't make it, his portion goes to whoever he says. That's the only way. No variables. None."

"Wow! You know, Deuce, I always knew you were a straight shooter. Honest as they come, but what you're doin' here don't seem honest. You're smugglin' shit."

"This is not illegal contraband, Solis. I made that very clear."

"I'll take your word on that, Deuce. But, the way you're treating this you're makin' me believe otherwise. You're goin' against the grain."

"Yes, well everyone has their price."

"That's what it always comes down ta. Price, money," Solis observed.

"Solis, just so there's no misunderstanding; this is not about money for me. In fact, this is what I'll do. I don't want the money. You keep whatever we make. Split it up between yourself, Heywood and Dobson. Add in my Air Force buddy. Keep it a four way split."

"No," Dobson said suddenly. "We said five ways. No variables."

"Fine. Here's how this is going to work. I'll have the load shipped to Arizona."

"You seem sure your buddy will ship it," Heywood observed.

"Well, if that white powder is ancient shit, his archaeologist buddy will ship it. He'll go along. You guys want that museum glory. Lookin' for big history. I think the sergeant already knows that. Right sergeant?" Solis observed.

"As I said, if he goes along with this and ships it, I'll hide it. It'll be safe. Once I get discharged, I'll start the testing process. I'm hoping to have final analysis by the time Heywood is discharged. Solis, if you want to come to Arizona and stay until this is all over, you're more than welcome. But remember it's hot in Arizona."

"No shit."

"The same goes for Dobson and Heywood. Upon discharge, you're more than welcome to come to Arizona. In fact, I would like it better if you did. But, you all know your own situations. I want each of us to take five or ten pounds and mail it home. That's our ace in the hole. Whoever you send it to, your mothers, fathers, wives, I don't care. Just tell them they are to put it somewhere where no one will find it. Don't keep it hanging around the house. Assure them it's completely legal and encourage them not to open it. But that's your call. You know your own families."

"How is the five pounds our ace in the hole?" Dobson asked.

"I think we can use it for a bargaining chip, if we have to. What I really need you all to understand is whoever controls the material controls the play."

"You're startin' to sound like a New York hustler," Solis said.

"You affect people that way, Solis," Heywood said.

"Then, we all agree;" Harrington said. "I'll talk with my Air Force buddy, Tommy Bowels. If he joins in, I'll find out when his next stateside flight is. He'll give us the logistics."

"Hey, Deuce, let me ask you somethin'," Solis said. "You said if somethin' happens ta one of us, you'll pass along our share ta our survivors. We still won't know what this shit is. What do we do if somethin' happens ta you?"

Harrington was suddenly confronted with a probability he hadn't anticipated. The not so subtle suggestion from Solis brought into question his own mortality. He also knew Solis was right. There was the possibility something dire could happen to him. But Solis' other point regarding museum glory and the potential of big history was accurate to the core. He felt an inner grimace at the possibility of a fateful, critical mass coming from the dry desert on a balmy, sunny day that may deny him the promising glory and history he desperately wanted.

"Well, sergeant, what do we do?" Dobson repeated.

Harrington knew there was no avoiding the perils of the desert or the onslaught of an alternate history. All the things of the world share the same space in equal measure. Consequently, he knew he stood an equal chance at glory or ruin.

"If something happens to me, what will you do?" Harrington repeated. "You'll have to decide that for yourselves."

THE military airbase in Mosul crops up out of the desert just north of Baghdad. The ribbon-like airstrip was more than a mile long, pot marked by dozens of Army green tents. A low wall of sand bags and flimsy chicken wire fence formed a perimeter around the canvas tents. The protection offered by the barrier against an enemy attack appeared to Harrington to be a grand illusion.

Private Heywood drove the squad's Humvee to the front of one of the eight aircraft shelters on the base. He stopped the vehicle and watched as an Army tow truck raised the front of a two-and-one-half-ton disabled cargo truck. Several soldiers were throwing around a football beyond the shelters. A maintenance crew offloaded field supply crates from the rear of a truck placing them on a row of pallets inside one of the tents. Rap music blared from a radio somewhere in the tent. The soldiers playing football seemed consumed by their rivalry. Those unloading the crates moved to the rhythm of the music. Neither group paid any attention to the Humvee or Harrington's squad.

"Look what we got here," Solis said looking at the soldiers playing football. "If I wasn't involved in a conspiracy with you, Deuce, I'd join that game and show them how it's really played."

"Why don't you shut up, Solis," Dobson said. "The only conspiracy here is the conspiracy of patience. Putting up with you."

"Is this the shelter, sergeant?" Heywood asked, slowing the vehicle.

"Yes. Drive around to the back. There's not as much activity there," Harrington replied.

Heywood drove the Humvee to the rear of the massive aircraft shelter. As he made the turn to the back of the shelter, an Iraqi Police Service jeep followed slowly at a measured distance. Haddad bin Nasab sat in the jeep with his cap pulled down. The Iraqi policeman focused his angry glare on every movement of the American soldiers.

Driving to the rear of the shelter, Harrington saw an F-16 in one of the other shelters and wondered if it was the same plane that bombed the village. Heywood stopped the vehicle by the cavernous opening of the shelter. The Iraqi Police Service vehicle continued past the hangar and stopped behind a tall row of crates. The driver positioned the jeep facing the rear of the hangar, remaining partially hidden by the crates. Haddar bin Nasab left the jeep. He carefully watched Harrington and his squad from a space between the crates.

"Okay," Harrington said. "Wait here. I want you guys out of the vehicle. You'll draw less attention. But, don't go far. I'll be back as soon as possible."

Harrington walked into the shelter, amazed by its unforgiving size. He felt small and irrelevant. The vastness took hold of Harrington convincing him most things considered significant could get overpowered and lost in it, especially one's thoughts. The only other vastness he could compare the shelter to was the broad desert and the night sky. In the center of the shelter was a C-5 Galaxy transport plane, surrounded by mounds of material covered with dusty tarpaulins. The large transport plane, with its massive body and wing span, could not compete in size to the shelter. It was swallowed whole by it and not allowed its own prominent perspective. Two Abrams Tanks were positioned by the opening ramp of the C-5. One tank showed dark burn marks on its belly. The other had deep gouges, suggesting it had been struck by high caliber rounds.

Harrington spotted Staff Sergeant, Tommy Bowles, draping a tarpaulin over the engine of a damaged AH-1 Cobra helicopter. He pulled hard on the tarpaulin, exposing exaggerated muscles, honed from years of weight training. His hair was cut close and exposure to the sun had tanned his scalp. The army issued T-shirt, Bowles was wearing, was wet from perspiration and clung tightly to his muscular body. Bowles looked up to see Harrington. He quickly removed a pair of canvas gloves to wipe his sweaty hands on his pants. Retrieving two bottles of water from a cooler, he threw one to Harrington.

"Hey, Mitchell, good to see you," Bowles said as he rolled the bottle of water across his forehead.

"Tommy, how are you? I'm glad you had time to see me," Harrington responded.

"I was glad you called," Bowles said. "It was great to hear from you. How are things with you?"

"So far so good. I've been lucky. I'm still in one piece. No candidate for a Purple Heart. How's the family back home?"

"Good. Molly's doing okay. Jenny's just turned two."

"Two? I don't believe it. Seems like Molly just gave birth."

"Yeah, time does pass, even here. Speaking of which, I believe you're discharging soon."

"I am. In two weeks."

"Good for you."

"I wanted to see you before I left."

"Come on, let's talk. I need a break." Bowles motioned to a group of chairs by the entrance way.

As Harrington approached the chairs, he noticed a King James Bible on the seat. He picked up the book and handed it to Bowles.

"Here, Tommy, I know this belongs to you."

"Yes. I was going to read it on my break."

"So Jesus still occupies a part of your life," Harrington observed.

"Now more than ever," Bowles responded. "Have you been reading Scripture?"

"No."

"You should. Here take this," Bowles handed the Bible back to Harrington.

"No, that's okay, Tom. It belongs to you."

"I have another. Besides, I know the book by heart."

"That's alright, Tom. You can keep it."

"Don't you believe in Jesus? Mitch, I remember when we were kids in Bible studies with Pastor Ford…"

"Pastor Bernard Dismas Ford," Harrington interrupted. "I haven't heard his name in a long time."

"He was a good teacher, and you were a good student. You were more receptive then."

"I was…then. Now, here with what I see going on, I question a bit more."

"Why?"

"Because I think Jesus avoids this place."

"Now, Mitch, you know you don't believe that."

"Tom, as I recall you always questioned the Bible. You were always challenging Pastor Ford as a kid."

"Yes, I did. I still have questions. I want to understand the past as best as I can. But what I see here now is clear cut."

"If you say so."

"It's not what I say. It's in the Bible. Do me a favor; take it even if you don't read it. At least you have it. When we get stateside, I'm going to work on your faith. You may be more receptive then."

"It's a deal. So how's your job going here," Harrington asked.

"Well, I don't get to see the war the way you see it. You're on the front lines. I just fly around the world. Sorry to say that's okay with me."

"Don't apologize. Just being away from your wife and daughter is hard enough."

"It is. So what was it you wanted to talk to me about?"

Harrington took a sip of water, then slowly and deliberately screwed the cap on.

"Tommy something came up," Harrington said. "We were called for a mission on a suspected enemy location outside the city. Two F Sixteens leveled the place. We just picked through it. A routine mission. It wasn't a suspected enemy camp, but the destruction exposed a pit. We found a cache of white powder…"

"Heroin?" Bowles interrupted.

"No. Not heroin. Remember the name Flinders Petrie?"

"Sure I do. Flinders Petrie, the famous Egyptologist."

"Remember his find in the Sinai?"

Bowles became excited. His eyes widened as he leaned close to Harrington. For an instant, he couldn't speak. He began to rock back and forward in his chair. The medal identification tags around his neck, along with a gold Crucifix, touched and jingled slightly. Harrington's attention was drawn to the odd melody. He was momentarily struck by a strange dichotomy generated by the icons. But Harrington quickly thought they were in some ways not opposites at all.

"What are you telling me, Mitch?" Bowles finally asked.

Harrington turned his attention from the dog tags and Crucifix and looked at Bowles.

"I may have found the Petrie find," he said.

"The Petrie find? Impossible," Bowles said. "The Flinders Petrie find was in nineteen hundred. He found it, and lost it the same year."

"Actually, the find was nineteen oh six."

"Still, it's over a hundred years ago. How could you be so sure it's the Petrie find?"

"I'm not. I suspect it is. When I get discharged, I'm having it tested. I'll know for sure then."

"Give me the background. How did you find it?" Bowles asked.

"We were on a mission. A village had been strafed by our jets. We were leaving the area when one of my squad fell into a pit. That's where I made the find."

"But Petrie's find was in Egypt, in the temple at Serabit."

"That's right. I believe the village was a cover. It appears the Petrie find, if that's what I found, was being transported from somewhere else. Maybe from Egypt, I don't know. I found pails I think were used to carry the stuff. I also found a pile of sacks. Quite possibly, the sacks were set to move the stuff somewhere else. Maybe to sell it."

"Was there anyone in the village?"

"No. But, the F Sixteen took out a van leaving the village. Everyone in the van was killed."

"Was there anything in the van?"

"I don't know. Another squad investigated it."

"Was there anything else to indicate it was the Petrie find? As I recall, he also found cups he believed to be from thirty-five hundred BC."

"That's correct. But, I didn't find the cups or the tube pots Petrie claimed to have found. The material I found was in several jugs. But I knew the jugs were recent pottery. You could buy them in any bazaar. The cloth wrappings around the jugs were modern fabric."

"You sure it wasn't alkali you found? Remember Petrie thought what he found could have been alkali from burnt plants."

"It wasn't alkali."

"Are you sure?" Bowles pressed. "How about burnt sacrificial animal bones?

Harrington reached into his pocket and produced a small envelope. He tapped it slightly redistributing its contents.

"Hold out your hand," he said to Bowles.

Opening the flap of the envelope, Harrington dropped the white powder into Bowles' rough and callous hand. Bowles looked at the powder, his mouth agape. His eyes widened more than ever. He felt a strange mystical energy. A force field gathered in his hand and commandeered his soul. The powder produced an energy that drained his strength making his breathing difficult. He clutched the artifact, like it was the true Eucharist, the actual cup of Christ filled with the Savior's blood.

"Mitch, could this be?" Bowles whispered

"It's not alkali, Tom. It's not burnt sacrificial animal bones. And, it's not heroin. It's nothing that I'm familiar with."

"Flinders Petrie's find. Could that be possible?" Bowles was excited. "Mitch, do you know what you might have here?"

"I know. It could be...It could be monoatomic gold," Harrington whispered.

"Can this be? How much did you find?"

"Well over a thousand pounds. Closer to two."

"What? That's a lot. Petrie said he found fifty tons."

"Actually, in his writings, he claims to have identified hundreds of tons."

"Do you think there is more out there?"

"Possibly. In the pit, I discovered empty jugs. I think those were slated to be filled, too."

"A ton of something that could be monoatomic gold. Mitch, where is it?" Bowles asked excitedly. "I hope you didn't leave it in the pit."

"No, I have it. All packed in sacks in a Humvee parked right out side."

"You're kidding?"

Bowles put out his hand, replacing the suspected monoatomic gold into the envelope. Bowles looked at the thin residue remaining on his hand, and started rubbing it into his skin. He couldn't feel the substance's texture. But his hands became warmer and his calluses immediately soften.

"Wow, so now you need to move it, right?"

"Yes. I'm hoping you could help me out. Can you fly it out of here?"

"It shouldn't be a problem. I'll have to figure out where I can store it. I can bring it aboard without anyone knowing about it. I fly with a straight crew. There's the pilot, co-pilot, the navigation officer and myself. That's it. We're a tight crew. I don't interfere with them, and they return the favor. Our first stop is Wiesbaden, Germany. We're not loaded with human cargo going back; only material. We drop a load there and wait for a load coming in from Afghanistan. Then we fly on to Luke."

"What's your schedule?"

"We arrive in Wiesbaden on the seventh. Two weeks from now. We have a five day layover there."

"Our schedules are almost identical. I'll be in Wiesbaden around the same time as you. I'm there the eighth, the day after you. That's my stop-over point. Then, I'm on to Fort Drum for my official discharge. We'll definitely hook up in Wiesbaden."

"Good idea. I'll arrive at Luke around the same time as your dis-charge."

"Will you be able to get the load out of Luke?"

"Once I get there, the rest will be easy. I'll drop the load off at the squadron duty station. Then come back with my pick up and cart the load off."

"It sounds a little too easy."

"Mitch, you have no idea what kind of contraband comes in and out of here. There are guys making money hand over fist. And, that's just what I know about."

"War makes money."

"Unfortunately, it's always at the expense of someone else's life."

"Listen, I have three guys in my squad that are in on this. We split evenly. No exceptions. You'll meet the guys. They're outside with the load. With you on board, it goes five ways."

"Do they know what you might have here?"

"No. If this does turn out to be monoatomic gold, then I'll explain it to them. Even then, they won't know the depth of it."

"Do we?"

"Something tells me, we're going to learn real fast."

"You know, Mitch, it's a shame Flinders Petrie didn't know what he found a century ago."

"Tom, nobody knew it back then. If this turns out to be monoatomic gold, there are a lot of people who are going to want to know about it. This discovery could disrupt established paradigms."

"For sure, but that's something they need to deal with. So, when I land at Luke and offload the material, where do you want it delivered?"

"First thing, I'm going to do when I get home, is find a safe place to store it. Once I establish that, we'll keep in touch. If I'm able to establish a good hiding place when we hook up in Wiesbaden, I'll let you know then. We'll plan this right. I have a bit of a back up plan should something go wrong on your end. I won't leave you out to dry."

"I appreciate it, but I don't expect anything to go wrong. I'll just have to figure out a place to hide the powder. Two thousand pounds you said?"

"Somewhere around that. Fifteen hundred to two thousand pounds. That's my guess."

"It's a good weight. I think I know how to hide it."

"Good. Thanks, Tom."

"Are you kidding, Mitch? Thanks for including me. Back in your vehicle, and we'll off load it. Let's keep the journey of the gold going. And keep alive Flinders Petrie's legacy."

"Yes. And let's keep alive the *true* legacy of the *real* gods."

Policeman bin Nasab watched from behind the crates as Harrington's squad unloaded the sacks from the Humvee onto a wooden pallet. The squad worked quickly. Once all the sacks were placed on the pallet, bin Nasab watched as Bowles strapped on a tarpaulin. Certain the pallet was going into the C-5, bin Nasab walked back to the jeep.

"What did you see?" the driver asked.

"The soldiers loaded the sacks onto the C-5 transport."

"They're taking it away. That's bad for us," the driver observed.

"No. It's good. That plane must be going to Wiesbaden," bin Nasab responded. "I don't suspect the soldiers would be taking it away from here if they were not leaving themselves. They may be on that transport traveling with the load. Maybe not. No matter how they travel, they will be going to Germany. Once they're in Germany, they won't be as protected. That's our best chance. If we miss them in Germany, it will be difficult to know where the load will end up."

"That means we have to leave?" the driver asked.

Haddad bin Nasab became angry. He turned quickly to the driver. A scowl contorted his face. His dark, oily skin became reddened. His jaw tightened.

"Do you have any reason to stay?" bin Nasab growled. "They took everything from you. Now is your chance to take something for yourself. Tell me now, do you want to stay? Tell me, brother," bin Nasab hissed.

"No. No. I'll leave," the driver said, uncertainty coursing through his expressions.

The policeman's anger did not waiver. His eyes remained hard and vindictive staring straight into the hangar and into the future.

"Once we meet up with the soldiers in Germany," bin Nasab said. "We'll show them how our customs deal with thieves."

ARIZONA

THE Alitalia flight departed Naples International Airport promptly on a rainy evening. The wet runway reflected the multicolored lights, sending geometric lines and formations dancing across the tarmac. After a moderate dinner, Segretti settled back into his first class seat. He gently held Gabriella's hand. Giving her a reassuring smile, he brought her hand up to kiss it. She reached over and unbuttoned the collar of his linen shirt.

Gabriella had traveled with Segretti many times on vacation and business. She always trusted in Segretti, and the level of her own instincts. But lately, Gabriella sensed threats lurking everywhere they traveled. She recalled a recent trip to Monte Carlo. Segretti was in the complicated process of selling beam weapon technology, when they were confronted by a United States Army General and several armed soldiers. Gabriella did not know the intricacies of the beam weapons or their sale, but she did recall the rage of the General and his name. He used his name as though yielding a weapon as an ominous threat when he confronted her. *"I'm General Bradshaw,"* she recalled him boldly shouting in her face.

The beam weapons were the most powerful and efficient weapons known to man. They were highly destructive as offensive and defensive weapons. The weapons operated on the highly advanced principle of electromagnetically charged beams of light. Traveling at the speed of light, they could disable any electrically operated weapon, missile or satellite station. The general feared, if foreign governments had access to these weapons, they could counter the advantage of the United States' military might. General Bradshaw's concern over the potential sale of the weapons to foreign nations, made him angry and belligerent. He boasted how easily he could have Segretti killed if the sales became final. The incident convinced Gabriella some form of surveillance had alerted the military of Segretti's intentions. The high-tech, Orwellian surveillance was difficult to avoid, and she feared the scrutiny would grow more intense. She addressed this reality in the only way she knew how; by keeping her concerns to herself.

Segretti turned to look at Gabriella and saw the trepidation in her eyes he didn't dare interpret. It was a look he had not seen before, and one he had difficulty addressing. The hypnotic sound of the jet engines did little to relax Gabriella. Her mind became a battleground for conflicting thoughts. At times, she was awakened by the sound of her own moaning. She leaned her head against Segretti's shoulder. From within the thin layers of sleep, she found herself restless and unable to exert her usual control over her vulnerability. There seemed to be a conspiracy forming in the night, exaggerated by the demons that plagued her during the day. Without the reassuring feel of Segretti's shoulder, she felt exposed and defenseless to the unseen forces she knew were tracking their every movement.

Gabriella became suspicious of the elderly couple seated across the aisle wearing sleeping masks. The profile of another man, standing up to reach into the overhead luggage compartment, resembled her nemesis of General Bradshaw. When he turned and smiled at her, she knew it wasn't Bradshaw, but the stranger's casual glance convinced her not all paranoia was unwarranted.

Segretti had read through the night. The book he chose for the flight was from his personal library, a reprinting of: Gaetano Mosca's *Theory of Governments and Parliamentary Governments*. Segretti had become familiar with Mosca's work after reading several of the political scientist's books. Mosca believed most societies were ruled by a numerical minority, a political class, or ruling elitists. Mosca observed that ruling elites possessed superior organizational and marketing skills, useful in gaining political power in a modern bureaucratic society. Through Mosca's writing, Segretti gained an insight into the theory of elitism, learning the ruling elite was not hereditary in nature. Instead, people from all classes of society could become part of the elite.

Segretti found Mosca's thesis enlightening. He believed it did not cover his own type of personality and nature. Segretti used the theorist's work to understand society, while helping him evaluate his own position within it. By operating outside the ruling political faction, and forming his own counter-caste that had a basis in wealth and independent power, Segretti felt certain he was not answerable to any ruling elite. That reminder was the soothing core to his sense of autonomy.

Segretti placed the book on his chest as Gabriella stretched seeking to relieve the tightness that engulfed her during the night. Sighing softly, she tried to squeeze through the layers of weariness that had taken hold of her. Her head and ears felt clogged and discomforted by the incessant moan of the jet engines and the stagnant cabin air. The elderly couple across the aisle had awakened and removed their sleeping masks. The stranger, who resembled Bradshaw, stood and walked by Gabriella on the way to the bathroom. Gabriella strained to see over the high backed seat to get a better look at the man's traveling companion who turned out to be a young boy wearing a baseball cap. Suddenly, with the morning light, the threats and suspicions of the previous night seemed unwarranted and frivolous.

"You didn't sleep well," Segretti whispered.

"No," Gabriella replied.

"We'll be landing soon. When we get to the hotel, you can sleep."

"Will your schedule permit it?"

"Of course."

The captain announced the plane would be landing shortly. Fastening her seat belt, Gabriella looked out the window as the earth came closer. Every detail of the buildings and the terminals became recognizable in the bright morning sun. Gabriella could see dozens of planes on the runways. One was taking off and another circling, preparing to land. What she could not see, no matter how hard she looked, was her own future.

TERMANAL 2 at Sky Harbor Airport was filled with travelers. Gabriella held Segretti's hand as they walked to the baggage area. A man rushed by brushing past Segretti.

"Excuse me," the man said.

"Quite alright," Segretti replied.

"We had a good flight," the man observed.

"Yes we did," Segretti responded.

The man quickly continued and disappeared into the crowd.

"Who was that?" Gabriella asked.

"He was on our flight; the front row. I don't believe traveling agreed with him. He held a rosary in his hand the entire flight."

"I didn't notice him," Gabriella said.

"I notice everyone," Segretti said.

As Segretti removed his luggage from the carousel, he noticed two men standing at the far end observing him. Within an instant, Segretti mentally recorded the ear pieces and the slight bulges at their hips. What became more glaring was their visual intensity. He scanned the baggage area, and saw another man with a woman at the opposite end. They, too, were watching him. Segretti realized their presence was not meant to be trivial or covert. By their very stillness, they conveyed a purpose that was meant to be unchallenged. Stepping away from the carousel, the four people scrutinizing Segretti approached.

"Pietro Segretti?" one of the men asked.

"Yes," Segretti acknowledged.

The second man reached for the luggage and handed it to someone standing in the crowd.

"Are you Gabriella DeCeasere?" the woman who came from the other direction asked.

"I am," Gabriella replied.

"Would you both mind coming with us?" the first man said.

"Certainly. Before we do, I'd like to know who each of you are and which department you represent."

"We are all with Homeland Security," the first man said. "I'm Agent Andrew Cummings. This is Agent Stewart Manning, and Agents Robert Heller and Jenny Tyler."

"Fine," Segretti concluded.

The group encircled Segretti and Gabriella. Agent Manning scrutinized Segretti closely while Agent Tyler watched Gabriella. The agents maintained a tight circle as they walked through the terminal to a gray corridor, and into a small windowless room. A long metal table was positioned in the center of the room. One agent placed the luggage in the center the table and stepped back against the cinderblock wall.

"Is this your only items of luggage?" Cummings asked.

"Yes," Segretti said.

"I'm sure you realize why you are of interest to us, Mister Segretti?"

"I can't imagine why. I'd like to have an explanation, if you don't mind."

"I do mind. What are you doing in Arizona?"

Segretti felt the forced heat of confrontation emitting from Cummings. His instinct was to embrace the challenge from the young agent and strike quickly with unbridled aggression. Deferring instead to his nature and the strategies of conflict, Segretti remained calm and calculating. He preferred to maintain strength in the illusion of compromise.

"I'm on holiday," Segretti responded with a steely insistence in his voice and his eyes.

"Why the United States? Why Arizona?"

"Why not Arizona?"

"Look Mister Segretti, your profession is no secret to us. And quite frankly, I find you and what you do despicable. We don't like your kind in this country."

"Is that so?" Segretti said, with control and resilience.

"That's so," Cummings growled, moving closer to Segretti.

"Do you also find what is being done in Abu Ghraib despicable?" Segretti said contemptuously.

Cummings' anger intensified as the muscles in his jaw tightened and his skin reddened. He moved his arm slightly touching the weapon strapped to his hip. Segretti was unmoved by the agent's intense temper. His instinct was to protect Gabriella.

"Which of these pieces of luggage belong to you Miss DeCeasere?" Agent Tyler said from behind Segretti. Her timely interruption slightly defused the potential confrontation. Without turning her stare from Cummings, Gabriella pointed to her piece of luggage.

"Good. Would you mind coming with me," Tyler said. "I'd like to examine the contents of it. I also need to search you."

Agent Tyler opened a door to an inner room and switched on the overhead lights. The man standing against the wall retrieved Gabriella's luggage and brought it into the second room.

"I'll need the mobile backscatter X-ray," Tyler said as the man passed her. "Miss DeCeasere, this way please."

Gabriella turned to Segretti and nodded her head.

"I'll be alright," she said.

Segretti nodded his head and took hold of Gabriella's hand. He walked with her to the inner room.

"Where do you think you're going?" Cummins shouted.

Segretti paid no attention to Cummings and looked into the second room. It too had no windows. There were no other doors and nothing to threaten Gabriella.

"Fine," Segretti said to Gabriella. "It will be alright."

Gabriella entered the room and Agent Tyler closed the door behind them. The two women were alone facing each other. The room was closet-small and solid. A cinderblock womb they both felt strangely at ease in. Yet, within the claustrophobic, silent space, the air of opposition was what they breathed. There was a knock on the door, and the man who had brought in the luggage entered with a black case. He handed it to Tyler and left the room. Agent Tyler opened the case and removed a strange looking camera with a small screen. Gabriella looked at the object and knew objects harbor various threats.

"I need to search you and your luggage, Gabriella. This is called a backscatter X-ray. It can see through your clothing, so there's no need to disrobe. I wanted to conduct this search away from the men. I trust you can appreciate that."

"Thank you," Gabriella said.

"Agent Cummings takes his job very seriously. I can't fault him for that. He takes the security of this country personal. I do also, and I take nothing for granted."

Agent Tyler turned on the equipment and aimed it at Gabriella.

"Please raise your arms out to the side," Tyler said.

Tyler looked at the screen which projected the details of Gabriella's nude body. The only object showing that was not human flesh, was the gold crucifix around Gabriella's neck.

"Please turn very slowly," Tyler said.

As Gabriella turned, the screen continued to reveal her body.

Turning the camera to the luggage, it revealed every layer of packed clothing from a three-dimensional perspective. It also revealed the contents of the zippered compartments. All that appeared on the video screen of the scanned area were three pairs of shoes in the lid of the suitcase. Tyler removed the shoes and scanned them with the back scanner. The heels of the shoes were not hollowed out, and the stitching of the straps was factory original.

"Please remove your shoes," Tyler asked. "Suddenly, shoes have become a threat. Even those as fashionable as yours."

Gabriella removed her shoes and placed them on the table. Tyler aimed the camera at them. They too revealed no anomalies. Agent Tyler knocked on the door and handed the camera back to the man who had brought it into her

"We're done here, Gabriella. They're going to check Mister Segretti the same way. Would you like to stay here until they're finished or would you like to go back in?"

"I'd like to return to Pietro," Gabriella said.

"I understand. I'll have the agent bring out your luggage when they're through inside."

Agent Tyler opened the door and motioned for Gabriella to enter the larger room. She walked straight to Segretti and put her hand in his.

"I'm fine," she whispered. "Everything will be okay."

"I know it will," Segretti said confidently.

After checking Segretti and his luggage with the back scanner, Agent Cummings' agitation had not subsided. Segretti studied him closely. He determined was more dejected and disappointed than angry.

"Are we free to go?" Segretti asked.

"I'll tell you when you're free to go," Cummings barked. "Do you know why we targeted you, Mister Segretti?" Cummings continued. "I'll tell you why, because as a known arms dealer, we monitor you constantly."

"If that's the case, then you must know I'm a legitimate business-man."

"And does your idea of being a legitimate businessman include the attempted sale of beam weapons to terrorist nations? We were very much aware of the Monte Carlo negotiations. A couple of good soldiers were killed trying to stop the deal. You're lucky we can't tie you to the killings.

It's only because the weapons didn't show up on foreign soil, you're still alive. I tell you all this because if you're trying to sell the weapons again, we'll be watching and waiting."

"Good, continue to watch and wait. You're agency is good at chasing down the wrong roads. It's what you do best."

Cummings flirted with the strong temptation to draw his weapon and shoot Segretti without regard for the consequences. Only the weight of the law countered his rage, but the internal struggle was making Cummings rattle and nearly implode.

"Go on, get out of here," the angry agent growled. "But the road I'm on is not wrong. It will bring us face to face again. And it will be a dark road with no witnesses."

"That's good," Segretti responded. "As long as it is a face to face meeting, and you don't sneak up behind me."

ALEX Kenneth Barnes sat in his jeep in front of his mine at the foot of the twenty-three mile long Cerbat Mountain range in northwest Arizona. He leaned his head back and took a long drink of water from a tin canteen covered with red and white embroidered Navajo designs. Given to him by his father on their first camping trip, the embroidered designs showed years of dirt and faded colors. The long day's work was exhausting. However, Barnes felt a sense of peace and accomplishment. He liked the pleasant ache in his arms from swinging a pick axe. The smell of rock dust, and the echoes in the cool confines of the mine, combined nicely with the majesty of the mountain and its secrets.

Barnes felt a spiritual connection to the mine. He worked it with a clergyman's dedication. Barnes believed the mine was the womb of the earth, a magical place of gestation. Each swing and strike with his pick axe was done with ceremonial respect to the mountain and the mine. The sound of chipping rock echoed a solemn sermon meant to express his worthiness and acceptance. For his labors, the mountain yielded to a ritual of solidarity. The mutually composed concert was framed within the only context that Barnes could hope for.

Barnes shared the chores of the mine with Billy Hayden. Though he was just a teenager, Hayden seemed to share Barnes' enthusiasm. Together, they managed to chip out three ore cars full of supracrustal rock, load the ore cars and roll them to the leaching pit. Barnes had worked the mine for about a year without help. Only the encouragement of his wife, and after a leg injury, was he convinced to take on help.

Hayden, a freshman in high school, was small in stature, but had large ambitions of going to college to study journalism. As a freelance writer for the local newspaper, Hayden wanted to write an article about mining. He approached Barnes with the idea. Barnes suggested Hayden work in the mine to gain firsthand experience. Hayden agreed, and the experience proved invaluable. After the article was finished, Hayden asked if he could continue helping at the mine to earn money for college. The relationship worked well, and Barnes felt a fatherly nature toward the boy. He admired the fact Hayden worked hard and didn't have a sense of youthful entitlement.

Barnes taught the young Hayden how to swing the pick axe and load the ore cars. When filled, each ore car carried about 200 pounds. Hayden enjoyed riding the quad Barnes used to pull the ore cars. Barnes had advised Hayden the most important piece of equipment was the quad. To ensure they would never be without equipment, Barnes purchased two of the four wheeled, all-terrain vehicles. One was to be used to haul the ore cars along the tracks. The other was a backup. But, rather than keeping the second quad idle, Barnes suggested Hayden use it whenever he wanted for transportation and recreation.

Barnes watched as Hayden hooked one of the quads to the lead ore car with a short, sturdy chain. He fastened each end with a thick metal dowel through the eyelets.

"Should I drive the load to the heap pit?" Hayden shouted.

"No. Leave the quad hitched. We'll move the ore cars tomorrow. We did enough for today," Barnes responded.

Hayden removed his work gloves and slapped the rock dust from his jeans. Approaching the second quad, he placed the gloves into the helmet resting on the seat and walked toward Barnes.

"Good work today, Billy," Barnes said.

"Yes, sir. We maxed out the ore cars. It's a shame, with all that work and all that ore, we won't be extracting much gold."

"Billy, do you know why? Why there's very little gold in the rocks?"

"Is it a geological scale of reduction?"

Barnes chuckled.

"No, Billy. That's not the reason. The reason there's a disproportionate ratio between gold and rock is because it's the rock's way of telling you to stay in school and get a good education. Your riches will not be found in the kind of hard labor we're doing now. Become a journalist. Report on important stories. The kind of stories that concern peoples' lives. Hopefully, through your reporting, you can change people's lives for the better. That will be your best reward. Call it a journalist's scale of economy. Do you understand?"

"Yes I do. I'll try, Mister Barnes."

"Good. I know you will."

"Mister Barnes, can I ride the quad here tonight with some friends?"

"Sure, go ahead. There's going to be a full moon. That should make for a good night of riding. Just remember, you and your friends must honor the no beer rule."

"Don't worry about that. We always do. Plus, I'm too young to buy beer. As a matter of fact, Mister Barnes, I've never tasted beer. I had wine once at one of my mother's birthday party, but never beer."

"Good for you. Then go ahead, enjoy."

"Thanks. Good night, Mister Barnes. You know, I forgot to mention to you, I saw a car parked here the other night. I thought it was you."

"It wasn't me, Billy."

"I was quadding with Henry Fuller when I saw the car. I saw flashlights too. Like somebody was walking around near the mine."

"I have an unpatented claim. Anyone can ride on this property. It could have been anyone. Campers and hikers come here on occasion."

"Yes, I know, but this wasn't campers or hikers. It just seemed peculiar."

"How do you know it wasn't campers or hikers?"

"Guess I really don't know, but the car didn't stay long. The light from the flashlight was like somebody was looking for something. I just wanted to let you know. Okay, see you tomorrow."

Barnes watched as Billy put on his helmet, mounted the spare quad, and drove away. The lights on the quad were swallowed in the cloud of dust it created as it faded into the distance. Pouring water on to his bandana, Barnes wiped the dust from his face and looked back at the mine. He felt a sense of pride in his labor with the earth. The mingling of tradition, ore dust and hard useful work, bore rewards placing him beyond complacent rules. For Barnes, it was a landscape of nostalgia and an inheritance of freedom.

Retiring early at age 55, Barnes had amassed a small fortune by manufacturing injection and blow mold products for sale to the electronics, medical and automotive industries. His injection mold facility utilized seven injection mold presses ranging in capacity from 40 to 100 tons. Through the lucrative sale of his company and prudent investments in commodities and real estate, Barnes had accumulated enough money to indulge in his hobby of mining.

His fascination with mining had begun at a very early age. As a boy, his father would take him camping in the Tipton Wilderness in the northern section of the Cerbat Mountains. They would hike in the pristine beauty of the wilderness and marvel at the terrain, especially the Cerbat Pinnacles.

Barnes' father would tantalize his son by telling him the tusk-like rows of the maroon colored spires were reminiscent of huge veins of gold.

Their camping and hiking trips would last for days and cover many miles. They would wander among the pinyon and manzanita pines. As they climbed to the higher elevations, they would camp among the white chaparral and expansive ponderosa pines. The elder Barnes would tell his son stories of how old mountain men and his Navajo ancestors lived in the beautiful, but sometimes, harsh environment. Stories of old prospectors mining for gold filled the young Barnes with a romantic longing.

On one such camping trip, while sitting in front of a camp fire, young Barnes made a promise to his father he would buy a mine claim and dig for gold. After discovering gold, he would build a home in the wilderness that looked out on the Cerbat Pinnacles. The elder Barnes told his son, it would be prudent to first get a good education, then earn enough money before pursuing that goal.

With enough money from the sale of his production company, Barnes kept his promise to his father. He purchased a mine claim in the mountains and began his quest for mining. It wasn't for the gold or as a hedge against inflation that Barnes worked hard. It was just the sense of being one with the open landscape. It was the authority and natural placement and order he felt swinging a pick axe and indulging in hard rock mining. There was an untold gratification he felt from extracting mineral bearing rock from host rock.

Using the hard rock method, Barnes created underground rooms or "stopes" supported by surrounding pillars of standing rock. He was able to muck out coarse ore using gravity to help move it down raises or shafts to his ore cars. The ore cars were then used to carry the ore out of the dark belly of the mine into the bright light and open landscape.

Barnes used the heap leaching method to extract gold from the ore. He had purchased a flat piece of land adjacent to the mine for that purpose. There, Barnes piled the crushed ore onto large plastic sheeting, then sprinkled cyanide onto the heap. Barnes had been told by his father, gold was recoverable because it dissolved in a cyanide solution like sugar in warm water. Using this process, he allowed the cyanide to percolate through the heap, and then collected the mixture through a pipe. The mixture passed through carbon filters separating the gold. The solution, without the gold, was then piped back to be reused. The cycle was the repeated.

With high grade ore containing only 0.05 ounces per ton of gold, Barnes was not concerned with value. He felt connected to something beyond money or wealth. He felt a kinship to the tales of the old prospecting days, and the ancestors his father spoke of when they camped in the

Tipton Wilderness. But more importantly, he felt a connection to his father whose spirit he felt along the white chaparral and the rugged foothills.

Barnes brushed his long white hair off his neck and shoulders with his fingers. He bunched it up, tying it with a red elastic band. Working with the traditional tools of mining, his hands felt rough and strong. His hands provided a distinct purity to his labor, far removed from manufacturing, sales and quotas from blow molds. The corporate and manufacturing world had changed before his eyes. But mining was a constant. A standard time had no power to alter. There was a sense of stability in being a partner with the earth. It was as immovable as the mountains themselves.

Other than the cell phone he kept on his belt, there was little in the way of modern equipment Barnes utilized. He preferred an uncomplicated world. He longed for the simplicity of hiking and camping in the wilderness. He preferred the memory of melancholy innocence, sitting with his father under the ponderosa pines listening to camp fire tales.

Barnes watched the sun as it started to descend toward the Black Mountains in the west. Painted light poured over him as the sun settled into a divide between the sky and the line of the mountains. He liked to sit quietly and watch the sun set. On occasion, he would sit back in his jeep and sleep for a while under the dark sky.

Dangling a foot outside the jeep, he noticed a set of lights off in the distance. Because he had placed an unpatented claim on the mine, anyone could use the land for any legal purpose. His real purpose for the unpatented claim was that he felt it immoral to have personal ownership of the landscape. The unpatented claim also allowed Billy and his friends the right to use the site to ride their quads. Campers used the area, leaving remnants of burnt out camp fires. When Barnes saw a doused camp fire, he would wonder if it had been left by a father taking his young son camping and hiking in the wilderness. With the decreasing camp fires and the increase of tire tracks from the quads and dirt bikes, Barnes realized modern recreation was replacing old traditions. As the vehicle approached, Barnes reached down and gripped the handle of a shovel. The vehicle slowed and stopped next to him.

"Good evening," one of the occupants said.

"Hi," Barnes responded suspiciously.

"Are you Alex Barnes?" the visitor said.

"Yes. And who might you be?" Barnes asked.

"My name is Erik Dawson. This is Timothy Finley. We're from the Department of Defense."

"Department of Defense? Is that so? How did you find me here?"

"Actually, we stopped at your house. Your wife, Mrs. Barnes, told us you were here."

"That's not what I meant. How did I get the attention of the Department of Defense?"

"Is this your mine?" Dawson asked pointing to the mine.

"It is. What's your interest in it?"

"We'd like to talk to you, Mister Barnes. Is this a good time and place?" Dawson said.

"Are you sure you want to speak with me?"

"We're sure," Dawson said. A distrust and tension, that grew without effort emanated from him.

Barnes studied the agents, allowing his suspicion to persist.

"Tell you what, gentlemen," Barnes said, releasing his grip on the shovel. "It will be dark soon. Let's go to my home. We can talk there. Obviously, you know where I live."

"Yes, sir, we do."

"Good, I'll see you there."

Barnes started his jeep and drove away from the mine. A glance in the rear view mirror showed Dawson's car following closely. Barnes drove to Route 93 and headed toward his home in Butler. The cool air blew through his long hair and dried the perspiration on his clothes. Barnes could not understand why he had attracted the attention of the Department of Defense. Chipping at rock in a hole in a mountain was not a national security threat he figured. Suddenly, he recalled the report from the Brookhaven Laboratory and the Niels Bohr Institute. He tried to understand what was so significant in the report. It was an in depth study on a high technical level. But Barnes began to suspect there was more to it. As Barnes drove, he kept checking on the car following him. He wondered if the men behind him were plotting a vile saga and already deciding his fate.

MARIO Orisi replaced the rented car with the car he had stolen. He drove from the Wayfarer Inn in Kingman as the sun began to set. Orisi drove slowly and carefully trying not to jostle the three containers Umberto Nunarro had placed in the trunk. One container was filed with acetone, the other with concentrated hydrogen peroxide. The last one contained hydrochloric acid. Jostling them individually would not cause a problem, but when mixed it became another matter. Nunarro had prepared the proper ratios for each in order to form the explosive triacetone triperoxide. As an explosive expert, Nunarro knew the mixture would become extremely volatile and create an entropy burst. The explosion would produce hundreds of liters of gas in a fraction of a second with little heat. He knew it would be the type of event perfect for the mine, achieving the maximum result he wanted.

Nunarro had weighed his options regarding explosives. He considered the problem of transportation and availability. After investigating and conducting surveillance of the mine and several stopes within it, Nunarro decided the TATP was the best choice. To detonate the mixture, Nunarro needed a charge. He wanted one that could be easily purchased without prompting suspicion. From a firearms dealer, Nunarro purchased a case of twelve gauge shotgun shells. He had also purchased one box of Silver Salutes M-88s at a local fireworks store to use as the primary detonator. In the hotel, he laid out the shotgun shells and painstakingly removed the powder from them. He sprinkled out the black powder and tightly wrapped it with a strip of oil cloth; then rolled it to form a long self-sealing wick.

Nunarro's components lacked the sophistication he was accustomed. Given the logistics, he figured his planning was creative. The combination of materials would produce a final explosive event with maximum efficiency. Unwinding several feet of wick, Nunarro bound one end of the main wick with the two M-88s using highly reactive flash paper. He tugged lightly on the fire crackers to ensure they were held securely by the paper. He then placed the oily roll into a small box.

"What's the burn time on the wick?" Orisi asked.

"No more than ten minutes," Nunarro answered.

"That may be too long. We're only going in ten yards. It won't take ten minutes to get out."

"I'm really not sure how long it will actually take. Ten minutes for sure. This wick may be erratic. We still have to drive away."

"What about the explosion?"

"The first two stopes will blow out and bring the wood and stone frames with them. We'll get a large volume of mountain rock to come down, too. I don't know exactly how much. It should cause the entrance way to seal up tight."

"Does the Monsignor think this will permanently shut down the mine?"

"That's not our concern."

"His scheme doesn't seem to be well thought out."

"Again, that's not our concern. Our concern is our plan."

"What if our plan doesn't close the mine?"

"If not, then we'll deal with Barnes personally."

Orisi drove slowly concealing his impatience to get to the Barnes mine. He felt himself set and bound to something personal, yet heroic, and at the same time, comfortable with damage and mayhem. Both fit easily into his nature. It was a fraternal pairing that held its own secrets and rewards. Orisi felt chaste by his endeavor, but somewhat miscast in a mission not of his choosing. It was a bit disconcerting for him to feel a puppet-string pull on his guile and vanity by a man of religion.

"Umberto?" Orisi said quietly. "What do you think of the Monsignor? What are your feelings about his motives?"

"Does it matter?"

"No. I was just curious. I realize people will always be who and what they are. But the Monsignor is a man that represents something different."

"Just what do you think he represents?"

"Tolerance."

"Tolerance? He represents no such thing. It's only what we assume he is that allows his deception. He's just a man. His collar, his vows, all the novenas and prayers he says can't hide that. The world may expect something different from him, but we know better….His true nature shows with this man, Barnes, and his mine. The Monsignor made the sign of the cross on both of them. And we know what that means."

BILLY Hayden twisted the hand throttle of the Kawasaki quad. It responded with a loud roar. The quad's crackling sound provided Hayden with pure excitement. The machine's response displayed unhinged power and the promise of joy, speed and flight. The ageless Cerbat Mountains acknowledged the sound and responded with a ghostly echo. Through eons of time, the mountains maintained a stoic vigil of all movements and sounds. Hayden strapped on his helmet, lowered the goggles over his eyes. He raised his thumb toward his riding partner, Henry Fuller.

The boys rode out along the base of the Cerbat Mountains with a fervor the desert could not contain. It was an unrestrained vitality, jolting as electricity, punctuated by youth. Hayden stood up on his quad like a jockey riding a true bloodline thoroughbred. The machine responded to every twist of the throttle. He was one with the quad, flowing effortlessly with every sharp turn, hitting a full gallop on the open range. Hayden maneuvered the quad over dirt mounds and arroyos, dodging thorny saguaro cactus. The lights from the quads illuminated the landscape in measured parcels. Along with the glare of the moon, enough visibility was provided to prevent doom.

The two boys found themselves chasing each other, catching up and then speeding away. It was a mechanical version of the ageless game of tag. They gave the quads full throttle on the straight-aways and slowed when maneuvering hairpin turns. Hayden had mastered the art of riding the quad; letting up on the throttle and slowing down on some of the sharper turns. He instinctively knew his limits against the pull of centrifugal force.

The boys did not establish a prearranged course, but made the entire desert their track. Hayden was familiar with the terrain and knew where the Barnes' mine was. Spotting a light in that direction, he stopped the quad and lifted his goggles. He suspected it was close to the mine. Perhaps, it was Barnes checking on the ore cars or driving them to the leach pit.

"What's the matter, Billy?" Henry Fuller asked over the hum of the idling quad engines.

"See that light?" Billy said, pointing in the direction of the mine.

"Yeah. What is it? A car?"

"I think so."

"Is it coming this way?"

"It looks like it's parked. From here, I can't tell for sure. I wonder if it's Mister Barnes."

"What would he be doing out there?"

"I don't know. I saw a car by the mine the last time we were riding."

"What do you suppose a car would be doing there, if it's not Barnes?"

"I don't know. Let's check it out."

Orisi stood outside the stolen Volvo at the opening of the mine. He looked off into the distance observing pearls of light twisting along the desert. Their movement was erratic without form or pattern. He heard the muted sounds of engines as it crossed the long distance.

Nunarro was hunched over the car's trunk carefully mixing the acetone, hydrogen peroxide and hydrochloric acid. The ample light from the trunk allowed him to perform his task with laboratory precision. His hands were firm and steady, pouring each premeasured chemical into a beaker, then sealing it with a soft cork. Nunarro carefully bound the preassembled wick to the beaker with a strip of masking tape along with the M-88s. Once the completed package of triacetone triperoxide was assembled, he lifted it gently from the trunk of the car. Approaching Orisi, he noticed the distant lights from the quads.

"What is that?" Nunarro whispered.

"I think it's those kids we saw the other night."

"Do you make out two of them?"

"Yes. They're coming this way. Should we wait and get rid of them?" Orisi asked.

"No. Let's get this into the mine and get it over with."

Orisi and Nunarro walked into the mine and stopped by the ore cars. Removing some of the stones on the rear car, Nunarro provided a flat base for the explosives. He carefully placed the beaker of explosives onto the ore positioning the M-88s next to them. He then guided the wick along the other two cars letting the end hang slightly off the lead car.

"Are you ready?" Nunarro asked.

"Light it," Orisi responded.

Nunarro reached into his pocket and removed the gold cigarette lighter given to him by the emir. He looked at the lighter and for a brief moment thoughts of the emir, and his daughter, Adilah, passed through his mind. Nunarro could not help but harbor the nagging regret for past choices. He wondered what Adilah was doing at the instant he lit the fuse, and if she could envision the indignity he felt being in this dark place, destroying the toil and dreams of another man.

A phosphorous glow filled the section of the mine as the wick began to burn. The burning wick crackled and hissed like a serpent full of defiance and menace. A line of smoke and the acrid smell of sulfur confirmed the presence of danger and doom. Nunarro saw the wick as something alive, burning with fierce self-consumption and faster than he anticipated. Orisi kept a flashlight pointed to the ground as they walked out of the mine. Nunarro looked at his watch measuring the time from the lighting of the wick to the explosion. They got into the stolen car and began to drive away slowly. Nunarro looked over his shoulder to see the mine entrance aglow against the dark outline of the mountain. It resembled a placid, benign beast with one fierce eye. The glow became more intense as the wick continued to burn. The gun powder and oil cloth wrapping combined to create taunting bursts and a crawling string of fire.

Billy Hayden saw the lights of the Volvo at the same time that Orisi and Nunarro saw the lights of the quads. The night had squeezed the machines toward each other on a collision course. The mechanical masses were drawing into a prescribed rendezvous, marked indelibly with clear intentions. Each vehicle maintained its own purpose and direction, moving forward with brute force and a new conflict.

Orisi watched as the quad swerved away from the onrushing Volvo. Hayden spun his quad abruptly and stopped. He saw Nunarro turn and look in his direction. Then beyond to the glowing mine entrance. Hayden turned to see the glow in the mine. Instinctively, he knew the mine was on fire, but couldn't imagine what could be burning. At first, he thought someone had set a camp fire. Then he tried to recall if there were barrels of cyanide in the mine. The factors then gave way to a string of tiny sequences. Hayden turned sharply toward the Volvo, noticing it had stopped. He thought he saw someone from within the darkness of the car still looking at the mine. Instinctively he twisted the quad's throttle.

"Run," he shouted at Henry Fuller. "Run."

The quads lurched forward and roared away.

The wick burned down to a tiny nub then ignited the flash paper around the M-88s. The wicks of the fire crackers ignited; burned quickly and then exploded. The burst caused a deep guttural rumble from the mountain. A chain reaction of heat and violent movement caused by the mixture Nunarro had prepared to go off in an extreme explosion. The secondary burst was a full-throated moan from the mountain. Its loud, painful cry traveled to the high chaparral and every space before it. The booming sound curdled the air, prompting coyotes and wolves, miles away to howl at the sky.

Nitrogen gas expanded rapidly with a great force into the mine, collapsing the wood and stone frames of the stopes. Large chunks of rock were jarred loose and fell. The percussion expanded to the mouth of the mine, throwing out hundreds of yards of rock and dirt from deep within its belly. The mountain's regurgitation was an extreme response to the foul abuse. The angry blast and the force of a gale wind carried the debris into the night and open desert, creating a new topography.

Billy and Henry had not escaped the reach of the blast and were pelted by flying dust and bits of rock. The rushing wind lifted Billy's quad, tossing it into a shallow arroyo. Billy released the quad and was at the mercy of a formless tumble. He crashed into the warm wash of the earth, rolling in it without the benefit of feeling or motion. His head skidded into the earth as he tried to crawl away.

Disoriented, Billy patted the earth seeking out the quad. Wherever he touched, there seemed to be no earth. Had he lost his hands he wondered. The surge of dirt surrounded him, filling his goggles. He could not see. The roar of the explosion had left a high pitched ringing in his ears. He choked and gasped for air, then felt a tug on his shoulders and a force gripping him around his chest. Henry Fuller had picked Billy up and set him on the back of his quad. Henry pushed the quad faster than he had thought it could go, driving beyond the sea of dust.

Gradually, Billy began hearing the low moan of the quad's engine. It sounded strained, muffled and distant. He felt his hands gripping Henry's jacket, and moved his fingers to convince himself they were still attached. Billy still could not see. Sand was in his goggles. He kept his eyes shut tightly and buried his face in Henry's back.

Nunarro heard the explosion. He watched as the dirt and rock belch from the mine. At the exact instant of the blast, Nunarro thought he heard Adilah gasp. The spirit of her disbelief and sorrow traveled through him residing in his mind. Nunarro felt an abject shame saturate him. His guilt was in direct proportion to his actions. There was a normalcy to the coarse emptiness he had been feeling up to the moment of the explosion. Then suddenly, he saw his rage, a fist shaken not at a capricious fate, but instead turned inward toward his own wounded nature.

Nunarro turned from the mine as Orisi drove away. They continued in silence. Neither man had a feeling of satisfaction or a plan for what they would do next. Exploding the mine seemed like a crazy dare carried out by two adolescents motivated by the grip of fear. The alignment of Monsignor Clementi's whims and his own capabilities to make explosives seemed to serve no purpose for Nunarro. A small displacement of rocks proved to be a fragile excuse to justify nothing.

Nunarro lit a cigarette with the gold lighter. The soft glow from the cigarette was quickly swallowed by the darkness of the car. Holding the cigarette, he watched as it burned leaving a crooked line of gray ash. Nunarro opened the window and flicked the cigarette out. He looked at the gold lighter still in his hand and began tapping it on his knee. Gripping it tightly with his fist, he brought it close to his lips. In one smooth motion, Nunarro put his arm out the window. He let it hang down resting on the door. Slowly, he opened his fist and let the lighter drop from his hand. As it hit the ground, he thought he heard himself say: *"I'm sorry, Adilah."*

ALEX Barnes went around lighting the tiki torches that lined his patio. His wife, Morgana, poured ice tea for the two Department of Defense agents from a hand painted terra cotta pot. The black images on the pot depicted the sun and moon, trees and stalks of wheat. Morgana had crafted the pot in a style and tradition of ancient Navajo stone drawings. Retrieving a buckskin pouch from the soft leather vest she wore, Morgana sprinkled pinches of several herbs from a glass jar. Reaching into another jar, she removed two turquoise stones and several small pieces of shell. She placed them into the pouch as well. She drew the string on the pouch, and placed it on the table.

Agent Dawson carefully observed Morgana's movements. He noticed her absolute confidence in the simplest tasks she performed. He was impressed with the way she moved with a natural command and assurance. Morgana sat on a cloth-covered ottoman opposite Dawson, legs crossed, shoulders back and chin up. As she stared at Dawson, she struck a regal pose like one of her Navajo ancestors. She was soft, yet statuesque with broad shoulders, long thick limbs and full breasts. Strength showed in her rounded jaw and full lips. Her dark eyes were penetrating, yet showed the capacity for compassion and forgiveness. Dawson knew Morgana was steeped in Navajo tradition. It was openly evident she partook of a traditional practice, done to protect against unexpected events or catastrophe.

Morgana's straight black hair was combed back and carefully tied with a strand of rawhide studded with small pieces of turquoise. She wore a silver necklace strung through the turquoise, white shell, abalone and jet; the traditional four sacred stones of the Navajo people.

"Thank you for the tea, Misses Barnes," Dawson said. "I hope we are not intruding."

"What is it you want from me and my husband, Agent Dawson?" Morgana said with a hint of bluntness.

Dawson knew he could not underestimate Morgana. There was a brutal elegance to her directness. It carried the weight and effortless force that matched her stature and stare. She offered an impenetrable defense of herself and her husband. He knew she was ready to defy him and the agency he represented.

"Okay. Let me start by asking how long have you owned the mine?" he asked turning to Barnes.

"I bought the claim sixteen months ago." Barnes answered.

"And, you also own your own heap leaching area?"

"You already know I do. I prefer heap leaching as opposed to vat leaching. That way, I can control my own leaching process."

"I see," Dawson said.

"But, you still have not answered my question," Morgana interrupted. "I'll repeat it just in case you gentlemen didn't hear it the first time. Why is the Department of Defense interested in us?"

"We were getting around to that," Dawson said. "You recently sent a sample of slag to the Niels Bohr Institute in Copenhagen."

Barnes nodded his head and sipped his ice tea.

"I'm just curious about something," Dawson continued. "Why did you send the sample to a laboratory in Copenhagen?"

"I had sent other samples to many domestic labs. Each report I received showed I had ghost gold."

"What's ghost gold?" Agent Finley asked.

"Ghost gold is like a slag that has the same chemistry as gold, but it's not yellow. The local labs had a history of seeing ghost gold and kept conducting standard testing. They always came back with the same results. The testing at the Bohr Institute included fractional vaporization which takes the testing to a different level."

"What made you think there was something more to the ghost gold?"

"What makes you so interested in their findings and my mine?" Barnes countered.

"You read the report," Dawson said. "What you sent to Niels Bohr was not ghost gold. Among the properties of the material from your mine is that of a superconductor."

"Superconductors are a concern to us," Finley said.

"Who else would they be a concern to?" Barnes asked.

"What do you mean?" Dawson asked.

"I received a phone call today from an international businessman who apparently heard about my mine. He wants to meet with me to discuss a business deal, an arrangement with me."

"What's his name?" Finley asked.

Barnes stood and left the patio. He walked into the living room to retrieve a note pad from his desk. After looking at the name he had jotted down earlier, he walked back out to the patio.

"His name is Pietro Segretti," Barnes announced.

Finley lifted his laptop computer from the floor and placed it on his knees. He went to the official site of the Department of Defense. After several prompts he typed in: *Segretti* then hit the "search" prompt. The D.O.D. logo disappeared and the screen immediately flashed to a folder with the heading *International Arms Dealers* followed by a list of names. Finley brought his cursor to Pietro Segretti's name and clicked on it. A screen opened and showed a lengthy bio on Segretti. Finley started reading an account of Segretti's most recent effort to broker a sale of beam weapons and looked over three pictures taken of Segretti in Monte Carlo, the scene of his attempted transaction. Within the bio, there was a link to Homeland Security. He opened the link and discovered a recent entry detailing an interrogation at Sky Harbor Airport conducted by Field Agent, Andrew Cummings. Finley closed the lid of the laptop and looked at Dawson. He was hoping not to reveal any reaction to the important information.

"Did Pietro Segretti give you any details about what he wanted to discuss with you?" Dawson asked.

"No. He was very polite. I knew immediately from our brief conversation he was an expert deal maker. I've dealt with his type all my life. This guy was very good."

"What do you mean by good?"

"Smooth. Confident. Probably very rich." Barnes thought for a moment. "He also sounded sincere," he concluded.

"Are you meeting with him?" Finley said.

"Yes, in two days."

"Getting back to the slag," Dawson said. "How much do you have, and how much did you mine out?"

The phone rang, interrupting Barnes' response. He waited as Morgana reached for it.

"Yes?" she said into the phone.

She heard an excited voice calling her name. "Misses Barnes! Misses Barnes! It's me, Billy Hayden," he screamed. "You have to come quick. Come quick! The mine blew up! I was riding with Henry Fuller! We got blown off our quads! I hit my head. My God, it was so loud…"

"Billy, slow down. Slow down." Morgana said calmly. "What happened?"

Barnes turned his attention to Morgana and rose from his chair.

"What is it?" Barnes asked, as Billy kept shouting over the phone.

"It blew up," she heard Billy say. "It just blew up. The whole mountain came down. I swear. We were just riding. Stuff is still coming out."

"Hold on, Billy, speak with Mister Barnes," Morgana said and handed the phone to Barnes.

"Mister Barnes, we were just riding our quads. The mine, the mountain, I can't believe it. It blew up."

"What do you mean a cave-in?"

"No. I don't know. It was loud. An explosion. God, it was loud," Billy said frantically.

"Where are you, Billy?" Barnes said maintaining control.

"I'm here. I'm with Henry Fuller. We both saw it blow up. We got thrown from our quads."

"Are you alright?"

"I can't hear so good. I can't see too well either. I hit my head. The quad's broke, I think. I saw a car. Remember, I told you I saw a car the last time. Well, I saw a car again."

"Forget the car. Forget the quad. Tell me you're alright."

"I'm alright, I guess. My ears, my eyes, but I'm alright."

"Is Henry okay?"

"Yes. He pulled me out. His quad works. You need to come quick."

"Was it just you and Henry riding? Is there anyone else with you or anyone in the mine?"

"No. It was just me and Henry. Nobody's in the mine. Come quick. Come quick."

"I will. I will. Is there a fire?"

"No."

"Is the leach pit damaged?"

"I don't know. I don't think so."

"You have to get as far away from there as you can. It's the leach pit that concerns me. That can be very dangerous. Do you understand?"

"Yes. I know. The leach pit was the first thing I thought about."

"Billy, this is important. Get out of there. Get going now."

"Are you coming here, Mister Barnes?"

"Yes. I don't want to see you there; you or Henry. Go now. Call my cell phone when you get home. I want to be sure you're okay. Go."

Barnes disconnected from the call and dialed a number.

"Sheriff's office," a voice said after the first ring.

"Sheriff St. Cloud, please. This is Alex Barnes. This is an emergency," Barnes said keeping his voice steady.

Barnes heard a click and a second voice.

"Yes, Alex, what's the problem?" the Sheriff said.

"Joseph, I just got a call from Billy Hayden. He was riding his quad out by my mine. He told me it blew up. I don't know if it was a cave-in or not."

"When did it happen?" the Sheriff asked.

"Just now. I'm on my way there."

"Alex, I can't allow that. We don't know if there is any damage to your leach pit?"

"I asked Billy. He said he didn't think so."

"Well, if there is, I don't want anybody in the area. Is Billy still there?"

"I told him to get out of there now. He's with Henry Fuller?"

"Was anyone in the mine? Workers, anyone?"

"No."

"Are you sure, Alex?"

"I just left there an hour ago…two hours ago at most. No one's in the mine."

"Let me call the fire department and toxic emergency service. Once they establish the leach pit is secure, I'll give you a call. Then you can go to the mine. It shouldn't take long to make a determination. Just sit tight. I'll get to you as soon as I know something."

SHERIFF Joseph St. Cloud drove his official vehicle along Route Ninety-three. Its emergency lights flashing. Two fire trucks, an EMS vehicle and an EPA inspector's car followed, disturbing the dark, quiet desert night. St. Cloud had been sheriff for more than ten years and loved the land of his Navajo ancestors. He felt his oath and personal responsibility made him guardian to it. Through his ancestry, he had become part of it. But, he could not avoid feeling a sense of treachery and subversion threatening the nature of inherent harmony it shares with his lineage.

When he was young, his grandparents had taught him that spirits were alive in all things. He was made aware the spirits spoke in languages accessible to those who knew how to listen. His grandfather, Still Cloud, often took young Joseph into the mountains and plains. They would remain still, listening to the howling of the wind, and the pouring rain. Still Cloud would encourage the young boy to hold his breath, while listening to the cries of animals, the squawk of birds, the run of the river or the decaying of plants. *"They all speak in their own special tongue,"* the old man would say. Young St. Cloud would remain in awed silence, open to the things he heard and felt. Each sound would be distinctive but would join together with him.

"Listen to these voices," Still Cloud would encourage. *"They are the sacred voices of harmony and renewal. They are the instruments of God played by His hand...Listen to the music."*

The lessons from Still Cloud resonated deeply within St. Cloud. He came to understand the sounds of the night differed from those of the day, and not all sounds were those of joy and renewal. The blaring of the sirens provided a distinct example. They spoke with a scared voice baptized in distrust and danger.

As he neared the mine, St. Cloud lowered the window and sniffed the air for signs of cyanide. The air appeared somewhat stale, marginally thicker than usual, laced with mine dust and a hint of burnt matches. But more noticeable to St. Cloud were the moans of the sirens. How different he thought they were from the sounds of nature, he was made aware of by his grandfather. The sirens were a mournful motif recounting a different message, meant as a severe warning; the kind his grandfather tried to teach.

St. Cloud drove to the mine where the dust from the explosion was still settling. He shone the headlights of his vehicle on the entrance, and noticed it had been blocked by large pieces of the mountain. The Sheriff had been familiar with the mine. As a long time friend to Barnes, St. Cloud had toured the mine on several visits. Seeing just a small portion of the rubble, he knew there was greater devastation behind the newly blocked entranced.

Two fire trucks parked on either side of St. Cloud's car. Their lights revealed more of the altered mountain side. Firemen approached the rocks blocking the entrance, and struggled hopelessly to create an opening.

"This is sealed up real good, Sheriff," said Acting Fire Chief, Paul Faulkner. "Are we sure this is not a rescue mission?"

"No. Alex told me there was no one in the mine," St. Cloud responded.

"Well, we've got to get in there," Faulkner said.

"We don't do anything until we learn the extent of a cyanide threat. We must be sure there was no cyanide in the mine."

The EMS and EPA vehicles skidded to a stop behind St. Cloud. Harold Becker, the driver of the EPA vehicle opened the door.

"Doesn't look good, Sheriff." Becker observed.

"It's not, Harold. But I need you to test the air. You know where the leach pit is. Check it. I don't suspect there's a leak. I don't get the odor of bitter almond from the cyanide. But, I need a contamination reading right away."

Becker quickly drove to the leach pit, removed his field cyanide probe from the trunk and set it up. He was familiar with various mines in the area, as well as the accompanying leach and vat pits and all sorts of contamination. For the past ten years, he had been involved with the regulation of leach and vat pits. He had studied the impact of abandoned uranium mines on the Navajo Nation. Resulting from his staff's research, the EPA, Department of Energy, Bureau of Indian Affairs, and the Nuclear Regulatory Commission, had finally reached an agreement to clean up the uranium mining waste. Becker had worked diligently to address the uranium contamination. His persistence was instrumental in cleaning up the contamination of local water sources and the area's mines. The mines had yielded more than four million tons of uranium over nearly 60 years. The legacy from the mining was untold sickness and immeasurable disaster to the Navajo people in the area. The grim requiem of the uranium mining was finally reaching a just conclusion. But Becker knew there would never be justice for the damage the uranium mining had caused the Navajo people and their land. Becker started to take readings of the air and checked the plastic sheeting for breaks or rips. He checked the main hoses and pipes noticing their fittings were properly connected and undamaged.

Mike Higgins, from the EMS Corps, stood by the fallen rock assessing the damage with Paul Faulkner and Sheriff St. Cloud.

"There's no question this blew out and not caved in," Higgins observed.

"I know," St. Cloud said.

"Who would do this to Barnes?" Faulkner said.

"The question is why," St. Cloud responded.

"Sheriff, did you contact Mine Safety and Health?" Faulkner asked.

"Yes. They should be getting here shortly."

"My guess is they'll close this mine up for good," Higgins said.

"Did Alex have dynamite in the mine he didn't secure properly?" Faulkner said.

"This is no accident involving a few sticks of dynamite. This mountain would only yield to something a lot stronger." St. Cloud said.

"Did Alex have any land squabbles?" Faulkner asked.

"None that I'm aware of."

"Was his claim coming in?" Higgins asked.

"Why?" St. Cloud questioned.

"If it was, maybe somebody got jealous."

"I doubt it. All the miners around here know each other. They're a small, close group."

"Who called in the explosion?" Faulkner asked.

"Billy Hayden."

"August Hayden's boy?"

"Yes. He was riding a quad with Henry Fuller. Apparently, they were here when it blew."

St. Cloud remembered his grandfather's urgings that all things have a purpose and spirit, and act in harmony with everything ever created. He was taught mining and the destruction he saw was in direct contrast to that harmony. Digging for minerals was a crude surgery; reckless gouging to plunder the earth's arteries and organs. He had come to understand rocks and dirt could not reproduce or replenish themselves. Perhaps, the collapse of the stone might have been the only way for the mountain to protect itself. Through the redesigned mosaic, the mountain was voicing a plea of defense, spoken in one syllable.

St. Cloud turned from the mountain to see the glow of lights from a vehicle heading toward him. As the vehicle drew near, St. Cloud recognized it as Alex Barnes' jeep. Barnes stopped the jeep next to St. Cloud and lowered the window. St. Cloud acknowledged Barnes and Morgana. He saw the two Department of Defense agents sitting in the rear as flashing lights from the fire trucks bathed them in colors of red and blue.

"Sorry, sheriff, I couldn't wait for your call," Barnes said. "I had to come and see what happened."

"It's bad, Alex. Your mine is sealed shut."

Barnes and Morgana stepped from the jeep and walked to the fallen rock. Barnes reached out and touched the stone. A remote sorrow, deep and personal engulfed him.

"Can you believe this?" Barnes whispered. "Who would do this?" Barnes' tone was hurt and incredulous.

"That's what we need to find out," St. Cloud said over his shoulder.

"How's the leach pit?" Morgana asked.

"Becker's checking it now."

"That should be alright," Barnes said, sniffing the air. "You would smell something if the pit was disturbed. It's been more than two hours since the explosion. If there's been a leak, the cyanide would have evaporated by now."

St. Cloud turned and saw Finley and Dawson standing beside Barnes' jeep, still being pelted by the pulsing lights.

"Who are they?" St. Cloud asked nodding in their direction.

"Agents from the Department of Defense," Barnes responded.

"Department of Defense? What are they doing here?"

"They were at the house when I got the call from Billy. They wanted to come and see what happened. Apparently, my mine has become an interest to them. All of a sudden, I've had a lot of interest in my mine."

"What do you mean?"

"I received a call earlier today from a businessman who said he was an international buyer. He said he has an interest in my mine."

"What else did he say?"

"Just that he wanted to have a meeting with me. Apparently, he knew a lot about me and my manufacturing business."

"How did he know that?"

"The sale of my company was touted in many trade magazines. The internet told the rest of the story. The guy did his homework"

"What's the man's name?"

"Pietro Segretti. I gave the name to the D.O.D. agents. I'm sure they know about him."

"I'll ask them. But what was the D.O.D. doing at your house?"

"Something about slag I brought out. I had it tested. It had superconducting prosperities."

"Why would that interest them?"

"Damned if I know. I'm not sure why Segretti is interested in it. I asked the D.O.D. guys why they were interested in it and still didn't get a straight answer. Maybe they think I'm building a terrorist weapon. I just care about my mine. This damn thing is a hobby with me, Joseph. You know that. I couldn't care less about superconductivity."

"Alex, right now I'm not concerned about those two guys. I need to know what may have been in the mine," Faulkner interrupted.

"What is it you need to know, Paul?"

"Did you have any dynamite in the mine that could have caused this?"

"Absolutely not. All my digging is done with drills and picks axes."

"How about cyanide? Did you have any canisters or anything stored in the mine?"

"Come on, Paul, you know that's not legal. There's no way I would have done that."

"Let's get back to the superconductors," St. Cloud said. "What's so special about them?"

"I don't know, Joseph," Barnes said. "Maybe it's not that at all. Maybe there's a different motive at work here. This was planned well in advance. I was gone from the mine not more than two hours. Do you know what type of product it would have taken to bring down this much rock?"

"Give me an idea."

"Dynamite is out. Somebody would have to load it on trucks and set charges. It would take a full day at best. Whoever it was, knew their explosives. They packed light, compact. There are a lot of new substances that could have been used."

Barnes touched the rock again with the tips of his calloused fingers.

"There's no heat," Barnes continued. "That eliminates certain explosives and gives probability to others. Without the presence of heat and fire, that would narrow down the product used."

"You say whoever it was packed light and compact. What volume are we talking about?"

"Joseph, now days a nuclear bomb can be packed in a briefcase. Whatever was used here could probably fit on the front seat of a car and be carried by one man."

"Billy Hayden was here with Henry Fuller when the mine blew." St. Cloud said. "Did he say he saw anything unusual?"

"He did say he saw a car. Come to think of it, he said he had seen a car a couple of nights before. I don't know if we can make a connection. You should talk to Billy about it."

"I will, but first I want to talk to the D.O.D. agents."

St. Cloud approached Finley and Dawson, noticing they were somber in the face of the settling dust and the disheveled landscape.

"Good evening," St. Cloud finally said. "I'm Sheriff Joseph St. Cloud. I understand you gentlemen are with the Department of Defense."

"That's correct, Sheriff," Dawson responded. "I'm Agent Dawson, and this is Agent Finley."

"I'm curious as to why the D.O.D. would be interested in Mister Barnes' mine?"

"We're interested because he mined a mineral that has the capabilities of being a superconductor. We were just investigating his find to determine how much he has mined."

"And is that a standard practice of the D.O.D.?"

"We investigate every incident where superconductors are concerned.

I know it's a bit preliminary, but do you have any idea what happened to the mine?"

"Aside from an explosion, I have no idea and no motives. What is the mineral that is a superconductor?"

"It's a form of gold."

"A form of gold? I'm not a miner, what form of gold are you referring to?"

"It's a single-atom gold. It's in the slag in his mine."

"Are you referring to ghost gold?"

"Not in Mister Barnes' case. His find is certainly not ghost gold."

"So how does this single atom gold become a superconductor?"

"To put it simply, the same way wind or water when harnessed properly becomes energy."

"So what's so special about the energy of superconductors?"

"They are pure energy...inexhaustible. That makes it more valuable than all the gold Barnes could get from his claim."

"Sheriff?" Becker called out from behind St. Cloud.

St. Cloud turned to see Becker raise a thumb. "All clear," he said. "No contamination. The readings are all normal. The leach pit is sound."

St. Cloud nodded. Then turned back to Dawson, and Finley trying to assess their knowledge, and peer into their departmental discretion.

"The Italian business man, Segretti. What can you tell me about him?" St. Cloud asked.

"He's a business man. Unfortunately, his business is in the illegal weapons market on a global scale. Apparently, he has quite a reputation in the circles he travels. He's very cunning and covert," Dawson answered.

"Sheriff," Finley said. "We know this is your jurisdiction and your investigation. But, we'd like to know how it proceeds. Anything you can share would be greatly appreciated."

"I will," St. Cloud responded. "I hope you would be forthcoming with information, as well. I'm sure, at the very least, you have a suspicion of what interest the Italian arms dealer has in Barnes' mine. That makes *your* guess better than mine."

Dawson nodded, aware of the level of distrust St. Cloud was measuring him with.

"The superconductivity is valuable to anyone," he finally announced. "We think he's looking to make a deal."

"Making direct contact with Barnes doesn't sound like the action of a cunning, covert dealer to me."

"Well, your guess is as good as ours."

St. Cloud turned to see Morgana and Barnes standing in front of the blocked mine entrance. They were motionless and silent, struck by the invasion in their lives. Barnes felt a deep nagging in his chest. He wished he had been present when the mountain collapsed so he could hear its crumbling song of loss or protest. Billy Hayden had heard that song but Barnes knew the boy did not hear it the way it was intended. Morgana clasped her husband's hand and pressed it to her side. From her vest pocket, she removed the buckskin pouch containing the turquoise stone, herbs and shells. She reached down and placed the pouch by the fallen rocks. She believed more than ever in the sacred legend of their ability to prevent unexpected events or catastrophe. The explosion caused the pieces of stone to fall on each other leaving a mammoth toll of heartbreak and devastation. Within this upheaval, Morgana believed a great catastrophe had ultimately been prevented by the influence of the contents of the pouch. Their forces guided her husband to a distance far from the mine where he was kept safe.

BILLY Hayden had never been inside the Mohave County Sheriff's barracks. He was in awe. Its hallowed halls had been a place reserved for those with a long tradition that went back to his Saturday serial heroes. It was a fraternity of peacekeeping men who always got the bad guy and tamed the West with an honest dead-eye aim of their six shooters. Billy entered the barracks with his father. He felt a strange excitement, but also a low level fear of the law and authority, that was out of place among the myth of old west lawmen.

The young boy noticed the flat screen computers, blinking modems and fax machines. To him, the battery of modern technology was the new digital-age posse used to chase and keep track of bad guys. Approaching the front desk, Billy saw the 9-mm semi-automatic on the hip of the desk deputy. He realized the gun was still the main method for keeping the peace.

"Good morning, Deputy," August Hayden said. "I'm here with my son to see Sheriff St. Cloud. We have an appointment."

"You're August and Billy Hayden?" the deputy asked.

"Yes, we are."

"Sign in," the deputy said, pointing to the appointment book on the desk.

August signed the book. The deputy handed him two visitors' passes.

"Sheriff St. Cloud's office is down the corridor. First office on your right."

August Hayden took the passes, and with his son, proceeded down the corridor to the Sheriff's office. Half the door to the office was frosted glass.

Printed in block letters was the word "SHERIFF". August knocked on the door and opened it.

"Sheriff?" August said.

St. Cloud was seated behind his desk; hunched over a report. He looked up and waived August and Billy to come in. Positioned in one corner of the office was the American flag. On the opposite side was the Arizona State flag with a brass plaque on the base of the flag holder. The plaque was inscribed: *"To Sheriff Joseph St. Cloud, for his tireless efforts in gaining freedom for Native American inmates to practice their traditional religious ceremonial rites. Presented 7/7/07 by the Navajo Nation Corrections Project."*

"Good morning, August," St. Cloud said.

"Hi, Sheriff."

"Billy, how are you?" St. Cloud asked.

"I'm okay," Billy responded tentatively.

"Sit here," St. Cloud said, pointing to the two chairs in front of his desk.

August noticed the oil painting hanging on the wall behind St. Cloud. In the center of the painting was a Navajo warrior in full feathered head-dress raising his hands to the blue sky. The Navajo warrior was depicted as an old man with dark, brooding eyes. His mouth was slightly open as though in prayer. In the background was a rocky mountain with a line of evergreen trees. The painting was strong and masculine. An eagle, its wings spread and curved to catch an updraft, was in the sky. The eagle looked out beyond the horizon. Its eyes showed the same brooding look as the old warrior's. There was a unity to their might and boldness. The open beak of the eagle seemed to suggest they were reciting the same ancient prayer. August observed the beautiful painting, but did not comment on it.

"Sorry, we couldn't meet with you last night at the hospital, Billy," St. Cloud said."

"Billy received a concussion from the blast and fall," August reported.

"How you feeling, Billy?" St. Cloud asked.

"I'm okay. I still have some ringing in my ears."

"Doctor said it would pass," August commented.

"How's Henry Fuller?"

"He's fine. He was a bit farther away from the blast than I was," Billy said.

"Well, I'm glad you're both okay....Billy, I hear you're writing an article about the explosion for the County paper."

"Yes. I am. I'm getting my own byline too."

"That's good. When is it due?"

"They want it for tomorrow's morning edition."

"Billy, I'm afraid I'm going to have to ask you to show me the article before you submit it."

"Why?"

"It's a criminal investigation. I wouldn't want the wrong information to come out."

"I understand. But, the paper only wants basic facts."

"That's good. So, what can you tell me about last night and the explosion?"

"Well, I first asked Mister Barnes if I could ride the quad on his property. He said I could. So me and Henry went riding."

"Before you went riding, were you working the mine with Mister Barnes?"

"Yes."

"What time did you stop working?"

"I don't know. We usually stop about six or six thirty. Doesn't Mister Barnes know what time we stopped?"

"Spoken like a true investigative reporter. Yes, he does. That's the time he said too. Sometimes the more witnesses the better. I like your journalistic instinct. Six-thirty. What time did you start riding?"

"We left Henry's house at eight."

"Sure?"

"Positive. I set my watch. I like to time my riding."

"What time was the blast?"

"That I'm not so sure of. It was probably around ten."

"Okay, let's get past all that. I understand you saw a car by the mine?"

"I did," Billy said and opened a notebook he had been carrying. He turned to a page where he had jotted some notes and handed it to St. Cloud.

"What's this?" St. Cloud asked.

"I wrote down the make of the car and the plate number."

St. Cloud stared at Billy with surprise.

"You saw the plate number?"

"I was real close to the car and the moon was very bright. I read the plate number and remembered it. I wrote it down when I was in the hospital. I didn't want to forget it."

"Billy, that was great work."

"The car stopped. Whoever was in it was looking back at the mine."

"You saw that while you were close to the car?"

"Yes."

"Did you get to see who was in the car?"

"Yes. Kinda. There were two men in the car. Only one turned around. He was the one I saw."

"Did he see you?"

"Yes."

"Do you think you would recognize him if you saw him again?"

"I hope I don't see him again. I'm afraid of him."

"I understand. So, why didn't you run when you saw him?"

"We did run. I mean everything happened so fast. We ran when I saw a light coming from the mine."

"What kind of light?"

"You know how the wick of a fire cracker sparkles when it burns? The kind of light, you know, bouncy light, but much brighter."

"So that's when you ran?"

"Yes. When I saw the light. I knew it was going to explode."

"Mister Barnes told me you also saw a car by the mine a couple of nights ago."

"Well, I saw lights from a car. And, I think a flashlight. Somebody was walking around with a flashlight."

"So, you can't be sure if it was the same car you saw last night?"

"No. I can't even be sure it was a car. It could have been a camper. Mister Barnes told me people camp on his land sometimes. Now I'm not sure. It could have been a camper I saw. That's why I wrote down the license plate number as soon as I could."

"Well, the information you gave me was very important. Especially, the license plate number."

"I'm glad."

"Billy, when you write your article for the County paper, I don't want you to mention the car or the license."

"How come?"

"It will interfere with my investigation."

"Can I quote a source as seeing a car at the mine?"

"Do you think that's honest reporting?"

"No."

"Sheriff, about the article?" August said. "Do you think whoever blew up the mine will know it was my son that was there?"

"These men were interested only in the mine. They knew the layout of the mine. I believe the car Billy saw two nights ago was the same car. The flashlight Billy saw suggests to me they were planning everything. The mine is all they were concerned with. They did what they had to do. My guess is they're gone. But, you may not want to allow Billy to go back there quadding for a while."

"Don't worry about that," August said. "He's not getting out of my sight for a long time."

"Billy, thanks again. Your information is going to be very helpful. Don't forget to show me the article, and no mention of the car and license plate number."

PIETRO Segretti and Gabriella DeCeasere drove to a roadside restaurant in Kingman. They had been driving since early morning. Segretti was relaxed and not concerned with the possibility of surveillance by Homeland Security or the presence of Agent Cummings. His trip was aimed at a legitimate, though unusual purchase.

Before entering the restaurant, Segretti noticed a colorful hot air balloon. The balloon seemed to glide peacefully, unencumbered by any sort of restraints.

Sitting at a table by the window, Gabriella sipped a cold glass of ice tea and patted her forehead with the cloth napkin. In the desert heat, her cheeks were more flushed than usual. Her hair clung to her bare shoulders. Gabriella took an ice cube and wrapped it in the napkin. She then applied it to her wrists. Segretti took satisfaction in the details of her movements. He was very much aware of the delicate grace she possessed, underlined by her steady strength and extreme loyalty. Commonplace matters concerning Gabriella were of interest to him. He felt privileged to witness them.

"Is the desert heat bothering you?" Segretti asked.

"Somewhat," she replied.

"Hopefully, we won't be staying too long."

"That's alright. I find the landscape beautiful."

"You seem a bit uncomfortable."

"It's warm."

"It's not the weather I think is bothering you," he observed. "What is it?"

Gabriella took the napkin from her wrist. She sipped her ice tea. She tried avoiding Segretti's stare, which seemed to reach beyond her thoughts to her inner most feelings and apprehensions.

"Tell me. What is it?" Segretti continued.

"I'm a bit uncomfortable in this country. Not the heat, I just get a sense of threat. The agents at the airport made me feel unsafe."

"Gabriella, we're here on legitimate business. There's no threat facing us. Let's make this deal and go home. I'll talk to the miner, Barnes, and make the deal. It should be a straight forward process."

"When you spoke to him yesterday, did you explain why you wanted to meet with him?"

"Yes, I told him I was an international buyer with a unique interest in his mining capabilities. I told him I had the purchasing power. My conversation was open and frank. It was part of the lure. He is seeing us only because he's a businessman who still likes the challenge of the deal. From the research I've done on him, he is a very good negotiator. He sold his manufacturing equipment company for a very large profit. He sees business dealings as an adventure. It makes up a good part of his nature."

"Why were you so open in your approach to him?"

"This is a legitimate business deal. There is nothing to hide. There was no other way but to be out in the open."

Gabriella smiled trying to scale down her weariness and anxiety. Without trying, she differed to the grit of her elegance to combat her inner voices of doubt. She finished two glasses of ice tea and started on a third before leaning back and succumbing to an uneasy peace.

Leaving the restaurant, Segretti stopped in front of a newspaper rack. The lead headlines of the *Mohave County News and Community Information* caught his eye. He inserted a coin and removed the paper. Gabriella leaned over his shoulder and read along with Segretti.

"A mine explosion," Gabriella said.

"Yes. The Barnes mine," Segretti responded reading the story.

"What happened?"

"According to this article, it was a deliberate explosion."

"Was Barnes injured?"

"No. The article says there were no injuries. The Sheriff, Joseph St. Cloud, was quoted as saying there was no one in the mine at the time."

"That seems like a strange coincidence, you were interested in the mine and then someone blew it up."

"Gabriella, I don't think this was a coincidence."

"What do you think it was?"

"I don't know."

"Will you still meet with Barnes?"

"Yes. Now I'm curious."

"Pietro, this doesn't feel right. This whole trip is wrong. First, the agents at the airport. Now the explosion. Agent Cummings is sure to come after us now. Let's just leave because now we can."

"I can't now. I've come this far. Just allow me this meeting with Barnes. Then we'll go. I promise. After the meeting, we'll go."

"But this changes things. The mine is shut down. There's nothing for you to buy."

"I don't know that. We need to adapt to the situation. Machiavelli once said, for men who rise to ambition first, they should seek to secure themselves against attack. We need to try to get a little more protection."

"How do we do that?" Gabriella asked.

"We'll have a meeting with someone else before we meet with Barnes. We need to form an alliance."

Gabriella felt an old fear rise to her throat, sensing the global game of chance Segretti had played over the years was starting to turn on him. The phenomena of circumstance fell into a strange dimension where no amount of hope and prayer could exert influence. The hot, heavy desert air carried with it a possessed determination that closed in on Gabriella. It had a firm grip on her; a foretelling of a categorical prediction of life expectancy. Segretti folded the newspaper and threw it into the iron mesh wastebasket. He looked up and noticed the hot air balloon was gone. Gabriella watched as the newspaper slowly settled to the bottom, mixing with all the other discarded waste. She cringed inwardly, hoping the sinking paper was not a foreboding to her life.

SHERIFF St. Cloud removed the lid from his coffee cup as his computer booted up. He took a few sips, then logged onto his e-mail. Of the twelve messages; one was from the Department of Motor Vehicles. St. Cloud had requested information on the vehicle Billy Hayden had seen at the mine. The Motor Vehicle Department's e-mail response reported the vehicle was registered to Ronald Clay of Bull Head City. St. Cloud paused for a moment, studying the information. Suddenly, a flash of suspicion registered in his mind. His experience, in law enforcement, had honed his instincts to a sharp edge. He knew there was a deeper mystery to the car and its owner. He recalled what Billy Hayden had said when he looked at the car in the bright moonlight. The car had stopped, and obviously, the occupants were unconcerned whether the vehicle or the license plate was seen. St. Cloud closed the e-mail message then started a search for stolen car reports. He typed in the license plate and found the car owned by Ronald Clay had been reported stolen two days before the explosion of Barnes' mine.

St. Cloud's suspicion grew. He felt the ancient subject of law and order, crime and criminals facing off once more in a battle of wits. He kept close to the concept, something deeper than a grudge or jealousy, was behind the explosion. The two crimes were not perpetrated on an amateurish scale. It was too soon to expect an outcome. A knock on St. Cloud's door interrupted his thoughts. He looked up to see Marjorie Henning, the secretary for the office staff, standing with a stack of folders in her arms.

"Sorry to disturb you, Sheriff. Deputy Foster wanted me to tell you there's a visitor at the front desk for you."

"Who is it?" St. Cloud asked with a hint of annoyance.

"Pietro Segretti."

St. Cloud's first reaction was surprise which slowly mixed with caution.

"Do you want to see him or should I tell him you're busy?" Marjorie asked.

"No. I'll see him," St. Cloud said thoughtfully.

Segretti entered the office with an air of poise and dominance. For an instant, they were wordless, exchanging looks. Upon shaking his hand, St. Cloud immediately sensed something imposing about Segretti. An unnamable quality emitted from Segretti as an aura of refinement, like a blade piercing silk. There was no misplaced contradiction about Segretti. He quietly presented himself as astute in the art of confrontation and ennobled with confidence from past victories.

"Sheriff, I hope I'm not interrupting you," Segretti said.

"No, not at all, Mister Segretti."

"This is Gabriella DeCeasere, my fiancée," Segretti announced.

"Hello, Miss DeCeasere. Please come in. Sit."

Segretti moved into the room and quickly read the plaque from the Navajo Nation Corrections Project at the base of the State flag of Arizona. From the inscription on the plaque and the painting, Segretti quickly sized up the Sheriff. He knew they represented the best parts of the lawman and would be a grave mistake to underestimate him.

"So tell me, Mister Segretti, how can I help you?" St. Cloud said knowing Segretti had already made a preliminary assessment of him.

"I read the article in the local newspaper about the explosion in the mine. The one owned by Mister Barnes. I'm sure you know by now, I had a meeting scheduled with Alex Barnes."

"Go on," St. Cloud said, cautiously observing Segretti's every gesture.

Segretti sensed St. Cloud was restrained, holding back what he had already learned.

"My meeting with Mister Barnes was to discuss the possibility of purchasing substance from his mine?"

"It's a gold mine. What can you purchase from Barnes' mine that you can't purchase anywhere else? Surely, there's no shortage of Italian gold."

"Not in the form that Barnes has mined."

"I'm listening," St. Cloud said.

"I understand he has mined a pure form of gold. Well, maybe pure is not the proper term. I believe the correct term is single-atom gold."

"So I've been told."

"Have you also been told what properties it possesses?"

"Suppose you tell me."

"It acts as a superconductor. That may be a concern to others, but that's not my interest at all. I've been told this form of gold can cure many ills. I have family members who could benefit from this product."

"I'm sure Barnes' mine is not the only source for this product."

"From what I know, his is of the highest quality available."

"So, Mister Segretti, I'm still not sure I understand why you came to see me."

"First, to tell you that is the only reason I want to purchase the substance from Mister Barnes. But, with the explosion, my deal may have been compromised. However, there is another reason. From my line of work and experience, I have a great many contacts. I may be in a position to help you with your investigation."

"Is it also because you wouldn't want to be suspected in the explosion?"

"Something like that. My direct approach to Barnes would clearly indicate I had nothing to do with the explosion. Common sense would show I have no motive or inclination."

"Clearly, I could see that to be the case. But, times are different in this country. No one is overlooked where an explosion is concerned. Homeland Security suspects everyone."

"That's an expression of deep paranoia."

"We have reasons to be paranoid."

"Yes, but they're the wrong reasons. As a descendant of Native American people, you should know better than anyone."

St. Cloud was suddenly reminded of the history long ingrained in his spirit. A deep exposure brought up by Segretti, made all memories current and proved certain truths do have a journey all their own.

"But it is because of that paranoia or suspicion," Segretti continued, "I came to see you first. To establish I had nothing to do with it."

St. Cloud leaned back in his chair and drew a sharp bead on Segretti. There were no terms to their meeting. St. Cloud felt free to press Segretti.

"No other reason?"

"None."

"Tell me, Mister Segretti, you appear to be a man of refinement. Do you know anything about music?"

"Somewhat."

"Do you know what a glissando is?"

"Yes, I do."

"Well, you'll forgive me if I suggest that I get the feeling you're trying to play me like a fine glissando."

"I'm trying to get the word out I had nothing to do with the explosion. And given my background, I want it clearly known I have no other interest in Mister Barnes' mine other than the possible benefit for my family."

"So, you've said. But with the mine not operational, there seems to be nothing for you to buy from Barnes."

"Well, I don't know that. He may have stockpiled some of the material. But when and if he starts up production again, I'd like to buy from him. That is, of course, if it's not too late for my family. And that's my only interest, which has nothing to do with playing you like a glissando."

"Fair enough. So given your background, immediately after you have your meeting with Barnes, I suggest you return to Italy."

"That's my intention."

"Good. And if you or your contacts can supply information regarding the explosion, I would be interested. This office would keep your name confidential. I'm sure that's important in your line of work,"

Segretti knew he had to create an alliance. The cutting remark by St. Cloud was what he had to endure for it.

"In that event, I would appreciate all the confidentiality you could provide, Sheriff."

"You know where to find me," St. Cloud concluded.

St. Cloud was not convinced there were no distortions or bent shadows to Segretti's claims. He was part of a criminal society where one had to be adept at deception and bluff. Although St. Cloud appreciated Segretti's apparent fine elegance and gentlemanly exterior, he realized they were adversaries in a festering antagonism. They were rooted in diverse philosophies and opposing ideologies with no possibility for the lines to blur between them.

St. Cloud looked at a photo on his desk of his wife, Jennifer. He recognized the playfulness, deep feelings and commitment in her eyes. St. Cloud's connection to Jennifer started with their first meeting. He knew their link was ordained by the spirits to last their earthly lifetime and beyond. With Jennifer, there was no reason for pretense or defensiveness. She was an affirmation in the protocols of peace, constantly showing him there were still people in the world to trust, and not everyone was filled with treachery and deceit.

GERMANY

THE Neroberg Tower, located on a hill overlooking Wiesbaden, was the only remnant of a fire that destroyed the 150 year old hotel. The tower looked out to the chestnut and almond groves of the Taunus Mountain range. Thousand year old oak trees shaded rustic benches, tables and gardens at the Neroberg Café. Peaceful walkways, edged with azaleas and white lilacs led to the Neroberg Temple and the 250 year old Russian Church. The tranquility of the grounds was disturbed only occasionally, when the wire and rope carriages of the mountain railway rumbled up and down the steep grade of the mountain.

A group of women walked along the shaded path around the tower, keeping watch over their young children playing on the grass. A young girl in a white cotton dress knelt behind one of the oaks, hiding from the other children. The others ran along the path and screamed upon discovering the hidden girl. Their playful screams rose up through the trees and off the mountain. But the girl was not concerned about being discovered. She was focused on the daisy in her hand. One of the women bent over to tie a ribbon that had come loose from the girl's hair. The child handed the daisy to the woman, who smiled and put the flower through a button hole of her blouse. She patted the girl's head, and cautioned the other children, to run slowly and be careful.

The mountain café, dotted with colorful garden umbrellas, was located at an elevation of 245 meters. Mitchell Harrington sat under one of the umbrellas. He could see the entire city of Wiesbaden and a portion of the Rhine River. It was late in the afternoon and most of the tables were empty.

As the women and children made their way along the path, they passed four men walking from the area of the mountain railway. The men, with stern, angry expressions, wore rumpled clothing. One looked into the distance, spotting a familiar face at the café. He motioned the other men to spread out from the path and follow him. The four walked slowly and deliberately toward the open area of the café and the familiar face.

Harrington felt strangely comfortable in a pair of beige cotton slacks and black linen shirt. It was one of the few times, in the past two years, he had worn civilian clothing. Harrington marginally trusted the feel of the clothing and the transition it signified into his civilian life. Discarding his body armor, helmet and army issued clothing, made him feel free and unthreatened. There was a space beyond the danger of combat that was opened up by a simple pair of comfortable pants and soft shirt. He sat back and sipped Oettinger beer from a decorative stein. A waiter placed a plate of Munich white sausage in front of him.

Solis had traded his helmet for a forest green hunter's hat. It sported a green cord around the base. He sat next to Harrington, casually tipping back the hat on his head. The transition from combat, for Solis, was not as smooth. He still felt the need to duck when he heard the sound of children shrieking playfully on the grounds of the café. Solis felt danger had become his constant companion. It had ingrained itself deeper into his skin than the desert sand. The streets of the Bronx showed Solis the world was full of good and bad things. The desert of Iraq, demonstrated more clearly, the gap between them closed and the lines overlapped. All those things he learned had a memory and took turns repeating, which meant they never really went away. He quickly drank three steins of beer, hoping to insulate himself from the sting should something go bad.

Tommy Bowles appeared more at ease, relaxed by the familiar surroundings. The low whistle of the wind, as it passed through the tall oak trees, reminded him of the steady din of the C-5 engines. The tones intersected and sank into a single note. He found safety in the elevation that was constantly supported by his many flights. The sense of openness and distance, unforced motion and the consistency of air felt like freedom to him, all blending with the inner shell of peace.

"This country sure is pretty," Harrington observed.

"That's for sure," Bowles responded. "I enjoy crew rest here. This place in particular is my favorite spot. I love the view from here. The café is quiet and peaceful."

"Not when those kids start screamin'," Solis said.

"It's better than the explosions we've been hearing for the last two years," Harrington offered.

"Always the optimist, Deuce."

"So, there was no problem getting the load out of Iraq?" Harrington asked.

"None, Mitch. I replaced one of the life rafts on the plane with the load. We came over with a sixty count of human cargo. I had to carry three, twenty-man rafts for them. Going back we had no human cargo, so I didn't need all the rafts. I took one off. It was a simple replacement. The weights between our load and the raft were almost the same. I wrapped the load in a raft sack. Labeled it. Sealed it. Real simple."

"How about when you get state side?"

"When I get into Luke, U.S. Customs will confirm my cargo and check my manifest. But the raft is considered part of the plane and not cargo. So, they won't even check. I'll have the life support crew unload the pallet. I'll transfer it to my truck and away I go."

"Piece of cake," Solis said.

"Let's not celebrate yet," Harrington said. "We still have a long way to go. It's always the things you don't anticipate that hurt you."

"Hey, Deuce, we got out of Iraq alive. Everything from now on is a celebration."

"Tommy, what was the final weight of the load?"

"It came in at eighteen hundred and eighty-four pounds. That's weighing the sacks and the pallet."

"That's about what I figured."

"Once I get the load off in Luke, where do you want it delivered, Mitch?"

"Hey Tommy, let me ask you something," Solis interrupted. "Do you know what that load is? The Deuce ain't tellin'."

"Yes, I know what it is," Bowles said. "It's *his* load," Bowles continued pointing to Harrington.

Solis shook his head and repositioned the hunter's hat to fit properly on his head.

"I should know better. White boys always stick together," Solis said.

"Fortunately, we don't need a large area to store it," Harrington said, ignoring Solis. "I have my sister looking for a self-storage facility. I think that will work. I just told her if she does rent one, not to do it in her name. I don't want to leave a trail that can be traced, just in case."

"Good idea," Bowles said.

"Deuce, who will want to trace the load?" Solis asked.

"I just want to keep it safe."

"From who?"

Harrington tipped the lid of the stein and sipped the beer. When he put the stein on the table, a shadow fell across his arm. He looked up to see a man come around and sit in the chair next to him. The face was vaguely familiar. Harrington tried to put the features into context. He spotted three others moving around the table. One positioned himself behind Solis. Harrington turned to the man in the chair, feeling some concern as he began to recall the man's face. Harrington started to move, but the man pressed a .45-caliber handgun into his leg.

"I wouldn't do anything, if I were you," the man said.

Solis reached for a knife on the table. The men standing behind Solis pressed a .45 to his back.

"Tell the black man to leave the knife alone," the seated man said.

Harrington looked at Solis and nodded. Solis felt the knife breath in his hand, but replaced it before it generated any auxiliary danger. The man standing over him leaned in and brushed the knife to the ground.

"What's going on?" Solis said.

"Shut up," the seated man said. "Don't anybody say a word, and nobody will die today. Understood?"

Harrington and Bowles were assessing the enemy and anticipating a counterattack. Solis kept looking at the knife on the ground.

"I said, do you all understand?" the seated man repeated.

"Yes," Harrington responded, deciding any counterattack would be disastrous.

"Good. The last time we met, you held a rifle to my head, remember?" the seated man said to Harrington.

Harrington studied the man trying to connect the dots in his mind. The vagueness gave way and the gravure image gained clarity. Suddenly, he recalled the sweaty face in the desert. He remembered the man's negotiating in open defiance of Captain Hicks' orders. But, what suddenly became clearer, was the reason for the man's eagerness. His interest was motivated by a different degree of loyalty.

"You're Iraqi Police Service," Harrington said. "Your name is Haddad something."

"You remember. Good. My name is Haddad bin Nasab." Haddad said and pressed the .45 harder into Harrington's leg.

"You're a sergeant. Your captain called you Harrington. Harrington is your name. I told you, Sergeant Harrington, we'd meet again. The prophecy of that day is fulfilled. I didn't like the idea you holding a gun to my head, Sergeant Harrington," Haddad continued. "How does it feel to have a gun pointed at you?"

"What is it you want, Haddad?" Harrington asked, hoping to spark a negotiation that would ease the threat.

"I want you to feel this gun. I want you to know I can kill you right now. That serves me well for the moment. So, let me just sit here and make up my mind, if I shoot you in the face right now."

Harrington's mind fought off the fear. His impulse was to attack Haddad. However, his seated position was awkward and unbalanced. His strike would be slow and ineffective.

"I don't think you want to kill me here," Harrington said. "You may have difficulty getting off the mountain."

"Do you think a few mothers walking with their children, or the waiters of the café, will stop us from getting off the mountain?"

"No," Harrington said trying to appease Haddad.

"No. I don't think so, either."

"Then what do you want?" Harrington said.

"You know what I want. I want what you took from my village and put in his plane," Haddad said motioning to Bowles. "What you stole belongs to me. I want it back," Haddad continued.

"I can't do that," Harrington said.

"Oh, what a typical boring response. Not only can you do it, but you will. You put it on the plane and flew away. Now, you can take it off the plane and fly away."

"It's not that simple," Bowles said.

"Oh, it's not? Then let me make it simple for you," Haddad said, repositioning the gun under the table and pressing it into Bowles' leg. "Either I get what belongs to me, or you all die. It's that simple."

"You don't understand," Bowles said. "The plane is locked down. We're getting a shipment from Afghanistan Friday. I can't get on the plane until then."

"Friday is three days from now. You get to the plane tomorrow, not a day later."

"It's not that easy to do."

"Just do it and get my property back to me. Be in front of the Luisenplat, the green horse. Do you know where that is?"

"Yes I do," Bowles responded.

"Good. Be there tomorrow by noon. To make sure you keep our appointment, the black man comes with us. When you get me what is mine, then you get him back. Anything after tomorrow and he dies. You all die. Remember, I followed you from Iraq. Do you know how easy you were to find? Don't try anything stupid. We have been watching you. We will continue to watch you."

"Listen, Haddad," Harrington said. "Can we make another arrangement? Can we become business partners?" Harrington continued, probing.

"Don't try to make a fool of me. I can kill you and still get what I want. You're not that important to my plans."

"Can we buy a portion from you?"

"Tell me, is your father a millionaire? Does he have a fortune? If your father doesn't have boundless wealth, you can't afford one of the sacks on that plane. There are no other terms but mine."

Harrington felt detached from the art of negotiation, but clung to a wisp of hope and the possibility of deception.

"Agreed. But I want to be able to talk to my soldier," Harrington said and slowly reached for his cell phone. "Here, take this. I need to talk to him and you when we get the load off the plane. How else can I make arrangements?"

Haddad grabbed the phone from Harrington and stuffed it into his jacket pocket.

"When you call, no one will answer the phone but me."

"I still need to know he's alive. If I don't speak with him, we'll take your load and drop it from the plane over the ocean. See if you can follow it then," Harrington said, glaring at Haddad.

"What makes you think you'll get to the plane? I said we're watching you."

"We can work this out. Let's not get prideful. You want what's on the plane. I want my soldier. This can work."

"See, I said it was simple."

Haddad stood and grabbed Solis by the shoulder. He pulled hard knocking the hunter's hat from Solis' head. The four men surrounded Solis and started to back away from the table.

Before they left, Solis retrieved his hunter's hat. He placed it firmly on his head in an act of defiance.

Harrington jumped up from the chair trying to control his anger and aggression. He reached down and picked up the knife that was knocked to the ground.

"Take it easy," Bowles said holding Harrington's arm. "The wrong action will get us all killed," he continued.

"I can't let them do this. I've got to protect Solis."

"Right now, they have the advantage. They won't do anything to Solis and compromise their advantage. Settle down. Let's think about this."

Harrington forced himself to consider the situation. His strong sense of discipline could reconcile the powerful forces that pressed against him. He took solace in the fact he had already fooled Haddad and put the first phase of his secret plan of attack into motion.

"You're right," Harrington said firmly. "But we're not done yet. It's those things we don't anticipate that hurt us. I just didn't expect them to come around so soon. Let's get out of here and figure how we can get out of this."

Harrington threw the knife on the table. He felt isolated in the unfamiliar surroundings. He was hopeful his training had prepared him for this new mission. He felt the works of a particular science behind all events. An unknown danger found its way to the German mountain and scratched at his skin. It was meant to be a personal plague promising to attack. But, he hoped it would not leave a deep, lasting scar. He put his hand into the pocket of his beige pants, and woefully thought it may have been too soon to replace his army issued combat uniform with civilian clothing.

THE Amelia Earhart Hotel was situated in the center of Wiesbaden. The hotel accommodated mostly military personnel on layover, awaiting deployment to the Middle East, or returning to the stateside camps for discharge from service. Stays at the hotel were either filled with relief and joy, or laced with anticipation and anxiety. Either way, a form of detachment ran through the halls. Even for those going home, there was a different brand of dread lurking in the cover of thankfulness. Most times an observer could discern the difference.

Sitting in Tommy Bowles' room, Harrington waited for the borrowed laptop to boot up. His leg twitched nervously as he sensed time had become his biggest enemy.

"Tom, before we go any further, I want to say something," Harrington announced.

"I know what you're going to say, but you don't have to," Bowles responded.

"I'm going to anyway. I brought you into this. You don't have to stay. I'll understand. You can go billet at the airbase, and go home with the load. You'll be out of this--safe. If anything happens to me and Solis, you know what the load might be and what to do with it. Make your split three ways."

"That's not an option, Mitch. I'm in this all the way. Forget the three ways. It's five ways, like you said in the beginning."

"And, what if something happens to you? The load is lost."

"No. It's not. I'll make arrangements so the load gets delivered wherever you say."

"But, you've got Molly home and…"

"We're wasting too much effort on this. We have very little time. Let's work this out so we all get home. There's no honor in running. You're the military strategist. Put together an operation that works for us. That's all I want to hear."

"It's not going to be easy. Somebody is going to get killed," Harrington cautioned.

"The military taught us how to kill. When the time is right, I'll ask Jesus to reclaim my soul."

"Okay, let's piece this together. The first thing to establish now this is a rescue mission. Solis is the priority. The load is a non-issue."

"That's how I see it," Bowles concurred.

"If we give up the load or we don't, Haddad is going to kill Solis and us. That makes the load unimportant. There's no other conclusion here. What we don't know is how many men he has. I suspect only the four we encountered today. I didn't see anyone else as backup."

"I didn't notice."

"When I saw him in the bombed village, it was just him and his driver. The guy standing behind Solis was the driver. There was a truck with four casualties leaving the village. It's unclear if they were part of his squad. If they were, that makes eight. My instinct tells me that was the extent of his squad."

"So four left."

"Four. But, let's be prepared for more," Harrington warned.

"He did say he has us watched. I wouldn't take too much from that," Bowles observed. "He was part of the Iraqi Special Police. He had to be familiar with our military procedures. A plane leaving Iraq will come here to Wiesbaden before going any place else. It's standard procedure. He had to see us load it up and knew when we took off. Billeting here is part of that procedure. So, he was right. He was following me, and I wasn't hard to find."

"He seemed surprised to see me at the café," Harrington said. "I don't think he expected to see me there. So, maybe he's not following me. I was just a good bonus for him."

"What's a good bonus for us?"

"We know his name. That can be huge for us. We can call Homeland Security and feed him to them. My guess is this guy, Haddad bin Nasab and his driver, deserted from the Iraqi police."

"Homeland Security will find him, but they may not go after him immediately. We only have one day. Then there's Solis. As their prisoner, he presents different problems. If Homeland Security does track them down, he's in the middle. They might also take him for a terrorist," Bowles reasoned.

"So that leaves us. The biggest bonus is the cell phone I gave them. It has GPS. Whatever we can do, it has to be done tonight. You in?" Harrington asked.

"I thought we cleared that up already," Bowles responded.

THE screen on the laptop displayed the United States Air Force logo. The audio played the Star Spangled Banner. Navigating to the internet, Harrington found a GPS tracking site, logged on, entered the cell phone information, and selected "find." A grid map of Wiesbaden appeared. Harrington went to the pull-down menu in the information bar and selected "show signs". The revised screen showed the city map, complete with street names and routes. A red dot, indicating the location of Harrington's cell phone, appeared and moved slowly along the streets.

"The red dot represents the location of my cell phone," Harrington said.

"He's moving south on route two-sixty-three, past Wiesbaden Sudost. He's approaching Mainzer Strabe. That's not far from us," Bowles whispered, leaning in closer to the screen.

"Why is he so close? I would have thought he'd be much further away," Harrington said.

"Maybe he made sure we came back to the hotel. Or, he could have left someone behind to watch us."

"Possible. Let's assume he did. We'll have to deal with that. Where's he heading now?"

Bowles stared at the screen. The images were temporarily burning into his eyes.

"He's still on two sixty three, passing Siegriendring and heading toward Rhein-main Schnellweg."

"Do you know the area he's driving on?"

"Yes, I've driven around the area many times. It's all small villages."

"Okay," Bowles continued. "He's now on Route six-seventy-one, parallel to Wiesbadener-Lindstrabe. He's also driving parallel to the Rhine River."

"Is he driving like he knows the area and knows where he's going?"

"Hard to tell. He's on a straight run."

The pulsing red dot passed steadily along the screen as though it had a heartbeat of its own. The electronic dot continued along a steady course, creating a remote defiance that was perfectly positioned within the chaotic web of the world.

"He's still heading south," Bowles continued. "He passed Wiesbaden StraBe to RampenstraBe. Now he's heading west to Ludwigsrame. That's Route four-fifty-five."

Bowles repositioned himself in the chair giving him a broader view of the screen. The dwarf representation of the city was overtaken by the drama unfolding. The movement of the red dot swept across the screen in a single shade of villainy. There were no arguments or theories to be made about the trajectory of the dot, only painstaking observation.

"He's heading north on four-fifty-five now. It looks to me as though he's lost or made a wrong turn," Bowles said. "No wait," he continued.

Bowles leaned close to the screen seeking a better understanding of the journey.

"He's going to Ludwigsplatz which is a rotary," Bowles whispered. "I see what he's doing. He took the rotary and still heading south. He's on Route forty-three."

"Any idea where he's heading?" Harrington asked.

"If he continues south on Forty Three, the only place he can go is the Main River. That's the southern most point. The Main River feeds into the Rhine."

They continued watching the red dot as it stayed on a straight, unbroken course. The density and pulse of the dot did not change. It stayed alive, true to its own blind rush.

"They passed Admiral-scheer-StraBe," Bowles observed quietly. "Still on forty-three. They're now passing Kostheimer LandstraBe. Still bearing south toward the Main."

"Why the river?" Harrington asked rhetorically.

"It's a good place to hide out. If they have a boat, no one will see them come and go. It's better than staying in a hotel in the city."

"If they have a boat that tells me they hooked up with someone here. Let's not count on there being only four of them."

Bowles kept looking at the screen hoping to deduce something from the trip. He knew the area well leading him to an interesting speculation.

"You know, Mitch, the four guys at the café were all Iraqi police. What are the chances they ever left Iraq and were here before?"

"I would say little. What are you getting at?"

"They're driving like they know the area."

"I know. It looks like they may have hooked up with people here who know the area. Four is definitely out."

"That's my point. They passed Am Mainzer Weg, LuisenstraBe, Maaraustrabe and passed Maniufer. The river is the only place they can go now."

"Are they off city streets?"

"Yes. There are no street labels after Maniufer."

"What's after that?"

"A park, a row of trees, and a small sandy beach. Then comes the river."

Harrington pointed the cursor to the information bar and clicked on the heading: "satellite". The grid map changed to an aerial view of the area. He zoomed in until he could see the park, the row of trees and small sandy beach. The red dot moved in real time through the park, under the trees and along the beach until it stopped at the river's edge.

"I see what you described. Do you know the area?"

"Sure I do. I know exactly where they are. My guess is they have a boat."

"That may work for us. There's a line of trees we can use for cover. The only exposure we'll have is the beach."

"It's small. We might be able to crawl to the boat without being seen."

"Is there a dock?"

"I'm not certain."

"We'll compensate. We need weapons and night vision equipment."

"I can get everything you need. Are side arms better?"

"Yes. Knives too. Don't forget protective vests."

"We have them."

Harrington looked at his watch then out the window to measure the level of darkness.

"Let's prepare to leave at twenty four hundred hours. I'll keep watching the screen, see if they go on the move. There's nothing to do now but wait and watch.

THE midnight air was cool and damp. Bowles made his way out from the hotel's basement door to the parking lot. Then sat quietly in the car. He looked around the dark, enclosed parking area, slipped a pair of night vision goggles over his head and scanned the area again. Convinced there was no one watching, he removed the goggles, started the vehicle, and drove slowly to the door. Harrington emerged quickly and settled into the front seat. He too scanned the parking area, then looked behind them as they drove out of the parking lot.

The city was awash with an electric glow. Muted lights shone from everywhere, causing Bowles to fear their operation would be exposed. Bowles drove on to Bismarckcking and turned onto Dotzheimer StraBe. They had decided they would not follow the same route bin Nasab took to the river. Harrington looked in the back seat, checking the two holstered .45-caliber hand guns and the two belts of ammunition. Two fixed-blade knives of stock tool steel, two pair of night vision binoculars were on the floor behind each seat, along with body armor vests. Harrington reached behind the seat and retrieved one of the vests. He maneuvered it over his body. As he strapped it over the black t-shirt he wore, he felt a sense of irony. His civilian clothing did not seem appropriate for the traditional form of combat. But once he strapped the .45-caliber pistol to his hip and the knife to his leg, he became convinced it was not attire that was the true designation of combat.

"Did anyone see you put the gear in the car?" Harrington asked.

"I had a buddy do it for me."

"Did he ask any questions?"

"One. He asked if he could help."

Harrington placed the computer on his lap. He stared at the pulsating red dot on the computer screen.

"Are they still camped out on the river?" Bowles asked.

"Yes," Harrington responded.

Bowles knew the route to the river and did not have to refer to the map. He was familiar with the picturesque villages they passed. He could not discern any details of the houses as they were hidden, shrouded in the night. All that was noticeable were their dark outlines and phantom gasps as he passed. He hoped the conspiracy of silence and darkness boded well for him. If not, he would have to rely on his instincts and strength, but mostly on the benevolence of fate. Harrington saw Bowles touch the crucifix hanging from his neck. In the darkness of the car, he could see the worry etched deeply on his face.

"The element of surprise should work in our favor," Harrington assured. "We strike fast and hard. We'll be out of there and back before they blow reveille."

"Reveille. I haven't heard that term since boot camp."

"Are we getting close to the river?" Harrington asked.

"Yes. It's just beyond those trees," Bowles said, pointing out Harrington's window.

Bowles slowed the car and turned off the lights. He then continued slowly coming to a slight inlet by a thin line of trees edging the river. He stopped the car and turned off the engine. Harrington took a last look at the computer and saw the red dot was stationary but continued to pulse. He reached for the night-vision binoculars and turned to Bowles, noticing the worry on his face had deepened. Suddenly, Harrington regretted involving Bowles, but he forced down his feelings, knowing they would only get in the way.

"Gear up and follow close to me," Harrington whispered. "Remember, don't hesitate and we'll be back by reveille. Repeat, don't hesitate. Say it," Harrington ordered.

"Don't hesitate," Bowles repeated.

"Good. Trust me. Those men on that boat will not hesitate with your life."

"Don't hesitate. Don't hesitate," Bowles whispered nervously to himself.

Harrington rolled smoothly out of the car, crouched and hurried to the line of trees by the beach. Bowles stayed closer than his shadow. Kneeling behind a tree, Harrington looked down river through the binoculars. He saw two boats moored at a small wooden dock. The boats were identical with square living quarters on flat hulls. The boats had low railings around their decks and small windows on each side of the cabins. One of the boats was completely dark. A dim light from the other vessel's cabin shown on two men seated at the bow. Harrington adjusted the focus, but couldn't discern their features. He looked at the windows of the illuminated cabin. He could see shadows and a small portion of what looked like a slumped head topped by a hunter's hat that resembled Solis'. He watched the cabin until he was convinced there was no movement. He then focused on the darkened boat, which created more suspicion for Harrington.

"There are two men on the bow of the boat with a light," Harrington said lowering the binoculars. "I think Solis is in that boat. I see the top of a head. I'm going into the river, ease my way to the dock and take out the two men. As I'm swimming, you make your way closer to the boat staying behind the cover of the trees. Once I take out the two men, I'm going in. When I do, you follow."

"Let me come with you," Bowles suggested.

"No. I'm better trained for this. I can deal with the two men."

"Are they the same guys from the café?"

"I can't tell. When you come in, stay low. Keep your eye on the second boat. I don't think it's hostile, but I can't be sure. Just remember, don't hesitate. Shoot whatever moves."

Harrington put the binoculars down and turned to Bowles.

"We'll be alright," he said confidently. "Follow my lead. I can't stress enough, don't hesitate….Ready?"

"Go." Bowles confirmed.

Harrington removed the knife from its sheath and held it with his teeth. He ducked away from the tree and eased onto his stomach. Slithering along the sand, Harrington kept his eyes on the two boats. He controlled his breathing and stilled his emotions. Keeping his thoughts on the operational tactics was at the core of his skills. Solis, and the men that held him captive, were academic. He had been well trained in the strategy and philosophy of combat. He had accepted the military training until it had become second nature. Harrington went beyond the many martial drills. He morphed into another being. One that hovered above the details of his actions that kept him true to the offerings of victory. But, it was his nature, and the Huguenot heritage that fueled his perspective and heightened his sense of mission.

He felt the sand growing firmer and wet, then slipped into the river. Moving with the current, he eased down river swiftly. He watched the boats, constantly looking for any movement and listened for the slightest sound.

The lighted boat was tethered to the dock by ropes from the fore and aft. Its bow faced down river, toward the convergence with the Rhine. A ladder, near the boat's stern, extended from the dock to the water. As Harrington floated by the dock, he grabbed the ladder and paused. Gathering his resolution, Harrington pulled himself up the ladder in a series of controlled and silent motions. He moved so slowly, the water flowed off him without a sound.

Once out of the water, he peered from the dock to the boat. The two men sitting on the bow were hidden behind the cabin. He looked into the rear cabin window and still could not detect any movement or sound. Climbing onto the dock, he crouched below the window and moved forward. He took the knife from his teeth, and gripped the hard, brushed-steel handle embracing the natural unfolding perspective of power and control it offered. Arriving at the stern of the boat, he stepped slowly, trying to move with the gentle motion of the river. Moving quietly to the bow, he passed the cabin and heard a low, painful moan. His attention to the sound made him certain it was Solis.

Harrington did not allow himself any distractions. Solis would have to endure the pain and torture. Harrington continued toward the bow and paused only briefly to see the two men still sitting with their backs to him. On the deck, beside their chairs were two AK-47s, along with several empty beer cans. Directly behind the men was the closed cabin door.

All the patterns and history of his life had led Harrington to this one distinct moment. The combined input of family linage and combat experience that had molded his nature and instincts were now ready to frame his action.

Harrington took to the moment with a mix of restraint and ease. He walked from the cabin and approached the seated men. One of the men turned as he approached. As the man stood, Harrington took a powerful swipe slitting the man's throat so deeply his head flew backward nearly coming free from his shoulders. The man made a gasping sound and started to fall toward the railing. Harrington quickly grabbed the man by the shirt preventing his fall and a loud splash.

The second man tried to reach down for the weapon by his seat, but

Harrington shifted quickly. Still holding the dead man, he drove the knife down into the back of the second man, puncturing his heart.

Time moved at a jerky pace. It triangulated somewhere within the boundaries of chaos, panic and folly. In the darkness, Harrington saw the faces of both men clearly and knew they had not been among the four at the café. He noticed Bowles running from the line of trees toward the boat. The door to the cabin burst open and someone aimed and fired hitting Harrington in the back. The bullet struck the body armor with a bludgeoning force knocking Harrington forward. Harrington spun around positioning the partially decapitated man in front of him as the man from the cabin continued shooting. The bullets struck the dead man, splattering blood into the night and on Harrington. Regaining his balance, Harrington reached around the dead man and fired one shot, hitting the gunman on the bridge of his nose. The impact lifted the man from his feet, throwing him back into the cabin.

Harrington dropped the decapitated man, ran to the side of the cabin and crashed the window. He saw two men in the cabin along with Solis who was tied to a chair with rope. A thick piece of tape was across his mouth. Harrington fired twice at one of the men, knocking him back onto a cot. Harrington did not take time to notice the blood from the man soaking the sheet. It was enough for him to know he had delivered the kill shot.

The window on the starboard side of the boat crashed open. Bowles shot at the second man. The first bullet struck the man in the arm, shattering his elbow. Fragments of bone were embedded into the cabin wall. Another fragment struck Harrington's cheek. The man stumbled back falling onto the cot. The second bullet Bowles fired struck the man in the leg. The man screamed from the pain but managed to retrieve the gun from the floor. Harrington tried to shoot the man, but his position did not offer him a clear shot. As the wounded man raised his gun, Bowles fired two more shots, striking the man in the chest and face. The man slumped on the cot, bleeding on the other dead man.

Harrington recognized the men in the cabin as those at the café, but neither was bin Nasab or his driver. He turned quickly, in time to hear a gunshot. He saw a flash at the stern of the second boat and felt a bullet strike him in the chest. The bludgeoning force knocked Harrington backward onto the deck. The adrenalin filled his body, yet he remained lucid. Dismissing all pain and burning he felt under the protective equipment, he fired back from a prone position. His bullets shattered the cabin and crashed into a stack of deck chairs. He heard the roar of gunfire coming from the other side of the cabin where Bowles was positioned.

Harrington rolled off the deck into the river, using the water as an illusion of cover and protection. From his vantage point, the river would be more favorable. From that position, he could also maneuver and adjust his angle of attack. Once in the water, he knew there were only two men on the second boat; bin Nasab and his driver. Harrington felt clarity overcome him, giving him the ability to know he had only two more rounds in his weapon.

Moving farther into the river, Harrington gained a better angle for his intended targets. He aimed and fired a single shot, hitting bin Nasab's driver in the neck. Upon seeing the driver fall, bin Nasab jumped up from behind the stack of deck chairs and fired at Harrington. Lacking cover, Harrington took a clear aim at bin Nasab and fired his remaining bullet, striking bin Nasab in the chest. The force of the impact sent bin Nasab flying back, arms flailing. He bounced off the cabin wall then fell to the deck. One hand caught the stack of chairs, knocking them to the deck with him.

There was no motion on either boat. Suddenly the night became silent and eerie. The echoes of the gunshots faded, lost to the two converging rivers. The final cries and moans of the dead men wafted off to somewhere, Harrington suspected was either the beginning of creation or the end of it.

Harrington paddled to the dock and climbed on to the boat. Bowles came from the starboard side and looked at Harrington with an expression of relief and disgust. Harrington knew killing someone for the first time had that affect. Touching Bowles' shoulder, Harrington conveyed the message of safety, but he knew it would be a lifetime before they could leave the incident behind.

"Good work," Harrington said. "You didn't hesitate."

"How many did you count, Mitch?" Bowles asked.

"Seven," Harrington confirmed as though reciting a simple calculation.

Harrington removed the fixed blade from the dead man and walked into the cabin. He carefully approached Solis noticing bruises on his cheek. His left eye was swollen and almost closed. He removed the tape from Solis' mouth and began cutting the rope that bound him to the chair.

"Deuce, thank you. Thank you. Thank you. I thought I was goin' ta die," Solis said, his voice weak and raspy. "They were goin' ta kill me and you all. You, Bowles, everybody. We were all goin' ta die. They kept sayin' that and laughin' about it," Solis concluded weakly.

"I know. I know."

"The guys here," Solis nodded toward the two dead men on the cot. "They're Germans. They're mechanics and work at the airbase. They knew when our plane came in. They followed Bowles ta the hotel. Haddad deserted from the Iraqi police. The driver is his brother."

"I knew they deserted."

"Well, did you know they were gonna sell that white powder ta an Arab emir for twenty million dollars? We busted up that deal. They were pissed."

Harrington finished cutting Solis free and helped him from the chair.

"Are you okay?"

"Roughed up a bit. But, Good. Deuce, I told you those guys would kill or die for the powder. I told you. Twenty million dollars and a bunch a dead guys. What is that white powder?"

"Come on," Harrington said and led Solis by the arm.

"Never mind, come on," Solis protested and pulled away from Harrington. "What is that powder? Twenty million. It's worth twenty million. But you knew that, Deuce, and you're not telling. Why?"

"I would think you would want to know how we found you. So, we could save your sorry life."

"Deuce, if there was anybody gonna find me, it was you. I had no doubt about that. How did you find me?"

"Let's get out of here fast," Harrington said. "I'll explain everything later."

"You'll explain the white powder too?"

"Can you walk?"

"Walk? Man, watch me run outta here."

Harrington grabbed Solis again and helped him out of the cabin on to the deck.

"Go on," he said to Bowles. "Take Solis to the car, I need to get my cell phone."

"Hurry up, we'll wait," Bowles said.

Harrington walked across the dock to the second boat. He knelt beside the lifeless body of Haddad bin Nasab. He reached into the dead man's jacket pockets and found his cell phone, smeared with blood. He looked at the dead man and realized every encounter they had was centered in threat, violence, anger and now death. The lifeless body of bin Nasab represented an inevitable outcome to those encounters. Harrington rose and stood over bin Nasab. His standing symbolized a victory; but one he could not celebrate.

The three men left the boat and ran across the sand. Harrington led them to a point in the tree line where he had entered the river. He looked over the ground and retrieved the pair of binoculars he had left earlier.

Carrying them away, he hoped to remove all traces that could connect him to the terrible scene. However, the gunshots and cries uttered an accusatory pledge to resonate for a lifetime. Only some future interpretation and consciousness could render any justice or dole out clemency.

They got into the car and Bowles drove away. Only when they were far from the beach did he turn on the lights of the car. Solis slouched in the rear seat, touching the wounds on his face. He placed his hand over his chest and felt his heart beating in chaotic spasms. Perhaps it was rapidly juxtaposing between the prospect of death and the joy of survival. He was amazed by his confusion between fear and jubilation. Readjusting his hunter's hat, Solis sat quietly, content with the wonder of survival.

Harrington looked at the cell phone in his hand. He was thankful modern technology helped him realize there were no alternatives or optional solutions to his situation. The mission was just and the extreme protocol served to ensure survival. He placed his head on the back of the seat and came to terms with the blood of Haddad bin Nasab on his phone. Slowly, his thoughts turned to the sacks of white powder on the plane. The twenty million dollars the Arab emir was willing to pay Haddad had no real meaning for Harrington. Money could never determine the powder's value. The powder that may contain an ancient history had suddenly acquired a modern legacy and became another probability Harrington had to deal with.

Bowles rolled down the window and was thankful to smell the damp night air. In the distance he heard the dim wail of police sirens. He knew they were headed in the direction of the beach. The homes of the villages he had passed earlier were still shrouded in the same darkness, sequestered in the same dense shadows as if to suggest no time had passed. But Bowles could not be fooled. He knew time had passed. He also knew what horrible things had transpired within that time. Bowles knew many forms of wickedness came with their own contradictions and pleas for forgiveness. For the moment, he could not take up arms against those ironies. The will to fight had left him. But what had not left him was the quest for his own salvation. He struggled on with a gallant effort to acknowledge the rightful pursuit of morality. It needed to be accomplished but his strength was lacking. His intentions tainted. He touched the gold crucifix around his neck. He knew it was time to ask Jesus to reclaim his soul.

ARIZONA

GABRIELLA DeCeasere sat opposite Morgana Barnes on the patio of Morgana's home. Both women harbored a similar secret arrangement allowing them to guard their personal dramas. They could not permit themselves involvement in the many perils and treasures of the outside world. They only remained committed to their human relationships. In doing so, the problem for them was always in spacing. The closeness which they allowed themselves to the proximity of their feelings was the true extent of their world.

Gabriella watched how Morgana turned the spoon in her cup of chamomile tea and gently wiped it with a napkin before placing it on the saucer. Gabriella knew every gesture of Morgana's was identical to the way she prepared her demitasse coffee. Their commonality expanded beyond their similar expressions to the knowing way they looked at each other. They were women who understood each other. Their strong doubt about the present threatened their once vigorous sense of the future. In addition to sharing a similar turn of a spoon, they also shared a sense of sadness. The tone of the wind blowing off the desert was not lost on them. It had a dry, dense feel of measured time they would not be part of. The wind also brought an acrid hint of sulfur causing Morgana to look out across the desert in the direction of the destroyed mine. The mine's strange contents and mysterious demolition caused Gabriella and Morgana to form an odd pact and adopt a keen wisdom, allowing them to divert their attention to a simple turning of a spoon.

"Gabriella, let's take a walk into the desert," Morgana suggested. "I like it there this time of evening."

"Do you walk in the desert often?" Gabriella asked.

"Yes, mostly after dinner. It gets a bit chilly at night. I can get you a jacket to wear, but I'm afraid it won't go with your lovely dress. It looks expensive."

"Thank you. I will welcome your jacket," Gabriella said. "The cost of my dress is not what you might think. It was made by Pietro's aunt. The value is more sentimental."

Morgana walked into the house where Barnes and Segretti were seated in the living room. They were sipping beer and stopped talking when Morgana entered.

"Gabriella and I are taking a bit of a walk," Morgana announced.

"It's cool out. You better put on a jacket," Alex suggested. "Get one for Gabriella as well."

"I will," she said reaching into a closet and withdrawing two rawhide jackets.

Gabriella liked the odor of the rawhide. She put the jacket on and spread her arms, admiring the many strands of dangling tassels.

"This is a lovely jacket. It appears hand sewn," Gabriella observed.

"It was hand sewn by a local seamstress. She's a tribal friend."

Gabriella touched the two embroidered symbols on each of the breast pockets.

"What are these symbols?" Gabriella asked.

"One is 'The Twins'," Morgana said. "It depicts the duality between emergence and creation. The Twins are represented as small boys. The legend is they overcome great odds and protect people from monsters," Morgana concluded.

"And the second one?" Gabriella asked.

"That's the 'Horned Lizard'. In traditional Navajo stories, it preserves ancient secrets."

Morgana led Gabriella through the sandy garden beyond the patio. The garden was the width of the house and extended 100 feet to the beginning of the desert. The garden was enclosed by an iron fence with four lighted posts. Several russet-colored sandstone rocks of various sizes were decoratively placed at the two far corners of the garden. The rocks were surrounded by small cactus plants and several creosote bushes. In the center of the garden was a meditation bench under an Emory oak tree. A brass plaque, inlaid into a flat stone under the oak, was simply inscribed: *Kenneth Timothy Barnes.* As Gabriella passed the Emory oak, she noticed the brass plaque. Instinctively, Gabriella knew the plaque represented the most personal of losses. She continued walking next to Morgana hoping not to trespass on her life.

"It is beautiful here," Gabriella observed. "Quiet and peaceful. Almost spiritual in a way. That's what I sense."

"Yes it is."

"Do you like the solitude?" Gabriella asked.

"I have my hobbies and my crafts. They keep me busy."

Morgana lifted the collar of her jacket. She took a deep breath. A forlorn cry from a desert coyote echoed from the distance. It did not have the longing of a mating cry; a sound Morgana was familiar with. The pitch and tone of the cry was more sorrowful, as if the coyote was in anguish from a trap or mourning a mate. She listened until the howl faded away.

"You're asking me if I'm lonely," Morgana continued.

"Not in a way that would be prying. I'm sorry. That's not something I should be asking of you."

"It's quite alright. I like your honesty. You have an easy approach to it. Your concern is genuine. Yes, it is a bit lonely for me. Even with my hobbies. You noticed the plaque by the tree."

"Yes, I did."

"You didn't ask about it."

"I was afraid to ask."

"Alex planted the tree the day we lost our son. Kenneth Timothy."

"I'm sorry," Gabriella said with genuine compassion.

Morgana paused, saddened by the memory.

"He would have been eight years old. We married late in life. My pregnancy was a surprise. It opened a whole new world. We were excited. Our lives took on a different meaning. We were content with our lives before the pregnancy. Our son survived one week after birth. His tiny heart just stopped. I blamed myself for not making him stronger during the pregnancy. I still blame myself. The void Kenneth Timothy's passing created has not closed....Now Alex and I are not as content."

"Your torment cannot be helping you," Gabriella said nearly pleading. It doesn't serve to keep you close to your son. It distorts your relation to him. It keeps his spirit from a sense of forgiveness. His spirit does not need that pain. You don't need that pain."

"I know. After my son's death, Alex sold his business and bought the mine. The mine was good for him in many ways. The boy, Billy, who helps him at the mine, is like a son to Alex. He tries to teach him and encourage him. The way he would have done with his own son."

"I could see how much the mine meant. You didn't need this trouble."

"Why was Pietro interested in the mine?"

"He's interested in the powder Alex mines from it. Pietro was told it had healing powers. He has sick relatives. Two aunts. They are people he loves. He hoped it would help them."

"Do you have any idea who would want to destroy the mine?" Morgana's words were framed with hope.

"No. But Pietro knows a lot of people. He will try to find the people who did this."

"What line of work is Pietro in that gives him the ability to find them? I'm sorry, I should not have asked that," Morgana added quickly.

"It's alright," Gabriella assured. "He's retired. Before he retired, he was in the arms business. He was an arms dealer. Weapons. He bought and sold weapons to nations."

Morgana stopped and turned to Gabriella. There was no hint of judgment or condemnation in her eyes. She was only amazed by Gabriella's candor and trust. It caused a soft joy to settle in to her like a sisterly clutch that blended with the night wind embracing her with an old familiarity.

"What will Pietro do now to help his ailing aunts?" Morgana asked.

"He will have to let fate take its course. Death like life has its predetermined appointments. Powders from the earth or prayers to heaven can't change that. He'll have to find out for himself."

"Men search for foolish things," Morgana observed.

"Yes, they do."

"Yet, Pietro still wants the powder?"

"Yes. If your husband reopens the mine, Pietro would want to buy from him. Does he have some that wasn't buried in the explosion?"

"Alex only has the small amount he sent to the lab. They returned it. I'll get it for you. I hope it will help."

"Thank you."

"Alex hasn't decided to reopen the mine. I don't want him to. You tell me the powder has healing power. Then why would someone want to destroy it? Clearly, if Pietro knew about the powder, someone else knew about it too. I read the report from the laboratory. It does have strange properties beyond healing. There would be dozens of industries interested in buying it from Alex. I don't understand who would want it destroyed. I don't believe in conspiracy, but if someone wanted the mine sealed and the powder buried, that leads me to believe there's more to the history of the powder and its ability to heal. There's got to be something secret.... Something very secret and ancient about it. But, if there is, the secrets will be protected by the horned lizard," Morgana said.

"How about Alex, does he think there's an ancient secret to it?"

"I don't know," Morgana said. "He hasn't said anything to me. If it's true and there's more of a secret history to the powder, we may want to learn what it is. After all, isn't that what this is all about, protecting secrets?"

"I thought you didn't believe in conspiracy?"

"Not believing in something is not the same as it not being real."

"It's funny," Gabriella said. "I think we're getting caught up in the search for foolish things," she observed.

"Perhaps we are, but finding the truth is never a foolish search," Morgana said.

Gabriella sensed Morgana struggled with the things she preferred over those she possessed. Like most people, Morgana preferred an exchange of life experiences. Yet, a single experience worked in many unusual ways. For the moment, it was enough for Morgana to make Gabriella understand some things about her.

"It's time we went back," Gabriella said. "Thank you for the jacket," she continued as she started to remove it.

"No," Morgana said. "I want you to keep the jacket. I want you to have it."

Gabriella felt overwhelmed by the expression of Morgana's generosity. The offer was unrehearsed and authentic, stemming from the limits of Morgana's need to connect. Gabriella ran her hand down the soft hide. She touched the embroidered symbols once more. She understood what the jacket meant. There were no words to describe her appreciation.

"Thank you. I'll treasure it always," Gabriella said. "I wish I could give you something in return."

"You already have, Gabriella," Morgana said. "More than you know."

The women started back toward the house. Gabriella slipped her arm under Morgana's. They clung to each other, each grateful for the other's presence.

Morgana opened the gate and walked into the garden. As they passed the Emory oak tree with the brass plaque, Gabriella gripped Morgana's arm more tightly. Morgana understood the meaning of Gabriella's gesture. She turned to look at Gabriella and smiled. It was a smile filled with assurance and a complacent rule of belief. That simple, enigmatical smile helped them to narrow their lives to simple gestures and forged an unencumbered friendship.

For the first time in a long time, Morgana did not feel guarded. She had a sense of alliance. Of those things left unsaid, were things she still revealed. It was the spoken truths and the language of expression Morgana entrusted to a stranger allowing her to abandon her weary hold on her private secrets.

Gabriella did not allow their spoken or unspoken words to be held for ransom. She used them to let their connection spread beyond the thin exterior of formality. Their unexpected bond took hold, giving rise to a welcoming sense of safety and connection. Gabriella was first linked to Morgana by a rude explosion meant to keep an ancient secret concealed. The connection was strengthened by a turn of a spoon, a rawhide jacket and a brass plaque inscribed with a boy's name. They didn't plan to have these small things contain tremendous meaning. Nor did they suspect their small compassions and passing generosities to be measured in lifetimes.

PIETRO Segretti looked out at the distance Cerbat and Mayswell peaks as he drove from the Barnes' house. The bold outline traces of the peaks jutted into the dark sky. Black clouds mixed with the peaks. Their muted shapes could be imagined as other things. Segretti could not be fooled by the dark, shifting patterns. The midnight clouds could not conceal the farce played on a crumbled mine. The laws of the mountain and desert were void of spontaneity and impulse. They contained their own plan to be carried out through timely evolution. Segretti believed the nature of things came in endless sequences. It unfolded without contradiction. He saw the grievous interruption to the natural line of fruition in the form of a calculated demolition to the mine as the workings of an alternate plan. On a parallel scale, the newly devised scheme was more complex. It contained the elements of human frailty, distorted logic most probably rooted in fear.

As he looked blankly out at the road, Segretti pondered the perplexing nature of the explosion. He wondered how it interfered with his purpose. He knew it was too soon to question the elaborate draw it might have upon him. Gabriella folded her arms and leaned against the car door. It was an unconscious attempt to move away from Segretti and remain close to the newly acquired solidarity with Morgana. Their alliance was forged since they were unwillingly drawn to the center of a drama solely because of their allegiance to others. She lowered her head so she could get closer to the soft hide. She breathed in its distinct odor. Her intimacy with the jacket had acquired a vast commentary that Gabriella was becoming familiar with.

"Are you alright?" Segretti asked.

Gabriella drew in a long breath and reluctantly lifted her head. She remained quiet, allowing herself time to disengage from her thoughts.

"Gabriella, are you okay?" Segretti asked again.

"Yes," she responded quietly. "Why?"

"You seem upset. Preoccupied."

"I'm fine."

"Was Morgana upset about the mine?"

"She was upset for Alex. Not the mine."

"Well, it was the explosion of the mine that started all this."

"No it wasn't. It was the act of fearful people that caused his distress. Morgana and Alex have enough loss in their lives. It wasn't just a mine that got destroyed. It was the truest part of Alex's life that got affected. The mine was something personal to him. And more than anything, the explosion destroyed Morgana's delicate sense of peace. It was something she was trying to hold on to. Now she's defenseless. Not because of the mine, but because of the secrets of the mine people try to keep."

"What secrets?"

"The white powder. The white gold has its secrets. Whatever they are. Who cares about those secrets? It's all foolishness. In the end, people will see and believe only what they want."

"You're angry," Segretti observed.

"Yes, I'm angry. It doesn't stop. People destroying people. That's the worst part of all. Destroying something that someone holds dear is like killing a part of them. No one has the right to hurt another. God does a good enough job."

"Gabriella, what brought this on?"

"How can you remain so detached?" Gabriella responded.

"I'm not detached," Segretti countered. "Obviously, my conversation with Alex was different than the one you had with Morgana. We spoke about business. My focus didn't change. I'm concerned only for Rosa and Melia."

"Pietro, did you ask Rosa and Melia what they want? Suppose they want their lives to end naturally. Suppose they refuse to accept the white powder, then what?"

"Why would they not want to accept something that can help them?"

"Help them, how? To live longer? They both lost husbands. Maybe they want to pass on before they bear the grief of another loss. Maybe they don't want to outlive their hopes and their failures. There are times when living is a curse."

"Well, suppose they want my help?"

"Ask them. That seems like something you should have done before we left."

"If you felt that way, why didn't you say that earlier?"

"Because, it's something I just discovered."

"When? Tonight? By talking to Morgana?"

"I don't know. Maybe."

Segretti could not be certain what troubled Gabriella. It was unusual for her to be overcome by confusion and dominated by irritation. Her mood was alien to him. He wanted to intercede and manage whatever philosophy suddenly became unbearable for her.

"Gabriella, what's really bothering you?" Segretti asked quietly. "It can't be the secrets of Alex's mine or the true wishes of Rosa and Melia."

"Maybe it's all that or none of it," Gabriella responded, a mild tempest arching just under her skin.

Segretti knew Gabriella's world was filled with things that were better left in her care. She was able to address the things that troubled her and patient enough to allow the time needed for all unknown ghosts to reveal themselves.

"Well, there's nothing for us here," Segretti said. "Let's go back home. Will you feel better knowing we're going home?" he said.

Gabriella could not respond to Segretti's gently offer of safekeeping. Nor could she identify the source of her angst. She gave up on exploring its importance and realized, for the moment, silence was her best companion. She kept looking ahead at the dark sky and responded by shrugging her shoulders. She gathered all of her unspoken feelings, and folded them neatly within herself. A vision of home, and her own silence, gave her a sense of retreat.

Segretti looked out at the changing shapes of the dark clouds altering the outline of the mountain peaks. The changing landscape suggested nothing was designed to last. If there was an ancient secret to the white powder, some day it would be revealed, and those discoveries would eventually yield to something greater. He suspected Gabriella was right about Rosa and Melia. Perhaps, the elderly women were content accepting their fate, unafraid of death and at peace with their lives.

The lights in the rear view mirror diverted Segretti's attention. At first, the lights mingled with the stars. As he watched the lights rapidly approaching, they appeared to gain with ominous aggression. Instinctively, Segretti reached for his hip, but realized he was unarmed. He pressed down on the gas. The car gained speed. Gabriella sensed the increased speed. She looked out the passenger window to confirm her suspicions.

"Pietro, slow down," she whispered.

She noticed Segretti looking in the mirror and turned to see the car gaining on them.

"Who's that?" She asked.

"I don't know. I'm not taking any chances."

Suddenly, flashes of blue and red lights burst from the oncoming car. It drew parallel to Segretti. The car continued past, then turned into Segretti's lane, screeching to a halt. Segretti applied the brakes coming to a stop, almost hitting the car. The doors of the official vehicle flew open. Two men jumped out, pointing guns at Segretti. In the light from his vehicle, Segretti recognized Andrew Cummings and Stewart Manning, the agents from Homeland Security.

"Don't move!" Cummings shouted, approaching Segretti.

Manning approached Gabriella's door and pointed a gun at her face.

"Why didn't you stop when you saw my flashing lights? Cummings shouted. "Turn off the ignition and put your hands on the steering wheel," he continued.

Segretti followed the instruction and gave Cummings a steel hard glare.

"Keep your hands where I can see them. Step from the vehicle slowly," Cummings ordered.

Segretti turned and looked at Gabriella noticing she was calm but angry.

"Don't worry, Gabriella," Segretti whispered. "Everything will be alright."

"Come on. Step out of the vehicle. Now," Cummings shouted.

Segretti moved slowly keeping his hands in front of him. As he stepped from the vehicle, he became acutely aware of the darkness and desolation of the road. The desert seemed endless in all directions; an abyss void of light, sound or life. It was a setting made for mayhem.

"I told you we'd meet again," Cummings sneered as he approached Segretti.

"Do you want to tell me what this is about, Agent Cummings? Segretti said calmly.

"How about transporting explosives for starters," Cummings responded.

"Explosives?"

"Yes. What did you use to blow up Alex Barnes' mine?"

"I'm afraid you're mistaken," Segretti reasoned.

"I don't think so. Stewart," Cummings shouted over his shoulder to Manning. "Remove the passenger and bring her here."

Gabriella pulled the rawhide jacket around herself touching the embroidered image of The Twins. She recalled Morgana had said the Navajo legend of The Twins protected people from monsters. She hoped the legend was true. She walked to the front of the vehicle passing through a clump of moths wildly attacking the headlights. Manning followed her and kept his gun pointed at her back. When Gabriella reached Segretti, she leaned her shoulder into his. Segretti reached out and held Gabriella's arm.

"Keep your hands where I can see them," Cummings barked. "You're both coming with me," he continued. "I want to know what you used to blow up the mine and who gave you the explosives."

"I already told you. I had nothing at all to do with it," Segretti said

"You don't seem to understand. I don't care if you did or if you didn't. I have a probable cause. I can take you in."

"What purpose would that serve?" Segretti said.

"Well, let me break it down for you in a way you'll understand. You're an arms dealer. I take you in. You're one less threat to our security. I put an end to your enterprise. Maybe in the process, you give up somebody else and then they give up somebody. That's how it works. We keep doing that until there's none of your kind left."

"And that's what you think will happen?" Segretti scowled.

"Why, you don't think you will?"

"Once again you're mistaken," Segretti said.

"Trust me, when you're locked away in a dark cell, your sense of bravery will be eaten away. You'll look to make a deal. Guys like you can't give up the good life."

Gabriella stepped away from Segretti and moved close to Cummings.

"Do you think you're going to destroy our lives as easily as that?" Gabriella said, controlling her rage. "You're not a Homeland Security agent. You're a smug little elitist. You don't care for your country. All you care about is your career and your vanity. I'm turning around and going back in my car."

"Don't do that," Segretti said. "This man is a coward. He will shoot you in the back, because he can't shoot you while you're looking at him."

"I'll shoot you both right here and now," Cummings said raising the gun to Gabriella's head. "I'll drag you into the desert where no one will ever find you."

Gabriella looked at Cummings and leaned her head closer to the gun. Her delicate, loving features turned hard and cold. She tapped into a demeanor of direct defiance. Her inner force generated a resistance designed to contest aggression.

"Pietro is right," Gabriella sneered at Cummings. "You're nothing but a coward. Without that gun you're a clerk with a cheap suit and tie. You better not even try to put a hand on me. You're not going to put me in a cell. Not because I like the good life. It's because I won't allow you to control my life. You don't have that right. I won't give you that right. So, why don't you put down that gun and go after real terrorists. Do your job. But not here and not tonight."

Cummings became enraged. A gauntlet had been thrown, blurring the space between his ego and his duty. The incendiary challenge lit up the dark desert with the flames of hostility and belligerence. A commensurate response was not enough. He had to exceed the challenge. He stepped closer to Gabriella and pressed the gun to her forehead.

"You bitch," he growled at Gabriella, hoping for further provocation.

Gabriella did not flinch. Nor did she plead for anything passing as leniency. She did not forfeit her quiet might. Her slight grin doused all authority Cummings thought he held over her. Cummings knew he made an error in judgment. Gabriella was formidable in ways for which he was not prepared. All that was available to him was the further pursuit of aggression aimed at disguising his defeat. He shifted the weapon slightly and fired a shot past Gabriella's ear attempting to reclaim his influence. The sound of the shot resonated through Gabriella, yet she remained stoic. Her slight smile shamed Cummings.

Echoing ominously between the distant mountain peaks, the gun shot filled the desert with menace. If left unchallenged, the menacing action by Cummings would grow into something monstrous and uncontrollable. Segretti acted quickly. His grip was strong. He pulled Cummings' arm high, away from Gabriella and toward Manning. He twisted the weapon loose from Cummings and swept forward hitting Manning on the bridge of the nose with the butt of the weapon. The sound of crunching bone filled the night. Blood spurted from Manning's nose. Manning dropped his weapon and fell to his knees, holding his face. Segretti forced Cummings against the rented car. Cummings brought his free arm around Segretti's neck, getting him in a choke hold. Segretti did not resist. Leaning backward into the hold, Segretti drove his elbow into Cummings' ribs. After the third powerful blow, Cummings released his grip allowing Segretti to turn. He punched Cummings in the face three times knocking him to the ground. Segretti quickly spun around and kicked Manning in the side of the face, leaving him sprawled on the road.

Gabriella retrieved Manning's weapon from the ground. It was the first time she ever held a gun. She felt the weapon's vile contours. Its hateful purpose sent a disturbing chill through her. She ran beyond the road and dropped the weapon on the sand. With one foot, she kicked up the sand burying the weapon, hoping it would never be discovered, and in time, would rot away. Gabriella turned to see Segretti kneeling over Cummings, holding him by the throat in a grip crushing his larynx. She ran to him and bent close.

"Pietro, that's enough," she whispered calmly. "That's enough. Enough."

Segretti relaxed his grip and stepped away from Cummings. Looking down, he felt a bolt of justice and triumph as Cummings struggled to draw breath. His eye and cheek were swollen and discolored. Blood spilled from his nose. His lower lip was split. There were scrapes on his chin. His neck, showed bruises and angry red welts.

Segretti turned from Cummings. He reached up and touched Gabriella's forehead where Cummings had placed the gun. In the light from the car, Segretti saw a small circular bruise on her soft, smooth skin. Gabriella quickly grabbed his hand hoping her delicate touch would turn off the violent force that had taken control of him.

"Are you alright?" Segretti asked.

"Yes. I'm fine," she said. "No more, Pietro. These men can't resist you any longer. Let them be."

Segretti lowered his hand and hugged Gabriella. Over his shoulder he heard Cummings moan. Gabriella saw Cummings struggling to rise to one knee. She quickly walked over to him and crouched in front of him. She grabbed his bloody face and raised it up close to hers.

"Leave us alone," she said. "We had nothing to do with the explosion. Don't make this a personal hatred. Just do the work you're supposed to do. We're no threat to you."

Cummings tried to stand, but he staggered forward hitting into Manning who was kneeling on the ground dazed and disoriented. Segretti stood over Cummings, knowing the agent's defeat was humiliating. He reached down and retrieved Cummings' weapon. He threw it into the night. Grabbing Gabriella by the arm, he helped her up and walked to the car.

"Get in," he said.

Segretti went to Cummings' vehicle, and removed the keys. He went back to his car and drove away. After he had driven for a while, he lowered the window and threw out Cummings' keys.

"Are you alright, Gabriella?" he asked.

"Yes, I'm fine," she responded.

"There was no other way out," he said apologetically.

"Yes, I know. It wasn't your fault."

"I'm sorry I involved you in all this."

"It's alright. There was no way to know how things would turn out. But you know, we'll never get out of this country now," she said.

"I'm not so sure about that. I have friends that are very prominent with far-reaching influence."

"But this is the U.S. government that needs to be influenced. That doesn't seem likely."

"Gabriella, influence manipulates the world. I'll make a phone call."

"But who do you know that will…?"

"Don't worry," Segretti interrupted. "Just leave this to me. I have a special friend who works closely with the Ministry of Foreign Affairs in Saudi Arabia. He's in a powerful position and knows how these things work."

Segretti reached into his pocket for his cell phone. He quickly tapped in a number and heard it ring. Gabriella leaned her head back against the headrest. She felt tired and fragmented; apart from her body. Every deep breath she took had two possible realities. She noticed spots of blood on the jacket that looked black in the dim light. Gabriella touched her forehead where Cummings pressed the gun wondering if the blood belonged to her. There were no stains on her finger tips, only a thin film of sweat and dirt. She became indifferent to the possibility the blood belonged to Cummings or Manning. The only conjecture that stirred Gabriella was the likelihood the dark stains were Morgana's embedded grief. They revealed themselves to Gabriella, entrusting her as the proper keeper of its history. She concentrated on what she sensed of the jacket's saga, oblivious to Segretti's conversation. From somewhere in the distance she thought she heard her name being called.

"Gabriella? Gabriella?" she heard it more distinctly and closer than she suspected.

"Gabriella? Gabriella? Are you alright?" Segretti called out, severing her connection to her distant thoughts. "Are you alright?"

"Yes," she said slowly, easing back within her own space.

"You seem lost. Are you okay? "

"I'm fine."

"Are you sure?"

"Yes, I'm fine. You told me everything will be alright. Is it?"

"Yes." Everything has been arranged. We have to drive to Phoenix tonight. I have an address. We're expected. A private Saudi plane will be at Sky Harbor Airport tomorrow night."

"And, what about Agent Cummings and Homeland Security?"

"That will be taken care of. Influence is the measure of cooperation. We'll be escorted to the plane with no interference from Customs or Homeland Security. We'll be under diplomatic protection."

Gabriella was not influenced by Segretti's confidence. She was still overwhelmed by a vague uncertainty that kept her surrounded in a chamber of echoes.

"Gabriella, did you hear me? There's nothing to worry about. We will be home and safe."

Gabriella heard Segretti's voice overlapping with the one in her head. The voices did not conflict. They joined to become a fragile reminder that danger was powerless against the ambiguity of time.

The motion of the car, and the sound of the wind blowing against it, was comforting for Gabriella. It made escape through momentum and time a reality. She knew that in a short time, she would be in Phoenix, then home, and shelter. There, she could ponder time as she never had before. Time and the horned lizard shared a commonality of secrets. Both may never reveal the true origins of the stains on Morgana's jacket and the secrets of the white powder. She didn't need those mysteries to be revealed. She had a better advantage. The message she learned from the jacket, was one she had been searching for. It told her things had their own momentum and consciousness, and to accept them as they were.

That's what made sense to Gabriella and eased her longing. She also realized what Morgana silently revealed through every gesture, conversation, and in particular, her assuring smile by the Emory oak tree. Gabriella was more grateful than ever to Morgana. She knew they had created their personal legacy.

Segretti turned to Gabriella, a look of impatience registering in his eyes.

"Gabriella?" he said.

"Yes," she responded in a low, soft voice. "I heard you, Pietro."

MONTE CARLO

UMBERTO Nunarro walked across the marble floor of the atrium in the Monte Carlo Casino. Dozens of tourists milled about looking at the bas-reliefs, frescoes and sculptures. As he passed the tourists, he heard bits of conversations in a variety of foreign languages. He walked between the onyx columns, past the auditorium dedicated to opera and ballet, and entered one of the gaming rooms. The broad stained glass windows, sculptures, allegorical paintings and bronze lamps gave the room a unique sophistication. The ambience and refinement of the casino suited Nunarro. It matched his black tailored silk suit, white shirt with gold cuff links and urbane mood. He made his way to an empty chair at one of the roulette tables and unbuttoned his jacket. He took five thousand Euros from his pocket and placed it on the table.

"One hundred," he announced to the croupier.

He looked around the table noticing an elderly couple at the far end. Seated next to the couple was a young woman wearing a low cut dress, a thick diamond necklace, gold bracelets and a large diamond ring. The croupier pushed a stack of one hundred Euros each to Nunarro.

"Good luck, sir," the croupier said.

Nunarro turned his attention to the stack of chips. He fingered one of the stacks. Reaching over the green felt covered table, he placed five, one hundred Euro chips on number six. He made three pair bets with the six: three, five and nine each valued at one hundred Euros.

The elderly couple placed twenty five Euros each on numbers ten, twenty and thirty. The diamond clad woman recklessly placed stacks of chips on almost every number except those Nunarro had bet. Nunarro knew there was no pattern to her betting. He suspected it was just a wanton display of excess and privilege. The croupier spun the ball in its track as the wheel turned. Gambling had a special lure for Nunarro. It was the offsetting factors of probability and chance ruled by actuality that intrigued him.

As the ball dropped from its track it sounded a melody all its own.

"Six," the croupier announced and mounted a crystal peg on the stack of chips Nunarro had placed on the number.

"Damn," the elderly man said. "I was going to bet that."

"Oh well," the lady with the diamonds announced. "I guess this is not my lucky night."

Before leaving the table, she looked at Nunarro, smiled and touched the diamond necklace hanging between her breasts.

The croupier counted out the proper amount of chips, stacked them in four equal piles, then pushed them toward Nunarro. Purposefully, he removed two chips valued at one hundred Euros each and slid them across the felt table as a gratuity for the croupier.

"Thank you, sir," the croupier said, showing his excitement.

A statement of energy and entitlement filled the room. It was pronounced, recognizable by the restrained laughter and the demands of a honed culture. Nunarro was sensitive to the energy around him, making it easy for him to detect a deviation of purpose from a man who sat down next to him and from another who stood behind him. The men showed no interest in gaming or kinship to the refined surroundings. They projected a stark energy and seemed to cast a chill about them. Their collective presence amounted to a kind of challenge, communicating a silent menace. In a conscience effort to ignore them, Nunarro aligned his chips preparing for another wager.

"Umberto Nunarro," the seated man said in a low tone.

Nunarro turned to look at the man. Then he looked over his shoulder at the man standing behind him.

"Who wants to know?" Nunarro asked with an edge of defensiveness.

"I'm not asking you. I know who you are."

"What is it you want?" Nunarro asked.

"Someone would like to speak with you. In exactly one hour, a car will be waiting for you outside the casino."

"Why don't you tell whoever wants to speak with me to come into the casino?"

The stranger looked at his watch and then back to Nunarro.

"In *exactly* one hour," the stranger said, stood and with the man standing behind Nunarro, walked away.

Nunarro could not imagine the source of the clandestine approach. He suspected it could not be a threat or represent danger, as attacks usually came without warning. His mind began to run through the likely possibilities. His business with Monsignor Clementi had been complete. He had been paid well. This was not the approach the Monsignor would take if he needed something else done. The more Nunarro tried to think of what was behind the mysterious meeting, the more likely his guess would be futile. Nunarro sensed he was being watched. He chose to remain casual yet attentive to the people around him. He continued betting, but was too preoccupied to be concerned with the outcome of the wheel or the philosophical nature of gambling. Casually, he kept looking at his watch until it was time to leave. He pushed his chips into the center of the table.

"Cash me out," he demanded.

The pit manager stepped from behind the croupier and approached Nunarro.

"Will you be leaving with the cash, sir?" the pit manager asked.

"No. I will come by another time to claim my winnings," Nunarro responded.

"Fine, sir," the pit manager said handing Nunarro a receipt. "Please present this claim and your winnings will be disbursed per your request. Is there anything we can provide you, sir?"

"No. Thank you. If I'm not back in twenty-four hours, give one thousand Euros to the croupier. Take five hundred for yourself and give the rest to the hospital." Nunarro said.

"Sir, that is a bit unusual. We would need you to put that in writing for us. We need some sort of proof or documentation to validate your request."

"I just gave it to you. Just do it. Twenty-four hours," Nunarro said and left the room.

Nunarro stood at the top of the stairs of the casino overlooking the fountains and gardens. He heard the flapping from the flags above him, and the water spraying from the lighted fountains. In the courtyard was a row of expensive Italian and British cars. People strolled casually around the fountains. Nunarro took a cigarette from his jacket pocket, but replaced it when he saw the door to a black Bentley open. The man, who had sat next to him at the roulette table, got out of the front of the car and opened the back door as Nunarro descended the stairs. He reached the car and climbed in. The man closed the door behind Nunarro, then climbed in the front seat and drove away.

Nunarro did not speak, but watched as the car drove down Avenue de Monte Carlo to the Boulevard Louis II. He suspected the car was heading toward the Monte Carlo Bay. At the foot of the dock, the car came to a stop. The door opened from the outside. Nunarro climbed out of the car and was escorted by two other men to a launch. There were many yachts in the bay, but Nunarro focused on one that flew an Emirate flag. From the lights of city that shone on the yacht, Nunarro could see the name, ADILAH, on the stern. He knew the yacht belonged to the emir; Adilah's father.

Reaching the yacht, Nunarro was helped aboard and escorted into the stateroom. The room was elegant beyond measure. The expression of wealth was emphatic and excessive. The marble floor was inlaid with gold. Four gold leaf columns stood at each corner of the stateroom. An ornate crystal chandelier hung in the center. To one side of the stateroom stood a table bearing dishes of sliced sturgeon, a silver bowl filled with caviar and a temperature controlled wine case. Gold adorned the utensils and glassware. The yacht, and its contents, was an extension of the opulence of the emir's home. Nunarro recalled it vividly.

Nunarro stood in the room as the past came rushing back to him. The sights, smiles, touches and scents of Adilah were everywhere. She was here. The sense of her permeated him. He felt her breath. Was she on deck with the sea breeze blowing on her face, swirling her hair and the pure silk gown around her? Was she just beyond the door? Did she go through this elaborate plan just to see him again? Why? What would he say to her? What would she say to him? Would they say anything at all, kiss, or consummate a longing and abolish a festering loneliness? He was filled with questions that raced through his mind in one long aching moan. He heard the door open and the emir entered. For an instant, Nunarro was disappointed. He looked past the emir hoping to see Adilah, but the emir smiled and closed the door behind him. The sound of the closing door was climatic, dashing a passion that filled every pore of his body.

"Hello, Umberto," the emir said.

Nunarro felt a knot of regret in his chest. It took him a moment to gain control of himself.

"Hello," he said trying to manage the years of regret that had settled in his voice.

"I apologize for the elaborate approach of my men. I hope they didn't alarm you."

The emir's voice sounded dry and scratchy. His face was rounder than Nunarro recalled. There were more creases on his neck. His eyes appeared tired. Nunarro wanted to stop all conversation except for one. He wanted to know about Adilah. He wanted to ask if she was well. He wanted to know if she was on deck waiting for him. But Nunarro knew it would be insulting to ask about Adilah. He also sensed his questions and desires would be answered with disappointing shrugs. That part of his life had passed. Adilah would always be a windblown image just beyond a door. Her scent, breath and kiss would continue to plague his memory.

"No," he said weakly. "Your men didn't alarm me."

"Good. Can I offer you something to eat?"

"Perhaps later," Nunarro said.

"Which means you're anxious to know why I brought you here? Come.

Sit," the emir said, leading Nunarro to a couch upholstered with Persian silk. "Can I offer you some wine?" The emir continued.

"No, thank you," Nunarro responded.

"You look successful. Have things been going well for you?" the emir asked as a formality.

"Yes. You look well," Nunarro observed.

"Thank you. Time is my enemy. It reaches a point when it starts to take things from us. Our youth worst of all. You were lucky in the casino tonight."

Nunarro sensed the emir was making a number of pointed observations.

"Gambling is unpredictable," Nunarro said, choosing to respond to only one observation.

"Only for those who don't understand its true nature," the emir retorted. "Umberto, I'll get to the point. I recently hired two soldiers in the Iraqi Police Service. Haddar bin Nasab and his brother. These men were to fulfill a contract we had entered into. It was to be a simple transaction. They were to transport goods from Iraq to Saudi Arabia, where I was to relieve them of the goods. There, I was to pay them and the deal was to be complete. Unfortunately, the goods wound up in Germany..."

"Why Germany?"

"Well it seems the goods changed hands. Several U.S. soldiers came across the goods before Haddar bin Nasab was able to transport them to my destination."

"Was Haddar bin Nasab trying to broker a different deal with the soldiers?"

"I suspect not. He was being paid very well. I was offering him twenty million dollars. I doubt the American soldiers could make a better offer. No, the American soldiers just happened upon the material and tried to take it for themselves."

"Twenty million. I would assume these goods are important to you?"

"You could say that."

"Are they just as important to the American soldiers?"

"I'm not so sure they know the actual value."

"Why don't you offer the soldiers the twenty million?"

"It's not that easy."

"I guess I'm missing something. The goods are in Germany, and you can't go there to retrieve them. Why can't you make the same deal with the soldiers?"

"Well, back to Haddar bin Nasab. Unfortunately, he and his brother, along with several others, met with resistance. I can only assume from the soldiers. More to the point, I suspect Haddar bin Nasab was weak and unprepared. Because of his weakness, the goods are no longer in Germany. They are on a military transport, either on their way, or have already arrived in the United States."

"Where in the United States?"

"We believe Arizona."

"Arizona?"

"Yes. You just had a recent trip to Arizona. You and Mario Orisi." the emir said, looking hard at Nunarro.

There was a knowing judgment in the emir's eyes. They no longer looked tired. They pierced Nunarro leaving him violated and exposed. He also felt a wave of guilt and shame over the things the emir had forced him to see he was withholding from himself. He felt corrupted and betrayed by his own failings. There was no hiding or pretending. More importantly, his actions at the Barnes mine had condemned him forever with Adilah.

"You did that job for the Catholic Monsignor," the emir continued. "I don't question your motives. After all, you need to provide a living for yourself. Nor do I question the reasoning and motives of the Monsignor. I just know his judgments are lodged in the Dark ages. His guilt is allowed to persist in the name of tradition. It's nonsense what he chooses to believe."

Nunarro knew he couldn't ask how the emir knew of his dealings with Monsignor Clementi. He just accepted the emir's honesty, making him feel dissatisfied with himself.

"So where do I come in?" Nunarro asked, seeking salvation and hoping to reclaim his dignity.

"I need you to find the soldiers and retrieve my goods. The offer I made with Haddar bin Nasab, I will extend to you. Whatever you need will be made available."

"Do you know the names of the soldiers?"

"Haddar bin Nasab took too much for granted. He did not get all the information when he had the chance. It would have been easy. He had the means to get the information. Not the will. That's why he was weak. He had the name and rank of only one soldier. Harrington. A sergeant"

"How do you know the goods are in Arizona?"

"Because Arizona is the destination of the military transport plane. Luke Air Force. That's the starting point."

Nunarro sat back in the luxurious chair. He never concerned himself with wariness over things that didn't feel right. This night brought on new perspectives and possibilities. He felt the outstretched offer was a chance to establish himself if he was successful in returning the goods. The proposal offered redemption of honor, a restoration of pride that could become his constant source of reference. But failure would cast him into obscurity forever. The level of self-chastising would be severe and could not be ignored or withheld. This was gambling on a much higher level than the frivolous turn of a slotted wheel.

"So, Umberto, can I count on you?" the emir asked.

Nunarro felt an inner fumbling for the right choice. A mistake or miscalculation could not be part of this process. He needed to recognize the possibilities and consequences with his eyes closed. He also had to assess his limits and trust blowing up Barnes' mine had not compromised those limits. He settled the matter by relying on his instincts. There was nothing to reason and no proven formula. It was just a primordial choice that relied on the knowledge etched in his DNA. Nunarro regained his self-assuredness; finding it at the appropriate moment as he had expected.

"Of course you can count on me," he said with the conviction of a zealot.

"Good. I knew I could."

"Can we discuss the nature of the goods?" Nunarro asked.

"By all means."

The emirs manner became mysterious, possessed by a secret obsession that gathered around him, shifting him into a sort of trance.

"It is an ancient relic from a different world," he whispered. "It's from the land of the pharaohs, the true cradle of civilization."

"Is it an icon?"

"It's greater than an icon. It's magical. It will redefine the limits and perceptions of the human experience. Imagine living without dread; without loss of any kind. Imagine living in a world where time has no influence."

The emir paused to consider the full weight of possibilities and discoveries. He awakened to a new dawn, with pure light and endless horizons.

"Bliss," the emir continued. "Pure and total bliss. To be one with Allah...Immortal. No icon has that ability."

"What is it, a drug?" Nunarro asked.

"A drug? No, not a drug. But it can heal. It can cure the body. It can cure the mind and the soul. It can end suffering. It is the true source of alchemy. Desire for it can create war. Proper use of it can end war. It is all things. It is everything. It is the source of life. It is the blood of Allah."

The emir's passion raised the material to an exalted status. His desire to claim it bridged obsession and desire. His display held a specific energy, a desperation striving for possession and control. Nunarro found the emir's craving mystifying and out of character. The emir was a man who would not allow himself the overt display of emotion or the expression of his thoughts.

He even controlled the expressions of those around him. Nunarro recalled when the emir's simple gesture stopped his wife, Aaminah, from displaying gratitude to Nunarro after saving their daughter's life.

"I see this means a great deal to you," Nunarro observed.

"Yes," the emir said. "That's why I don't want it to be taken from me again. I'll give you anything you need to bring it back to me. Even an army."

"Can you tell me what I'll be looking for?"

"Yes…its white powder…*Pure* white…White and soft like talcum. I was told by Haddar bin Nasab, the soldiers put my powder into sacks. Crude sacks. Not the appropriate vessel for something so pure. Find this soldier, Harrington, and you'll find my sacks. Eternity is in those sacks, Umberto. Two thousand pounds of it."

"I will find Harrington. I will get you your white powder."

"I know you will. I trust you, Umberto. Let me know where you are at all times. I will also be sending twenty-five of my guards as back up. They will assist you only if you ask for them. Otherwise, you will not know they are there. They will have strict orders. You are in total command of this operation."

"That's good. Their support will be welcomed. May I suggest you send less. Twenty-five is too much. They'll attract attention."

"How many do you suggest?"

"Five of the best. That will be enough."

"Done. Once you have possession of the powder, bring it to Phoenix," the emir said, handing Nunarro an envelope. "That is the name and address of an import and export company that is at my disposal. There is a phone number there as well. Just say my name, and the man who answers the phone will know what to do. Once you bring the load to him, he will make arrangements to get it to me. From that point, there will be no problems with the export of the product. Understood?"

"Yes," Nunarro responded and put the envelope in his pocket.

"Good."

"I will be working with Orisi."

"I suspected that. He is already on my plane on his way here from Italy. There are two first class tickets in your hotel room. You and Orisi will be leaving tomorrow night. I've made all the arrangements. I hope you don't mind."

Nunarro felt as though his fate had been commandeered and held for ransom. He was an integral rook, carefully maneuvered and painstakingly aligned by a grand master to ensure total victory.

"No I don't mind," he responded.

"Good. My car will take you back to your hotel. But first, it will take you to the casino where you can claim your winnings."

NUNARRO held on as the launch returned him to the dock. Standing on the bow, he felt the soft, salty spray on his face. The engine's din added a melodic lament to an unsettling tune playing in his head. More than ever, he pondered the factors of chance and probability that competed for dominance in his life. He knew they were in a tight race. Standing by to observe as they converged to reveal his fate was his best option. Nunarro stepped out onto the dock and was escorted to the Bentley.

In the car, it was the familiar scent that first alerted Nunarro to her presence. It was the sweet, haunting smell opening a flood of memories. A torrent of bittersweet reminiscences forced themselves upon him, leaving him at the mercy of the past. Suddenly, he was confronted with the task of trying to find the missing time and the emotion lost to it. But first, he had to anchor himself to the present. He had to be certain it was Adilah seated in the dark corner of the Bentley. He had to know with every cell of his being the sad eyes watching him belonged to Adilah. But there was no way for him to confirm it was her. He couldn't move to touch her. He couldn't speak to call out her name. A numbing astonishment took hold of his senses.

The door closed behind him and the car rolled away from the dock. Nunarro had to take control of his thoughts. He had to separate dream from fantasy before he could adjust to his own presence in the car. He needed a moment to collect himself. Then, he would focus on Adilah; assuring himself of her proportions and depth. He needed something tangible, something like the touch of her flesh to demystify his bewilderment. Adilah helped whisk away his struggle. She simply called his name. In a breathless whisper the sound of her voice provided a connection to the failings and sweetness of the past. She took the initiative and led him from a collection of old regrets and faded joys to a place where they no longer mattered. The vast bend of time brought him back to the beginning.

"Adilah," he said, his mind slowly clearing.

"It's good to see you again, Umberto," she said.

Nunarro became aware of the deep, luxurious interior of the Bentley and the boundaries it created, encasing the uneasiness between Adilah and himself. The dark glass created a tight compartment hiding them from the driver. It encapsulated, encouraging the revival of an old intimacy.

"You knew I was here," he said.

"I've know where you've been since the last time we spoke."

Nunarro could still recall the look on her face. It was a look not much different from the one she showed now. The same hurt still evident in her eyes. A similar wisp of anger notched into her clenched jaw. An old line of sadness became edged by a new drop-shadow of hope and determination.

"You had me followed?" he asked, hoping she never abandoned him.

"I just knew about you," she said hiding all implications.

Nunarro did not draw any conclusions from her interest. He just let it be until he could better assess her intentions.

"So did your father," he said. "He knew about me and seemed to always know where I was. I suspect he watches me constantly."

"Not now," she said, offering Nunarro a reprieve from his suspicions.

"I'm not certain," Nunarro said searching for more assurances. "He has eyes everywhere."

"Don't project," Adilah's tone was dismissive.

"Why is he watching me?" Nunarro pressed.

"He watches you because he needs to know and understand your frailties."

"Why is that so important to him?"

"He has his reasons."

"All he has to do is ask."

"No, by watching you, he will discover things you don't know about yourself."

"He watches even to the extent he knows what I win in a casino?"

"Winning, as much as losing, tells a great deal about a person."

Nunarro felt raw, exposed to the elements of the silent observation that provided no flattery or sense of self-importance.

"Maybe so, but I feel like my life is not my own."

"Then you should have given it to me when I asked for it."

"At the time, your life was not your own."

"It wasn't mine because you took the choice from me."

A new shame took hold of Nunarro. Its grip was fierce, shutting off the flow of forgiveness to his soul. It was a constriction that kept him immobile, frozen with self-torment.

"Adilah, I didn't mean to. I saw your independence as strength. I admired that about you."

Adilah's lip quivered. She raised her head in a proud, dismissive gesture serving to look above the pain lying at her feet.

"You admired it, but not enough to build upon it and grasp the future," she whispered as tears filled her eyes.

"How can I make it up to you?" he asked hopelessly.

Adilah knew it was a fool's quest to bargain for the past. It was the same sort of folly to set a claim for the future. She tried to align herself with hope and be open to all possibilities.

"You can't. Not now," Adilah said.

"Why?" Nunarro asked, his hope turning to desperation.

"First, you have to retrieve my father's powder."

"Is that what this is all about, the powder?"

"Not for me," Adilah said, looking out the dark window at the muted lights of the passing cars.

"But it is for him. That's why he watches me," Nunarro said in a tone of protest.

"I told you why he watches you" Adilah said bringing her focus back to the dark compartment.

"To see if I'm worthy for his needs. I get it."

"Do you really? He has hundreds of mercenaries at his disposal to retrieve the powder," she said. "Men who are merciless. He wants someone who could show restraint. He doesn't want blood on the powder. That's why he wants you. When you are successful, it will be a different story."

"How so?"

"Because then he will be indebted to you."

"Indebted to me...over the powder? Why wasn't he indebted to me the day I saved your life?"

"Because then he had more to control. His pride and traditions were the most important things to him. In a cultural way, Aaminah was the reason behind his stronghold. Many factors justified his purpose, but none more than her. When Aaminah was well it was easy for him. He derived his strength from her. Now that she's ill..."

"Adilah," Nunarro interrupted. "Your mother is not well?"

"Not at all. The doctors say her time is short."

"What happened?"

"She has been ill for a while. She had been diagnosed shortly after you left. She has seen specialists all over the world. They tried everything. Now, there's nothing the doctors can do."

"I'm sorry," Nunarro said and touched Adilah's hand.

"Don't you see?" Adilah said. "That's why my father asked you to retrieve the powder. If you're successful, you've proven yourself. You redeemed yourself, and to some degree, you redeem my father. You saved his family.... Again. Because of that, he can let go of his traditions. It will be his turn to repay you. The money is just a token gesture of good will. His pact has already been made. He needs you to make it all happen. I know what my father wants. That's the easy part for me. I don't know what you want?"

Nunarro had not let go of Adilah's hand. He held it softly. The feel of her flesh assuaged all his doubts. He studied her face; the contour of her cheek and the line of her neck. Beneath her soft, delicate features was a noble strength that came from the core bloodline of Aaminah.

"Does not knowing what I want the hardest part for you?"

"It's the frightening part."

"Well let me ease your fears," he said. "I no longer want to take away your choices. I want your choices and mine to be the same. No separate paths. No time away from each other. Your father will have to find his own reason to re-examine his traditions. If I'm instrumental in that, fine. But he can keep the money. I don't want his token gesture."

Adilah wrapped her arms around Nunarro. He felt her soft skin and warm breath on his cheek. He turned to face her and kissed her. She folded herself into his arms, releasing her hurt. It was the way he always remembered her, giving freely of her passion without caution. He felt her full body rapture pass through him to the place where his emotions lay dormant. Nunarro held her tightly promising to keep her near. There were no more traditions to uphold. No more honorable goodbyes that served the wrong purposes.

"My father is convinced the powder will save Aaminah." Adilah finally said. "He believes in its power."

"Do you?"

Adilah thought for a moment, searching for what made sense to her. She didn't need to second guess the emir. Nor did she want to carry any guilt or regret for Aaminah.

"I believe whatever will unfold for Aaminah will have an indirect result to what you do. All good intentions could be brought to bear, but they must align with what is beyond our control."

"And this powder can help Aaminah when all the best doctors in the world can't?"

"We'll see."

Nunarro felt a demanding pull. In the past, he accepted less for himself at a time when he wanted more. He wanted something specific. He wanted control of his life. He suspected Adilah was offering it to him.

"What is the powder?" he asked trying to acquaint himself with the key to his freedom.

"My father calls it Allah's gold," Adilah said.

"Allah's gold? He told me it was from the time of the pharaohs. So it's ancient."

"Yes. It has its own history. For centuries, it had been buried, unknown and undiscovered. Now, it has come to life."

"Come to life for a man like your father to claim it for himself?"

"No. For men like my father to understand the history of the ancients. To be enlightened by it. It belongs to the world."

"But, your father will keep it for himself."

"Right now, it's not his to keep. He needs you to get it for him. What he does after will be a matter of prophecy."

"For the moment, prophecy has taken the powder away from your father."

"The prophecy is yet to be played out. You're not seeing all its workings. Bringing you back is a part of it. Prophecy has made you a priority."

Nunarro could not allow himself to think of all that was placed before him. It was too complex for him to understand. He accepted Adilah's perspective and began to suspect his decisions may have already been ordained well in advance of his acceptance. Nunarro nodded his head slowly. He looked down at Adilah's hand still cupped in his.

"The matter of priority forces me to leave tomorrow night," he said.

"Yes, I know. A lot is expected of you. I also know you expect a lot from yourself."

"What do you expect, Adilah?"

"I expect you to return. I expect you to keep your promise about my choices. Don't let me down."

Nunarro saw his reflection in the darkened glass. He nodded his head, acknowledging something within himself. It was an improbable image of a tapestry loomed from a single skein into a full circle bringing him back to Adilah. Within that tapestry, he found himself caught in the framework of ancient history, and the truth behind that history. It was there for him within his reach. Perhaps, it would be the final workings of the prophecy Adilah spoke of. A credible prophecy sanctioned by the gods to dispel prevailing myths and distortions.

Nunarro suspected a different reason the emir had chosen him to retrieve the powder. The emir had studied his frailties and believed they had no bearing on the quest. But more importantly, the emir needed an excuse for his personal enlightenment before he could offer enlightenment to his family and to the world. Once more, the stakes Nunarro gambled for climbed unbearably higher and squeezed with unrelenting pressure.

Adilah had decided she would no longer forfeit her choices, leaving them to someone else. She compiled them neatly, presenting them with the persuasion of her conviction. Her demeanor showed no hint of moderation. The excesses she called for were to ensure they would meet her singular need. She took command. Now, all she had to reckon with was the influence of fate which she had to trust.

She turned to Nunarro as if seeing him for the first time, but having known him for an eternity. She needed to address their familiarity with a strangeness that took hold of her. Adilah could not just rely on words because words could have a tendency to be misconstrued, and would then have no effect or power. She resorted to the look in her eyes to convey a message to Nunarro. The look wasn't just about something specific, it was about everything. In case the meaning proved difficult to comprehend, she drew Nunarro's face close to her own. She wanted no misunderstanding to fall into the space between them.

"Allah be with you," was all Adilah could say. She meant it to express a profound meaning, and hoped it would serve as a personal prayer of gratefulness for all the blessings she was open to receive.

ARIZONA

THE giant C-5 transport plane, arriving from Germany, touched down at Luke Air Force Base. The craft taxied on the runway to the blocking area assigned by the control tower. Captain Fred Abrams, Aircraft Commander, watched the ground crew block the C-5's wheels. The engines idled to a whisper then went silent, as the plane came to a full rest from its arduous journey.

Abrams held to procedures and, as commander, was the only person allowed off the plane before customs agents could review the cargo. The captain disembarked from the plane, and found the customs agents standing under the massive wing. He handed over the customs packet supplied by the load master. The military and civilian customs agents reviewed the packet taking half an hour to confirm and approve the contents of the C-5. As Bowles had suspected, the life rafts were part of the life support material and considered part of the plane. It did not raise suspicion.

After the customs agents finished, Abrams thanked the crew for their cooperation on the routine flight. The crew disembarked leaving Bowles with the responsibility to off-load the plane. Bowles did not think the trip and smooth landing were routine. The flight kept him dealing with an adrenaline rush of danger. The possibility the white powder could be discovered worried him. Although well hidden, a part of him felt insecure about its concealment.

The ground crew drove the forklifts onto the tarmac and began off-loading the plane according to Bowles' instructions. The crew worked efficiently and quickly. Several pallets of medical supplies Bowles ordered to the base hospital. A pallet of munitions went to Security Police. The damaged engine from an AH-1 Cobra helicopter and two Abrams tanks were directed to maintenance. A fleet of Humvees, with varying degrees of combat damage, rolled out from the belly of the C-5. Bowles ordered the vehicles sent to motor maintenance where they would be repaired and retro fitted with enhanced armor.

The last item Bowles had removed was the pallet of powder. He directed the forklift driver to leave the pallet on the edge of the tarmac. After the ground crew had completed their tasks and left, Bowles removed the life raft seal and cover from the pallet. He carried them back onto the C-5 then drove the forklift with the pallet containing the powder to his van, where he had parked before leaving for Iraq. After loading the pallet into the van, he drove the forklift back onto the tarmac where he called for a crew bus to take him to his squadron's quarters.

As the crew bus slowly passed the front of his squadron's duty station, Bowles spotted the engraved bronze plaque bearing the name of Lieutenant Frank Luke, Jr. Luke was the first aviator to win the Medal of Honor for his valor in World War I and became the airbase's namesake.

After checking out with the squadron commander, Bowles had the crew bus drive him back to his van. Once in the van, Bowles took several deep breaths and allowed the anxiety to subside. He drove from the air base to North Litchfield Road. After leaving the base, he wound his way onto route seventeen. The road stretched ahead, heading into a ball of setting sun. The road brought him to the Agua Fria National Monument. As a boy, Bowles would take trips to Agua Fria long before it was designated a monument. With his dad and uncle, he saw the many petroglyphs scattered across the Pueblo ruins. His dad knew the area well and told his son the petroglyphs had been drawn when several thousand Native Americans, known as the Perry Mesa Tradition, inhabited the region. The petroglyphs, depicting animals, geometric figures and abstract symbols, fascinated Bowles.

When the terrible sights and sounds of Iraq became overwhelming, Bowles would find comfort in reading the Bible and recalling the petroglyphs. He would force himself not to try and find comfort with thoughts of his wife and child. He knew, when he was no longer in the military; he would not want to associate his family with the horrors of Iraq.

Dusk began to settle on the Thumb Butte and the Granite Dells as low crimson clouds covered their peaks. Bowles thought the streaks of red and black clouds were a form of art; a medley of forms and patterns offering a different ending to each day.

Continuing on route seventeen, Bowles finally reached Prescott. As he drove by the familiar sights of his home town he felt a strange welcome. He expected the town to have changed. Since he was away, he was no longer the same. The homes, streets and stores were exactly as he remembered. Bowles welcomed the familiar streets and used them to recall the past. Old images were revived, used as a key to detoxify himself against the effects Iraq had exacted on him. Faces lost in time flashed before him. Teachers, who exposed him to the wonders of literature, held a special place for him. The books he read, introduced him to all places and times that helped him grow and formed his opinions and ideology.

He drove past the Pentecostal Church of Jesus, where he and Harrington attended Bible studies as boys. Atop the steeple was a large bronze cross. It stretched up and blended with the darkening sky. Bowles remembered how the sun reflected off the bronze cross. The reflection would cast a blinding starburst.

Bowles remembered the Pastor. It was easy recalling his short white hair, the creases of his face and the veins that showed on his neck when he preached. Pastor Bernard Dismas Ford had taught the Bible to the young Bowles with brimstone and passion. Ford's teachings were faith-based and absolute. They offered a searing perspective to the young Bowles whose inquisitive mind struggled with the contradictions.

He looked at the sacks behind him and was drawn into the saga of their contents. The white powder was unique and cast a spell over him. Its timeless pulse invaded his thoughts, redefining his logic and beliefs with a paradigm rooted in true antiquity. In some strange way, Bowles equated the sacks with the Bible studies of his youth. He had many questions regarding the Bible. Now, his probing mind needed to unlock the mystery of the powder.

"Pastor Ford," he whispered in a way that was personal and private.

The visions of Pastor Ford standing before a group of young, impressionable boys filled his mind. Echoes of the questions he had raised with the Pastor still registered in his mind.

"*If there is only one God,*" he heard his young voice call out from years ago. "*Why in Genesis does it says, 'Let us make man in our image after our likeness? What does that mean?*" asked the young and confused Bowles.

"*There is only one God. One Jesus,*" Bowles could still recall Ford's response and tone.

"*Then why the reference to us and our likeness?*" Bowles remembered asking.

"*Scripture refers to the Holy Trinity, Mister Bowles,*" the Pastor's voice echoed in his mind. "*Father, Son and Holy Spirit. That's the us and the our in your question.*"

"*Three in one?*" Bowles questioned. "*Like an equal-sided triangle?*"

"*Faith is not mathematics or geometry, Mister Bowles. Faith is more finite than any number and more acute than all given formulas and equations.*"

Bowles looked at the church envisioning Pastor Ford standing on the steps, calling out his response again as he drove by. Shouting to remind him that concepts, images, and faith in God did not change.

"*But how do I know what three in one really is?*" Bowles remembered asking the Pastor. The same question he would ask, if Ford had been standing on the steps of the church as he passed.

"You're not supposed to know. You need only to believe."

That response stayed with Bowles. Pastor Ford tried to make him understand that was the capstone to his search for meaning.

As Bowles stopped for a red light, he stared back at the church and the past it represented. He recalled himself as a boy walking through the doors, sitting in the third row from the front. Looking up he could see the Pastor, rigid, an improbable messiah baptized in fanatic certainty. Bowles saw himself through the gauze of memory, sitting with the Bible on his lap turning the page and coming upon something else that confused him.

"What about Genesis, three, five?" he heard himself ask.

"What about it, Mister Bowles?"

"Referring to man it says here: '...your eyes shall be open and ye shall be as gods.' That's confusing to me. But, then in the same book chapter three twenty-two, 'The Lord God said, 'behold the man has become one of us.' I thought there was only one God."

"There is only one God," Pastor Ford said, the vein in his neck protruding from intolerance and anger.

"Then why is Genesis referring to multiple gods?"

"The reference is not about multiple gods, Mister Bowles, How could it be? There is only one God. The reference challenges your faith."

His questions did not stay in the past. Over the years, they became part of him, nagging his perceptions and taxing his notions of certainty. Perhaps, Pastor Ford was right, it was all about belief.

Bowles did not see the light had changed. He remained lost, captured by distant voices. They came in streams of perfect recollection and instant clarity offering proof that everything that ever was, remains contained somewhere. A car horn blared behind him freeing him from the hold of old ghosts. Bowles let the past slide back into itself and began to rely on his ability to cope with the present. But as he drove away, the questions from his past lingered. The book that gave rise to his questions would be the same book he hoped would provide him with answers. The same held true for the contents of the sacks behind him. Their presence made him feel closer to the answers that had evaded him all his life. He wondered if an oddity of nature, in the form of white powder, would ever provide him with the clarification and enlightenment to the mysteries of Genesis and the past. He hoped the sacks offered lessons and understandings beyond the flawed explanations given to him many years ago by Pastor Bernard Dismas Ford.

Flashing lights pulsated in the rear view mirror distracting Bowles from his thoughts. His thoughts about Scripture and the sacks shifted instantly to the flashing lights. Bowles became alert and cautious. A van pulled along side him. Bowles recognized Hector Solis and Mitchell Harrington. Solis extended his hand out the window and motioned for Bowles to follow. As Harrington drove through town, Bowles followed. Both headed south in the direction of the Sandretto Hills storage facility.

The storage complex was made up of rows of low buildings, each containing up to ten storage units. Harrington drove to the last row and stopped next to one of the storage bays. Bowles parked next to Harrington and stepped from his van.

"Tommy, you made it," Harrington said, punching Bowles lightly on the shoulder and patting him hard on the back. "How did it go?"

"Smooth. No problems at all," Bowles responded.

"Got through customs?"

"Routine search. When I get back to Iraq, I'll reload the raft and no one will know."

"Good. Real good. You remember Hector Solis?"

"Sure I do," Bowles said, shaking hands with Solis.

"You guys okay? No trouble with any more Iraqi Police?"

"None," Harrington said.

"Do you think we're done with them?"

"I don't know. We still should be very cautious."

"You can bet somebody is gonna come lookin' for this stuff," Solis said.

"That's why we have to be careful; anticipate what's lurking around corners," Harrington replied.

"It's just going to be you two," Bowles said. "I'm deploying back to Iraq in one week. That's the end of my crew rest. What about your group? Dobson and Heywood?"

"They'll be out in a few months, if they don't get stop-lossed."

"Do you have any other backup until then?"

"No. That's why we have to be very careful. Let me see the stuff," Harrington said, barely containing his excitement.

They walked to the back of Bowles' van. He pulled hard and opened both doors. Harrington looked in and paused before touching one of the sacks. The pile of sacks seemed sacred and iconic, alive with a captivating spirit. He felt it was the breath of God passing purely through time and distance, ultimately stopping before him.

"Oh, I can't believe this," Harrington said quietly, as though whispering a prayer. "I can't believe this."

He could not overcome the urge to open one of the sacks. Reaching in, he pulled a sack toward him and loosened the drawstring. The sight of the white powder drew him in, causing his breathing to change and his pulse to rise. Its silent, compressed power bore down on him, making him understand the reasons armies marched into battle and extinct civilizations carved their legacies in stone. He felt overcome with glory and caught up in a surge that was exciting and addictive. The illumination, offered by the powder, was like a new dawn and a different light, that made his legs go weak. The quake he felt in the ground was finally about to give up its long-held secrets. He suddenly felt a true ownership of the powder that could yield unbelievable possibilities.

"Do you believe we have this?" Bowles asked.

"No," Harrington said, mesmerized by the lure of the powder. "No, I can't."

"Looks ta me you guys already know what that stuff is," Solis observed. "You got the look of fame an' fortune right there all over your faces."

"Solis, some day you'll understand our joy," Harrington said.

"Sorry, Deuce, I'm celebratin' comin' away from Iraq and Germany alive. Right now that's joy enough for me. I could see that stuff's got you wrapped up good an' tight. I hope it don't turn in on ya."

"We'll see, Solis," Harrington said. "We'll see."

"Don't jinx it, Solis," Bowles said.

"Makes no difference what I do," Solis responded. "Seems ta me that stuff's got a mind of its own. It ain't heroin, but it's got you addicted. Trust me, man; anything that's got control of you; got a mind. If it don't got a mind, then it's got a soul. And I know you can't kill a soul."

"We don't want to kill it, Solis," Harrington responded.

"I know you don't. But if you can't kill it, you can't own it. Alls you can do is sell it. That's why I'm along. You need ta find that emir who wants ta pay twenty million. Take the money an' run, man. That's what I say, Deuce."

"I assume you rented this storage?" Bowles asked pointing to the garage door and ignoring Solis.

"Actually, I rented the first three spots. I didn't want somebody to be on the other side of me," Harrington said.

"What's in there?" Bowles asked nodding toward the storage space.

"My old flat bed truck. I mounted a steel construction case for the powder. I can transport it quickly," Harrington said.

"You think this place is safe?" Bowles asked.

"Not safe enough for me," Solis said. "The Iraqi guys thought they had a safe place and look how that turned out."

"I also rented space in six other locations. If need be, I'll separate the load or move it around." Harrington said.

"Are the locations traceable to you?"

"No."

"What do we do about testing the powder?" Bowles asked.

"That's the scary part. There's no way around this. We've got to expose the powder. That's the only way we're really going to know if this is the Flinders Petrie find. Once we bring it to a lab, the powder and all of us are exposed. Who knows what will come down?"

"You can be sure it's going to be a fire storm," Bowles said.

"I'm sure. That's the corner we've got to be able to see around."

"Am I missin' somethin' here," Solis said. "I thought the guys that got themselves killed in Germany proved this stuff is what you think it is," Solis said. "Why not have a museum curator get it tested. You stay out of it. This way you'll be real low key," Solis concluded.

"That's a good idea. I didn't think about that" Harrington said.

"Solis is right, Mitchell," Bowles said. "We can be in the background. In addition to showing it around to museums, we can go to a university that specializes in Egyptology. Maybe an anthropological organization could be the way to go."

"Wait a minute. What am I thinking about?" Harrington said startling himself. "Analisa Scotti."

"Who's she?" Bowles asked.

"Analisa, she was in my college program at the University of Arizona She's from Italy. We dated for a while. She's an Associate Professor of Anthropology. An adjunct at U.A. in Tucson. I studied with her. We shared research interests in Paleolithic archeology and human evolution. Get this…she also did research in social and ecological contexts for evolutionary change in hominid technologies. She was big on sociocultural anthropology and her geographic interest was Africa."

"Then she's got to know about Petrie's work in Egypt," Bowles commented.

"I don't know. That conversation never came up between us. But, I'd be hard pressed to think she doesn't know about him."

"Yes, it wouldn't make sense not knowing about Petrie. Did she do a lot of lab work or was she primarily field oriented?"

"Both. She did it all."

"Great. If she's familiar with the principles of lab work, she could be exactly who we're looking for. She could run the tests."

"Hold on, Tom. I'll have to think about this."

"What's to think about?" Bowles questioned.

"I'm not sure I want to bring her into this."

"Why?"

"Well, we don't want to draw exposure, and I certainly don't want to put her out there. Last I heard, she was in Chad doing archaeological research work."

"Call her. See if she's back. Tell her what we have and let her decide if it's something she wants to get involved in. If not, she may give us another direction."

"I don't know. I'm not sure I want to contact her," Harrington persisted.

"Listen, Mitch, no matter what we do we're going to draw attention. That's a fact we can't get around. We have to know for sure what we have here. Let's just go for it."

"Tommy, you know if she's familiar with Petrie's work and suspects, as we do, this is a part of his discovery that has been lost for over a century, she'll jump at this. I don't want her reacting out of scientific curiosity and lose sight of any potential danger."

"Mitch, I don't know what she'll do. And, I certainly don't want to expose her to any danger. Getting involved will be her call. But, if this is part of the Petrie find, and you don't tell her you have it, then what?"

"It's not as though we're still involved. We were really close but went our own ways because of Iraq and her work."

"Mitch, I don't mean to make a case for calling her, but this is part of her work. This could open a whole new vista for her."

"That's another thing. If this proves out to be the Petrie discovery, if she supports the hypothesis of its origins, she could find herself in a battle over the status quo of science, religion and academia. Analisa could find herself in the middle of a controversy that could overwhelm her."

"But there will be segments of the scientific community that will welcome this discovery. Especially, if it disproves all myths. But, any anthropologist would love the chance to be on the forefront of this."

Harrington didn't move. He stood there letting Bowles' words hit him hard opening him to a fundamental reality. A strange temptation had turned into some transparent thing his excuses and concerns could not hide behind. Harrington felt an odd sorrow for something unrecognizable and nonspecific. It left him groping to understand his inner turmoil.

"Was it a bad break up?" Bowles continued.

"No. We still care for each other. We're still friends. We talked and texted while I was in Iraq. The messages were mildly personal but guarded."

"I understand given the uncertainty of war. But listen, Mitch, I see your point about not getting Analisa involved in this. If you don't want to contact her, I'm sure there's another way. We'll find it."

"Sure, there's another way," Solis said. "You could just tell me what the stuff is, and I'll go back home ta Gun Hill Road, and sell it on the street. I know somethin' about fencin' swag."

"I bet you can, Solis," Harrington said. "But this is a little different. I'm not so sure your contacts on Gun Hill Road will know what to do with it."

"Trust me, Deuce, if you ever told me what this stuff was, I'd find a buyer."

Many voices ran through Harrington's head, but he listened to only one. It spoke of a miracle journey he hoped would prove all the things he believed in, and disprove all things that were lies. The lone voice spoke to his intellect and spirit. He wanted it to ultimately cry out and correct centuries of misperceptions. In the end, all he could hope for was to hear the voice speak in the universal language of truth.

"I'm sure you can, Hector," Harrington said after a brief deliberation. "But, I'll call Analisa. I want to see her as soon as possible. I guess I miss her. I would like to get back with her."

"Go see her, Deuce. You need a little romance after Iraq," Solis said.

"You're coming with me, Hector. Before we go, Tommy, I'll ask my sister to make you an extra set of keys for all the storage spaces I rented and for the truck. I want everyone involved to have their own set of keys. Swing by to get the keys from Laura before you leave. I'll go see Analisa. If she's able to do the testing, I'll text you the results."

"Do you think it's safe to be so far away from the powder?" Bowles asked. "The University is a long drive."

"It should be okay. But, I'm not taking anything for granted. That's why I want to go see Analisa right away. The sooner I get back here, the better. Just don't forget to come by and get the keys from my sister."

"I won't."

"Hopefully, Analisa will be able to do the testing quickly. Then, we'll know if we have a credible find here."

Harrington tied the sack and looked around the area. The sun had long set behind the peak of Mt. Title. Thunder sounded in the distance and a flash of lightening cracked the dark, western sky. Harrington removed the key to the storage door from his pocket and looked up at the angry sky. A storm was coming, off the mountain peak and across the plains. It was forming fast and headed his way.

"Come on, let's put these sacks away," was all he said.

UMERTO Nunarro figured many things were firmly anchored in the imbalance of power. There were no limits to its tyrannical grip and its domain was far reaching. Power was a force folded in upon itself, until it created an untenable illusion. It had no conscience, gobbling up reason, defiling established law and undoing sanctified paradigms. There was no true measure to the rule of power. It was obsessed with its own single minded id, ignoring any containment or governance. Yet, in spite of itself, it was a falsehood that caused Nunarro not to trust.

He questioned if he should rely solely on his own strength, backed by the emir's small band to retrieve the powder. He hoped the power he and the emir's group produced would discourage any challenge from Harrington. Deception, guile or stealth would be other resources Nunarro could rely upon. He knew he had choices he could draw upon and plans he could implement. But he knew remaining spontaneous would be his best option.

Finding Harrington became a simple matter of researching the state's directory. There were only three listings with his exact name. He called all three, pretending to be conducting a survey for an Undersecretary of the Veterans Administration. He was able to locate the right Mitchell Harrington. He claimed the purpose of the survey was to provide information that would be incorporated into annual VA projections of enrollment, utilization and expenditures as well as high level budget and policy analyses. Harrington was not suspicious of the call. He admitted he had recently been discharged from the military, but declined to partake in the survey.

Nunarro tore up the printed survey he had downloaded from the Internet. Along with Mario Orisi, he checked into the High Plains Motel, several miles from Harrington's home. Nunarro and Orisi each rented cars; determining different cars would draw less suspicion should they have to depend on surveillance of Harrington. He also made contact with Ubaid, the leader of the band of mercenaries, the emir had hired. Nunarro arranged to meet Ubaid in the lobby of the High Plains Motel.

The lobby of the motel was rustic with terra cotta tile floors and a high cathedral ceiling of chaparral pine. Several tables and chairs of Arizona white oak were placed around the lobby. Hanging in the center of the Entrada sandstone fireplace was a large oil painting of a Native American hunting party. A young man was registering at the front desk, while the woman with him retrieved brochures from a display and a local newspaper from the stand. Nunarro looked around the lobby. He waited for the couple to enter the elevator before he and Orisi approached Ubaid, who was seated in front of the fireplace. Nunarro sat down across from Ubaid, and introduced himself and Orisi. Ubaid acknowledged them with a nod of his head, remaining silent and stoic. His dark eyes were piercing and ferocious. A crimson scar on his left eyebrow continued down to his cheek. Its appearance was like a permanent tear drop. Ubaid's legs were stretched out, his hands rested on his knees. He was tall with a long reach. The inexpensive grey suit was tight, accentuating the thick muscles of his arms and legs. He wore a white shirt, buttoned tightly at the neck. Ubaid's features were strong and pronounced, as if chiseled from the same stone used for the fireplace.

Nunarro avoided concentrating on Ubaid's scar. He preferred to pay attention to his demeanor. While Ubaid tried to conceal much about his nature, he still allowed Nunarro to see a great deal about him. When he spoke, his tone was impatient, yet controlled. Nunarro recognized an underlying annoyance probably from an early history of abuse, making him vengeful and intolerant. Over the years, he mastered the art of control and intimidation. Whatever the early abuses, Ubaid appeared to have grown to ensure they would never be repeated.

Ubaid's silence, brief conversation, and indifference provided much insight. Nunarro sensed Ubaid's philosophy was mostly based in doom, and possessed a deep rooted scorn for forgiveness and mercy. Ubaid appeared friendless, yet he had to be trustworthy, or the emir would never have chosen him for the operation.

There appeared to be less calculation and caution in Ubaid's nature and more impulse and cunning. But, what truly disturbed Nunarro about Ubaid was he gave no indication he was constrained by the thought of sin or burdened by any act of retribution. Ubaid seemed programmed for the tasks of destruction. In short, Ubaid was a robotic blend of soulless apathy with brutal tendencies.

"Here's Harrington's address," Nunarro said handing Ubaid a slip of paper. "We need to follow him. I don't suspect he has the product in his house. But, I don't think it's far. He'll lead us to it, I'm sure. When he does, I'll find a way to take it. I don't want any alternate plan activated before then."

"Do it your way," Ubaid said. "If it doesn't work, I'm taking Harrington. He'll give me what I want."

There was a cold declaration to Ubaid's words. He offered no pretense for his boldness. He was giving notice. He made it clear, violence and evil were well within his capabilities and experience.

"We shouldn't underestimate this man. We saw what he was capable of with the incident in Germany."

"I don't care about Germany," Ubaid said. "I'm the one who should not be underestimated."

"We know he's not alone. Other soldiers were with him. We need to know what we're up against. I want to know the size of his group."

"When you find out, tell me. If his group is too much for you, I'll handle it."

Ubaid used the command of his words to draw a clear picture of his position. There was no shading or potential misconception in his language and tone. His intention was brutally formed and presented a riveting chill.

"It'll be best if we don't confront him," Nunarro said. "There's more to be gained if we just take it away from him without a struggle. I don't want to get the attention of the local sheriff. Then we'll have a second fight to deal with. We still have to take the product out of the country."

"I don't see a problem at all."

"That could be a mistake. We should anticipate and have a response."

"The mistake is being too careful," Ubaid said. "It makes your enemy stronger. You patronize your enemy; you make your own downfall."

"I do not patronize my enemy. I only recognize what I need to do to defeat him."

"Crushing him completely is the way to defeat him."

"The objective is to retrieve the powder. That's the only objective. There are different ways to get it done."

"Don't complicate the operation. There's no complexity to confrontation. It comes down to might and the first strike. I think Harrington knows that. That's why he was successful in Germany."

"It's because of what happened in Germany he may be expecting an assault. He's military and no stranger to combat. Being a soldier in Iraq had to teach him something about warfare."

"When he was in Iraq, he was conditioned to warfare. He had to maintain a military perspective to stay alive. Now that he's home, it's something he wants to put behind him. That makes him weaker."

"How do you know? He still has to protect the powder. His military instincts will show him how. That's why strategy may serve us well here."

"Then choose your strategy. But, it better be the best strategy. My life and the lives of my men are involved."

"We need to work together on this," Nunarro said.

"The emir has my word on that. But, I have a responsibility to myself and my men. Don't put me in a position where I have to choose. And, don't make me go against my word."

Nunarro determined in spite of Ubaid's potential for recklessness, there was a level of trust about him. He was predictable to the extent he would do anything to retrieve the powder.

"I won't," Nunarro said.

"Good. We understand each other," Ubaid said.

"Tell me," Nunarro said, "what do you know about the powder?"

"Whatever the powder is; has no importance to me. My only concern is to make sure it all goes back to the emir."

"Do you think I have a different objective?"

"If you don't, why bring the matter up?"

It was clear Ubaid was assessing Nunarro, looking for flaws and something that could prompt his retreat. Ubaid's scrutiny was intense. The two men sat facing each other, joined through common loyalty, but searching for a logic and reason to be adversaries.

There was a crude upheaval to Ubaid's perspective that connected to a vile conviction. When Nunarro witnessed Ubaid roll his hands into tight fists, suspecting it was a reflex triggered by paranoia, he realized the emir's emissary shared an overt alliance to everything hostile and anything criminal. Nunarro knew the only way he could contain Ubaid was to maintain his own command and purpose. Should he falter, show any sign of doubt or weakness, Ubaid would overrun him with the total support of the emir.

The meeting was brief, but for Nunarro it proved to be a way to understand Ubaid's willful limits. Nunarro knew those limits were far reaching. They could be exploited and useful. Ubaid easily grasped that a struggle was taking place. Its narrative set up temporary boundaries, but would not deter an all out conflict.

Nunarro told Ubaid to have his group rent rooms in different hotels in the area. An annoyed look on Ubaid's face conveyed such a minor point had not been overlooked. His look also persuaded Nunarro to refrain from suggesting they not indulge in alcohol and women. At the conclusion of the meeting, Ubaid rose and left the lobby without saying a word.

Nunarro and Orisi sat back in their chairs and watched Ubaid walk through the automatic glass doors, disappearing into the night. They were gripped in the wake of an awkward silence. Both men needed a moment to collect themselves and breathe in air not tainted by the subtle hint of confrontation. Nunarro reluctantly understood the balance between Ubaid's value and threat. Being so dedicated to the emir made him useful, being so angry made him volatile. Even poisoned air can be useful if pointed in the proper direction.

He had little choice but to welcome the force the emir had assembled. With them in place, there was nothing for Nunarro to consider other than follow Harrington. In a sense, Ubaid was right. There was little complexity in confrontation.

There were many reasons Nunarro knew he could not fail in retrieving the white powder for the emir. After meeting with Ubaid, he realized one more reason. One that required his best preparation. His success was the only thing that would keep Mitchell Harrington alive.

AGENT Andrew Cummings sat at his desk in the Phoenix branch office of Homeland Security. It was midday. The sun shone through the office window facing Bolin Memorial Park. He looked out his window and saw the flag mast and anchor of the USS Arizona, the Vietnam War Memorial and the Capitol building with its tall, sculptured wind vane. Showing no interest in the park, Cummings sat back in his swivel chair, and looked at the bookcase beside him. Nestled between the bookcase and the window was a blue flag trimmed with gold piping and tassels bearing the Homeland Security insignia. On the opposite side of the office, was an American flag, given to him by his uncle, a congressional district leader. The flag, sewn from imported silk from Kanchipuram, India, was in recognition for completing his honors fellowship, and attaining a permanent position within the department.

Cummings stared blankly beyond the bookcase. He felt a nagging rhythm permeating his body, miring him in despondency and distress. Recalling the incident in the desert with Pietro Segretti gave him root cause for his irritation.

His jacket was carelessly draped over the back of the chair. His tie was loose and shirt unbuttoned at the neck. Cummings needed to feel unfettered by the boundaries of his job. But, he knew he couldn't move to far beyond the protocols the flags around him brought to mind.

He turned from the bookcase and looked at the scrapes on his hands. He could not remember feeling the trauma during his altercation with Segretti. As he thought about it, he remembered not feeling any pain in the struggle. The pain that followed was delayed. Now, aches were everywhere in his body. Two days after the incident, the gash to his inner lip still oozed. He could taste blood whenever he ate. But, more disturbing than the physical pain was the injury to his pride and ego. His sense of defeat and abuse was overwhelming, and gnawed at him constantly. It was an open wound where all his hatred and need for revenge gathered. He internalized his anger, feeling it as something alive and consuming. It pressed in on his lungs, causing him to breathe deeply at the recollection of Segretti's face. The preoccupation with reprisal contorted his inner fascia and devoured his aura. In order to relieve the physical and emotional discomfort, he made a reckoning on any level to be his quest. The scope of the department would help him find and apprehend Segretti. The authority of his office would ensure him retribution. Cummings could not move away from his obsession. It allowed him to remain confrontational. He was convinced he would be the final arbiter of Segretti's fate.

Cummings turned in his chair to face his computer. He accepted this spell of obsession, but needed to hide it within the stack of folders on his desk. He clicked the mouse and the screen image changed to his personal e-mail. Cummings saw he had forty seven messages. As he moved the cursor down the list, he noticed more than half of them were from Branch Director, Henrietta Dell. Looking at the earliest date of the e-mails, he realized a response was overdue.

He had worked under Dell for three years and always found her competent, efficient and extremely professional. Failure to respond to her messages would be unacceptable. Cummings was very familiar with Dell's career. Her rapid promotions were a matter of record. He was very aware how they paralleled his career. Before he had enrolled in the Honors Fellowship Program, Dell had been serving as co-director of Arizona's Department of Liquor Licenses and Control. When he was midway through the Fellowship Program, Dell was promoted and appointed to Arizona's Counter Terrorism Information and Oversight Committee. She stayed in the position until just two months before he received his fellowship. It was at this time, Dell was appointed to Homeland Security and Border Safety on a local and national level. She also became co-chairperson of the Border Security Committee of the National Governors Association's Homeland Security Advisors Council. In addition, she became the co-chairperson of the Arizona's Emergency Preparedness Oversight Council.

Cummings respected her achievements and work. Not showing her professional courteously was something he had to rectify. He positioned the cursor on her earliest message and clicked on it. Before the message opened, there was a knock at the door. Henrietta Dell leaned into his office and declared: "Anybody home?" Cummings looked up as Henrietta entered.

"Yes," Cummings said. "Come in, please. I was just going through my e-mails and getting to yours. Sorry, I didn't get to them sooner."

"Quite alright. I know you've been out of the office recently on assignment and have had some difficulty because of it."

"That's no excuse. I should have gotten to your messages sooner."

Dell moved into the office carrying three folders. She sat in one of the two chairs in front of Cummings' desk. Dressed in a dark blue suit with a pink silk blouse, Dell looked like a runway model for the Senior Executive Branch. A former track star, Dell had let the flesh of her figure fill out to compliment her age. She felt it was time to trade the gaunt look of an athlete for the curvy trend of a successful executive. Dell found a natural way to keep her professionalism and womanhood separate, and for each to have a point of reference. There was a certain sensuality to her authority and poise she could not avoid, but did not acknowledge.

Her chestnut hair, with increasing grey, hung just past her neck, and a whisper above her shoulders. It was thick and layered, pushed back as if she styled it by running her fingers meticulously through it. She wore a thin gold loop chain around her neck and one on her wrist, accentuating her gold watch. The only ring she wore was a simple band with a delicate, antique scroll. The ring had been given to her by her grandmother just before she died. Plain and simple, the ring could create an intricate and insightful story. In the telling, it would say a great deal about Henrietta.

The antique ring originally belonged to Henrietta's great-grandmother; given to her by her young husband before he went to fight in the Battle of Vicksburg. After a warm, sunny day in June had passed, and the moon shown down on the mist-covered bucolic hills of Warren County, Mississippi, the ring was all Henrietta's great-grandmother had left of the young soldier. On that day, Henrietta's great-grandmother wrote in her diary that death had a life of its own. Her hand written lament concluded that the principles of conflict formed a legacy of consequences and anguish. She further described that war voraciously fed on rage and grief, lustfully giving birth to orphans and widows.

When she was old enough, the ring went to Henrietta's grandmother. The ring became a bittersweet heirloom, accumulating memories and legend. Henrietta's grandmother grew up never knowing her father. The stories she heard of him always came in remorseful rhyme and with a fair amount of nostalgic lore. Barely a teen ager, Henrietta's grandmother met a soldier in the 7th Calvary, and fell in love with his stout bravery. Henrietta's great-grandmother and grandmother were drawn to military men. With its deceptive history, the attraction of imposing uniforms, colorful ribbons, shiny medals, and the possessive nature of all sorts of weapons, the military could attract an ample supply of willing soldiers.

Henrietta had once seen a creased and faded sepia tintype of her grandfather. He was dressed in his regimental uniform. Brass buttons were displayed down the front of his jacket. A long saber was strapped to his waist. Stars were affixed on the epaulets, covering both shoulders. He was young and stood straight, with one hand on the back of an empty brocade chair; the other holding his hat and long white gloves.

Henrietta's grandmother spent a summer on a Dakota farm with the photogenic soldier. They were caught in the natural spree of waving wheat fields and late day rains. The two swam naked in a nearby lake, enjoying their meek freedom from guilt. Henrietta's grandmother removed the ring from her finger and tied it to a thin hemp cord. She placed the cord over the soldier's neck and the ring hung just above his heart.

On a day in December 1890, shortly after Christmas, the young soldier was in South Dakota. Following an incident during a disarmament inspection at a Lakota Sioux encampment near Wounded Knee Creek, eighty-nine Sioux were killed. The army casualties were numbered at twenty-five. It took three weeks before Henrietta's grandmother received a tattered box wrapped with soiled paper and a crude rope. In the box was a brass button, embossed with the image of an eagle from his uniform, an epaulet with stars and the scroll ring. A small blue thread hung from the button. A burn mark singed the end of the torn epaulet. The stars were stained, with what Henrietta's grandmother thought was blood. Tiny bits of dirt lodged in the scrollwork, hallowed earth from a far away place where the soldier fell and died.

Henrietta's grandmother put the ring in a cedar box, along with the stained brass button and the singed epaulet. She locked the box, and hid it in a cedar chest, forcing herself to come to terms with the complicated betrayal the concealment represented. It was only on the day she passed the ring along to Henrietta, that she opened the box. The unlocking was like a ritual; a personal unveiling. It came with harsh memories and a hopeful legacy. Her wrinkled and spotted hands shook as she removed the articles from the box. The old woman noticed the singe on the epaulet had faded and the brass button had tarnished.

"*These were from his uniform,*" Henrietta's grandmother had said softly. "*They were on him the day he died.*"

She gently picked up the ring, noticing particles of dirt still remained in the scrollwork. With no other reference, she recalled her husband as youthful on the day she gave him the ring. It was a testimony that time had passed, but somehow remained still.

"*I gave him this ring,*" she said. "*It was a promise we were to love forever.*" the old woman continued, as a sad smile crossed her face.

Henrietta held the articles in her hand for a long while. She felt their history, and the strong force still present. She understood how people remained connected through time and sorrow. She carefully replaced the button and epaulet back in the box. When the dirt was removed from within the scrollwork, she put each grain in a small glass tube and kept it in a case on her desk. Her grandmother did not pass the ring along to Henrietta's mother. She believed, by skipping a generation, the curse would fade away.

Henrietta wore no other rings. Nor did she wear an inscribed bracelet or a locket bearing a loved one's photo. Henrietta cherished the ring, and knew its journey would end with her. The ring would remain on her finger for eternity as she had no one else to pass it onto. In a way, Henrietta's grandmother was right. There was no modern soldier to receive the ring along with vows of love; leaving no potential for grief. But with no heir for Henrietta to bequeath the ring, that remained a curse of a different kind.

Henrietta noticed the unruly appearance of Cummings' tie, and the haphazard manner his jacket was slung over the chair. To Henrietta, they were signs of his troubling thoughts.

"Are you okay, Andrew?" Henrietta asked.

"Yes. Why do you ask?"

"No lingering effects from your altercation with Segretti?"

"I still feel some pain in my face. My ribs hurt a bit, but that's it."

The glint in Henrietta's light blue eyes softened as she looked at the bruises on Cummings' face.

"Anything beyond that?"

"No."

"What about your mind?" Henrietta's tone was probing and direct. "I know sometimes an altercation could have a psychological affect."

"Listen, if you're asking me if I'm still pissed off I let him get the better of me, the answer is yes. But, I don't think I need to get an evaluation regarding my state of mind. I wasn't as badly beaten as Agent Manning."

"Sometimes the extent of injury does not equate with the level of mental distress."

"I know, but I can deal with it."

"Are you sure? Everything I see about you tells me otherwise."

"Why, because I didn't answer your e-mails promptly enough?"

"That's one thing."

"What else?" Cummings responded. His tone was dismissive and almost condescending.

"That, right there," Henrietta observed. "You're angry, defensive."

"I told you, I'm still a bit pissed. I don't like the idea of being beaten up. I'll get over it. When I do I'll lose the attitude."

"You have too. I don't want your anger to interfere with your judgment. Quite frankly, your attitude is contrary to your psychological profile. Is there anything else bothering you? Something you would like to talk about?"

"Like what?"

"I don't know. Something personal you can't work through?"

"No. Everything's alright, Henrietta. I just need a little more distance from the incident with Segretti." Cummings said, making an immediate adjustment to his behavior.

"Good. I read your report regarding the events of that evening. It coincides with Agent Manning's account. This leads us to the issue of Pietro Segretti and the explosion in Alex Barnes' mine. While you uncovered no direct evidence linking Segretti to the explosion, it is your belief he holds some complicity to the incident?"

"Yes, I do."

"In the report, you indicate Segretti met with Barnes to negotiate the purchase of gold Barnes had mined."

"That's true."

"What I don't understand is why would Segretti approach Barnes with a potential deal, bring exposure to himself, and then destroy the mine containing the product Segretti wants to purchase. With the extent of destruction to the mine, the product would be buried for a long time. That defies logic."

"Let me pose a question. Why did Segretti choose to fight with me and Manning, and then go into hiding?"

"Segretti is not in hiding. Well, not here anyway. He flew out of Sky Harbor Airport on a private Saudi plane the next day. He's in Italy now."

"He did?" Cummings responded, letting a hint of surprise and anger show.

"Yes, he did."

"How did he pull that off?"

"Obviously, he knows how the system works. He knows the people who make it work."

"I'll be damned," Cummings said his tone angry.

"Why did he fight with you and Agent Manning?"

"What do you mean?"

"Did he fight because he perceived a threat from you?"

"Are you making excuses for Segretti?"

"I just want to get a better understanding to all this."

"If Segretti felt threatened then maybe he was guilty of something. I met him in the airport earlier before the incident in the desert."

"Yes, I know. I understand there were some tense moments."

"So are you suggesting our first meeting was the cause of the threat he felt?"

"I'm not suggesting anything. I just want to understand."

Henrietta allowed her instincts to feed her suspicions. She was clever enough to conceal it. She also knew Cummings was limited by what had been left unresolved with Segretti. It was for him to work out.

"I think it best if we move away from this," Henrietta continued.

"Agent Cummings, do you know anything about the gold Segretti wanted to purchase from Barnes?"

"No. What about it?"

"It's called monoatomic gold. It's special and rare. It's gold in its purest form. This form of gold, in abundance, is worth the wealth of a realm. That's if it can be found or mined. The earth does not yield it up easily, nor is it found in great quantities. So, if Segretti came to this country to purchase it, and by all accounts Barnes could only muster a small quantity, it seems illogical for him to destroy the potential source."

"So who would want to destroy a mine that produces monoatomic gold?"

"Now, that's just part of the question. The other part is *why* would someone want to destroy a mine that produces monoatomic gold. Certainly, Segretti is not likely to destroy the mine. That's a given. The question is why would he want to buy the gold? Let's examine that. He's an international arms dealer. We have to assume he has a buyer of enormous wealth and sophistication who can utilize the gold for all manner of armament. Let's not forget, he flew away from here on a private Saudi plane. The connection could easily be made Segretti is the middle man for the Saudis."

"How can the gold be used for armament?"

"In unimaginable ways," Henrietta said. "Ways that defy comprehension."

Cummings sat back. He felt rejected by the realization some of the world's secrets were kept from him. Henrietta seemed to have already made discoveries that were enlightening and tormenting.

"So, how does Segretti fit into the explosion?" Cummings asked with fermenting rejection.

"I don't believe he does. I believe it was just a matter of coincidence. He happened to be here while a plot hatched around him."

Cummings observed Henrietta and recognized her perceptions.

"So, maybe someone didn't want Segretti to get hold of the gold," Cummings said. "Or maybe it was a plot to prevent the Saudis from obtaining it too."

"That's a possibility."

"But, you don't think so."

"No, I don't."

"So, what is it you're not telling me?" he asked.

Henrietta saw clearly that Cummings felt mauled by bureaucracy and exclusion.

"We had a very interesting surveillance that came across our database," she informed. "Two Italian nationals were in Arizona at the time of the explosion. Mario Orisi and Umberto Nunarro. It's important to know they stayed at the Wayfarer Inn in Kingman, which is in close proximity to the Barnes mine. Here's a little history on Orisi," Henrietta continued, opening one of the folders she held.

"Orisi was a member of the Italian army serving as part of a NATO force in Afghanistan," she read from the folder. "For his services, he was awarded the military order of Italy in the Knight class. The report goes into detail regarding the circumstances surrounding the award. But for now, I'll pass over them. You can familiarize yourself with them later."

Henrietta flipped a page and continued. "After his discharge from NATO, he joined the Carabinieri. He was on assignment in Vicenza under the Sea Island Conference where he received a career ending injury. Again, there's greater detail to the injury. It's unimportant for the purposes of this conversation. There is not much more information about him after his discharge from the Carabinieri. We are still inquiring about him. But, what is known, is his association with Umberto Nunarro," Henrietta said. She then closed one folder and opened the other.

"Umberto Nunarro is even more interesting," Henrietta began reading from the second folder. "He was a demolition engineer, working in Dubai on the construction of the Central Library. He abruptly left the position he held in Dubai. No other information is available on him."

"Any banking records on them?" Cummings asked.

"None. It appears that Orisi and Nunarro know how to conceal themselves. As of now, the background information trail ended. That is, until they both showed up together in Arizona, prior to the Barnes incident. We are probing deeper for a background on both and their personal association. However, in all of the information gathered, we did determine neither Nunarro nor Orisi has any connection with Pietro Segretti."

"Are Nunarro and Orisi suspects in the explosion?" Cummings asked.

"Sheriff St. Cloud's investigation turned up an eyewitness, who saw a vehicle at the site of the explosion. The vehicle turned out to be stolen. There were traces of acetone and hydrogen peroxide, along with grains of gun powder in the vehicle. Acetone and hydrogen peroxide along with hydrochloric acid, when combined, make an explosive known as triacetone triperoxide. Because we can't get into the mine, we can't determine if triacetone triperoxide was used as the explosive material. Nunarro did rent a car. There were traces of gun powder and hydrogen peroxide in it."

"So, now, all we have to do is place Nunarro and Orisi at the mine. Who was the eyewitness?"

"A local boy, Billy Hayden. He had been questioned by St. Cloud. Two agents, from the Department of Defense, were also at the site. Agents Erik Dawson and Timothy Finley."

"What were they doing there?"

"They had an interest in the product Barnes was mining. They were with Barnes at the time of the explosion."

"What was their interest?"

"Mister Barnes had sent samples of his mined slag to the Niels Bohr Institute in Copenhagen. The slag was identified as monoatomic gold. The Niels Bohr Institute is affiliated with Brookhaven Institute in New York. They had to send the results to Brookhaven. Brookhaven had to forward it to the D.O.D. This is procedure, because the monatomic gold has unusual properties, which make it consistent with a superconductor."

"Why did Barnes send this slag all the way to Copenhagen? Why didn't he submit the slag to local laboratories? Was he trying to conceal something?"

"We don't think so. He did submit the slag many times to local laboratories. Each time, he was told the slag was nothing. The scientists, at Niels Bohr, conducted more sophisticated testing. Consequently, their results were different. What is interesting, of the two scientists at Niels Bohr, one is very important. His name is Nicola Bounetti. Well, perhaps it's not Bounetti who is so important. But, his wife is. Her maiden name is a Lucia Scotti. She's a concert violinist. Scotti has a cousin. We know the cousin as Pietro Segretti," Henrietta said, trying to shift her inflection away from the dramatic.

Cummings heard Henrietta's voice, but he couldn't determine if it was her voice or just a sound she made. It could have been a scream, but he couldn't be sure if the scream came from within him. Henrietta looked closely at Cummings and detected an unconscious wince.

"Are you okay?" she asked.

"Sure. Why wouldn't I be?"

Henrietta looked beyond the staged layers of his detachment and was not convinced. She had cultivated her own perceptions seeking to understand the reasons behind the slightest bodily movement. Henrietta garnered a different insight into Cummings, but elected to quietly move past the subject.

"So, I want you to coordinate with Sheriff St. Cloud, Dawson and Finley. It might also be important to know Lucia Scotti has a sister who is an adjunct professor at the University of Arizona. Her name is Analisa Scotti. That is a bit of information we got on our own. The D.O.D did not supply it."

"I'll keep it in mind."

"Italian police gave us pictures of Nunarro and Orisi," Henrietta said, handing them to Cummings. "Hopefully, Billy Hayden can identify them."

Cummings looked at the pictures and placed them on his desk. He struggled to gain his composure.

"Are Orisi or Nunarro associated with any known terrorist organizations?"

"At this point, that's unlikely, but remains unproven. Once we identify the motive, we'll make sense of it. But, in a way, the answer to that question may be on our doorstep. It was our cross-reference in our database that flagged Nunarro and Orisi. They're back in Arizona. They've checked into a Hampton Inn. We have them under surveillance. I want you involved. But first, I need to know you're not distracted by Segretti. Right now, I don't see him as a player."

"My focus will not be on Segretti."

"Good. He will only be a distraction. Orisi and Nunarro are the prize."

"What has surveillance turned up on them?"

"We located their rental cars and examined them. Nunarro rented one car, Orisi another. There's nothing of interest in either vehicle. We placed GPS tracking on each vehicle. We also examined their hotel rooms. Nothing unusual was found. Orisi and Nunarro did meet with a national from Oman. His name is Ubaid," Henrietta said, opening the last folder.

"He was born in Oman, the eldest of twelve children. His grandfather founded a local Islamic school. He was a devout Muslin, but left Oman to get a scholarship in an Islamic School in Iran. His bid was unsuccessful, so he went to Afghanistan. After the war with the Russians, he was instrumental in organizing the movement of radical extremists and finding them safe houses in Pakistan. He moved to East Africa and worked with a Mogadishu-based facilitation network. Once again, he located safe houses for radical extremist leaders, as well as assisting in the transfer of funds and procuring weapons and explosives. He is an accomplished document forger," Henrietta said, then turned the page in the folder.

"Ubaid was there for two years and moved to the United Arab Emirates," she continued. "He lived in Abu Dhabi. There, he became friends with local radical extremists. We believe he had some sort of disagreement with certain members of the cell over a plot to crash a plane into a Western navy vessel in Port Rashid in U.A.E. Once again, we're unclear as to what provoked the disagreement. However, he was injured in the fight, which caused damage to one eye. Nonetheless, he did manage to kill three of the extremists. Why there was never any retribution toward him by members of the group is still a question…"

"Maybe he was more than a facilitator," Cummings observed.

"Could be. There's missing intelligence on Ubaid for the next two years. We do pick up his trail when he showed up as a bodyguard for Khallad Mukhtar. Mukhtar was a successful businessman in Dubai responsible for overseeing business licensing and free trade zone registration. Two years after his employment, Mukhtar died of a heart attack."

"Was the heart attack natural?"

"As far as we have been able to determine, yes it was."

"Did Ubaid leave Dubai after that?"

"No. He lives quite well there."

"Is it possible he met Umberto Nunarro in Dubai?"

"Intelligence has no evidence of that. All Ubaid's travels, and given his relationships with extremists groups, intelligence suggests he was never involved in operational missions in Mogadishu. His operational involvement with extremists in Abu Dhabi is unclear. However, the fight, that left three extremists dead, may indicate he was."

"It appears as though Ubaid had many influential connections and is able to transition between extremists and legitimate businessmen."

"My reading is Ubaid is a rogue mercenary with materialistic leanings. He seems to hold his own ideology and is not ashamed to amass wealth."

"So, there has to be a third party bringing them together."

"That's how it appears. The question is not so much who the third party might be, but for what purpose."

"And why here?"

"These are questions we will have answers to shortly."

"Since he's been here, has Ubaid had any communications we can trace?"

"None. He's made no telephone calls nor has he sent any e-mails. He's familiar with clandestine protocols. I wouldn't expect him to make too many mistakes."

"What have we learned of the meeting between Ubaid, Nunarro and Orisi?"

"We were not able to obtain audio surveillance. Their meeting was conducted in the lobby of Nunarro's hotel. It was a brief meeting. Sheriff St. Cloud is working with us. I want you to coordinate with him, as well as Agents Finney and Dawson."

"What is your intuition about what's going on?"

"Why are you interested in my intuition as opposed to the intelligence we have so far?"

"Because our intelligence is sorely lacking. We have fragmented bios that offer only hints to these people. There's a strange force aligning these men our intelligence has not uncovered. Their convergence appears to have little to do with National Security, yet it does. Monoatomic gold can be used for unimaginable armament, yet a mine that can produce only small quantities is blown up. I don't understand it. So, what's left to help plane the edges but your intuition?"

"There is a great deal that's missing. We need to uncover the purpose for the strange convergence of Orisi, Nunarro and Ubaid. I don't discount my intuition. I feel monoatomic gold is still the prize."

"But, if Orisi and Nunarro destroyed it in Barnes' mine, what makes you think they want to acquire it now?"

"Because, I believe, they've changed alliances and are at cross purposes. Ubaid came along to support their new agenda."

"You still think Ubaid has ties to radical extremists?"

"That's a possibility. But his strengths are procurement."

"If this gold is so damn valuable, it suggests there's a rush to procure it," Cummings rationalized. "Ubaid could be working against Segretti for control of it."

"Segretti doesn't fit into this the way you would like him to," Henrietta said. "If there is another quantity out there, I don't think he's aware of it."

"Okay, forget Segretti. But, if the monoatomic gold has such amazing capabilities, why aren't our scientists on a fast track mining or manufacturing it?"

"Because, the gold doesn't fit into the military's paradigm. Other technologies are in the forefront of war and generate more revenue. The gold doesn't have the capability to produce the peripheral industries, nor is it a force of destruction. The other answer is; there's profit in its destruction."

"Profit to whom?" Cummings asked. "What are the secrets of disclosure or conflicts over destroying it?"

Henrietta pulled back from the possibilities. The truth behind the gold, as Henrietta knew it, could not be restricted to thought or conversation. The enemies of disclosure were everywhere. They possessed resources that could take a large truth and shrink it to smug indifference. Those same enemies evoked an edict that ensured the monoatomic gold was exclusively theirs. They owned its properties and its legacy. They controlled its history, as well as its fate. That understanding gave Henrietta perspective to her own strength. She found an assuring comfort, mostly because they could not control the things she already knew.

Henrietta gathered the three folders and placed them on Cummings' desk. She stood and straightened her jacket. Unconsciously, she touched the scroll ring on her finger and twisted it gently. She saw the look on Cummings' face gradually shift from anticipation to disappointment in increments relating to her hesitation. His look did not persuade her to give up any of her knowledge, nor would she allow it to accuse her of omission. It just remained part of a cycle between the forces of command and doubt.

"Possession and destruction," Henrietta said almost in a whisper. "I'll save that explanation for another briefing."

MITCHELL Harrington was familiar with the drive to Tucson and the University of Arizona. He had driven it many times in the past. The route played in his mind like a video. He compared the things he saw through his memory. The sights were not different from what he remembered. All that had changed was the level of his anticipation and excitement.

He was somewhat anxious to see Analisa again. He didn't know how she would greet him, or if she would consider the possibility of rekindling their relationship. He felt he would like to have her back in his life. Before that could occur, he had to readjust to the protocols of civilian life. Knowing how he would behave under the recall of the sights and sounds of the war was critical for him. He couldn't allow the sudden invasions of memory to claim his relationship with Analisa as another casualty.

Pushing these concerns aside, he was excited about presenting Analisa with the twenty-five pounds of white powder packed in the briefcase on the back seat. Their first reintroduction, since coming home from Iraq, would be as colleagues and scientists researching an unusual relic. That was easier for him to bear than dealing with the challenges of civilian life. He needed to allow himself time to fight a second war against his ghosts.

He tried to imagine her reaction to the possibilities of the white powder; remembering how joyous she would become whenever presented with small gifts, he suspected she would not be able to contain her enthusiasm. No matter what he remembered of Analisa, he still couldn't guess what impact the white powder would have, if it proved everything she believed and imagined, turned out to be true. The thought alone assuaged all his other anticipations and concerns.

"Hey Deuce," Solis said distracting Harrington. "This is a different world than where I come from," he continued looking out the window. "Man, look out there," he said pointing to the landscape. "Where are we?" he continued.

"Outside Chandler. That's the San Tan Mountain range," Harrington said.

"Man, this sure is nice. I look around, and I see open space. Look in any direction, and all I see are mountains so far away they look impossible ta get ta. That makes 'em not seem real. Nothin' about this place seems real, and if it ain't real it can't hurt ya. I like that. Everythin' on Gun Hill Road is close and real as real gets."

"But you miss it, Hector."

"Not any more I don't. Iraq had a way of changin' me. I don't know where I belong. All I know is I want quiet. I want clean, fresh and quiet. I don't wanna smell sand or blood."

"There's sand in Arizona, Hector."

"Yeah, but it ain't the same. You know, Deuce, I still can't get the smell a blood outta my nose. Remember, I told you I was always smellin' blood? Well, I still smell blood. You think it's in my nose or in my memory?"

"I don't know, Hector."

Solis became disturbed at his own question. It was something beyond his senses and reasoning, raising a conflict between his mind and his heart, dislodging any measure of contentment he hoped for.

"What do you remember about the war, Deuce?"

"I don't know how to answer that. My mind can certainly recall things, but that's not how the visions unfold for me. It's hard to describe."

"Hard because you don't wanna talk about it, or you feel like it ain't the soldier's way?"

"Perhaps both."

"We got new lives, Deuce. These new lives got nothin' ta do with Iraq."

"Do you really think we'll ever put enough distance between ourselves and the war?"

"I don't know, but that don't mean we gotta still fight it. It's over for us, Deuce. So I think we should start actin' like it. And, the best way ta start should be by talkin'. We gotta be brave ta do that."

Harrington allowed himself to embrace the redefinition of bravery that Solis believed required full disclosure.

"Deuce?" Solis continued. "Go for it. There ain't nothin' left ta do."

"Everything I saw found its way into my being," Harrington confessed with sudden and uncontrolled candor. "It's all in my body, my heart and my soul. That is, if I have a soul left. It's like an indelible watermark….The watermark looks like a skeleton. It shows no sign of fading. I think the worst part of everything I experienced_in Iraq was allowing myself to go along with it. I can make an excuse for it, but it's not that simple."

"You got a way of puttin' it, Deuce, which I can understand. That was what I was strugglin' with. You gave me orders in Iraq that kept me alive. I only wish you could give orders ta get me normal."

"That's above my rank, Hector. You need to learn how to do that on your own."

"You know what stays in my mind, Deuce? It's that time the Iraqi police had me on the boat in Germany. Here I was gone through the war, and now I was gonna get killed after the war. That bothered me. It was unfair. I was gonna' get killed for the white powder you got sittin' in the back seat. That didn't make any sense ta me."

Solis looked out at the landscape, where the plains meet the mountains. The colors of the hills and sky had as much meaning to his life as a watercolor hanging on a museum wall or on someone's refrigerator. He felt lost and displaced. Before he could understand his surroundings, he had to rediscover himself. That became his priority. Suddenly, the mystery of the white powder no longer had any significance to him.

"Seems like we been drivin' for days," Solis whispered for no apparent reason.

Looking out to the road and beyond, Solis began to accept the space, the distance and his proximity to them. The San Tan Mountains and the landscape appeared friendlier than he could imagine. He closed his eyes, knowing he was not threatened and no attack would come.

"Hey, Hector, tell me something," Harrington asked. "I noticed something about you."

"What's that?" Solis responded from a slight daze.

"I noticed you no longer use foul language," Harrington observed. "Why is that?"

Solis turned and looked at Harrington. He knew Harrington's observation was simple yet staggering. It related to something much larger than words and connected to something very personal.

"Yeah, I don't," Solis confirmed. "You notice it, right? You know why that is, Deuce? Let me tell ya. It's because I'm outta that hell in Iraq. I don't need ta curse any more."

"What did the cursing represent? Your hostility? Your anger?"

"I guess you could say both."

"So, your hostility and anger are gone?"

"If my cursin's gone, then I guess so's my hostility….I ain't so sure about my anger, though. Sometimes I still feel like I need ta bust somethin'. But you know what I'm left with, Deuce?"

"No what?"

"Now, I just have bad dreams."

AGENT Cummings swiped his identification card through the magnetic reader. It allowed him access to the restricted surveillance area. He and

Agent Manning briskly walked down the long corridor to the Central Surveillance Command Center. The command center was several levels below ground at the Homeland Security building. It was built into the earth as an impregnable fortress. The walls were reinforced cement, and the lighting was stagnant, artificially creating a permanent twilight. The employees, with security clearance to the area, referred to the space as the "tomb".

Cummings felt a deep compression entering the area. To him, it was a vast underworld known only to those who took oaths and kept secrets. Henrietta Dell stood outside the door leading to the command center as the agents approached. Her appearance communicated urgency and command. The compression of the tomb did not have an effect on her. The door behind Henrietta framed her elegance and control. The lighted sign above the door read, AUTHORIZED PERSONNEL ONLY, confirming Henrietta's authority.

"Thank you for coming on such short notice," Henrietta said. "Earlier, I had ordered specific surveillance on Orisi and Nunarro. I just wanted you to be included in the preliminary surveillance," she concluded.

Henrietta pressed her thumb on the fingerprint recognition pad, entered her personal code, and then opened the door. They entered a small corridor leading to another door with a camera mounted above it. Manning walked with a limp as they crossed the darkened surveillance room. His eyes were swollen and discolored. His nose was still purplish. A thin line of black sutures extended from his upper lip to one cheek; the remnants from his altercation with Pietro Segretti.

Henrietta and the two agents noticed the large video monitors on the wall. The monitors were fronted by a contoured console lined with smaller monitors, three keyboards and a computer. A greenish tint emanated from the screen and monitors. Seated in a swivel chair at the console was Acting Supervisor of Surveillance, Ryan Collins.

"Good morning, Ray," Henrietta said, as she approached.

"Good morning, Henrietta," the supervisor responded, keeping his attention focused on the screens.

The optical technology, Collins operated, was like an Orwellian prophecy dimming the lines between protection and invasion. Cummings was unconcerned with moral technicalities or the potential of totalitarian dangers. He just liked the pure accessibility to power. For him, the new world of surveillance signified deep control, aligning with his sense of voyeurism and ownership.

"How is the surveillance coming along?" Henrietta asked.

Typing in coordinates, Collins directed a satellite surveillance system to focus on two cars, each appearing on a split screen. Through GPS tracking, Collins was able to identify the vehicles rented by Mario Orisi and Umberto Nunarro.

"Very good. The vehicle on the left is traveling south on Route Seventeen," Collins announced, without turning his head to Henrietta. "It has passed Chandler and Casa Grande, and is nearing Eloy. The vehicle on the right is in Prescott. It has been parked for an hour and thirty-seven minutes."

"Where did the first vehicle originate from?" Henrietta asked.

"They both originated in Prescott. I have their routes recorded in detail," Collins said, removing an ear piece attached to a thin microphone by his mouth. "I'll give you the complete printout of the movement."

"No. Give it to Agent Cummings," Henrietta said.

"What about the second car?" Cummings asked. "The parked car? Is anyone in that vehicle?"

"It's difficult to say. Most of the vehicle is obscured by the overhang of the trees. The angle of surveillance is unable to determine any occupants."

"I hate to think parking under the trees was deliberate," Cummings observed. "That would mean they suspect something."

"It could be they're lucky," Henrietta replied.

"Did you follow the car to that location?" Cummings asked.

"Yes," Collins responded.

"Were you able to see who entered the vehicle?"

"No, sir. The vehicle left from a parking facility located under the High Plains Motel in Prescott where the suspects are staying."

"Can you focus on the license plate?"

Collins typed in the revised information. The image adjusted showing just a portion of the front of the vehicle. To capture the license plate, the image zoomed in increments until the numbers on the license were displayed clearly.

"That car is rented by Mario Orisi," Henrietta informed. "I remember the license number."

"Rented cars? Our suspects are not doing a good job of concealing themselves," Cummings announced.

"Don't underestimate them," Henrietta warned. "I think they know exactly what they're doing."

"Would it be in our best interest to apprehend Orisi and Nunarro?" Manning asked. "I know it may show our hand, but we might be able to get information from them and short circuit whatever they're planning."

"We don't have probable cause," Henrietta said. "Not that we need probable cause in the new age of terrorism. I just don't think it's prudent at this time."

"Even if we do apprehend Orisi and Nunarro, there's no guarantee they're going to tell us what we need to know," Cummings said.

"If Billy Hayden can place Nunarro and Orisi at the scene of the Barnes mine, that's all the probable cause we're going to need," Manning said.

"When you meet with Billy Hayden, and should he confirm they were at the mine, then we should revisit the possibility of apprehending them. But, I think we should see what surveillance gives us. What may be unfolding here is something we're not thinking about, and may surprise us. I believe the answer we're looking for will appear on that screen."

Cummings studied the split screen trying to determine the purpose and motivation of the vehicles' operators. His suspicion led him to believe he was observing secret arrangements unfolding toward a destructive plot.

"The surveillance indicates the stationary vehicle is located between South Alacron Street and Carelton Street," Collins advised.

"That area is all residential," Cummings observed.

"There's a reason they're at that location. Their purpose raises all sorts of suspicions. Maybe someone in that neighborhood is part of it," Manning said.

"Run a background check on the residents where the car is parked," Henrietta ordered.

"We have movement," Manning said, watching the screen. The car parked under the trees began moving slowly down South Alacron Street.

"Good. Can you get a tight visual?" Henrietta asked.

Collins began typing, causing the visual on one half of the screen to zoom in on the car.

"The car is passing under a row of trees. It's going to be hard to see inside the car," the technician said.

"Then just follow the car for now. That's more important," Henrietta said. "Where is the second vehicle? Nunarro's vehicle," Henrietta asked.

The technician looked at the other portion of the screen and adjusted the information, displaying the location.

"It just passed the Marana town line and is driving toward Tucson."

"Tucson," Henrietta said quizzically. "Pull back and give me a visual of other vehicles on the road. Put it on the entire screen. I want to get a bigger picture of what's around Nunarro's vehicle. I still want visuals on the Orisi vehicle. Can you do that?"

"Yes. I'll put the Orisi vehicle on monitor two," Collins said.

He typed in new coordinates. The scene of the road Nunarro was driving on filled the screen.

"Highlight Nunarro's vehicle," Henrietta said.

With one keystroke from the technician, a thin red circle appeared around Nunarro's vehicle.

"He's driving south on Interstate Ten. The vehicle has just passed Cortaro," Collins reported.

"There's not much traffic on the road. I need license plate numbers on the vehicles in front of Nunarro's vehicle. I count six in both lanes. Those appear to be the closest to him."

Collins referred to a scale on the bottom of the screen and measured the distance and speed of the vehicles.

"The furthest vehicle is three quarters of a mile from Nunarro's vehicle," Collins said. "That vehicle is traveling nine miles per hour faster than the other five vehicles. The other five are within a half mile, traveling at a speed varying between two and half to three miles per hour. There are two trailer trucks. Do you want the licenses on those also?"

"No, just the cars. One vehicle appears to be an SUV. Get that one, too."

"Henrietta, fill me in what you're thinking," Cummings said.

"Something tells me Orisi and Nunarro are doing exactly what we're doing…conducting surveillance."

The screen zoomed in on the image of the first vehicle in front of Nunarro's car. Manning quickly jotted down the license plate number, as well as other vehicles close to Nunarro's.

"I've got all of them," Manning advised.

"Good. Give me an overview of all six vehicles, including Nunarro's," Henrietta said.

Everyone watched the screen as the cars continued south on Interstate Ten. They stayed in formation maintaining consistent distances to each other. The lead vehicle began to slow down and turned off Interstate Ten.

"The first vehicle is exiting West River Road," the technician announced. "Do you want continued surveillance on that vehicle?"

"No. Let it go," Henrietta responded.

The remaining vehicles continued on. A second vehicle moved closer to Nunarro's vehicle, slowed and exited on West River Road.

"Let that one go, too," Henrietta said.

"Two down," Manning said making a notation next to the license numbers he had jotted down.

The remaining caravan continued for a reasonable distance. The agents watched as three of the vehicles grew closer. They joined to exit as the remaining two vehicles sped passed them.

"Was that the West Prince Road exit?" Henrietta asked.

"Yes," Collins replied.

"Now, one left," Henrietta said. "These are the vehicles I'm interested in."

The images of both vehicles were clear as surveillance spied down on them. At one point, a sharp glare reflected off the top of both vehicles briefly hiding them from view. The land mass passed quickly revealing the topography in a long uneventful blur. The modern tracking Collins came to rely on could be mundane and tedious, but when measured against the possibility of threat, for him it was an absorbing necessity. Henrietta and the agents became mesmerized by the image on the screen. They were drawn with a sober eye into a mosaic of events. There was an underlying theme connecting the moving images in front of them with the potential for failure and destruction. Knowing a successful outcome required more than just technology and skill. They also need luck. The agents watched the screen as both cars continued south. They eventually slowed and finally turned. The agents shared a silent anticipation.

"They just turned off at West Grant Road," Collins announced.

"If they go to North Park Avenue, they will be on the campus of the university," Henrietta commented.

"Yes, and that's where we can find Analisa Scotti. She's the professor and cousin to Pietro Segretti," Cummings announced.

Henrietta turned away from the screen. She looked at Cummings, who seemed to be connected to an undisclosed point somewhere beyond the images of the screen.

"That's right," Henrietta said to him.

Nunarro's car seemed to keep a measured distance from the car in front of him. It was a defined space Henrietta sensed was chosen to maintain a level of inconspicuousness.

"Maintain visual contact on both vehicles," Henrietta said. "Do we know the license plate number of the first vehicle?"

"Yes," Manning responded.

"Good," she said turning to Cummings.

"Call security at the university. Instruct them to maintain surveillance on Nunarro's vehicle, without arousing suspicion. Stress they are not to approach the vehicle. They are to apply strict surveillance on the other vehicle. I don't suspect the vehicle is a threat, but I believe it's a key to the puzzle. I want periodic updates. If anything unusual occurs, I want to be informed immediately."

"Understood," Cummings said.

"Also, keep Sheriff St. Cloud advised. He should have some presence on South Alacron Street, but not until we do a background check on the residents there."

Cummings studied Henrietta, noticing how her composure blended into the darkly tinted room. He detected her sense of authority, along with distinct traces of formidable intuition that seemed to support her position.

"What's your feeling about what's going on there?" Cummings asked, nodding to the screen.

"As I said, this looks like surveillance by Orisi and Nunarro. I wouldn't be surprised if the driver of the car that went into the university also lives on South Alacron Street."

"So, that would mean there's a connection between him, Orisi and Nunarro."

"Perhaps, but that doesn't mean it's a friendly connection."

Henrietta gave the screen a final glance. She knew there was an ominous reference between the video and the theatre of reality. Theories drifted across the screen suggesting conflict and danger. She let the images and theories mix with her judgment, hoping they would form an insight. It disturbed her to know the world was filled with the potential for endless catastrophe. The images of the vehicles on the screen could be in the preliminary stages of impending ruin. She looked up at the air vent blowing down on her, and wondered if it caused the chill to her body.

The confines of the tomb suddenly had an effect on her. The thick walls exaggerated everything, amplifying her inner voice, thoughts and fears. But Henrietta knew how to offset her apprehensions. First, she had to disconnect from the things that didn't exist, and become intimate with those that did. That was a reference point from which she assessed her most important judgments. Henrietta put her hand on Collins' shoulder, thanked him and left the room.

Cummings did not dismiss Henrietta's observations. But he had his own impulse and reflections that could prove valid. His skepticism and hunches went a long way, tapping into experience and knowledge. But more importantly, his dark obsession floated to a memory he could not ignore. The wounds to his face and body brought an aching for revenge. He hoped that somehow, Orisi, Nunarro and the mysterious driver were somehow related to Pietro Segretti.

MITCHELL Harrington drove to Old Main in the northern quadrant of the University of Arizona. The familiar buildings, that were once part of him, welcomed him as an old friend. Harrington felt the density of the energy. The campus had solidarity with the rhythms of his own feelings.

Every building he saw came with a history and memory. But more than anything, he knew what it felt like to have finally come home. The red brick of Centennial Hall, the Student Union Memorial Building, dedicated to students who died in the first and second world wars, and the State Museum all seemed to shrink in stature, yet grow in prominence, as they represented his past innocence. Harrington opened the window and let the hot air with its fresh, earthly smells of cut grass wave over him. He embraced the familiarity around him with an eagerness he had never felt before. His thoughts unfolded in rapidly changing scenarios. Images flashed in his mind, seemingly without reason or connection. A place of learning with its various academic halls mythically transmuted to rows of pastoral cathedrals. He concluded it was the white powder, with all its unusual power, that brought him to the campus of cathedrals.

"Hey, Deuce," Solis' said interrupting Harrington's thoughts.

Harrington welcomed every breath that brought a gradual reversal to his past virtue. He was holding onto something delicate and soothing. The slightest acknowledgement to Solis would severely disturb it. The campus knew him as a young student long before he became a soldier. He remained silent, waiting for the warps and bends to work out the necessary logistics and timing, so he could feel unburdened again.

Solis looked out at the clean streets and finely trimmed grass. He looked at the buildings, plants and trees. It was unlike anything he had ever seen. Except for certain trees he recalled seeing in Iraq. He spotted a group of young girls walking, dressed in cut-off jeans and tank tops. A young Asian girl played a violin, entertaining a small group of students sitting on the grass around her. A blue banner hanging from Yuma Hall caught his attention. It read: FRATERNITY AND SORORITY - BROTHERS AND SISTERS JOIN US. The banner suggested a kind of solidarity and acceptance for which he was unaccustomed, even as a soldier.

"Hey, Deuce, you with me?" Solis asked.

"Yes, what is it, Hector?" Harrington said, seemingly from a distant place.

"You listen' ta me, Deuce? It's like your minds back in the desert."

"Hector, this was a long ride. Don't end it by getting on my nerves. What is it?"

"Nothin'. I was just callin' out ta ask you, this is where you went ta school?"

"Yes, it is. Why?"

"It's really impressive lookin'. What do they teach here?" Solis asked, with a sense of perplexity.

"Anything anyone wants to learn."

"This where you learned about diggin' up bones?"

"This is where I did my anthropology studies."

"Do they teach common sense here?"

Harrington turned to Solis as a sliver of annoyance cut across his face.

"Hector, what kind of a question is that?"

"Well, if they taught you common sense, why did you go fight in Iraq?"

"In a sense, Iraq was a higher education for me. I needed to be there, so I could learn about the philosophy of war."

"War ain't got philosophy, Deuce. Don't you know that? When you apply philosophy ta war, it means war's got thought, understanding… humanity. War ain't got none a those."

Harrington turned to Solis and smiled. He recognized his friend in a different way. The universal disguise of pretense a soldier carries had faded from Solis' face. He appeared innocent, but not naive. He genuinely showed what was beneath the ethics of his pain.

"You know what, Hector? I think you should have gone to this university instead of me."

"Yeah, well, if I get rich from the white powder you got sittin' on the back seat, I just might enroll here."

HARRINGTON drove slowly around the campus. He was hoping to reacquaint himself with the surroundings, and connect to his own memories. In a sense, he wanted to go back through the esthetic of time to when he first met Analisa. It was a magical day that he recalled with total clarity. Nothing that had ever happened to him, from then on, gave him more to hope for. As he drove around the campus, the hope he once enjoyed became edged in doubt.

"Hey, Deuce you been drivin' around for an hour. You musta circled the campus ten times. I thought you knew where you were goin'."

"I just want to see the campus again. I've been away from it for a long time. I want to see if anything's changed."

"No. No, you don't."

"What do you mean I don't?" Harrington asked with a defensive tone.

"You know what I mean. You stallin' for time. It's like you're afraid ta see your girlfriend again."

"You're nuts," Harrington responded, with a trace of irony.

"Am I? Tell me I'm not, and in a way I can believe you," Solis challenged.

Harrington became evasive.

"Deuce," Solis continued. "She'll take you back or she won't. Those are her only two choices. You got two choices, too. Run away or fight. Whatever you do, do it quick. Cause I'll tell you this, if you keep her waitin' any longer she'll dump you for sure. Now, you called her and told her you was gonna meet her in front a library."

"Museum. I said I would meet with her in front of the State Museum," Harrington said.

"Whatever. Only difference between 'em is one's got books, the other's got bones. Real question is why you lookin' ta back out now? Cause in your mind this ain't about givin' her the white powder. It's all about her. Seein' her again. That's what you're worried about."

Harrington stopped the vehicle and looked at Solis, who had turned toward him with a wry judgment in his eyes. Solis had made a simple assessment, to which he also offered a straightforward resolution. Within the nuance of accusation and encouragement from Solis, Harrington backed up the vehicle to University Boulevard and drove toward the State Museum.

University Boulevard was awash in bright sunlight. The sidewalk leading to the State Museum was lined with tall palm trees. The trees were perfectly aligned, uniform in height, thickness and age.

"Hey, Deuce, these trees look like the same trees they got in Baghdad," Solis observed.

Harrington did not look at the trees. He saw a woman standing on the sidewalk in front of the columned archway of the museum. The woman appeared lost, yet excited and hopeful. She became attentive to Harrington's car, and tried to look past the glare coming off the windshield. The woman raised her hand to shade her eyes from the glare. Upon recognizing Harrington, her graceful movement became her way of saluting him and welcoming him home.

"Is that Analisa?" Solis asked.

From a distance, Harrington was able to lip read the name she formed, "Mitchell."

"Yes," Harrington replied. "That's her. That's Analisa."

The sun made Analisa's auburn hair glow with a soft golden hue. She wore a white cotton dress with thin shoulder straps. The stream of bright daylight, coming from behind her, accentuated the sheerness of her dress, slightly exposing the curvy outline of her body. A gentle breeze caused her dress to flutter slightly. Analisa looked strong but delicate, with firm arms and soft, full breasts. The bronze skin of her arms and shoulders glistened from a crystal-fine layer of perspiration. Her cheeks and jaw line were softly rounded and seemed to be molded from an artisan's delicate breath of blown glass. Standing erect, her statuesque figure cast a shadow, doubling her as a perfect deity of feminine mythology. As Solis looked at Analisa, he knew she was born beautiful.

"Hey, Deuce," Solis said with his mouth slightly agape. "I'll tell you right up, she's too beautiful for you. You're outta your league with that fine lady."

"You think?"

"What do you mean, 'I think'? Trust me, Deuce. She's too fine a lady ta be seen with the likes a you. Your hands are too rough ta touch a delicate face like that."

Harrington stopped no more than ten yards from Analisa. He paused for an instant, and then slowly stepped out of the car. He stepped onto the sidewalk and just watched her.

Upon seeing Harrington, Analisa slowly lowered her hand from her eyes. She squinted against the sun, trying to make his image clear, more real. She took a tentative step toward him, then another. She hoped his image was not a cruel deception. A wide smile crossed her face, and then her lips began to quiver. She felt somewhat confused and disbelieving at what she was seeing. But in an instant, she knew it was truly Harrington, and she was happy.

They walked quickly toward each other and embraced. The sunglasses, Analisa was holding fell to the ground. She began to cry in a way that mixed joy with laughter. Her voice cracked when she whispered, "Mitchell. Mitchell."

She held him tightly without breathing. Subconsciously, she moved her hands from his shoulders, to his arms and back to convince herself there were no wounds to his body. She ran her hand along his face to confirm he was not disfigured. She touched his head, noticing the only physical change was his short prickly hair.

"Mitchell, I'm so, so glad you're home. I'm glad you're safe and whole. You are alright? You're not wounded or hurt?"

"No. No. I'm fine," he responded.

Harrington felt Analisa's embrace. They hugged for a long while without speaking or breathing. Harrington stayed within the wordless state connecting to the fibers of her intimacy and mystery. Suddenly, he felt capable of sheltering the bond with Analisa that had been in question and was long overdue. More importantly, he knew he could do it, because this was the final phase of his redemption. It was now complete. He achieved forgiveness through the complexities of a silent embrace. There was no need for time to be turned back, yet in a sense, it had. Through her touch, all his doubt had been replaced by hope.

"Are you back to stay?" Analisa asked.

"I would like to be," Harrington responded tentatively.

Analisa smiled fully understanding the distinction between presumption and acceptance.

"Good. I've missed you so much, Mitchell."

"I missed you too, Analisa."

"God, I can't believe I was able to get by all this time without seeing you. I didn't realize how much you were a part of me until this very moment. You feel so, so good."

"I thought of you a lot while I was away, Analisa. I feared I would never see you again. I felt it from the first day I deployed overseas. The feeling never left me."

"There was so much I wanted to say to you the day you left for Iraq. So much I should have said but was afraid to say."

"Afraid of what?"

"Afraid to commit. I was afraid you weren't going to return. I needed to turn away from my feelings for you. I couldn't bear having to deal with you never returning. I can say that now that you're here. It was selfish and weak of me."

"No, you weren't. You were right to do what you did. War taught me to do anything reasonable to survive. Your choice was reasonable."

"I regret it now. I feel like a coward. Like I let you down."

"The only way you can let me down is if you send me away right now."

Analisa took hold of Harrington's face and kissed him. She held him tightly, offering him exclusivity to the orb of her being through unreserved mime. It was a burning and honest passion Harrington was familiar with. It was a direct and concise expression, leaving no margin for misinterpretation or doubt.

"Stay," was all Analisa said.

The inflection in Analisa's tone captivated Harrington. Her expression was a breathless consummation overriding the past and fused to the future. A world of commitment resided in a single word. It was poetry that rhymed with all aspects of his life.

"It's like I never left," Harrington said.

Analisa put her arm around Harrington and began walking back toward the State Museum.

"I have to give a lecture to a group of students. Actually, I'm a bit late. You can come and stand in the back. For some reason, the students were interested in my lecture. I have a full roster. No seats available."

"I'd love to listen in."

"Good. After the lecture, we'll go out. You can tell me what you found in the desert. Your vagueness on the phone caught my interest."

"I'm with a friend who was with me in Iraq when I made the discovery. He's a guy I trust. He's here now."

"Good. He can come along."

"What's your lecture about?"

"Do you really want to know?"

"Sure I do. I miss being around the conversations about digs and finds."

"Is that why you're here to see me?"

"No. Well, in a way. What I have to show you was an excuse to see you. But really, I had to know we would pick up where we left off."

"Funny, but I wouldn't categorize us as ever leaving off. You were in my thoughts every day you were away. We can talk about all that later. I'm glad whatever it is you found was your excuse to look me up again. But, Mitchell, you didn't need an excuse to see me. All you had to do was walk right back into my life, with or without whatever it is you found."

"That's good to know. What's your lecture about?" Harrington asked.

"This is the last of four lectures involving the new behavioral and biological perspectives on the origins and dispersal of ancient humans," she said proudly.

"So this is what you've been doing since I've been away."

ANALISA stood in the wings of the stage, looking out over the students filing into the auditorium. With no seats available, Harrington stood in the rear of the hall; his back against the wall. After parking the car, Solis entered the hall, carrying the case with the white powder. He spotted Harrington standing in the rear and joined him, setting the case down at his feet.

The lighting in the hall came from a double row of overhead globes of tinted white glass. A row of spotlights hung from the high ceiling in front of the hall and were aimed at the podium. Several other spotlights aligned along either side of the hall, accentuating several exhibits. The hall, purposely designed without windows, so the natural light could not fade the displays of pottery, jewelry, baskets and textiles, which were further protected by Plexiglas cases. The artifacts, in the cases, were unearthed during archaeological excavations by the museum staff and other professionals. The rest of the objects were ethnological items donated by Native American tribes. Textiles, embroidered rawhide moccasins and small blankets were draped over stone pedestals. Larger, more elaborate blankets were affixed to the deep luxurious cherry wood walls.

There was a rustling in the auditorium as students took their seats. The swell of activity began to subside as the spotlight illuminated the podium where Analisa was about to approach. When the students had completely settled, Analisa emerged from the left wing of the auditorium to their polite applause. Harrington studied her confident walk, her appreciative smile and the way she adjusted the pages on the podium. She had a grace and sensuality he knew on an intimate level. It felt good to be near her again.

"Thank you. Thank you," Analisa said to the students, as their applause began to fade.

"Thank you for coming to the last of my four lectures. I assume you've found the lectures interesting, because there is no extra credit relating to your attendance," she quipped.

"As you remember from our past lectures," Analisa continued. "We investigated the origins and dispersal of ancient humans. This final segment is the most mysterious of all. It's the mystery of the missing link.

"Before I get into that, I just want to stress anthropology is often defined as being holistic and based on a four field approach. It is holistic, because it is concerned with all human beings across time and places, and with all dimensions of humanity. The breakdown is inclusive of physical anthropology, archaeology, cultural and or social anthropology and linguistics. In the case of linguists, a category that is inclusive, but not necessarily exclusive of the way many ancient cultures use images as language. They inscribe, chisel, scratch and burn images on tablets and walls, which we have interpreted today. Then, there is another language. It's the language of early construction. Temples, pyramids, walls, monoliths and the like, have their own secret language. That language is spoken in every part of the world by every ancient civilization. This language is far more difficult to decipher. But make no mistake about it, it is a language nonetheless. It says a great deal about the ancients. It has a haunting cadence and, in some cases, it defies translation.

"Now, before I begin with this final lecture, I'm sure you all know Darwin coined the term 'missing link.' But what I'd like to see, by a show of hands, is how many of you think Darwin taught that humans had descended from early apes such as chimps or gorillas."

With the exception of just a few, most students raised their hands. Analisa looked out over the students and made a quick assessment of the ratio between those with opposing beliefs.

"How many of you are not sure what Darwin taught at all."

One student raised her hand; then bowed her head slightly embarrassed.

"How many of you never heard of Darwin?" Analisa asked with a chuckle.

"That's okay. It's okay. It doesn't make a difference," Analisa continued.

"Whatever your beliefs are, ponder this," Analisa continued. "Would it be a reasonable assumption if man was a descendent of a chimp or a gorilla, would there still be chimps or gorillas around today? Clearly, there are chimps, gorillas, and monkeys, orangutans of all sorts roaming the wilds, living on preserves and in captivity. No, Darwin never taught that theory. In fact, it was logically believed humans must have evolved from a different type of ape. A bipedal ape for sure. But the problem is there is no archaeological discovery that supports this theory. So, what are we left with?" Analisa asked, letting the question hang in the air. "The missing link," she said, answering her own question.

"But, that's contrary to Genesis," one of the students in the front of the hall called out. One of the same students who raised his hand to the question of Darwin teaching humans descended from apes.

"That's correct. It is contrary to Genesis. That is a very good observation. Certainly, there are religions that take extreme exception to the concept of human evolution from apes. And as you suggest, Genesis describes how man, in this case Adam, was created. Genesis also notes Adam was created in adult form," Analisa said without judgment or ridicule.

"However, this lecture is anthropologically based and not theological in nature," Analisa continued. "I would certainly encourage those of you who have doubts and questions to take theological courses and come to your own conclusions. In your search, you may want to locate the great, albeit brief, debate between Thomas Henry Huxley, an Oxford scientist, who was a proponent of Darwin, and Bishop Samuel Wilberforce. You may find that debate quite interesting."

"But what about the Piltdown Man skull?" another student asked.

"Yes. That skull you're referring to was found in Piltdown, Sussex, several years after Darwin's death. If you know about the skull, you also know it was a hoax. The skull of a gorilla was joined with that of a human. That was the extent of the Piltdown Man," Analisa informed.

"Hoaxes are always counter-productive and rarely humorous," she continued. "So, for the purposes of my lectures, I will try to stay on track with my perspectives of origins. It is difficult enough to have to contend with only limited hints from what we dig up to make such a large connection. That brings us to the purpose of my lectures. I want to focus on the specific time frame of thirty-five thousand to thirty thousand BC. This is the time of the Neanderthal and Cro-Magnon man. It has been proven both these species did exist for a time as contemporaries. Which means what?" Analisa asked rhetorically. "It means they did not evolve from each other," she concluded.

"Excuse me, Miss Scotti," another student said, with a slightly raised hand. "I read that Neanderthals did share a common ancestry with Homo sapiens six hundred thousand years ago. Can you clarify that?"

"On a scientific basis, the claim could not be proven," Analisa replied. "Another thing to consider is Cro-Magnon man developed out of Africa, Asia, perhaps the Balkans and spread throughout Europe. Their ancestry has not been established or discovered. Nor does it appear their physical appearance, such as those humans share today, without the protruding brow, had any forerunners....By the way, skulls of Homo Erectus were found in Indonesia more than forty thousand years ago. The finding also suggests Homo erectus did not evolve into Neanderthals....I hope that answers your question?"

The student nodded her head, but raised her shoulders at the same time.

"Confused?" Analisa asked.

"A little," the student responded.

"All this means is the DNA evidence concludes Cro-Magnon Homo Sapiens have no ancestral link to Neanderthals," Analisa emphasized. "There was no interbreeding between Neanderthals and Cro-Magnon. They were reproductively incompatible. I further suggest this can be a problem for Darwinism and Creationism. For those of you who would like to do more research on this subject, I suggest you go to the internet and look at The Times for July eleventh, nineteen ninety-seven..."

"Hey, Deuce," Solis whispered in Harrington's ear. "Your girlfriend knows alota stuff."

"Yes. Obviously, she is very intelligent."

"Do you know what's she's talkin' about?"

"Yes. I do."

"What's she sayin'?"

"She's trying to explain, we really don't know who our ancestors were."

"Why's that so important? You Caucasian people can't figure that out because you might be afraid ta learn you all got some African blood in you. That much a what she's sayin' I understand. Me, it don't make a difference. My grandfather was black on my father's side. He was a big black guy right from Africa. My grandmother's people were racist. They wouldn't let my grandma marry no African. So, I only got a little bit of African blood. But

Deuce, I got it, and all you Caucasian people do. That's what your girl's sayin, so get over it."

Harrington tried to tune out Solis. His aimless banter was distracting him from Analisa. Her poise and command were ethereal. She somehow existed within the context of the ancient history she was lecturing about. He felt her beauty and sensuality were timeless.

As she spoke, Harrington sensed the students were enthralled with her as well. Every face angled up toward her, in some kind of special homage. Some students were hanging on every word, while others jotted notes. Harrington noticed one student holding a tape recorder, while another took a picture of her with a mobile camera. Understanding and mystery traveled through each row of students. Analisa gained their trust and engaged their quest for knowledge. She captured, so eloquently, the primal relationship between teacher and student.

Harrington was familiar with her academic passion. He saw it many times when they were students involved in a common dig or specific research. Her personal quest for knowledge and insight was not limited by any preconceptions or prevailing bias. Rather, she remained open and accepting of new discoveries, no matter how challenging or controversial. She once conveyed to him, while digging in Syria, all the mysteries she wanted to uncover were all the mysteries she needed to transcend.

As he listened to her lecture, he began to believe she was in a state of transcendence. Clearly, there were many more mysteries she had uncovered since they were students together. There were those mysteries that still remained undiscovered and beyond her grasp. Yet, they were the mysteries to which she instinctively knew the answer.

"... The DNA that is passed down through the generations is unchanged," Analisa continued. "All humans have similar sequences, unchanged from mothers to children. There are, however, random mutations. But it's worth repeating, all humans have similar sequences. The DNA of the Neanderthals, on the other hand, is that of a separate species entirely. It is also important to note, the Neanderthal DNA is a DNA that has run its course... a deadend. So, it appears humans are descended from Afro-Asian, Cro-Magnon types."

"See, what did I tell you," Solis whispered into Harrington's ear. "We all got Afro blood. I don't know about that Asian blood though. You sure she's right about that?"

"Quiet, Hector," Harrington whispered to Solis. "She's just about finishing her lecture. I want to hear the end of it."

"...So in conclusion," Analisa said. "The real question is; from what species did Afro-Asian, Cro-Magnon man evolve?" Analisa said. "That's the question, the real mystery that has eluded archaeologists and anthropologists over the centuries. That's the quest for what Darwin termed, to find the missing link."

The students gave Analisa another round of applause. She folded her papers and waved at the students.

"Thank you all for coming," she said, as she moved to the front of the stage. "Thank you," she said once more and smiled.

Several students walked up to her and shook her hand. The student with the mobile camera continued taking her picture. One student handed her a paper to autograph. Analisa seemed genuinely pleased with the response the students offered. It was satisfying for Analisa, but in the end, all she wanted was to try to get them to think. She wanted to instill in them the initiative and desire to learn, and be open to all possibilities. She knew their quest for discovery had no guarantees. In addition to the difficulty of finding what earth and time had buried, Analisa knew, they would also have to deal with those who have the desire to protect the status quo. The traditionalists who entrenched themselves in every phase of academia, religion, and politics were formidable. They could not bear the forward motion of evolutionary thoughts and ground breaking ideas. They were entrenched in the wretchedness of control for the sake of outdated superstitions. To her, they were the same army of suppressors who struggled to thwart advances of imagination and stifle a man like Darwin.

But for the moment, that struggle didn't matter to her. She raised her head and looked out over the students to see Harrington standing against the back wall. He nodded his head and smiled at her. It was a loving expression of pride and approval. She smiled back. It was a smile that displaced all her longing. Through the smile, she indicated her overriding joy and deep need to be with him once again.

ANALISA changed into a faded pair of jeans. She slipped on a plaid shirt, unbuttoned at the neck. She thought about how she was going to prepare a dinner of stuffed eggplant and pasta with toasted bread crumbs and olive oil. Both recipes were her grandmother's from Calabria, Italy. They were the elderly woman's favorite recipes served as a tradition on Christmas Eve. Whenever Analisa prepared this recipe, she would always recall her Italian grandmother fondly. The true lesson taught by her grandmother was that food served as a form of nurturing and an expression of love in the security of home. With Mitchell now home, she chose the deep tradition of this particular recipe to express her love for him.

Analisa's hands prepared the meal with the loving memory of her grandmother. She placed a bottle of red wine on a tray with three glasses, and walked out to the rear porch of her ranch style home. Earlier, Analisa had lit several candles around the large open porch. She had fired up the outdoor fireplace she often used as a defense against the desert chill. She placed the tray on the table between two burning candles and poured the wine.

"Welcome home," she said raising her glass. "Welcome home to both of you."

"Good to be home," Mitchell said.

"This sure is a nice home ta come home ta," Solis said. "Especially, the way you got it set up."

"Thank you. I set up the guest room for you, Hector. Both of you are staying here tonight," she said and looked at Harrington with a hint of seduction.

"Fine with me. It's a long drive back," Solis said and sipped his wine.

"Where are you from, Hector? I suspect you're not from Arizona," Analisa asked.

"New York. I'm from the Bronx…New York. But I like it here a lot. I just might make Arizona my home."

Analisa sipped her wine and sat next to Mitchell. She rested her head back against his shoulder, and he drew her close to kiss her forehead.

"What did you do in New York, Hector?" Analisa asked.

"I was an artist. I worked in oils mostly. I did city scenes and people. I was also a photographer. Shot mostly in black and white. Picture shoots of every day people. Workers, homeless people mostly. I tried to capture their human qualities, their struggles. I would shoot them goin' ta work in the mornin', getting' on the buses, and trains. Stuff like that. Then I'd try to find the same people comin' home at night and shoot them again. Somebody could look at the pictures of the same people just eight hours later, and they could fill in a lifetime. I know I did."

"I didn't know that's what you did, Hector," Harrington looked surprised.

"Yeah, well that's because there ain't too much you wanna say as a soldier that could make you look like you got your own identity. Guys in our outfit can turn it against you."

"Did you ever sell any of your photos or paintings?" Analisa asked.

"My art wasn't about sellin'. It was about creatin'. But yeah, I sold some of my stuff ta a gallery in Manhattan. Got a few dollars for 'em. I made some money. I had a showin' once at the gallery."

"That's wonderful. What type of painting did you do?"

"It's hard ta describe my work. Abstract mixed with a little bit of impressionism. I'm still settlin' inta my style. I was told my paintings were a cross between Jean Michel Basquiat and Amedeo Modigliani. When the art dealer, in Manhattan, told me that, I couldn't believe it. I liked both those guys. I really couldn't see the connection to Basquiat though. His work was more out there than mine. He's too hard edge for me. Modigliani? I don't know. I was familiar with his work. Our techniques might've been similar, but my strokes were a little lighter than his. Anyway, this dealer saw a connection somewhere, but I didn't see it. Not with Basquiat, anyway. What can I say? Everybody sees somethin' different in art. Did you ever hear of them, Deuce, Basquiat and Modigliani?"

"Yes. Well, I heard of Modigliani at least."

"Yeah, Modigliani was more of a world artist. Basquait was a New York guy. Troubled soul. So was Modigliani for that matter. Both a them were tormented. Both died real young."

"How about your photos?" Analisa asked.

"Yeah, same dealer said my photos were like Garry Winogrand's. The dealer liked ta compare my work with other guys. Winogrand was another New York guy. His work was good, top ta bottom. I didn't mind bein' compared ta Winogrand. Not that I minded being' compared ta Modigliani either. But I don't know, seems if my work is like other guys, no matter how good, it's like I'll always come in second best. But that's okay. For me, it's about the art. I may stay out here and paint. Take photos of the desert. You sure got some pretty sights out here. Sunsets are awesome."

"I'm surprised you never painted or took photos in Iraq," Harrington said. "There certainly was no shortage of drama there."

"Yeah, well, maybe I just didn't wanna paint or shoot somethin' and have it remind me of what went on there. The way I approach art, I don't want it ta come from a perspective of violence. Tragedy and struggle, that's okay. But not violence."

"There was some triumph in Iraq," Harrington commented. "You could have painted or photographed it."

"Not from the way I saw things back there, Deuce. I never saw triumph. And the tragedy... there just wasn't what I was used ta. It all came from violence." Solis retorted, taking several sips of his wine. "No. That wasn't for me," he concluded.

Harrington found Solis' revelation surprising. The mystery of his life could be found in tubes of oil paints, fine sable brushes, a blank canvas, and the shuttering of a lens. The core of Solis was not limited to those objects. More precisely, truth about Solis was to be found in the way he used them. They were tools to his inner expressions, observations and sensitivities. They were also weapons capable of conquering the torment in his soul.

The same torture he seemed so familiar with that troubled Basquiat and Modigliani.

"But explain something to me," Harrington said. "If you were so opposed to violence, why did you get yourself involved in Iraq?"

Solis knew he could not try to explain away the question. If he was able to, it would be in ways Harrington could never understand. He was also very much aware he could not satisfactorily explain that probing enigma to himself. Consequently, Solis just contorted his face to a quizzical and regretful cringe, and shrugged his shoulders pathetically. It was a mimed expression that carried its own explanation. In a way, it was all the explanation Harrington needed.

"Is it too much of a ridiculous question to ask how your time in Iraq was?" Analisa said.

Solis looked at Harrington and nodded his head. It was another gesture offered as a deferment to the question. The bafflement proved to be something else he just couldn't explain.

"I'll leave that one to you, Deuce," Solis responded.

Harrington sipped his wine and leaned forward. He noticed the light from the candles and fireplace illuminated the open porch in a golden tint. It made Analisa's hair glow, much the same way the sun had earlier in the day. The shadows softened the contours of her face. Her eyes seemed dreamy and sensual, combining to create a sense of tranquility and obsession he hadn't felt in two years. Consequently, he didn't want the awful memories of war revived.

"Well," Harrington said. "It's hard to describe. I'm not sure it's worth the effort. But it did have a potential reward I would have never expected in a million years," he said.

Analisa turned and sat on the edge of couch to face Harrington. The shadows on her face shifted. From any angle, she projected an irresistible allure.

"Then I assume we're finally getting down to whatever it is you're excited about showing me."

"Let me get straight to the point," Harrington said. "Suppose I told you I found what I think could be something so valuable and important, history would be rewritten."

Analisa grew more attentive. The soft curves of her face began to tighten. Her eyes grew hard and anxious causing an odd strain in her pause.

"Tell me, what it is, Mitchell," she demanded.

Harrington reached under the bench producing a small case. He placed it on the table. He withdrew one of five clear pouches containing the white powder. Undoing the seal, he opened it and showed it to Analisa.

Instantly, her eyes widened. She became excited, almost frightened. A sense of disbelief gripped her.

"Oh my God," she said breathlessly. "Is this what I think it is?" she said, reaching in and touching the powder.

"What do you think it is?" Harrington asked.

"What do I think this is? My God, Mitchell, my God," Analisa's excitement began to grow. She began to shout. "What have you found here? It's the powder? The Flinders Petrie powder...white ash. Is that what it is? Is that what you think it is?"

"Yes. That's exactly what I think."

"I knew it! I knew it! I knew that's what you thought. I can't believe this. My, God, how did you find this? It's been lost for more than a century," Analisa continued excitedly, not giving Harrington a chance to respond.

"When I was recently in the Chad and Niger," she continued. "I took several days and went to Egypt. I followed Petrie's path to the Temple of Serabit, trying to locate any remnants of his white powder. I also looked for a fuel source or charcoal. But like Petrie, I saw there were none to be discovered. There was no residue or indication of fire on the rocks or in caves. Petrie thought the white powder was just ash. Consequently, he concluded the fires were for religious sacrifices. I'm not convinced the fires were used for sacrifices at all. I was hoping to find some traces of what he had found. Who figured it would drop in my lap."

"Analisa, I don't think we should make any assumptions about this," Harrington cautioned. "We can't be certain it's Petrie's discovery."

"It's hard not to assume anything. But you obviously made the same assumption. It makes perfect sense. I'll have to test this to be sure. Is that why you brought it to me?"

"Yes."

"Well, I'm glad you did. How did you find this? I assume you found it in Iraq," Analisa said, her excitement overtaking her.

"Well actually, Hector found it. He fell into a hole while we were on patrol."

Analisa looked at Solis and reached out and touched his hand.

"Hector, you realize what you have found? Do you know what this could possibly be? Have you any idea?"

"Listen, I'm still askin' Deuce ta tell me what it is. He's sayin' nothin' ta me. So no, I don't know what it is. Are you gonna tell me?"

"I wanted to be sure this is the Petrie find before I say anything," Harrington interrupted.

"I agree," Analisa said. "Just a few tests will confirm or deny our assumptions. What kind of a hole was it? Was it a cave? Some sort of an ancient temple?"

"No. It was a hole the size of a small room dug under a house. It wasn't an ancient temple or a place of sacrifices."

"Do you know where it came from? Could it have come from the Temple of Serabit?"

"There was no way to tell where it came from. It's conceivable it could have been moved from the Sinai. That's not out of the question."

"No, it's not out of the question. What is remarkable is that it survived at all. Petrie claimed it all had gotten lost."

"Maybe this came from a different source than what Petrie saw."

"That's quite possible. How much did you find?" Analisa asked.

"We brought up about a ton."

"What? A ton? That's a lot. But compared to what Petrie describes seeing, it's not much. His notes indicated he measured the ash powder to be eighteen inches deep for over a hundred feet. He saw the ash that deep and spread out in several other locations. That would be more than a ton. But it's still a lot. How much is here?"

"I brought twenty-five pounds with me."

"Where is the rest of it?"

"I have it hidden in a storage facility."

"I hope you have the storage facility secured."

"Yes. I took a few hundred pounds and hid it in a separate place, just in case."

Analisa took the clear plastic bag from Harrington. She held it out to the light of the fireplace. The golden honey light shimmered through the plastic in abstract forms. The light seemed to make the powder glow beyond white. She felt the powder was a grail, an apparition of all things sacred and revealing. A mythical potion blended by the gods of legend. If her tests confirmed what she suspected, she would be overcome by the world of possibilities.

"There were two other empty jugs in the hole, which I suspect were going to be filled with more powder."

"So, there could be more?"

"Possibly."

"How did you get it shipped here from Iraq?"

Harrington felt the solemn weight of conflict, but remained silent.

"We had somebody help us out," Solis intervened. "We ran inta a bit of a problem, but it all worked out in the end."

"My God, Mitchell, this is astounding. If this is Flinders Petrie's find, and if it was the alchemy of the ancients, this could enhance our knowledge dramatically," Analisa announced.

"I know," Harrington responded.

"Alchemy, I know about that," Solis said. "That's when guys turn stone into gold."

"Not exactly, Hector. The alchemist, Eirenaeus Philalethes, claimed the Philosopher's Stone is no stone at all. It's called a stone by virtue of its fixed nature. But, its appearance is that of a very fine powder. Impalpable to the touch, dry yet oily, just like this," Analisa said rubbing a slight amount of the powder between her fingers.

"Philalethes described it as a potency penetrating to the spirit," she continued. "Philalethes says the stone does not exist in nature, but must be prepared by art, in obedience of nature's law."

"I don't get it," Solis said. "If it don't exist in nature, but its gotta be prepared by nature's laws, what's that all about? And, if it don't exist, what's that in that plastic bag you got in your hand?"

"That is the mystery of alchemy," Analisa said. "The ancients knew about alchemy, especially the Philosophers Stone or the Paradise Stone. It's all the same. The last ones that knew about alchemy were the alchemists of the Knights Templar. They made colored glass for the Notre Dame cathedral in France in the twelfth century. Their secret was the Spiritus Mundi – the breath of the universe – the white light of the Paradise Stone.

"The Paradise Stone for the glass of the cathedral was made from gold. It was subjected to specific heat that transformed it into glass. But not only was the glass clear, it was missing forty-four percent light – the Spiritus Mundi. The breath reappears in the glass, which means the forty-four percent never disappeared, it just moved into a state of weightlessness…. Alchemy is so much more than turning stone into gold."

"So wait a minute," Solis said. "Let me see if I get this. The Paradise Stone or the Philosophers Stone is not really a stone, but a powder that don't exist. Even though that powder is right there in your hand…"

"We don't know that yet," Analisa interrupted.

"Fine, we don't know that yet. But, if you test it out and it proves ta be the Paradise, and that other stone, and then it's somethin'. It's there, it's somethin'. I see it. And, let me tell you somethin' else. That stuff does have weight ta it. I know. I carried it outta the hole I fell inta. That's another way I know its somethin'."

"Well, it is something, Hector, that's for sure," Analisa said "The alchemists, as late as the twelfth century, knew how to prepare it. It wasn't *just* something, it was everything."

"But the twelfth century ain't that long ago. So, why don't we have the secrets of their alchemy? There's gotta be somethin' written down. You would think somethin' that important, somebody woulda kept a copy of the recipe. Why don't we have it?"

"Because, it wasn't their secret. It doesn't date to them. It goes back long before them."

"Back how far? Back to who?" Solis asked.

"That's the mystery, Hector….That's the great mystery."

A dull rationale raked over Solis. It was an awkward presumption joined with the elusive secrets of alchemy that simultaneously undulated forward and backward in time. In its movements, he suspected alchemy had to leave an imprint or a hint of its formula, and its true nature somewhere in history. He wondered if somewhere in the chronicles of ambiguity, alchemy, and the white powder were umbilicaly bound, and had an established link to their common origins.

Suddenly, Solis began to feel the trappings of a strange realization. It grew on him, like a compelling clash of fragmented details straining for connection. He equated his gradual awareness to the images of the many photos he had developed in a dark room. Those blank sheets of photographic paper, he placed in a pan of solution, gradually began to show images until they became more defined and ultimately revealed a complete picture--an undeniably recorded truth.

"Hey, Analisa," Solis said slowly and deliberately, his mind developing a new clarity. "This powder looks ordinary ta me. Just ordinary. But does the white powder have somethin' ta do with the ancient people you was talkin' about today?" Solis continued. "Does the white powder have anything ta do with the missin' link?"

Analisa embraced the logic and the possibilities of Solis' question. The answer was one she had always cataloged somewhere in the realm of promise, hoping one day to gain confirmation. Yes, the white powder seemed ordinary. But, Analisa knew it was not ordinary. It became less so when connected to the past. Suddenly, the powder offered Analisa a shrinking gap between her, and the history she pursued. It had the potential to bring her to the convergence of myth and revelation. Analisa knew the white powder had the capability of becoming, among other things, pure light. She hoped it also had the extraordinary capability of becoming the light of a pure and vivid description.

"Yes, Hector," Analisa said quietly and firmly. "I believe the white powder has everything to do with the missing link."

BILLY Hayden appeared nervous when he and his father, August, entered Sheriff St. Cloud's office. August placed his hand on his son's shoulder, causing Billy to feel as though he was being lead into an adult-size struggle for which he was unprepared. Everyone was taller than him, making Billy uneasy. Everything he said, and the way he said it, was going to be scrutinized.

Young Hayden had difficulty standing still. He secretly wished he was riding his quad in the desert. But, he thought, it was because of riding his quad, he was in the thick of the situation. Sitting behind his desk, Sheriff St. Cloud looked serious, and officially threatening. He could feel the hands in his pockets beginning to twitch and sweat.

Billy's fear mounted, when he saw the bruises on the faces of Homeland Security agents, Cummings and Manning. He quickly assumed they were attacked by the men he saw at the mine. They were going to find him, and beat him, once they learned he had identified them. For support and reassurance, Billy quickly turned and looked at his father. He was hoping arrangements were already made that would keep him safe.

St. Cloud noticed Billy was nervous and frightened. He saw the boy looking around the room. His eyes were wide, as though a threat was lurking. The Sheriff was aware of Billy's isolation and tried to ease his anxiety.

"Billy, come in," Sheriff St. Cloud said, making his tone friendly. "No one is going to hurt you. We just want to ask you a few more questions. Okay?"

Billy's father led his son to a chair. August removed his hand from his son's shoulder as the boy sat down.

"Thank you for coming to see me again," St. Cloud said. "Billy, it must seem to you we have difficulty getting things done. That's why we called you in again."

"I don't know," the boy responded.

"Well, we just need to be sure we have all the information we need to move forward. Now, these two men are here to help us. They're with the United States government," St. Cloud said motioning to Cummings and Manning. "They want to ask you about the explosion at Mister Barnes' mine the other night. They really need your help. Are you okay with that?"

"Yes," Billy said.

"Good. There's no reason to be afraid. You'll be doing them a real favor by answering all their questions the best you can."

"I'll try."

"Thank you, Billy, I'm Agent Andrew Cummings. This is Agent Stewart Manning," Cummings announced.

"We're with Homeland Security," Cummings continued. "I know you've heard of Homeland Security?"

"I've been studying about Homeland Security in social studies."

"That's good. I'm sure you know we try to protect the country. Keep it safe so people could feel good about going to work and school, and play outside safely; riding bikes and quads."

"Yes."

"Well, that's exactly what we try to do. Keep people safe. Most times, we can do it by ourselves. We have lots of cool technology we use. But sometimes, we need people to help us. We often rely on citizens who may see things. Then they report to us, and we investigate it. You know what I mean?"

"Yes."

"Now, whenever citizens like you help us, we always keep their names and the names of their families secret. No one ever knows who gave us the information. I understand you were riding your quad out by Mister Barnes' mine the night somebody blew it up, right?"

"Yes, I was. Me and my friend, Henry Fuller."

"I was glad to hear you and your friend were not injured in the blast."

"I got a concussion," Billy said.

"You did? Are you feeling better?"

"Yes. The ringing in my ears went away."

"That's good. Now, I've been told, it was only you who saw a car and two men in it. Not your friend, Henry. Right?"

"Yes, sir. I saw the men. Well actually, I saw only one of the men in the car. He was looking back. Like looking back at me. The other man, the driver of the car, he didn't turn around. So, I really only saw one man in the car that night. I mean, I saw only one man's face and one man's head. But, there were two men in the car."

"That's good. If I showed you a picture, do you think you would know the man?"

"I think so. When I spoke to Sheriff St. Cloud, I told him about the car. I gave him a license plate number."

"Yes. Sheriff St. Cloud has given us that information."

"It was a Volvo. Model Seven-Forty," Billy confirmed.

"Are you sure about that?"

"I'm sure. I like cars and quads and motorcycles. I pay attention to them. I'm good at recognizing them."

"If you identified the car, then I'll bet you'll be able to identify a picture of the man you saw if his picture is here," Cummings said, raising a manila folder.

"I'll try."

"That was very helpful identifying the car, Billy. It's very helpful you're attentive to details. I understand you want to be a journalist," Cummings said.

"That's right. I do."

"Good. To be a good journalist, you have to be observant. You appear to notice details. Now, could you just tell me how you were able to see the car so clearly?"

"Yes. There was a full moon that night. A full moon on the desert makes everything look bright. It's really not hard to see things when the moon's that bright. The desert reflects the moon's light. And the lights from my quad were right on the car. But, even if not, I could tell a car just by the back lights. I didn't need to that night, because of the moon and lights from my quad."

"That's great. That's the kind of help we need from citizens. Now I'm going to show you pictures of several men. I need you to take your time when you look at the pictures. If the man you saw that night in the car is among these pictures, just let us know. Okay?"

Cummings removed the photos from the folder. Some of the photos were of men who were known criminals; some were office staff at Homeland Security. Other pictures were of suspected terrorists. Most of the photos were clear, while others were candid shots with a certain amount of distortion. The photos of Nunarro and Orisi were purposely placed in the center of the stack. In addition, the two photos lacked perfect detail and clarity. However, their images were recognizable.

"Here, take a look at these, Billy," Cummings said, handing the stack of photos to the boy. "Take your time. I want you to be sure you can identify the man you saw that night at the mine. His picture may be here, and it may not. We need you to tell us."

Billy took the photos from Cummings and started to look through them. As he went through the stack, he came upon the photo of Umberto Nunarro. Suddenly, Billy winced and sat back in his chair. The image was the exact likeness he held in his memory. There were no distortions, as his mind made the frightening connection. The photo of Nunarro seemed fierce and threatening. His face was a model of intimidation. Cummings noticed Billy's reaction, and the fright that appeared on his face.

"Is that the man?" Cummings asked. "Is that the man you saw at the mine that night?"

Billy was drawn to the photo. Although he wanted to push it away quickly, he held on to it, unable to move. It was the menace in Nunarro's glare he remembered so well. Once again, it was there, real and personal. The stare coming from the photo was penetrating; looking back at him.

"Yes, that's him," Billy whispered.

"Are you sure?" Cummings asked.

"If he said it's him, then it's him," Billy's father said abruptly.

"It's okay Billy," his father continued, taking the photo out of his son's hand and passing it to Cummings.

"Do you want to look at the rest of the photos?" Cummings said.

"My son said he only saw one man that night, and that's the man he just identified. There's no reason for him to look at the other photos," August Hayden said.

"We just want to be sure," Cummings said.

"He identified that man. That's as sure as it's going to get," August responded. "Besides, my son gave you the license plate number of the car. I would think that would have been all you needed to go after these guys. I don't see any reason to put my son through much more of this."

"You're right, Mister Hayden," Cummings said. "But, we just want to get as much information as possible. I hope you understand."

"Yes, I understand. But, if this gets out that it was my son who gave you this information, who's going to protect him from these guys? That's what I really need to understand."

"As I said, this meeting is strictly confidential. No one outside this office will ever know your son gave us this information," Cummings assured.

"August, Billy's under my jurisdiction," St. Cloud said. "I will guarantee you my office will protect Billy and your entire family."

St. Cloud turned to Billy and saw the concern in his eyes. He knew the boy had made his own connection to a plot that might be hatched against him. With little effort, the boy's imagination could make improbable things real. The world of violence and menace were not in the lexicon of a young, small boy who seemed to be growing smaller with each bit of information he imparted. But a glossy 8-by-12 photo suddenly gave his nightmares a basis for real possibilities.

"Billy, what you did here today was very brave," St. Cloud continued. "And it was very important. I don't want you to be frightened. With the identification of the photo, we will apprehend these men. I will make sure my deputies are looking for these men at all times. They will be easy to find now. Once we do, they will never be a threat to you. You will be able to go to school and go quadding like you have in the past. So please, don't worry."

"Billy, just so we're clear, along with the Sheriff and his deputies, I will also be around to protect you. So just trust me and the Sheriff. You'll be fine," his father said.

Billy looked at the men in the room and struggled to conclude they were telling him the truth. Without being fully aware, his sense of trust was in a raging battle with his belief in bad guys, villains and the overconfidence of authority. His personal safety had become threatened, and now, he seemed answerable to the face he saw on a desert night and in a grainy photograph.

"Do you at least know who the man in the photo is?" Billy asked.

Cummings started to put the stack of photos back in the folder.

"Yes, we do, Billy," he said.

"That will make it easier to catch him, right?" Billy pressed for more assurance.

"Yes, it will."

Cummings' response marginally assured Billy. He hoped the agents of Homeland Security, with all their cool technology, could live up to their responsibility and catch the bad guys before they could hurt someone like himself.

"Can you tell me his name?" Bill asked. "The man in the photo."

Cummings looked at Billy and then at his father. There seemed to be a conventional indifference Cummings was trying to protect. The things he saw as noble were not those things that could fall to lesser concerns.

"Billy, it's better if you don't know the man's name," Cummings said, indifferently.

AGENT Cummings walked through the corridor to the small conference room located next to Henrietta Dell's office. With two manila folders tucked under his arm, he carried a cardboard cup filled with hot coffee. His pace had a stern intensity. The glare in his eagle-like eyes conveyed his fiery thoughts. The information contained in the folders gave him a sense of order and command. The investigative results brought together an outline of related documentation, yet resulted in vague inferences. The reports he was prepared to present to Henrietta Dell were at a sharp angle to an intrigue being played out by a handful of people in a small section of the world not far from his office. Because of that close proximity, he felt a personal invasion; offset by the confidence the assumed tyranny was within his reach.

Cummings was glad to have a world of new technology at his disposal. Satellites and hidden surveillance cameras enabled him to see things that might otherwise slip through the world unnoticed. What he liked more was the freedom to employ the methods of observation from his perspective. The things in the world that could not rely on total concealment were the things Cummings trusted most. He felt the control of total scrutiny was always the way to force a show of honesty and have an impact on protection and domination.

He looked at his watch before opening the conference room door.

Henrietta stood beside the oblong mahogany desk, looking out the window. She held a cell phone to her ear, and turned as Cummings entered the conference room. With a wave of her hand, she instructed Cummings to enter, and motioned to a seat at the conference table.

"Yes," she said into the phone. "I am confirming I will be unavailable all next week. I will be co-chairing the annual Board of County Supervisors Meeting. Yes," she said, clearly responding to questioning that Cummings faintly heard.

"The agenda will address effective emergency response and recovery operations with other county agencies. We need to review and update the development preparedness materials for the public. Spokespersons from FEMA will be attending the meeting, as will spokespersons from Fort Huachuca, Provost Marshal's Office. Understand, I want to see the complete text of the article before it gets presented for publication."

From the flow of the conversation, Cummings assumed Henrietta was speaking with someone from the local press. He knew she had been the key spokesperson for a series of articles on Homeland Security.

"If the text of the article is not given to me before the meeting next week, it must be placed on hold," she continued. "One more thing. I do not want to see the text on Friday. I will not have the time to review it. I need at least twenty-four hours. Good. I'm glad you understand. Thank you," she said, and closed the lid of the phone.

"Sorry, about that," she said to Cummings. "The press," she added confirming his assumptions.

"No problem. Sorry I'm late," Cummings said. "I was watching for surveillance information from security at the University of Arizona. It seems as though they had computer problems."

"Have the problems been resolved?"

"Yes, I did get everything I needed at the last minute."

"Good."

Cummings moved the coffee cup aside and opened both manila folders. He slid one of the folders across the table to where Henrietta had taken a seat. The folder contained duplicates of the reports in his folder.

"The first bit of information you have shows a list of residents on South Alarcon Street," Cummings said. "You will notice one name is highlighted."

"Yes, I see it. Mitchell Harrington," Henrietta acknowledged.

"Mitchell Harrington. I'm still in the process of gathering information on other residents, but the main emphasis is being placed on Harrington. I have good reason. As we go further, you'll see why. To begin with, Harrington was driving the vehicle being followed by Umberto Nunarro.

Harrington drove to the University of Arizona. He had a companion in the car…"

"Was the companion identified?"

"Yes," Cummings said. "You'll notice on the second page…"

"Yes, I see it," Henrietta said, as she turned the page. "Hector Solis."

"Hector Solis," Cummings confirmed. "Solis is from the Bronx, New York. I think you'll find more information on Solis, but I'll get to it in a bit."

"What was the purpose of Harrington and Solis going to the University of Arizona?" Henrietta asked, prodding Cummings to reveal more of the surveillance.

"We don't know the exact purpose of his trip. Mitchell Harrington was a student at the university. We assume he went to visit a faculty member. One in particular, Analisa Scotti…"

"Analisa Scotti. Yes, of course. She's Pietro Segretti's cousin through the marriage of her sister to Nicola Bounetti," Henrietta said pointedly.

"Yes. It appears Harrington and Solis went to see her specifically. They stayed with her. It could be a coincidence that Harrington and Scotti met."

"I'm not a believer in coincidences, but in this case, that could be. Let's not try to read more into this than is actually here. However, we should keep an open mind. Did Nunarro and Harrington meet, or was my suspicion correct that Harrington was being followed?"

"It appears you were correct that Nunarro was conducting surveillance on Harrington. Nunarro drove around the campus, and then followed Harrington's car to Analisa Scotti's house."

"Analisa Scotti is attracting a great deal of attention. As I recall, Analisa was an adjunct professor at the University."

"That's correct," Cummings responded.

"Adjunct professor of what?"

Cummings looked through the report until he found the pertinent information.

"Here it is," he said. "She's an adjunct Associate Professor in Anthropology."

"Anthropology….Interesting. Good. What else do you have?"

Cummings removed a paper clip from a second stack of papers and took a sip of coffee.

"Here's where things get very interesting and start to draw a big picture" Cummings said.

"There's interest in the little things, too. Don't overlook anything."

"I won't. For now, I want to direct your attention to the report: 'Military Intel'. You have it there, grouped as section two."

"I see it," Henrietta confirmed.

"What you have offers us a little background to Harrington and Solis. Incidentally, it was through military intelligence, I was able to learn the identity of Hector Solis."

"Good."

"Let me start with Mitchell Harrington. Harrington's rank was staff sergeant. He was attached to the Second Squadron, the Seventh Cavalry, and Fourth Brigade Combat. He served a one two-year tour. By all indications, he was an exemplary soldier. Solis was in the same brigade and immediately under Staff Sergeant Harrington's command. They both were under the command of Captain Eli Hicks…"

"Where was the command?"

"Iraq."

"Did Solis serve a two-year tour?"

"Yes."

"Harrington and Solis were officially discharged from military service only fourteen days ago. Harrington took his discharge in Arizona. Solis took his in New York. Immediately after discharge, Solis came to Arizona. But before they took official discharge, they had a stop over in Wiesbaden, Germany. I'll get to that layover in a minute," Cummings said. "That's important.

"Now, through military intelligence, I was able to gain access to a report filed by Captain Eli Hicks, regarding an incident that occurred on the outskirts of Mosul," Cummings continued. "Two F Sixteens flew over a tiny hamlet near Mosul; the suspected outpost of enemy activity. After the jets laid waste to the hamlet, Captain Hicks along with Sergeant Harrington, Private Solis, and others in the operation, were involved in a clean-up and reconnaissance. As they were approaching the area, two soldiers from the Iraqi Police Service arrived. There was a standoff, and only under the threat of force, did the Iraqi policemen stand down. According to Captain Hicks' report, Sergeant Harrington was a pivotal part of the standoff when he approached one of the Iraqi policemen. Apparently, the policeman didn't like the idea that Sergeant Harrington's weapon was being pointed directly at his head. The Hicks report goes on to say the situation was defused after he, Captain Hicks, exerted command. The operation continued without further incident. No enemy or insurgents were found near the hamlet, and the incident ended. Captain Hicks recorded the name of only one of the policemen, after said policeman identified himself. The policeman's name was Haddad bin Nasab."

"When did this incident occur in relation to Harrington's tour of duty?" Henrietta asked.

"Just about two weeks before Harrington's discharge. His and Solis'. They were both discharged at the same time. It was the last report filed on them before their collective discharge. Let's fast forward to Wiesbaden, Germany, the debarkation point before final discharge in the states. On the banks of the Main River, just before it converges with the Rhine, German authorities discovered seven murdered victims on two small boats…"

"Let me guess," Henrietta interrupted. "One of the victims was Haddad bin Nasab."

"Yes. Along with Haddad bin Nasab was his brother, Dawud. Some of the other victims were Klaus Hoffer and Conrad Hultz. Both were mechanics at the airfield at Wiesbaden. Three of the seven victims remain unidentified at this time.

"Incidentally, Haddad bin Nasab and his brother Dawud, were deserters from the Iraqi Special Police. I was able to get limited information on them. It's located in the file denoted by 'Profile'."

"Fine."

"There's not much there and given the upheaval in that country, I would be sensitive to the reliability of the information."

"That makes sense."

"I will certainly cross-reference Haddad bin Nasab with other intelligence we have."

"Keep me updated on this. If something urgent develops, don't hesitate to call me at the conference."

"I'll let you know if anything develops. Now, what was also retrieved at the murder scene in Germany was spent ordinance. Guess what? Some of the ordinance was clearly identified as military issue. I spoke with Kurt Berker, a German police investigator, who was at the scene. He described it to me. He provided photos, as you can see there," Cummings said, pointing to the photos separated from the report.

Henrietta looked at the report, then at the photos with a jeweler's eye. She saw starkness in the photos she found repulsive, but could not turn away. She looked beyond the carnage, searching for something completely concealed. She knew the lifeless bodies had the forensic capability of telling a compelling story.

"I'm not an expert, but this looks like the effects of a military-style raid to me," she observed.

"Exactly. It also has all the fingerprints of a drug conspiracy that went awry," Cummings observed.

Henrietta's hand moved across the photos in a gesture meant to search for something to make it complete. From every angle and within every inch of each photo, she saw the undeniable human flaws and rage.

"Has it been established Sergeant Harrington and Private Solis were in Wiesbaden at the time of the murders?"

"Yes. They were billeted at the Amelia Earhart Hotel, which is the common hotel for service personnel on layovers."

"How long were they on layover?"

"Five days."

"I assume you've contacted the proper authorities at the hotel?" Henrietta questioned.

"Yes. I did. Other than confirming their stay, there was no other information. The soldiers were under no confinement while on layover. They were basically on their own, sort of a vacation."

"What did Harrington study at the University of Arizona?" Henrietta asked.

Cummings looked at Henrietta with a frozen curiosity. He struggled to find relevance and symmetry between the photos he knew Henrietta was studying and the possible interpretation she may be compiling from them.

"I'm sorry?" Cummings said, not understanding why Henrietta asked such an obscure question.

"What did Harrington study?" she repeated.

"I don't know," he said.

"Find out," she ordered.

"Is there a specific reason you should know this? I don't understand."

"You said Analisa Scotti is an adjunct professor in anthropology; cross-reference that with Harrington. That could be important. Drugs don't seem to be the motive for the murders in Wiesbaden. It's illogical to me," Henrietta said. "Here's my reason," she continued. "Haddad bin Nasab and his brother were members of the Iraqi Police Service who deserted their posts."

"Yes, that's correct."

"Then let's assume for a moment, Haddad and Dawud were involved in a drug trade. Perhaps, they were involved in a pipeline smuggling drugs out of Afghanistan, where we know large supplies of heroin originate. Where's the logic in the brothers leaving their posts? They're already in the center of a drug route. They're at the point of operation. Why go to Wiesbaden, Germany? For what purpose? If Haddad bin Nasab and his brother were involved in drugs surely they would be low-level and not apt to go to Germany. By leaving Iraq, they would never get back into their country without being arrested for desertion. Not to mention, incurring the ire of their fellow drug dealers. So for many reasons, leaving Iraq, if they're involved in drugs, has no upside for them. My suspicion is drugs are not the issue. Harrington is the key to all of this. He more so than Solis. I would also assume the standoff in the hamlet played a key role. The hamlet was bombed out correct?"

"Yes. Strafed by F Sixteens."

"Does your report indicate why two members of the Iraqi Police Service wanted to be part of the U.S. military clean-up operation?"

"No. The report only stated the policemen wanted to help."

"Yes. Help with what and why? Were the brothers hiding something in the hamlet they didn't want discovered? Something other than drugs? It appears Harrington was pivotal in the standoff. Why? I believe Harrington is at the center of this. Also, find out what relationship he has with Analisa Scotti."

"What are you suggesting?"

"I'm suggesting everything gets looked at. What kind of academic ties did they have, if any? Were they involved in any kind of business partnership? If so what? As I said, there's interest in little things. We need to do all the things we can as well as keep our eye in the sky on Harrington. Solis, Nunarro, Orisi and whoever else is involved could cause their operation to unfold without our intervention. When it does, we can just walk in and institute the final verdict. But, I want to try and have a preemptive option."

"I understand."

"How helpful was the eyewitness to the explosion at the Barnes mine?"

"Billy Hayden was the eyewitness. You'll see the notes of the interview in my report. He's a young boy, but he seemed very reliable. He confirms it was Umberto Nunarro at the Barnes mine the night of the explosion. He even identified the car Nunarro was in."

"Did you brief the Sheriff's department?"

"Yes, after we met with Billy Hayden, Agent Manning and I briefed St. Cloud. We also met with agents from DOD and briefed them. We told both agencies we had Nunarro, Orisi and Harrington under surveillance."

"Good work."

"In that briefing, St. Cloud gave us some information. The car, Billy Hayden identified at the Barnes mine, was different from the car rented by Umberto Nunarro. The car Billy saw, at the explosion site, had been stolen."

"Clever switch," Henrietta observed. "We didn't have that information earlier in our investigation. That's why we still need to improve our inter-agency communication capabilities. I intend to speak about it, at the annual Board of County Supervisors meeting, next week. We can't allow information like that to remain isolated."

Cummings witnessed a strange look come over Henrietta's face. Her eyes fluttered with a gnarly agitation as she wiped pensively at her forehead.

"Henrietta," Cummings said. "If you don't think drugs are at the core of this, what about terrorism?"

Henrietta paused, allowing her professional instincts to overcome notions that could be subject to faltering or uncertainty.

"Because I don't think drugs are involved," she said, with a reserve of control. "That doesn't mean they're not. As for the threat of terrorism, I never disregard the possibility under any circumstance. Clearly, if the eyewitness puts Umberto Nunarro at the mine, then it's conceivable he is a prime suspect in an act of terrorism. Certainly, the murder of seven Iraqi deserters carries a multitude of suspicions. I would never be so cavalier and overlook any links or think none existed between Nunarro, Harrington and a plot of terrorism. The possibility of terrorism is everywhere. It's a nagging paranoia that is consuming and must always be validated."

Cummings became acutely aware Henrietta examined intricacies where none could possibly exist. He understood, to Henrietta, nothing was simple. Yet, she tried to see the simplistic nature to all complex things. By doing so, her empirical sense taught her all problems shared the same common dominator. She had a way of showing him she was good at looking at photos of seven murdered men and seeing a dark pattern of humanity and an ancient awe. Even useless knowledge supported her concept that guile and specifics were finely interwoven. Henrietta was a master at the art of visual redundancy. She identified varying spaces and forms without losing concentration as to where a single fact resided. Cummings trusted the random essentials of her perception. She had a way of seeing history and recognizing the future.

Cummings removed the lid from the cup of coffee and took a sip. He sat back in his chair and closed the folder. He put the cup down and looked at Henrietta, studying her with a certain level of envy.

"So, what do you think this is all about?" He asked. "What could be the possible connection between Harrington, Solis, Nunarro, Orisi and the murdered Iraqi policemen? All of it?" Cummings concluded.

Henrietta tightened her lips indicating nothing specific came to mind. A wide band of skepticism formed across her brow. Her eyes went blank. She felt a fluttering disturbance that challenged her perceptions and all things that gave her joy. There were times, Henrietta wished the answers to complexities would be blown into her lap. This was one of those times.

"I don't really know, Agent Cummings," Henrietta responded. "But I suspect, when we do find out, the answers will surprise us."

THE day for Umberto Nunarro had been tiring. The long drive from Prescott had proved exhausting. Nunarro felt the tightness in his neck and shoulders. His arms ached from the tension. An overall weariness pressed hard on him. His body was clammy from perspiration. Nunarro's head ached from the constant glare of the sun on the windshield.

After following Harrington from the university, Nunarro parked at a safe distance from Analisa Scotti's house. His car remained partially hidden by the shrubs on a nearby neighbor's property. He was able to see Harrington's car parked in Analisa's driveway. Nunarro remained there until he was convinced Harrington and Solis would be staying the night. Abandoning his surveillance for the night, Nunarro and Ubaid chose to stay at a nearby hotel. The hotel was in close proximity to Analisa's house. They rented adjoining rooms on the top floor, where they could see Analisa's house clearly.

After using a false identity to check in, Nunarro went directly to his room. He took a warm shower to relieve the onslaught of the headache. Lowering his head, he let the water fall on to his head and shoulders. Hoping to drive away the pain, he rubbed his neck and the sides of his temples.

Shutting the lights in the room, Nunarro stepped onto the balcony and looked toward Analisa's house. In spite of the darkness, he was still able to discern the dim lights of candles in her backyard. Harrington's car was still parked in the driveway. Nunarro sensed a certain peace and tranquility surrounding Analisa's house. Its adobe walls and ocher tiled roof appeared to be in partnership with a neighborhood.

In the quiet of an early sleepless morning, Nunarro suddenly wondered why the obvious sense of unity and community filled his mind, causing him to become sentimental. He felt fragmented, but his own loneliness could not allow himself to fall prey to even the slightest amount of susceptibility. If revealed, the angry man, with the animal instincts in the next room, would sense the limp and pounce.

Nunarro drew in a deep breath of the cool night air and relaxed his shoulders. Slowly, the tightness in his neck began to recede, and his headache subsided. As he turned to go into his room, he noticed the muted light coming from Ubaid's room. The door to the balcony was shut and the drapes drawn. Nunarro sat in a chair in front of the open balcony door, allowing the breeze to blow over him. He dozed sporadically, sleeping no more than thirty minutes at a time. Each time he awoke, he walked out on the balcony to look at Analisa's house. By the third time, the candles were out and the lights in the house had gone off.

His final sleep was filled with visions of white powder being blown by a fierce sirocco sweeping across a desert floor. The powder blew past a naked image of Adilah standing with her arms spread Christ-like. The powder poured through the holes in Adilah's palms, and the hole in her torso, just below her breast. Adilah raised her head. The powder lodged in her hair turned it completely white. She smiled, and her face began to shrivel, mixing with the powder and disappearing into the horizon.

Nunarro flinched in the chair and called out Adilah's name. He turned quickly, feeling disoriented by the strange room. His desperation began to subside once he became reacquainted with his surroundings. The red readout from the clock blinked. It was 4:10 a.m.

Lighting a cigarette, he walked out to the balcony and looked out toward Analisa's house. He leaned over the railing and listened to the sounds of the desert. The breeze had ceased its low groan. It was replaced by an occasional nocturnal howl; the painful cry of a desert animal. The melody of the night was a natural pitch of struggle and survival. He stayed on the balcony smoking several more cigarettes, all the while watching Analisa's house. It remained dark and peaceful, refusing to yield to his intent.

The dawn moved in and spread out from the horizon. It was an easy transfer of power. The silent passing from night to dawn spelled a new phase in his own journey. Each moment brought him closer to a certain point he hoped included Adilah.

Nunarro finished his last cigarette and flicked it from the balcony waiting for the day to begin. The rising sunlight glared on the desert surface, as if it were a sheet of tinfoil. Nunarro saw the line of morning light accentuate the flatness of the terrain. He remained on the balcony, taking his time trying to understand the complexities of the desert.

Like the morphing landscape, with unseen threats lurking in the palm of creation, Nunarro knew there were perils before him. Acquiring the white powder for the emir was encased in doubt and fringed with danger. The formidable nature of menace was not limited to the forces of opposition. At times, they also included those that were found in the coalition of purpose.

"You stand looking at the desert when you should be taking things into your own hands," Ubaid said from behind him.

Nunarro turned to notice the door to Ubaid's room was open, but the drapes remained drawn. It appeared as a purposeful cloak designed to threaten Nunarro. The inconvenient circumstance was a grand plot that formed their union, and was a blatant mismatch of sorts with the potential for a terrible ending. Nunarro was aware Ubaid was controlled by impulsive urges to strike out at anything that went against his nature. Reason was a poor deterrent to Ubaid's tendencies. The use of intimidation and cunning were useless against him.

"I'm waiting for Harrington to move. I need him to play into me," Nunarro responded to the drapes.

"It should be clear to you what we need from him is somewhere in Prescott not here. Nothing is getting done here," Ubaid said, moving out from behind the drapes.

"That's why Orisi is in Prescott."

"But, you both wait like poor people hoping someone will hand you something," Ubaid accused.

Nunarro would not allow Ubaid to draw him into a confrontation. Once the powder was delivered, there would be time.

"That's right," Nunarro said. "We wait. By waiting, eventually Harrington will hand us exactly what we want."

It was only through denial that Ubaid could not understand the consequences of the moment. But, Nunarro's remarks registered clearly. They were calculated, and they fit harshly in the context of covert humiliation.

"You think I don't know why you wanted me to help you follow Harrington," Ubaid said. "You wanted to keep me in sight. You wanted to keep an eye on me. That's why Orisi is in Prescott, and I'm here."

"That's exactly right. The emir trusts you, Ubaid. I don't."

Ubaid moved closer to Nunarro and glared at him.

"That's right, you should not trust me," Ubaid said. "You should not trust me, because your methods disgust me. You test my patience, and I don't like you."

Nunarro paused and glared back at Ubaid. There was a stiff charge to the silence. It blended with the molecules of the air, generating a raw friction.

"I don't care who you don't like. As for my methods, you have no idea what my methods are," Nunarro responded in a cold, controlled tone.

"And what will be your method today?" Ubaid sneered.

"Same as yesterday, we follow Harrington. I know what we're looking for is in Prescott, but something brought Harrington here. Whatever the reason he's here, it's important to Harrington."

"Can't you see what was so important to Harrington," Ubaid said. "He came here to get laid. He's with his girlfriend. Down there, in that house," Ubaid continued, pointing to Analisa's house. "We go there now, put a knife to her throat. Then Harrington will give us everything we want. We get it without waiting and without begging."

"We don't know who that woman is. We're here for the powder, not to kill an innocent woman. Where's the honor in that?"

"The honor is in getting the powder. How we get it doesn't matter."

"It does to me. I'm not giving up more than I'm getting."

"Then in the long run, you'll lose. Your virtue will suffer just the same, along with Harrington's treachery. Or maybe, that's not it at all. Maybe you're afraid of confronting Harrington. Perhaps you're frightened of him because he killed those men in Germany."

"You think what you want, Ubaid. You're insignificant to me. If I need you to help me get the powder, then I'll use you. Until then, don't become a distraction."

Ubaid felt the convergence of tension and rivalry well up inside him. It was a familiar feeling, one he needed to embrace to feed his brutal nature.

"The only reason I don't leave you here is because I'm indebted to the emir."

"You choose your reasons carefully, but choose your actions wisely. Nothing in this world is harmless, and everything is dangerous."

Ubaid became rigid and tense, a habitual pose whenever a threat was near. He felt his body go through a rapid series of reactions, until it was locked and ready for combat.

"Spoken like a true fatalist. How do you want this to end?" Ubaid asked a glint of destruction in his eyes.

"Any way you want. But for now, get ready. We're going to the house where Harrington is staying to follow him again. I know you need things to happen faster, but this is the process that's best. Before this is over, your need for conflict will be met. Until then, we have to be very cautious. This powder Harrington has in his possession is of great interest to him. That makes him dangerous. A man will fight harder for his interests, than for his rights."

The cell phone in Nunarro's pocket rang, shattering the tension. Nunarro reached for the phone and flipped it open. It was a clear gesture to Ubaid the potential for something only partially related to the retrieval of the powder had ended.

"Yes." Nunarro said into the phone, turning his back to Ubaid.

Orisi was on the other end speaking rapidly in Italian. Nunarro heard the struggle for control in his voice.

"You should come back," Orisi said in a firm commanding tone.

"Why?" Nunarro asked, continuing the dialogue in Italian.

"Something changed at the house."

"What changed?"

"A woman left the house. She drove to a storage place about a half hour away. She met a man, and gave him a key to the garage door. I think what we want is in the storage place," Orisi said trying to limit his conversation.

"Are you sure?"

"They opened the door. I saw a truck inside."

Nunarro tempered his excitement in the face of the possibilities. He folded the sense of control to his favor and plans began to develop in his mind.

"Did they take the truck?" he asked.

"No," Orisi said.

"Did they take anything off the truck?"

"Nothing. They just opened the door. It was easy to see they were trying the key to make sure it opened the storage door. The man walked into the garage and looked at the metal box on the truck like it was the most important thing he saw. That was all he was interested in. The key and the truck, that's all."

"Did they try to conceal themselves?"

"No. The woman drove straight to the garage from the house. She didn't look around at anything."

"Was the man waiting for her?"

"Yes. He was just standing there."

"Was he alone?"

"Yes. When she drove up, they didn't pay attention to anything. If you ask me, they were careless."

"Don't count on it. Are they there now?"

"No. They both drove away. The man left with the key to the storage door."

"Where are you now?"

"I'm following the man with the key. Should I take it from him?"

"No. We don't know anything about this man. I'm too far away to help. See where he goes. We can always take the keys from him later. Did they see you?"

"No. But I saw a police car drive by the house just as we left."

"Did the police car stop by the house?"

"No. But it did slow down."

"Did the police see you?"

"I don't know. I can't be sure. It seemed suspicious they were there."

"That may complicate things. Did they follow the woman to the garage?"

"No."

"So, that means there's no need for me to be here. I'll meet you at the hotel," Nunarro said and flipped the phone closed. He looked out at the desert feeling a soft, gritty breeze on his face. His journey continued on course toward a culmination. A leeward wind seemed to be guiding him in the direction of the treasure. The powder was there before him, sitting in a small, dark garage. He felt it within his grasp, and it excited him.

"The poor and the patient sometimes get handed what they need," Nunarro said to Ubaid. "That was Orisi. He followed a woman to a garage not far from Harrington's house. She met a man there and gave him a key that opened the door. Orisi believes the powder is in that garage."

"Is Orisi sure the powder is in the garage?"

"Not absolutely sure. Not without actually going into the garage and seeing it. But he's confident it's there."

"I told you Harrington would keep it close. So we go back to Prescott," Ubaid ordered.

"I would still like to know what Harrington is doing here."

"He's no longer our concern. This has always been about getting the powder. That's what we're going to do, get the powder. Harrington is here, the powder there. He's far away from the powder, so he can't fight for his interests. Let's go. I'm tired of wasting time."

Nunarro understood the distinct clarity to Ubaid's declaration. Under the circumstances, their union was roughly reinforced. They were redirected to the universal quest no longer as adversaries, but not as friends either. Staged as they were by influences beyond their own control, their reactions were defined by their individual agendas. Nunarro wanted the powder, Ubaid wanted blood.

Through the alliances of duty and pride, they were cast into a rivalry between Harrington's need to own the powder, and their obligation to take it from him. An ageless conflict headed toward an inevitable conclusion. No matter the results, the overwhelming rule of conflict would bring loss. The virtues of valor and commitment would share space with casualty and anguish.

Nunarro relied on his temperament, and resilience to achieve his quest, and spare him the sting of defeat. Beyond his abilities, he trusted the warm rising sun appearing over the eastern horizon would shine on him and bring him luck.

ANALISA Scotti rested on her side. Her naked body curved, conforming to Harrington's. With her arm around his chest, she pressed into his back. Harrington could feel her soft breasts against his back. Crumpled white sheets covered her feet. She could feel the morning breeze coming through the open window. Analisa could still feel Harrington's tender but strong movements in the muscle memory of her legs and arms. She felt deep, satisfying warmth lulling her. Analisa felt as though she was in a parallel world, where nakedness and love were not subject to reason or time. The exchange of their wordless passion the night before was powerful and mysterious. Analisa felt their primal exchange of energy was a fulfillment close to divine. From the day Harrington left to go to Iraq, Analisa held her passion within herself. Consequently, her release to him was complete and selfless. Her response to his tenderness was pure and uncontrolled, raising her to the heights of her secret desires. Analisa moved her hand to Harrington's chest, feeling his heartbeat. It was rhythmic and stout, offering a pulsating oath that went beyond their physical union.

"Are you sleeping?" she whispered.

"Not any more," Harrington responded.

"I want you," she said breathlessly.

Harrington turned, positioning himself on top of her. Analisa quickly spread her legs and grabbed his shoulders. She held him tightly and her breathing became deep. For a moment, Harrington stopped and looked down at her.

"You're beautiful," he said. "I feel your beauty in my heart."

Analisa wrapped her arms around his torso and raised herself off the bed. She held her face against his cheek, feeling his rough stubble. Her embrace was an attempt to nullify the time they were separated, and to convey, through the force of her grip, a commitment to never be apart.

Analisa held her embrace, flowing in unison with Harrington's movements. She was caught up in his physical utterance, and lost to the intrigue of time and motion. Analisa could not identify the moment when their movements eased, and they became still. Their breathing became synchronized and their heart rates slowed in harmony. Looking into Harrington's eyes, she detected a patch of contradiction still swirling within him. She touched a bead of perspiration that had formed on his brow and wiped it onto her breast.

"Are you, okay?" Analisa said.

"Yes. Why?"

"You seem different from the way you were before you went away," Analisa whispered.

"I am," he responded with a troubled certainty.

"No. What I mean is; I expected a change. I'm sure being in Iraq affected you. You're gentler than I expected."

Harrington felt a strong need to explain what he truly felt. He was searching for a different understanding, and a truer intimacy with Analisa.

"The war fragmented me in ways I was unaware of," Harrington blurted out. "Killing, death, being away from you was eating me alive. In Iraq, soldiers have to bury their feelings deep. It's a silent code of survival. But, I've learned, no one can bury things deeply enough. You can't contain all the sights and deeds of war. Eventually they'll seep out into every cell in your body and get stronger and hurt more. I feel a hurt that keeps me on the verge of crying and killing. Perhaps if I quietly embrace them, neither one will control me. I just want you to know that seeing you again, and after last night, gentleness might be the way to manage the hurt."

"Do you still feel like crying or killing?" Analisa asked.

"I will never kill again. I've killed enough. Because of that, I know salvation is a long way off for me. I feel like crying for all the soldiers and innocent people whose deaths I can't justify."

"It's not for you to justify."

"I was a part of it. I need to justify my involvement in it."

"You already started by letting your feelings out. When your hurt goes, you'll allow yourself the freedom to see that real justice is beyond anyone's control. It must be left for a greater wisdom to deal with. Embrace that simple logic, Mitchell, and things will be easier for you."

Harrington knew the core of Analisa's observation was filled with love and forgiveness. That knowledge, and the trust he had in her, allowed him to begin to unravel from the torments that had wrapped around him in Iraq.

"I love you, Analisa," Harrington said. "I love you so deeply."

Analisa smiled. There was no enigma to her smile. It was an honest and open smile that broke down all her secrets. It was an interpretation of the true meaning of her tenderness. She began to feel complete and whole, belonging to something she was meant for.

"Mitchell," she said. "I was born in love with you. I knew your gentleness and your strength. I knew your passion, and I couldn't wait to give you mine."

Harrington kissed Analisa. He didn't want to feel any other sensation. Her lips and body was what he needed most. That was all that existed. He didn't want to feel himself move or think. There was no reason to breathe. It would have been a distraction. If he did not breathe, he would be content with dying that moment. The distant sound of breaking glass suddenly caused Harrington to stop and focus on the sound.

"What was that?" he said.

"Nothing. You're safe here, Mitchell," Analisa said. "Sounds like Hector."

Analisa rose from the bed and slipped on a pair of cotton shorts and a T-shirt. She took a brush from her dresser and ran it quickly through her long, auburn hair. She tied her hair behind her head.

"I better go make us some breakfast," Analisa said. "I have to get to the University."

Analisa crossed the room and bent over to kiss Harrington. He put his arms around her waist and held her hand until she walked toward the door.

"I have fresh clothes for you in the dresser," she said, before opening the door.

Analisa saw Solis sweeping up the broken glass as she entered the kitchen.

"Sorry about that, Analisa."

"No problem. Leave it. I'll sweep it up. Did you sleep well?" she asked.

"Man, did I ever. First time in a long time, I went ta sleep not hearin' nothin'."

"It's a quiet neighborhood."

"You been livin' here long?"

"About four years. What would you like for breakfast?"

"Coffee's good."

"No, it's not. You need something substantial. I usually make fresh vegetable juice, with oatmeal and fresh fruit."

"Oatmeal's like army food. I can't stand it."

"Not the way I make it with cinnamon and fresh berries."

"You a vegetarian?"

"As a matter of fact, I am."

"So, that means you ain't got bacon or breakfast sausage, right?"

"No, but I can stir fry you up some tempeh or scrambled tofu with organic hash browns?"

Harrington entered the room wearing a pair of neatly pressed cotton pants and shirt. Analisa had kept them when they were together before he left for Iraq.

"Thank you for keeping them," Harrington said pointing to the clothes.

"Thank you for coming back for them. They still look good on you."

"The pants are a little ta loose around the butt," Solis observed. "Looks like you took off a couple a pounds."

"That's okay, he'll put the weight back on in no time," Analisa said.

"Not eatin' tempeh and scrambled tofu he ain't," Solis replied.

Harrington poured a glass of vegetable juice and sat at the table.

"So, what do we have planned for today?" Harrington asked. "Can we get the powder tested?"

"Yes," Analisa said. "I've already arranged to have the laboratory at my disposal."

"Do you have any idea how you're going to test it?"

"Yes. I've been doing this testing in my mind for years. I'm going to focus on spectroscopic analysis," she said, allowing her enthusiasm to revive her girlish innocence. "I've set up all the equipment I'll need."

"How long are you going to do the spectroscopic testing?"

"I think to get reliable results three hundred seconds will be a minimum. I've read the reports the Soviet Academy of Sciences had done, but their time frame was much less. They did achieve fractional vaporization. That time frame was more than efficient and attained results. I will duplicate their methods, but I will go longer if I have to. The trick is taking the sample on a carbon electrode. When I run a second carbon electrode down and above it, all oxygen must be kept away from the DC arc for an extended period of time. Otherwise, the carbon will oxidize and the electrode will fall apart."

"Is there someone in the laboratory who can assist you?" Harrington asked.

"I'd like to have you there to see this, but I couldn't get you clearance. So it will be just me. I don't want to share this with anyone else just yet. Maybe my sister."

"How is she doing?" Harrington asked.

"Fine, I haven't spoken or e-mailed her in a while. I need to do so."

"Is she still on the concert tour?"

"Yes, she is. I can't keep up with her schedule."

"I used to listen to her CD when I was in Iraq."

"Deuce, that music we listened ta all the time was Analisa's sister?" Solis said.

"Yes," Harrington said, nodding his head.

"You never told me that was Analisa's sister. Your boyfriend gave me a CD of Lucia Bounetti's violin music," he said to Analisa. "Lucia Bounetti is your sister?"

"That's what I said, Hector," Harrington said.

"Imagine that. I remember on that CD she played Beethoven's violin concerto in three movements. *Allegro ma non troppo, Larghetto* and *Rondo allegro.* She plays the violin real good. I thought her playing was restrained but effective," Solis said.

Harrington looked at Solis with a bare exposure of astonishment.

"I'm surprised you remembered. You were familiar with it?" Harrington questioned.

"Why would think I wasn't?"

"I don't know. I'm just surprised, that's all. You never said anything to me about it. I wouldn't have thought you cared for that kind of music," Harrington said.

"No, Deuce. What you mean is you didn't think I ever heard classical music. That I don't know anything about it. You think all guys from the inner city are dumb. Like we only know hip hop."

Harrington felt exposed, caught between embarrassment and ridicule.

"No," Harrington responded. "What I meant was; I thought you never heard classical music, and you don't know anything about it...and my biased assumption was flawed."

"See, it feels good when you make confessions."

"Good, but let's forget Beethoven for now. Analisa, will you test all the weight of the samples?" Harrington said.

"No. I'll just use a portion of the samples. I don't need it all," Analisa responded.

"How deep will your testing go?"

"For now, I'll do the spectroscopic analysis. I'll run it through an annealing process. I'm going to video the testing so you can see it."

"Hey Analisa, what's so special about this powder?" Solis asked.

"Oh my God, Hector. Everything is special about it."

"Everything, like what?"

"Where do I begin? For starters, it's a superconductor. Simply put energy that never fails. It has amps but no voltage, as long as you're in resonance with it. It has the ability to create weightlessness in objects. That's significant, but it's scientific. Clearly, I'm interested in it, but that's not what fascinates me most. It's the non-science; the metaphysical that arouses my sense of awe. The powder has the ability to produce extra sensory powers and has properties associated with bi-location. But I can't test for that. I'm not sure I know how."

"What do you mean extra-sensory powers?"

"It's the ability to grasp things that are beyond the ordinary senses. To be able to tap into another world...other dimensions."

"I don't get it."

"For a guy who understands the complexities and intricacies of a Beethoven concerto, why are you having such a problem with this?" Harrington said.

"Because music I can hear. I can feel it. It's real," Solis responded.

"That's not really the reason, Hector," Analisa said.

"No, then what?"

"Music doesn't challenge you in the way the concept of the powder does. It doesn't go against your belief system."

"What are you sayin'? I know I been askin' the same question since we found the stuff. Deuce never told me what it is. Now you tell me I'll be able ta hear things that I couldn't hear before. Is it the same thing? Like Beethoven can hear music nobody else can? He's got the extra sensory thing goin' for him, right?"

"That's a great analogy. I never thought about it in those terms."

"I'm glad you think that, because I still don't understand."

"It's more than understanding. The powder is about enlightenment, Hector."

"Enlightenment? That's the new-age way of thinkin', right?"

"No, in my opinion, new age concepts have moved away from enlightenment. I believe in technological advancement, but I also feel there's a downside to it. We've become too technical. We believe we can solve everything through science and ego."

"But this powder, it's about science, right?"

"The powder is about more than just science. When Moses was on Mount Sinai, he was smelting the powder, I suspect to gain enlightenment. Understand that in the Old Kingdom of Egypt, eyelashes were called bushes. Check your Egyptian literature if you don't believe me. The burning bush was the enlightened Third Eye. Third Eye, as in extra sensory."

"So wait a minute. I know a little about the Bible like I know a little about classical music," Solis said. "As a kid in religious instruction, they told me Moses was on Mount Sinai and he checked out the burning bush. Now you tellin' me the bush ain't a bush, like with flowers and berries, but it's really eyebrows?"

"Yes. The term 'bush' is a mistranslation. The reference is actually to the Third Eye. Enlightenment and the Third Eye are synonymous. It was the opening of the Third Eye and God communicating to Moses through the powder. That was science coming to meet the metaphysical."

"Come on, Deuce, you believe all this?"

"She's got it right," Harrington responded.

"So, what you sayin' is with that powder we can talk ta God?"

"I'm saying it will bring about enlightenment. From there, who knows?"

"So what one man can do, another can do. What Moses did, somebody else can do. Talk ta God with the help of the powder. Is that it?"

"Why not?"

"So, Deuce, why was such a secret that you didn't want ta tell us about?"

"Because it goes much deeper than this. This is just the surface story of the powder."

"What do you mean surface story?"

"Just let this settle in first, Hector," Analisa said. "This information is already challenging to what you were taught in religion. You may not be ready for more."

"I wasn't ready for Iraq, but I did it."

"This is different."

"Well, if you know about this stuff, I would think all those priests and nuns who taught me about religion would know what you know. Why wasn't I told about this in religion? Does the church want ta be the only ones ta talk ta God? He's my God, too. I'd like ya ta know. What are they afraid of?"

"Control. The organized religions need to control," Analisa said.

"So, if they're so busy controllin', they can't be gettin' themselves enlightened. Those guys are defeatin' themselves. So what else don't I know?" Solis asked.

"It's not your fault you don't know all this, Hector. Suppression of truth is not a new thing," Analisa said.

"So why would anybody want ta keep the truth about this stuff all hidden?"

"For some people, the truth is an enemy."

"Ta me, it's not so much about suppressin' the truth, it's more like tellin' lies."

"However you look at it, Hector, it all comes out to mean the same thing."

"Sounds ta me we do things their way, and everybody comes out a loser."

"Well, let's hope that doesn't happen to us."

"So in three hundred seconds, you'll know if the powder is the Third Eye stuff?" Solis said.

"Well, that's over simplifying it. As I said, I can't test for that." Analisa responded.

"But, you'll know somethin'?"

"Yes, I'll know something."

"Will it take more than three hundred seconds ta tell me the deeper meaning of this stuff?" Solis asked.

"No. It shouldn't take much longer than that to explain the implications of this powder. But, I don't know how long it will take for you to accept the explanation."

"Why's that?" Solis asked.

"As I said, the truth is dangerous for some. That's why they think a lie is safer."

Analisa let the contradiction hang in the air. She didn't try to understand the forces of conspiracy. She was about to make her own discoveries and document them with no mistranslations. Her findings would become her truth, but she would not hold them as absolutes. She knew for every discovered truth there were more truths to be uncovered. It was a never-ending process. While her inquisitive mind wanted to know things, she knew she couldn't possibly know all things. Consequently, for her, it became more important to believe than to know.

Harrington sipped his vegetable juice. He remained aware the outcome of Analisa's testing would deepen his ambition and his responsibility. He would be forced to become more watchful and silent. Just as he was beginning to trust in joy, he knew he had to remain wary of the forces lurking, ready to control the powder.

In time, his fate would be revealed to him. He wondered how long it would take for it all to unfold. For now, he only focused on three hundred seconds. Three hundred seconds that seemed a lifetime.

ON the drive back to Prescott, Umberto Nunarro felt the wind of fortune blowing in his direction. The observation of the storage facility by Orisi happened in a flash of fate. Painstaking exploration of the small area was set in motion. Everything connected to the contents of the facility was slated for disclosure and confiscation primed to alter lives and define relationships. Nunarro wanted to remain the narrator of the events that were hovering between a visible reality and the reach of expectations. But, he knew he could not be fooled. The difference between those opposing paradigms was definable and challenged by risk. The things he believed in accounted for those risks, yet still remained in direct alignment with his conviction. He couldn't allow mistrust or speculation to interfere with his narrative. All his actions and plans referred to the retrieval of the powder, and the plausible quest he subscribed to.

The long drive made him weary. His fatigue produced vague and un-founded thoughts. He began to envision the powder as something alive, with its own thoughts and plans. It seemed to be laying a trap. Bringing together unsuspecting people, with a cruel purpose to draw the energy from their lives, and become stronger with a bloated legacy. Fanciful illusions fell into harmony with the monotonous tone of the road. The strange powder seemed to become a web that could entangle people who thought they were disconnected and just passing through. The boundaries could be proportional to whatever influence the powder might have. In such a case, there would be no room for alternative calculations; only the habit of collapse.

Nunarro revived his sleepy mind and reconsidered his thoughts. It was best not to give the powder too much credence or awe. Thinking of it as an inanimate object would demystify it; draining it of power and character. The convergence of people around the powder was not due to its pull, but rather a set of detached objectives. He was uncaring of the concerns of others. Reasons always complied with needs. His were no different. Because of that, the powder had the potential to take over his identity and defy his actions. As such, perhaps the powder wasn't totally alive. It could very well be gestating.

After driving Ubaid back to his hotel, Nunarro and Orisi returned their rented cars. Using still another false identification, Nunarro rented another car from a different company. He suspected the sheriff's car that passed Harrington's house was not following a routine, and was sure Orisi's car had been observed. Driving a different car under a different name, he felt less conspicuous.

Using several identifications he checked into a roadside motel. They stayed in the room until nightfall; then drove to the Sandretto Hills storage facility where Orisi had followed the woman from Harrington's house earlier in the day. Nunarro shut the lights of the car and drove slowly through the alleys of the storage bays. He studied the construction of the bays and placement of the overhead lights, discovering there were four security cameras on the perimeter of the facility. Orisi directed him to the specific door where he stopped briefly and inspected the other bays.

"This is where they were today," Orisi said. "That's the door they opened. Number ten" he said.

"The truck is inside?" Nunarro asked.

"It's here waiting for us," Orisi commented. "Just beyond that door. Let's get the key and take it away tonight."

"No. Getting the key tonight leaves us too spread out, too weak. What do we do with the people we take the key from? We can't leave them at the house. We can't take them here," he said.

"Then have Ubaid get the key."

"If he goes to the house to get the key, he'll kill whoever is there. I don't want that blood on the powder."

"Then we should find a way to take the powder now before it gets away from us."

"We'll take the powder, but not now," Nunarro responded. "I'm not prepared."

"How hard could it be to break the lock and hot wire the truck?" Orisi said.

"Not hard. But it's not right. Now is not the time. As long as Harrington is not here, the powder is going nowhere. I need to plan this. We'll come for it tomorrow night. We'll get into the garage without a key. We'll start the truck, and take it to the export company in Phoenix. Then we're done."

"And what if Harrington comes back sooner? We'll have to deal with him and whoever else is with him. We really don't know how many people he has with him."

"No, we don't. We will need Ubaid to be our backup."

"But you don't trust him."

"I don't, but he will be useful. I will use him even if Harrington does not come back."

"With him here, you know there could be blood on the powder. That's just what you don't want."

"I have to find a way to control Ubaid and whatever situation arises around him. We are taking the powder to Phoenix. I will make that happen. That is something Harrington, his men, and Ubaid will not prevent."

Nunarro continued out of the storage facility onto Commerce Drive and past Pioneer Park. He proceeded a short distance passing the roadside motel he had checked into earlier.

Before going to the motel, he went to a nearby gas station with a convenience store where he filled the tank. Next to the gas pump, he found a discarded plastic jug he filled with gas, and then placed it on the back seat of the car. Nunarro went into the convenience store and purchased six glass bottles of soda, five pounds of granulated sugar, masking tape and a box of wooden matches. He then found a local home goods store, and purchased a battery operated drill, a hammer and a heavy duty nail punch. He then purchased a flashlight and two tube-style painter's caps with protective face flaps with oval cut outs for vision.

Nunarro drove back to the motel. He parked in the rear beside a large Sargasso cactus. He and Orisi walked up the stairs to the second floor, carrying only the bag of supplies he had purchased, and the container of gas, leaving the material he purchased from the home goods store in the car.

Once inside the room, he placed the bag from the convenience store and the plastic container of gas on the table. Orisi walked to the window and drew the curtains. A floor lamp was lit, casting a yellow hue throughout the small room. The room was bleak, with no outstanding properties, except for being a final stop before their long launch toward a beckoning destination. Orisi looked at the material on the table. Although they appeared to be an assortment of unmatched items, he knew they would serve an important purpose.

"I would feel better if we had guns," Orisi observed.

"For what we need to do, guns wouldn't help us. Fire was the first weapon ever used. It's still the best," Nunarro said.

Orisi sat on the sofa listening intently for the slightest sound. He became aware of all sounds, distinguishing between footsteps on the stairs, the creak of a floor board or a pistol being removed from a belt. For Orisi, knowing noise was as good as knowing its meaning.

"How safe do you think we are?" Orisi asked.

"What do you mean?"

"The sheriff's car that passed in front of Harrington's house must have seen me."

"I'm sure they did."

"Which means we're not safe?"

"It means we can't be predictable.

"It means we should have guns."

Nunarro removed the material from the paper bag. He then separated the bottles of soda from the sugar, matches and masking tape. He saw the strange assortment for what they were, weapons meant for diversion and not destruction. They were assembled tools, when assigned properly, would bring him closer to his hope.

Standing over the table and looking down at the material, Nunarro began making preparations in his mind.

ACTING Supervisor of Surveillance, Ryan Collins, was the main focus of the staff meeting chaired by Agent Cummings. Agents Manning, Heller and Tyler were also present. It was a highly anticipated meeting needed to shed light on a compromised world. Collectively, the agents understood the theme of readiness was not the most basic way to prepare against the cruel intentions of others. Information and preemption would always be the best defense to ensure control and safety. There was no acceptable interchanging to the formula. Any form of stark variation was doomed by misjudgment. As Collins entered the room, the agents were seated around the conference table. He removed several folders from a pouch and placed them on the table.

"I trust all of you have seen the original surveillance report on subjects Umberto Nunarro, Mario Orisi and the man known as Ubaid," Collins began.

"Yes," Cummings responded. "We also have their bios."

Each folder Collins placed on the table contained several stacks of paper marked by red tape affixed to the edge of the cover sheet.

"As to my preliminary report," Collins said. "Original surveillance, on the subjects, was quite detailed. I trust everyone is familiar with those findings."

"Yes," Cummings responded.

"Unfortunately, the sequences involving continuing surveillance on said subjects have seemed to run their course. There is nothing current to be seen. The men have become phantoms, disappearing from all forms of tracking."

"How so?" Cummings inquired.

"As regards to their lodgings at the High Plains Inn, Umberto Nunarro used an online program to check out of his room. That is the last surveillance we have on him. The car he rented is now a stationary blip on our GPS monitoring system emanating from the rental service. Video surveillance on Alacron Street reveals no activity," Collins said.

The lack of continuing data made Cummings apprehensive. He hoped the strain he felt did not show as he moved with a bit of forced effort in his seat. Cummings began to feel as though he was losing his grip on his obsession. The natural flow of circumstances seemed to be deliberately bypassing him with no concern for his duty or plight.

"So we lost the trail of Nunarro and Orisi," Agent Manning said incredulously. "They're either smart or lucky," Manning concluded.

"Luck has nothing to do with this," Cummings shot back.

"Do you think they knew they were under surveillance?" Jenny Tyler asked.

"As of now, they're no longer under surveillance," Collins corrected. "Consequently, we can't determine if they pose any threat."

The frustration for Agent Cummings began to deepen. His suspicion began to mount. He imagined an underground cell of terrorists concealing Nunarro and Orisi. Exacerbating his growing dissatisfaction was the statement by Collins. Furthermore, Cummings knew anyone with a warped sense of eternity is a threat.

"Did we get any cross-reference hits from our database? Any likely terrorists with a connection to Nunarro or Ubaid?" Heller asked.

"None. They seem to be independent from any other activity," Cummings responded. "Ubaid is another matter. He has had prior connections with extremists. You are all familiar with them. Henrietta Dell, believes when we discover what they're plotting, it will surprise us," Cummings concluded.

"That's usually the way things end up," Collins said. "Surveillance shows us definitive things, but when we finally uncover the minute details, it's always a surprise."

"Well, I don't want to be surprised," Cummings announced, without concealing his annoyance. "Whatever is coming toward me, I want to see it from a mile away."

"Has the local sheriff filed any information with us?" Heller asked.

"His office only confirmed seeing the car rented by Orisi in front of Harrington's house. The car was turned in, and Sheriff St. Cloud investigated it. His report shows it was a routine return. The rental company remembered nothing unusual."

"It seems Harrington is the Pied Piper," Tyler observed. "Nunarro, Orisi and Ubaid appear to be just following him."

"That could be. But, Nunarro was here once before when Harrington was still overseas in Iraq," Cummings responded.

"So what's different between then and now?"

"The only thing different is the thing that will surprise us."

"It appears Harrington might also be surprised if he learns Nunarro is following him. I don't think he's consciously playing the role of Pied Piper."

"It might be time to confront Harrington," Heller offered.

"That's prudent if Harrington and Nunarro are not involved in something together. If they are, then everything goes away if we show our hand."

"That could be a good thing," Tyler said.

Cummings felt secrecy was the best way to continue. There was no sense of desperation to make him feel otherwise. Just his own discomfort.

"If things go away, it's only for the short term," Cummings said. "We need to remain clandestine. It's the only strategy that could allow us to gain insight to the bigger picture. Are they here on their own surveillance mission, preparing for something to follow? Either way, I believe they're preparing something illegal. That will not come as a surprise to me. We have to wait on this one. Ryan, I want you to contact me, immediately, if surveillance is reestablished. Call my cell phone, any time. Hopefully, we'll restore surveillance or things will pop up around Harrington."

Cummings did not acknowledge the family connections of Analisa Scotti. That was an enduring narrative he kept to himself. Whoever Harrington would attract, Cummings suspected, would be nothing compared to the specific family that would flock to Analisa. Whatever the unfolding plot; Cummings was moved to conclusions orchestrated by his own beliefs.

It would serve as an excuse for the compulsion that was at the center of his authority. Speculation was no longer something that concerned him. The crowded field had been cleared. All that remained were his concerns. Cummings no longer felt burdened by details. He became invigorated once again by the torrent of possibilities Pietro Segretti could be the unfolding surprise.

The staff meeting ended. Cummings went back to his office. He read through his e-mails. He sent an e-mail to Sheriff St. Cloud advising the subjects had eluded Homeland Security's surveillance. He asked if St. Cloud was continuing his observation of Harrington's house. St. Cloud responded, expressing disappointment over the lost surveillance. He assured his own department's observation of Harrington was continuing. He would share any information as it became available.

Cummings felt the most important point of surveillance was Analisa's phone and e-mails. Cummings made arrangements with a friend at the service provider that all calls and e-mails be monitored, and reports should be sent to his Blackberry. He sent a final e-mail to Henrietta Dell giving her a short synopsis of the meeting with Collins, and the unfortunate lapse in surveillance. He apprised her of his communication with St. Cloud. He concluded his message by wishing Henrietta success on her upcoming supervisors meeting.

Shutting down the computer, Cummings swiveled around in his chair and looked out the window. Night had settled over the city. He could see the lights illuminating the top of the Capital Building in Bolin Memorial Park. Cummings looked upon it as a serene sight suggesting justice and stability. The building was an inspiration to Cummings. It was a clear representation of triumph and spirit, much like the other war memorials in the park. Somewhere, in the shadow of the places, was a band of men whose philosophy was specifically designed for upheaval. They were adept at the worst kind of strategy and tactics, but surprise was their ultimate weapon. Their intentions were borne from anger, yet they gave him incentive and, in the process, defined him. It also brought into question the vulnerability he tried hard to disavow. It was real and nagging, fueled by his possible lack of control. That was what disturbed him most.

Cummings rose from his chair and walked to the window. Perhaps from this vantage point he could gain a better perspective, allowing him a clearer vision of Nunarro and Orisi. They were lurking somewhere, fostering unknown intentions. His inner need was not just designed for prevention, but to find his balance and restore his force.

He looked out beyond the Capital Building to the dark horizon. There was no distinction between the dark earth and sky. The proximity to them was lost to his reflection in the window. Nonetheless, it was a dimension he could not turn away from. He knew, somewhere within that measure, was something more definable than Nunarro and Orisi. There was a pulse that had a unique definition and a promissory glint of personal deliverance. His fixed gaze was a fierce determination to ensure that conclusion. Somehow, he knew he would get to see clearly into the dark void and ultimately find the elusive figure of Pietro Segretti.

ANALISA Scotti unbuttoned her lab coat and spread her arms away from her body. She felt as though she had to open herself up to accept the onslaught of hysteria and rapture brought on by the results of the testing. The powder proved to be what she hoped; a revelation of pure magic her eyes could not believe. Her mind had yet to comprehend its existence. For years, she had envisioned making this discovery and the elation she would feel. But no presumption could have prepared her for the numerous emotions swelling up within her. Elements of fright joined the cacophony of feelings, yielding to the hauntings and blessings administered by the presence of gods and ghosts.

The powder responded to the testing, bearing out the true character of an ancient legacy. Extruded from its metallic form, the powder never recreated metallic qualities, which was a testament to the intervention of knowing deities. It was when Analisa saw the lab table levitate; she became convinced the powder was the basis of mysticism. To her, it was a visible sign certain aspects of myths could be rooted in actuality. Within the confines of the laboratory, she also found a convincing argument for the possibility of immortality.

Something uncontrollable and wild needed to burst from her. She had to tell the world of her discovery. But first, she needed to be alone, quiet with the white powder. There was a prescribed reverence she needed to adhere to that would make her worthy. It took the best part of her self control to contain her exuberance.

Analisa's thoughts shot in different directions causing her hands to shake and her knees to go weak. She sat in a chair pressing her hands together. Bowing her head, she felt as if the laboratory had been converted to an ancient temple. She offered a profound prayer to the deities of myth. Holding herself tight, she embraced the peculiar bonds existing between science and miracles. Unfolding her trembling hands, Analisa touched a mound of powder she had placed on the laboratory workbench. She felt ecstasy beyond awe to be in the presence of the miraculous substance. Secrets of the world had been opened to which she was privileged, yet she felt humbled and penitent.

With a tissue, Analisa blotted the moisture from her eyes. She allowed her scientific mind to give way to something less formal and more primeval. Those deeper mysteries and elements of beauty were forces revealed by her test. It offered much in the way of assurances; going beyond the etiquette of debate to the potential for profound understanding. Analisa knew she was in the presence of true perfection. A light of purity guiding everything ever created.

Stunned, Analisa felt conflicted. She suddenly saw herself standing in the world as something more substantial, but less significant. Much would be made of the results of her testing. She knew contention would ensue. However, no matter the challenges, the powder would have the power to endure because of its own truth.

Analisa went to the three video cameras she had focused on her experiment and shut them off. She couldn't wait to call Harrington to share the results and show him the videos. Carefully and reverently, Analisa gathered the powder into the plastic bag, placing it into the briefcase Harrington had given her. Analisa stopped the audio recorder in the pocket of her lab coat. When she felt less overwhelmed, she would replay the recording, coordinate it with the video and write a report of her findings. For now, she just needed to feel the glow of her excitement and share it. Sitting in front of her computer, Analisa lifted the lid on her laptop computer. She went to the prompt of her e-mail and clicked on her sister's address.

"*Lucia,*" she typed. "*I hope you and Nicola are well. I hope all the family is well, Rosa and Melia. Sorry, I haven't communicated sooner. My work has occupied much of my time. I'm sure you understand. I read about your performance at Teatro Communale di Bologna. Rave reviews. I'm glad for you. Exciting. I too have encountered something exciting. As you know, I've been to the Sinai searching for something elusive. My expedition yielded no results. I gave up my quest, accepting some things will forever stay hidden from searching minds. Then, suddenly what I had been looking for dropped into my lap. Mitchell returned from Iraq and my search ended. Strange, the workings of fate. Nicola would be interested. Tell him I have in my possession the white nectar of the gods! He'll know what it is. Thanks to Mitchell, we have over one thousand pounds of it! Nicola would be interested in my testing of the relic. It is exactly what he would expect. Perhaps more. Something only the gods can create. I'm excited by this find. I need to tell Mitchell what he found. Give my best to Nicola. Tell him we should talk. Perhaps we can meet. Let me know your schedule. I can come to Italy. Actually, I would like to do that. I need to see you, Rosa and Melia too. Love, your sister.*"

Analisa closed the lid of her laptop and picked up the briefcase with the powder. She set the briefcase on her lap and hugged it gently. A nurturing joy accounted for the overwhelming contentment she felt. Cradling the briefcase, she rocked back and forth feeling the pulse within it. She accepted the tug that sought her out.

Analisa removed her lab coat. She retrieved the cassettes from the three cameras. Along with the audio recorder, she placed the cassettes in the briefcase and left the laboratory. Hurrying down the hall, she passed several students and faculty. Their greetings fell mutely on Analisa. She felt a desire to flail her arms wildly and run through the University shouting whatever came to her mind.

The bright sun was lingering low, sliding to the west when she left the building. There were only a few hours left to the day. Suddenly, Analisa felt it had all started over. It was the beginning of a new day, filled with promises and the revised history she had only hoped for. Going forward nothing would be the same and evolution would have a different meaning.

She opened the door of her car, and placed the briefcase on the front seat. She removed her cell phone from her pocket. At first, she had difficulty making her fingers press the correct numbers. The phone rang once and Harrington picked up.

"Hello," Harrington said.

Analisa looked up at the sky and twirled around, lost in the rhythm of a fine dance.

"Mitchell," she said, then paused not knowing what else to say.

"Analisa, what is it?" Harrington said when Analisa could not continue. "Are you okay?"

"Yes. Yes. I'm fine. I'm better than fine," she finally blurted out. "The powder is everything we thought it was. Mitchell, do you realize what you found? You found history."

WHEN Analisa reached her block, Harrington was standing in the driveway with a wide stance of anticipation. Solis was behind him, on the front porch, with an expression that showed a deep need for inclusion into the discovery. Analisa slowed as she drove into her driveway. Harrington ran his hand along the fender and opened the door for her. Stepping out, Analisa threw her arms around Harrington and kissed him. It was a wordless meeting, but their sly smiles revealed a conspiracy of absurdity. Harrington reached into the car and withdrew the briefcase.

"Come on, let's go inside," he said.

They walked through the house to the back patio, where Harrington placed the briefcase on the table.

"So?" Harrington said, as he sat next to Analisa.

"So?" Analisa said, uncapping a bottle of water.

Suddenly, that small word had large implications, filled with an over simplified term to express things that were staggering and momentous.

"Do we have Flinders Petrie's find?" Harrington asked, a childhood hope creeping into his demeanor.

"That guy again," Solis interrupted.

"Well, I can't be certain it was Petrie's find, but it probably was," Analisa responded. "It has to be what he claims to have seen."

"How could it have disappeared for all these years?" Harrington asked, trying to eliminate all possible doubts.

"Who knows," Analisa said. "He claimed it was lost to the winds, but perhaps it gathered somewhere, and someone just stored it away. Or, it could have been from a different location, part of a different load. It could have been unearthed by someone else. An accidental find like so many others. Like the Dead Sea Scrolls. I don't know the answer."

"So tell me, what happened during the experiments?" Harrington asked, his excitement threatening to take command of him.

"Oh, Mitchell, I can't wait to show you. Basically, I did sheath the electrode using Argon gas. That kept the oxygen away while the arc was struck. I was afraid the arc would fall apart, but my fears were unfounded. There was no reading for fifteen seconds, nothing conclusive. That is, of course, except for the emission of certain light frequencies. When I went beyond that to three hundred seconds, the testing became complete. Incidentally, argon gas was instrumental to sonoluminessence."

"What happened in the annealing process?" Harrington asked, trying hard to conceal an old stimulation that had taken hold of him ever since he read of Petrie's discovery.

"My God, Mitchell, not only did it levitate the vessel I had it in, but it took the table with it. Both were levitated."

"I can't believe it."

"Believe it."

"So it loses its weight as does its host."

"Yes."

"What was the ratio between the weight of the powder to the weight of the vessel and the table?"

"I believe the ratios are limitless based on the ease of levitation."

"Incredible."

"That's not all. As it cooled, it went to one hundred and fifty percent of its weight. I did that experiment twice. Twice the table levitated and twice the weight increased exponentially."

"Miraculous," Harrington whispered.

"Hey, let's not forget I'm in the room here," Solis said. "I really don't know what you're talkin' about. You scientists got your own way of talkin' that don't seem ta include us common folk. Do you mind tellin' me what's goin' on?"

"It means, the powder is exactly what I thought it was," Harrington responded.

"That's good. I'm glad for you. But I'm gonna' feel like a real fool if I ask what is it you thought it was, and I don't get a real answer. I'm getting' tired of askin' that question."

"It's monoatomic gold. That's what I thought it was all along."

"That much I know. The same stuff that Moses used ta see God? Ta talk ta him?"

"Yes."

"So this stuff doesn't belong ta that Petrie guy, it belongs ta Moses?"

"It goes back long before Moses."

"How far?"

"Who knows. No one knows."

"Back ta Jesus' time?"

"Well before Jesus."

"And whatever you did with it in the lab, it raised the table?"

"Yes," Analisa said.

"So, if Jesus had that stuff tucked under his robe or in his sandals he coulda' used it that day when he walked on water."

"I don't know," Analisa responded.

"But he coulda?" Solis pressed.

"I don't know."

"How 'bout Lazarus? I mean if this stuff is such a miracle like the Deuce says it is, maybe that's what brought Lazarus back from the dead."

"I don't know the answer to that, Hector."

"But, if this stuff can make Moses talk ta God, see The Almighty with his eyes, and if this stuff can lift tables, why not make Jesus walk on water and Lazarus to come back to life? That seems simple enough."

"It's not that simple, Hector," Harrington said.

"Why not? Or, maybe this is just part of what you're not tellin' me. But, you know what, I don't wanna know any more. I'm beginin' ta figure things out for myself. Yeah, this stuff goes back ta God givin' it ta who He liked best. He wanted ta give it only ta those people he felt worthy. His plan was maybe ta keep pagans on the outside. He left it up ta the righteous ta tell the unrighteous how to get inta heaven. But they used it ta keep the pagans down. Keep 'em outta everything that's due them. Not much has changed. The righteous thinkin' they're chosen. I saw enough a that in Iraq. That's why I don't care. You think I couldn't handle that? Well, it really don't make a difference ta me. Now, all I really wanna know is what does that make God?"

"What do you mean?"

"I mean He sees fit only ta bless certain people and have the others pound sand. Sounds ta me He didn't use good judgment, or maybe He's showin' favorites. I maybe didn't learn much growin' up in the Bronx. But this much I'll tell ya, I knew early on what a bigot is. What do you think?"

"I don't know," Harrington said.

"You don't know or you don't wanna know? Maybe that's because you're sittin' here with God's trump card. You feel like you're part of the chosen ones. Or, maybe with all that powder, you're the only chosen one."

"Once again, I don't know," Harrington responded.

"You don't know. Okay. That's fair. Then let me ask you this....Was that stuff worth what we went through ta bring it out a Iraq, and especially Germany?"

Analisa looked at Harrington. Judging by the veil of regret that shaded his eyes, she knew the powder had attracted another secret. She needed to know what occurred in Iraq and Germany, and how much of Harrington's soul the powder had claimed. Now was not the time to ask for explanations. She would save that for a time when she could confront the negative side to this joy. Analisa understood all things were subject to duality and ruin. She recalled even the once mighty Ozymandias succumbed to wreck and decay.

Harrington drew a deep breath. He knew part of the answer to Solis' question. But seven men had been killed outside Wiesbaden, Germany. That equation had to be factored in, and by doing so, it altered the scales of proportion.

He thought perhaps Solis was right. The powder did pit the righteous against the unrighteous. The chosen against those they needed to dominate. The laws of debasement were precise and ran contrary to the immense potential of the powder. But, that was not the fault of the powder or its alchemists. It was the need to possess the powder that was the basis of a false hierarchy.

Harrington could not turn away from the ramifications of what had happened in Germany. There would come a time he would have to confront all manner of accusations and deal with the consequences. He knew judgment was still far off, but was unsure how quickly it was closing in. He looked at Analisa and knew there was much he had to confess. He then looked at Solis and knew there was nothing he could explain.

"I don't know, Hector," Harrington said quietly. "This journey is not over yet."

ITALY

LUCIA Bounetti was glad to receive the e-mail from her sister, Analisa. It coincided with her own feelings of melancholy and loneliness. She became increasingly aware of the distance and stillness between herself and her sister. With each concert, her loneliness became more acute. She felt the adulation of audiences, but she needed something more intimate, something beyond what her husband could provide. Lucia needed the closeness of her biological family. However, all she seemed to be greeted with was separation. With the increasingly ill health of Rosa and Melia, the potential for a new void was becoming an ever greater cause for anxiety. Although Lucia was glad her sister had found a new excitement with the discovery of the powder, she focused on what Analisa said in the conclusion of her e-mail. "I need to see you, Rosa and Melia, too."

Pouring two cups of demitasse coffee, Lucia put them onto a tray and carried them to her bedroom. Bounetti sat in bed reading a book. He looked up, over his eyeglasses as she entered the room. She placed the tray on the night stand and handed a cup to Bounetti. He sipped it with a soft, slurping sound.

"Thank you," Bounetti said.

"What are you reading?" Lucia asked.

"The writings of Thomas Aquinas."

Lucia walked to the terrace doors as a soft breeze blew in from the Ionian Sea. She gathered the lace curtains billowing in the breeze and closed the glass doors. Next to the doors stood an antique Renaissance-style walnut dresser with reliefs of masked Cupids, scrolled foliage and a serpent. Lucia ran her fingers along the highly polished reliefs contemplating their meaning and intent. Some masks were tragic in form and design, while others were joyous. Each Cupid was joined by foliage wrapped around their feet and cherub legs. The serpent, coiled within itself, seemed to represent one of many vices that tempted and corrupted souls. There could have been many interpretations of the relief. Each one based upon the mood or temperament of the observer. Lucia saw only the sorrowful masks. They appeared dominant, taunting and accentuated her unsettled mood.

Bounetti closed the book and watched Lucia. She seemed to be lost within the fine scrollwork of the dresser, captured by its haunting declarations. Lucia was central to his existence. Consequently, he was highly attuned to anything that disturbed her. Part of her being was immersed in his core. He wasn't aware when or how this connection had occurred, but it was certain.

Lucia turned from the dresser and saw Bounetti watching her. She had become so familiar with his every glance and movement that none of his thoughts could remain a secret. They both shared an uncanny way of seeing each other's truths. She forced a smile, walked to the bed and took the cup of demitasse coffee from him.

"Finished?" she said.

He watched her take the cup and put it back on the tray, recognizing the conflicting grace that segregated her assurance from her distress. For someone so adept at being in the limelight, Lucia's movements were an obvious display of imbalance. Suddenly, Bounetti was reminded that everything between them was an act of intimacy and trust.

"What's the matter?" Bounetti asked.

"Nothing. Why?" Lucia responded.

"Nothing always means something," Bounetti responded.

Lucia walked around to her side of the bed. She then lit scented candles sitting in two cut crystal glasses. She took a tube of moisturizing cream and began to massage it into her hands.

"I've been considering cutting down on my concert touring," Lucia said.

Bounetti removed his glasses and rested them on the tray.

"Why?" he asked.

"I'm tired," she responded. "I'm tired of traveling and staying in strange hotels, different cities. I love performing. I don't like the isolation of the road tours."

Bounetti sat up, allowing Lucia to continue.

"I need to spend more time with my family," she concluded.

"How long have you been feeling like this?" Bounetti asked.

"I don't know. A while I guess. I don't really know. These things sneak up and find a way to mix with everything else. I don't like hearing about my sister's life by way of computer. I want to sit in front of her and talk. I haven't seen her in over a year. The last time we went to see Rosa and Melia; I was amazed how old they had gotten. I need to be around my family more. That's all."

"Have you mentioned this to your sister?"

"I don't have to. I know she feels the same way. Sisters know these things."

"Have you heard from her recently?"

"Yes. Tonight. She just sent me an e-mail. I hate those e-mails. I would rather receive a phone call. At least, I can get to hear her voice. E-mails are so impersonal. I don't like all this new technology. It takes away emotion. It allows only the expression of thoughts not feelings."

"Well, what were your sister's thoughts?"

"She needs to be near family, too. She needs to see Rosa and Melia."

"Then she should make time to come here. What else did she say?" Bounetti asked.

Lucia reached for the moisturizing cream, squeezed more into her hands and rubbed it into her elbows.

"She said Mitchell is home from Iraq. You remember Mitchell?"

"Yes, I remember him. Her old boyfriend. I thought since he left for the army, she had dropped him."

"Well, he's back in her life."

"That's good. I thought she was career minded and didn't have time for relationships. Digging in the sands in the Middle East may not be for her any longer."

"Everyone gets to a point where they need to reevaluate their lives. Analisa is no exception."

"Did she say she was glad to be back with Mitchell?"

"She didn't have to. I know she is. She said he came home from Iraq with something that might interest you."

"Something that might interest me?"

"Yes. She said to tell you, she has in her possession, the white nectar of the gods. She said you would know what that means."

Bounetti turned abruptly toward Lucia. The light from the flickering candles threw hard shadows across his face. He felt a rush; a sense of urgency, as if expecting a visitation from ghosts.

"What else did she say?" Bounetti said, sitting up higher in the bed.

"That you would be interested in the testing of the relic."

"That means she tested it," Bounetti said thoughtfully.

"She said it would be what you expected. Perhaps more. Then, she said something about it being a creation of the gods."

"Interesting she chose to describe it that way."

"What does it mean?"

"I'll explain later. What else did she say?"

"She said she needs to tell Mitchell about it."

"You mean about the results of her testing?"

"Yes."

"So he doesn't know?"

"I'm sure he does now. The e-mail was sent from her laboratory."

"Mitchell was an anthropologist as I recall. So Mitchell had to know, or at least suspect, what it was he brought home from Iraq."

"I don't know what Mitchell thought. Analisa said he brought in over one thousand pounds of it."

"That's a lot. He wouldn't have brought it if he didn't know what it was."

"Is this is the same type of powdered gold Pietro went to Arizona to buy from that miner?" Lucia asked.

"Yes."

"How did Mitchell come to have it if it comes from a mine?"

"There are different places it could come from. It doesn't come as a surprise Mitchell found it in the Middle East. What does surprise me is how much he has. I'm sure Pietro would want to know about this."

"Why?"

"It's something he wants. I'm sure he will want to go see your sister."

"But Gabriella told me when they were in Arizona they had a lot of trouble because of the powdered gold."

"That's a simple classification of it."

"Gabriella said they were threatened by U.S. Homeland Security. The gold can't be good if it causes that much trouble."

"The gold is good. That's why it causes trouble."

"Does Analisa know what kind of trouble this gold brings?"

"I don't know."

"God, Nicola, I don't want Analisa in trouble. Why did Mitchell bring it to her? I don't know if I trust him."

"Did she say what she's going to do with the gold?"

"No."

"If no one else knows she has the gold, then we can have Pietro contact her. He'll want to go there as soon as possible and offer to buy it from her."

"I doubt he'll want to go back to Arizona. I know Gabriella doesn't want to go back. She doesn't want to travel anywhere in the United States."

"You don't know Pietro as well as I do. He's not intimidated by Homeland Security," Bounetti said, as he reached for the phone. "If Pietro ever found out we knew your sister had the gold, and never told him, he would not forgive us. On the other hand, if he got involved with Analisa, he could protect her. Trust me. This is the way to go."

"But how is Pietro ever going to get into the United States. Homeland Security will be watching him. I know what that type of scrutiny is like."

"Don't underestimate Pietro. He has a great many connections."

"But what if Analisa has other plans for the gold? If it's a relic, she may want to donate it to a museum?"

"You're right. I shouldn't assume she will want to sell it to Pietro. But at the very least, she should know he's a prospective buyer."

"But Mitchell was the one who found the powder. He brought it back from Iraq. It belongs to him."

"Yes, that's true. Pietro will have to deal with it."

"Suppose Mitchell doesn't want to sell it to your cousin?" Lucia asked suspiciously.

"What do you mean?"

"I mean how far will Pietro go to get the powder?"

"Never so far that he would hurt your sister. As I said, he can protect her. Maybe even protect her from Mitchell. Listen, Lucia, if you don't trust Mitchell, then trust Pietro. He'll never harm your sister."

Lucia knew she couldn't treat her concerns with mistrust. She was aware she should not project her own doubts for fear they could attract those very things she wanted to keep from her sister.

"Is it too late to call Pietro?" Lucia asked.

"Not for this," Bounetti responded.

Bounetti became excited. He knew the gold was an exalted commodity. Its qualities were clearly linked to danger, but it was also rooted in life. It was the obsession of men to possess it, and their downfall to be manipulated by it. But the many failures surrounding this ageless relic were worth the attempt at one triumph. Ownership of the gold seemed to be saved not for the most cunning, but for the luckiest and the most deserving. Perhaps, Analisa, had already attained that coveted status. Perhaps, she had been chosen as the gold's rightful heir. If so, history would be of her making, and all the threats and pitfalls would be tempered by glory.

PIETRO Segretti sat next to Gabriella DeCeasere at the outdoor café, glancing through the brochure he had gotten at the Museo Nazional in Reggio. He and Gabriella had visited it earlier in the day. What he focused on were the Bronzes of Riace, found off the coast of Riace near Reggio. The Greek sculptures dating back to the fifth century BC, depicted two Greek warriors. The bronzes were believed to be sculptures of Tydeus and Amphiaraus, two members of The Seven against Thebes. The eyes of the bronzes were inlaid with bone and glass. The teeth were pure silver. Each bronze was life-like in size and proportion. They represented a bloodline marked to survive history.

What Segretti found most fascinating, was the ancient bronzes made him question the effects of time. They neither aged nor withered. The bronzes endured far beyond the motives of those who created them, generating scholarly speculation about art and war. But for Segretti, they implied philosophy.

Segretti added his own conjecture to the enigma of the bronzes. Perhaps they were not merely warriors against Thebes, but forged as true soldiers against the onslaught of time. From this perspective, perhaps the bronzes offered a way to understand time, or to make it more confusing.

Gabriella touched Segretti's hand, prompting him to shift his focus and thoughts. He looked at Gabriella, and became aware once more of the activity in the café. He heard the conversations of the other patrons as low, indiscernible whispers.

"I'm glad we saw the bronzes today," Gabriella said. "It was a nice trip."

"It turned out to be a long day. You must be tired," Segretti observed.

"A little," Gabriella said, adjusting the silver bracelet Segretti had bought her earlier.

A small, heart-shaped amulet dangled from the bracelet. In the amulet was a small amount of cimaruta. In Calabrian folklore, an amulet filled with cimaruta was said to protect the bearer against *maloccio* or intentional harm. Segretti bought the bracelet for Gabriella not because he believed in the centuries-old local lore, or was challenged by superstition, but because he felt it would help extend his protective influence over her.

A waiter cleaned off the table behind Segretti, tilting the chairs against the edge of the table. Several other patrons at another table began to leave, allowing Segretti to become comfortable with the silence and the ending of the day. Segretti sipped his wine and indulged in the luxury of connecting to the night and the city. He felt infused with a reverence; something about the sounds and smells he could trace back to his boyhood. It gave him a sense of identity and belonging. Nothing around him was distant or impersonal. He wanted to linger so everything could take hold of him again and perhaps bring him back in time.

"You seem to enjoy this city," Gabriella observed in a low voice.

"Yes, I do. Very much."

"What is it about being here that makes you enjoy it so much?"

"I feel a connection to this city," Segretti replied in a whisper. "Actually, I feel a connection to all of Calabria. I have roots in this part of the country. I have folk heroes that come from Reggio."

"Folk heroes? I would never have suspected you to have folk heroes. Which ones?"

"Giuseppe Musolino. Did you ever hear of him?"

"No."

"I read about him when I was a boy. He was a bandit. He lived right here in these very streets in the late nineteenth century. He stole from the rich and gave to the poor; to the monasteries. Giuseppe was falsely accused of a crime and sent to prison. He escaped and avenged himself on those who lied about him. To me, he was a symbol of the fight against injustice. He was the first person like that I had ever read about."

"But did he commit the crime he was accused of?"

"I'd like to think he didn't. That's what heightens his reputation for me."

"How did Musolino get revenge on those who bore false witness against him?"

"With extreme measures."

"Vengeance is unforgivable."

"What's more unforgivable than lying? There's no honor in it. I could excuse vengeance."

"Pietro, there were others who came from here that could have been better role models for you as a boy."

"Such as?"

"Well, Pope John the Seventh or Pope Zachary. What's wrong with them?"

"You know your local history, darling Gabriella."

"Did you know about them as a boy? Those popes?"

"No, they came to my attention later in life."

"When it was too late?"

"Too late for my salvation?"

"No. Too late for you to be influenced."

"Well then, yes," Segretti chuckled. "Way too late."

"In addition to John the Seventh and Zachary, there was also St. Bartholomew of Grottaferrata. Now these men would have been wonderful examples for a boy," Gabriella teased.

"They were all of Greek nationality. They would not have fit into my little Italian-minded world."

"Pity, there's even a feast day for Bartholomew."

"Yes, but they made a movie of Giuseppe Musolino."

Gabriella recognized an insight into one of Segretti's early influences that formed some of his adult philosophies. There was a direct correlation to the story of Giuseppe Musolino, no matter how romanticized, to Segretti's principles. They helped make him, and he made the world around him.

"Well, at least I learned a little about your boyhood," Gabriella said.

"My corrupted boyhood."

"You didn't turn out so badly, my dear."

"I'm glad you approve. Perhaps, we should go."

Segretti reached into his pocket and placed more than enough money on the table to pay for the wine and tea. As he rose, his cell phone rang.

"Yes," Segretti said into the phone.

"Pietro, it's me, Nicola," said the voice from the phone.

"Yes, Nicola. You're calling so late. Is everything alright?"

"Yes, yes it is. Am I calling too late?"

"No, not at all. We are just leaving a café. What's the matter?"

"Nothing. Nothing. I'm here with Lucia. She just received an e-mail from her sister, Analisa, in Arizona. Something very interesting came up. Something you might want to know."

"What is it?"

"Remember what you went to Arizona to buy from the miner?" Bounetti said, trying to be cautious.

"Yes."

"Well Analisa has acquired some of it."

"She did? Is it the same thing?"

"I haven't seen it, but Analisa says it is. You know her background. If she says it is, I believe her. She did tests on it."

"How did she get it?"

"An old boyfriend just came home from overseas. He brought it with him. She has a lot of it….Over one thousand pounds."

"I'm interested. I'm very interested."

"I thought you might be. I wanted to pass the information along to you."

"Did Analisa give any indication the product was for sale?"

"No. I don't think she has looked beyond the initial discovery of it. My guess is they're still evaluating its scientific significance."

"What do you think about it?"

"It's a scientific marvel. Nothing less. As for the quantity they have, that's an impossible amount to amass. This is once in a lifetime."

"I'm sure…I'd like to be considered as a primary buyer."

"I'm sure you would."

"This deal may require delicate negotiations."

"I can call her and make an overture for you," Bounetti offered.

"I would appreciate it. In the meantime, I need to make immediate plans. I'll leave tomorrow."

"I'll call her now. It's till early there. I'll tell her your plans. You can negotiate when you get there."

"Nicola, what can I say to you? Thank you."

"No need to thank me. When I call her, I'll discuss the testing she did. I should have more of a scientific insight then."

"Thank you."

"How is Gabriella?"

"She's fine. How's Lucia?"

"Worried about Analisa."

"Why?"

"Because of what we're talking about."

"Maybe I can offer some assistance and some safety for Analisa."

"That's what I told Lucia. I'm counting on it. Do what you do best. I'll get more information for you."

"Thank you, cousin," Segretti concluded and flipped the cell phone closed.

Gabriella saw the look in Segretti's eyes. His playful charm became tantalizing yet ominous. He made a sound in his throat, an exclamation of something foreboding that worried Gabriella. Apparently, Segretti was called to some duty of loyalty that required his intervention.

"What was that phone call about?" Gabriella asked.

"That was Nicola," he responded.

"I know. What did he want at this hour?"

"Lucia's sister, Analisa, has something I would like to have."

"What?"

"Analisa has a boyfriend. He's a war hero…"

"What does Analisa have that interests you?" Gabriella interrupted.

"Her boyfriend brought something back from Iraq."

"What did he bring back?" Gabriella asked impatiently.

"What I tried to buy from Alex Barnes. The same stuff. But he has a larger quantity of it."

"And where is this stuff?"

"Arizona, of course."

"Of course….So what does that mean?"

"Gabriella, I'm sorry. You know what I have to do."

"Pietro, don't be foolish. You know you can't go back to Arizona."

"I have to."

"Why? Why do you have to go?"

"Gabriella, you know better than to ask that question."

"But do you know how dangerous it is for you to go back. That man, Agent Cummings, is hunting you. All of Homeland Security is. You know Cummings has made this his personal vendetta against you. He's looking to exact the same vengeance that Musolino did to those men that put him in jail."

"Please don't equate me with those betrayers."

"I'm not. I would never do that. I'm just frightened."

"I know you are. I know how you feel. I know what measures Cummings is likely to take against me."

"And still you want to go back?"

"I have to go."

Gabriella looked around the plaza at the closed shops. A thin film of dew had settled on the ancient cobblestone. She needed to redirect her thoughts, focus on something that didn't frighten or threaten her. But, everything looked ominous, casting her with a lonely indifference.

"Gabriella," Segretti said, gently touching her hand.

A deep anxiety settled into Gabriella's chest. She heaved deeply. Her forced breath did not seem to be her own. She knew she had to show Segretti strength, present a stance he could trust. His was a world of control and self-reliance. There was no margin for the display of anything contrary. Gabriella had to navigate the space between her apprehension and what he silently demanded. Controlling her reaction to them was the primary expectation. Anything less would defile her image. Anything more would be an untruth he would not tolerate.

Gradually, Gabriella took control of her breathing and managed her troubling premonitions. She called upon an inner sense of control and realized her compliance and support were all Segretti would recognize. They had formed an alliance based on the protocols of reputation. Compromising this established standard would be seen by Segretti as a gross infidelity.

"When will we leave?" she asked.

"I can't take you this time."

"Why not?"

"You know why, Gabriella."

"And if I insisted?"

"Makes no difference."

Gabriella knew the limits she could go with Segretti. Anything more would be a violation. Crossing a line, he marked with his dignity and rule, was unacceptable.

"Will you take Gino and Alberto?" she asked.

"Yes, of course."

"How will you get into the United States?"

"I'll arrange to take a private jet."

"When?"

"As soon as possible. Tomorrow. Tomorrow night at the latest. The sooner I leave, the sooner I can return."

There was not an argument Gabriella could present that would dissuade Segretti. Whatever dangers lurked for him, she was powerless to stop. They would unfold according to influences far beyond her control. The workings had been set in motion. There was no turning back and no other decision to be made. Whatever dangers loomed, Gabriella hoped they would remain in perpetual motion and not settle on Segretti.

Under the circumstances, there were not many choices given to her. Gabriella had been governed by an alignment of things taking shape that had a potential for misfortune. There was nothing else she could draw from that would be a stand in for a reversal of events. Consequently, she focused on her choices. There were several. Yet she immediately clung to one. One that insisted she wait with a stoic resolve and trust in a positive result.

In contrast, Segretti had only one choice. It was one that had been made for him a long time ago. Gabriella realized boyhood influences were difficult to abandon. She wanted to curse the memory of Giuseppe Musolino. She felt an inner contempt for the rule his legacy had on an impressionable young boy, roaming the streets of Reggio searching for a hero. Gabriella knew she was powerless to revoke Musolino's lasting mandate. But she needed to find some way to combat his command.

She slid her arm into Segretti's as they walked away from the café. Discreetly, she removed the bracelet with the amulet and cimaruta and slipped it into his jacket pocket. There would be time to find an ancient church in town and pray for his safety. For the moment, she hoped the old Calabrian lore of the amulet and cimaruta would serve to protect him against the *maloccio*--the evil eyes.

ARIZONA

UMBERTO Nunarro unscrewed the cap from one of the bottles of soda he purchased at the convenience store. He poured the soda down the drain of the small sink in the motel. Then he fashioned a funnel from a paper cup and put it into the mouth of the bottle. Once the funnel was securely in place, he opened the five pound bag of sugar. Pouring some through the funnel, he filled the bottle to less than one quarter. When he was satisfied with the amount of sugar, he filled the rest of the bottle with gasoline. When the bottle was filled, he removed the makeshift funnel and replaced the cap tightly. With a towel, he wiped the bottle and cautiously set it down on the table.

He continued the same process with each bottle. When all the bottles were filled, he tore a strip of masking tape and placed it sticky side up on the table. Removing a handful of wooden matches, he carefully affixed a row to the tape allowing for only the heads of the matches to protrude beyond the edge of the tape. He butted each match to the next, creating an unbroken row around the base of the bottle. Working purposefully, he continued to affix the tape with the matches to each bottle. Then he applied a second layer of tape giving the matches added security.

Mario Orisi watched the care and precision Nunarro applied to his task. Nunarro worked silently with a deep single-mindedness, preparing the bottles for their purpose, when he would break into the storage facility. The contents of the bottles were now a rudimentary mixture designed to create a minor commotion. Simplistic in appearance, he stood back and looked at the bottles as though they were an every day treasure.

"I would still feel better if we had guns," Orisi said. "I could rely on guns."

"Speed is going to be our best ally," Nunarro responded.

"Ubaid is going to have guns."

"Fine. Then it's going to be up to him to shoot if that is what's needed. Our job is to drive away with the truck. Anything else will be a distraction."

"When do we call Ubaid?"

"Tonight, just before we leave. I don't want to give him time to think or to act on his own. I'll explain the plan to him as we get close to the storage site. We need to control him. But we can only do that for a short while. The less he knows, the safer we are."

"What do we do about the four security cameras around the perimeter of the garages?"

"We do nothing. They're placed too high up on poles. We can't disable them. We don't have to. If this goes the way I hope, it's a simple break in. We leave with the truck, and Harrington won't report it."

"If it doesn't go as you hope?"

"We react as best we can. But no matter what happens, we leave with the truck. Nothing alters that plan."

Nunarro carefully wrapped each bottle in long strands of paper towels and placed them in two paper bags. He showed a slight attachment to the bottles, as though they were instruments to help with his luck. Orisi started to light a cigarette. He stopped and tilted his head toward the sliding doors leading to the small balcony. He thought he heard something in the distance. As the sound grew louder, he realized it was the wail of angry sirens. Orisi knew they were police cars and other emergency vehicles. They moved with purpose and urgency, in concert with some sort of human catastrophe. For an instant, he suspected they were coming for him. The sirens were a coded message Orisi interpreted as a warning and danger.

Nunarro moved close behind him and opened the drapes to investigate the sirens. The sun burst into the room, accompanying the increasing level of sound. Momentarily, his vision was distorted. The blaring of the sirens was offensive. The noise and glare attacked him in a belligerent way. Nunarro opened the door and walked out onto the balcony. In the distance, he saw a line of emergency vehicles speeding down Commerce Drive. He noticed two fire trucks, an EMS vehicle, and several State police vehicles. They continued past the motel and Pioneer Park. Nunarro strained to watch the vehicles as they went beyond the Sandretto Hills storage facility. At a certain point beyond the storage facility, he heard the sirens gather.

"What's going on?" Orisi asked.

"I don't know."

"They're at the garages."

"No. I don't think so. But close."

Nunarro turned and walked back into the room. He quickly turned on the television and flipped the channels until he came to a local cable station. Letters ran across the bottom of the screen identifying the station as AZTV 13. A woman reporter was shouting into the camera over the sounds of the sirens. Confusion ensued as firemen and sheriff's deputies frantically ran around her.

"...I'm here reporting live on Commerce Drive," the reporter continued shouting. "Apparently, there's been a serious accident. I'm here with Ted Parker, who was driving on Commerce Drive, when the accident occurred."

The reporter turned to the man who entered the frame of the television screen. The man looked troubled, dusty and sweaty. He held a handkerchief and dabbed at his watery eyes and runny nose.

"Mister Parker, can you describe what happened?" she asked loudly over the background noise.

"Yes," the man responded in a strained, raspy voice. "I was driving north on Commerce Drive when this truck, you know like a fuel truck, was coming down toward me from the north. I saw the truck swerving erratically. Like the driver was losing control of the rig. Well, I swerved out of the way, and the tanker came into my lane. Then it tried to turn back into the right lane. I guess that's when the driver really lost control. The rig jackknifed and tumbled over."

"Keep those people back," someone shouted off camera.

"Move back. Move back," the sheriff's deputy said to the reporter and her crew.

The reporter, along with the man she was interviewing, and her film crew followed the orders from the deputy.

"What else did you see, Mister Parker?" the reporter asked as they walked.

"Well, I got out of the way of the truck and drove past it. I stopped and watched the truck slide down the road. Man, there were sparks everywhere. Even in the daylight, the sparks were bright. The rig rippled like it was made of rubber, and then it split. Thick green smoke came out of the truck. I stood there a while watching it, then all of a sudden, my eyes started to burn, and I began coughing. That's when I got in my car and drove further away."

"Did you see if there were other vehicles involved in the crash?"

"No, I didn't see. I don't remember. Everything happened so fast. I don't think there were other cars behind me," he said, dabbing at his eyes and nose again. "I do know there was no traffic coming down behind the truck," he continued.

"Do you know what happened to the driver of the truck? Did you see if he escaped the crash?"

"I really didn't see. I wanted to drive back to help him, but as I said, my eyes began to burn. I couldn't see. There was a lot of sand and green smoke. I figured the green smoke was bad news by the way my eyes burned. It made me cough."

"Thank you, Mister Parker," The reporter said, turning back to the camera.

"I'm waiting to speak to Fire Marshal, Fred Brand," the reporter continued.

"Fire Marshal Brand," the reporter shouted. "Fire Marshal Brand, can I ask you a question, please?"

The marshal wore a heavy protective coat with yellow stripes and a breathing mask. Goggles hung from his neck.

"Can you explain what occurred?" the reporter said.

"Yes. We have a chemical spill. It's one of the most severe kinds of chemical one could be exposed to."

"Can you give us details? Can you identify the chemicals?"

"The tanker was carrying a corrosive mixture of hydrochloric, nitric and hydrofluoric acids with chromic acid mixed in. The fumes are toxic to the lungs and could cause a severe reaction."

"Yes, I could smell it. It does have a rather pungent odor. It has an effect on my breathing."

"You should be positioned further back."

"Could you describe the extent of the damage?"

"The tanker truck was carrying eight thousand gallons of the chemicals. We don't know how much has already spilled. My men can't get close to the crash site due to the danger of exposure. Hazmat crews have been called in and will handle it. They're better equipped for such an emergency."

"What is usually the procedure in an accident like this?" the reporter asked.

"We've made an initial assessment, which I just described. Hazmat will confirm our findings. Then they will have to pump whatever is remaining from the damaged truck into another truck. That's the only way to contain this spill. If you'll excuse me," the fire marshal said, abruptly walking away.

The confusion from emergency personnel continued around the reporter. She looked through the crowd and appeared to recognize someone.

"Sheriff St. Cloud," the reporter called out. "Sheriff St. Cloud."

Sheriff Joseph St. Cloud appeared on camera. He appeared official and in control, determined to change the nature of the chaos.

"Move your vehicle to Tower Road," the Sheriff shouted to someone off camera. "Take up position at that intersection."

"Sheriff," the reporter said. "Sheriff, I've just spoken with Fire Marshal,

Fred Brand, and he described this as one of the worst kinds of chemical spill. Can you give us a report from your perspective?"

"As far as we can determine, it was a severe chemical spill. I've coordinated with Fire Marshal Brand, and we're waiting to confer with Hazmat officials."

"Do you know if anyone was injured?"

"The driver escaped the crash and was taken to the hospital."

"Were there any other vehicles involved in the crash?"

"It appears there are none. But we can't get close enough to the wreckage to confirm that."

"Sheriff, what plans do you have in terms of traffic, and the possibility of evacuating the area?"

"Because of the toxic effect of the chemicals, we are in the process of evacuating everyone within a one mile radius of the crash site. Traffic has been prohibited on Commerce Drive. We've also prohibited traffic from entering the roads feeding into Commerce Drive. Rose Lane, Aster Drive, Sunflower Drive and Marigold Drive have all been shut down. Also Tower Road. All these roads are southwest of Commerce Drive. On the east, we've shut down Spire Drive."

"How long will the traffic be shut down, sheriff?" the reporter asked.

"Until further notice. We have to confer with Hazmat officials, and with Fire Marshal Brand. Something more definitive will be determined then. For now, I need you and your news crew to vacate this area. You are just on the edge of the area we need to evacuate," the Sheriff said and walked away

"Certainly, we'll just wrap up and leave."

The reporter turned toward the direction of the camera. She cleared her throat and blinked her eyes several times as they were becoming irritated.

"That was Sheriff Joseph St. Cloud," the reporter said. "And as you've just heard, we've had a major chemical spill on Commerce Drive south of Pioneer Park and Spire Drive. According to Sheriff St. Cloud, a section of Commerce Drive and all arteries north and south leading into it will be closed to traffic until further notice. There is also a plan to evacuate the area. And I can tell you, we're standing a fair distance from the crash, and I can feel the effects of the chemicals. My eyes are burning and my throat is raw…"

Nunarro became angry and shut the television. He threw the remote control on the sofa and walked back out to the balcony. Standing next to Orisi, they looked in the direction of the crash and the Sandretto Hills storage facility. Suddenly, Nunarro felt a pull from the area. He wondered if the powdered gold had somehow devised a plot using the crash as a means to keep him from his intentions. He questioned if the powder had made a secret arrangement with someone other than himself to be a guardian and keep its true identity hidden? Was the crash a designed ploy to deny his access to the garage? If so, why? Nunarro refused to give into the possible hidden plan or potential will of the powder. He did not want to succumb to a fanciful superstition or incur any vile curse it may possess. Nor would he yield to any ancient order of exclusion. His need was the only thing he would bow to.

With the roads leading to the garages closed, he'd have to postpone his confrontation with destiny. For the moment, there was nothing for him to do but wait until the roads reopened. At that point, his journey would be free of obstacles. It would be a matter left to his influence and control. Whatever alternate plan the powder may have, was of no consequence to him. He held to a tight vision of his own glory. In the final moments, he would ride away leaving in his wake the ultimate expression of his own determination and the beginning of a new heritage.

AGENT Andrew Cummings made it a point to carefully monitor his actions as they related to the responsibility of his job. He was dutifully responsive to every bit of information he received via e-mails, and attentive to the results of surveillance reports and updated bureau initiatives. Not to be overlooked was information from other agencies, such as the CIA, FBI, and DOD. Whatever information, wiretaps, electronic intrusions, these agencies chose to share, Cummings read to brief himself. He was still searching for the slightest bit of information that could mingle with his obsession. He needed to be attentive to any potential threat from Nunarro and Orisi, but mostly he needed to find clues that could reveal the actions and location of his enemy for life…Pietro Segretti.

Information about Nunarro and Orisi went beyond facts and the actuality to truth. But, it was information about Segretti that would ultimately lead to personal relief. Practical information converted into special knowledge for Cummings. Combined, they resulted in a sequential advantage that was interchangeable and had no equal. Both would be harnessed and used for his benefit, giving him the freedom to act upon his urges.

Cummings drew from the details of every classified memo, thoughtfully and without distraction. Perhaps in the same way as shamans, while meditating. Every coded line had the potential to reveal to him the one name, the one person and one more opportunity to rearrange memories that best suited him.

The phone on his desk rang interrupting his thoughts. The caller identification indicated the call was from Bart Freeling, an executive with AT&T, the telecommunication company Cummings had chosen to monitor all correspondence from Analisa Scotti.

Freeling had been one of the phone company's personnel who had been authorized, through a secret Presidential order, allowing AT&T and other telecommunication companies to monitor all phone conversations after September 11, 2001. The operation was also given the approval to monitor e-mails, faxes and any other forms of communication.

With the help of ECHELON, the giant computer program, the age of technical eavesdropping had shrunk the world to instant transparency, and relieved it of its core freedoms in the name of protection and security. ECHELON controlled the download, dissemination and interception of all fiber-optic communications. The computers, designed for this purpose, had the capability to intercept and record telephone calls around the world, as well as faxes and e-mails.

Freeling had worked closely with Cummings for a long time. The two had become colleagues in a struggle against revolutionaries who insisted on their own version of cataclysmic change. The security agencies, along with strategically chosen corporate communication executives, ordained themselves the sole task of ensuring they maintained their authority as the most intrusive force known. Information was the key to their power. It was used to enshrine the executives and agents as high priests. Cummings shut down his computer and picked up the phone.

"Hello, Bart," he said.

"Hi, Andy," Freeling's voice said. "How are you?"

"I'm good."

"I heard you had some difficulty recently in the desert," Freeling commented.

"Yes, I did. How did you hear about it?"

"I was speaking with Stewart Manning the other day at the Conference of the Executive Board of Communications. He mentioned it to me. He's healing up, but he still didn't look so good."

"We were involved in a slight altercation. I'm working on resolving it. So what else did Stewart tell you?" Cummings asked.

"Well, clearly he's pissed that you guys came out on the short end of that incident. But beyond that he didn't say too much."

"Did you happen to mention to him what you're working on for me?"

"Absolutely not. I got the distinct impression this was something you didn't want announced."

"Good. I knew you would understand. How are things on your end, Bart?"

"Well, with the Senate breathing down our necks over our part in communications surveillance, things are getting a bit sticky. But, you know that."

"It's all smoke and noise. It will all go away."

"Until it does, guys on my end hope there's not a junior senator somewhere looking to make a name for himself."

"Don't worry about it. We've got our own guys on the Hill to make sure nothing ever comes of this. It's all headlines and parlor conversation. The real game is played on our field with our rules."

"That's comforting to know."

"Bart, that's not why you called."

"No, it's not. Listen Andy, did that incident in the desert have anything to do with the names of the people you gave me to put on my high priority watch list?"

"One name, the known arms dealer. The others are peripheral people he's known to associate with. Some are family, why?"

"The arms dealer, was he the guy in the desert? The guy you and Stewart had the altercation with?"

"Yes. Why?"

Cummings heard the ruffling of paper, then a long, quiet pause. He felt the silence was a separate communication, the core part of paranoia and distrust. Freeling used the silence as a protection against those little invasions he was complicit with. He feared these same forces he used on the rights of others could be just as easily turned on him. Caution and deception for Freeling were more than just prudent. They were the essence of his career.

"We need to talk," Freeling announced.

"This line is secure," Cummings assured.

"It may be, but I'm more comfortable with another arrangement. You know where to meet me?" Freeling said.

"Same place as last time?"

"Yes."

"I'm leaving now," Cummings said and hung up the phone.

CUMMINGS drove through the high ponderosa pines that were beginning to blend into the darkening sky. The setting sun painted a stretch of clouds with a deep ocher, black and blue. Such sunsets were familiar to Cummings. He had seen so many in the past. Each one was dramatic in tone and texture. But lately, he overlooked them, especially the one currently spread out before him. His attention was distracted by the anticipation of the information he hoped Freeling would provide. He continued among the

Granite Dells, following the roadway leading to the entrance of the Prescott Lakes Golf Club. The sprawling landscape was preserved for elite recreation and a refined, uncomplicated offer to a certain segment of society.

The road led Cummings past the main building. A vintage Conestoga wagon and a U.S. Cavalry wagon were set on either side of the walkway leading to the entrance. He noticed the front hitch of the coverless Conestoga wagon rested on the ground. The original cavalry wagon, complete with a faded emblem of crisscrossed Springfield Rifles, was accentuated by a bright spotlight. Both wagons were proud reminders how expansionism had come to the west.

Cummings parked in a deserted area beyond the main building, closer to the entrance to the bucolic golf course. A row of idle golf carts formed a barrier he felt comfortable behind. Beyond the cart, undulating spray of water arched across a manicured green from the sprinkler system. He shut the engine and absorbed the glow from the overhead light. The sounds of small field animals, the rhythmic spray of water and wind coming off the golf course, caused Cummings to rest for a moment. He tried to keep his anticipation at a distance. Rubbing his eyes, Cummings tried to relieve the twitching. The slight throb played on his fingertips and did not respond to his gentle massage. During the day, he was unaware of the involuntary movement. At night, his thoughts were usually more complex and seemed to produce the twitch.

Lights from an oncoming car diverted his attention. He watched as Freeling drove in and parked next to him. Cummings looked around, then quickly entered Freeling's vehicle. Freeling checked the rearview mirror as Cummings settled into the passenger's seat. The executive's suspicion was accentuated by a clench in his jaw. He glanced toward the row of golf carts, and the darkened fairway. The hint of criminal activity, no matter how patriotic, caused him to take a deep breath and question his sensibilities. The overhead light to the fairway was a distraction making Freeling feel vulnerable and exposed. He became a convert to the new system of compliance, yet it made him uncomfortable for his future. His tie was still tight around his neck. His jacket hung like a curtain from a hook on the door behind him.

"Sorry for the cloak and dagger, Andy," Freeling said.

"I understand, Bart. What do you have for me?" Cummings asked.

Freeling produced a large envelope from under the seat, and handed it to Cummings. He felt the envelope contained a grim potential that also harbored an implied accusation meant to gauge his conscience. The surveillance information had no such claim on Cummings. It was what he had been waiting for.

"That name you gave me, Segretti," Freeling announced. "You wanted special preference placed on his communications, as well as his associates and family."

"Yes."

"There it is. We did get European communications on his transmissions. Everything came from our DE CIX Internet exchange point in Frankfurt. That's our European intercept point. We followed a line of communications."

"That's great, thanks. I knew something would come of it."

"Andy, it appears the first communication originated from right here in Arizona. I personally checked it and followed the line of communication."

Cummings flipped on the light in Freeling's car and opened the envelope. He quickly read the first page of the report then turned to Freeling.

"I see here the first transmission was from Analisa Scotti," Cummings observed. "Is all this transcribed?"

"No, the transmission from Analisa Scotti was an e-mail. The actual text is on the second page."

Cummings read the e-mail carefully. He kept looking for key words, searching for something that would reveal anything beyond what he read.

"It was to her sister, Lucia," Cummings said.

"Yes. The e-mail initiated the ensuing correspondence. You have it all there. It's current up to just a few hours ago. The times of transmission are indicated."

Cummings continued reading. His look became more perplexed as he got deeper into the text. He wondered if the communication was some sort of coded message meant to mislead. But then Cummings realized the message was unguarded, unaware of interception.

"Did you read this?" Cummings asked.

"Yes."

"What do you think she means when she refers to the 'white nectar of the gods'?"

"I don't know. You'll have to figure it out."

"How did this get to Segretti?"

"There's a reversed chronology in the reports. You'll see them marked as such. The e-mail to Lucia mentions Nicola. I take it Nicola is Nicola Bounetti, Lucia's husband. They were on the watch list. Bounetti is actually Segretti's cousin. Analisa says to Lucia that Nicola would be interested in what Mitchell found in Iraq...."

"Mitchell Harrington," Cummings interrupted. "Mitchell Harrington is the soldier just discharged from the military. I should have had him on my watch list."

"I could add him," Freeling said.

"Yes. Do it."

"Analisa refers to whatever Mitchell brought back from Iraq as a relic," Freeling informed.

"Alright, that's the connection between Mitchell and Analisa. That's what I've been looking for." Cummings said. "Now the question is whether Nicola is interested in this relic for himself or is it something for Segretti."

"The other question is what is the relic?" Freeling said "Is it the nectar she refers to?"

Cummings read the report intently. Every line became a talisman with intentions meant specifically for harm. There was no reason to struggle against his instincts. Everything he needed was falling at his feet. Interplay with an unnamed relic found in Iraq by a solder was all part of an unraveling he was planning to take charge of.

"Bounetti clearly reacted to the e-mail and called Segretti shortly after Lucia received it," Freeling continued. "What you have there is a verbatim transcript of that conversation.

"Segretti is a known arms dealer. I wonder if the nectar of the gods is some sort of explosive."

"If it's an explosive, why refer to it as a relic?"

"Because it could be a code word. If it is explosives, then Analisa and Mitchell have over a thousand pounds of it. It looks like Segretti is about to get his hands on it."

"Who's the miner from Arizona that Bounetti mentions in the conversation?" Freeling asked.

"A guy by the name of Alex Barnes. He lives in Butler. Segretti was there when the mine Barnes owned blew up."

"I don't understand."

"It means Segretti is very shrewd," Cummings said, trying to be evasive.

"I'm not so sure. He's sending us an open invitation to his scheme. Look at the transcript," Freeling continued. "Segretti says openly he's coming here tomorrow on his own jet. How bright is that?"

"No, not very bright," Cummings agreed with a menacing glee. "Are you still monitoring these people?"

"Yes. And now Mitchell Harrington. How much longer do you want this to go on?"

Cummings understood there were formulas and time limits placed on these types of things. Through the results of technology at the European intercept point in Frankfurt, Cummings felt he was finding a way to control formulas and manipulate surprise. What could be an unbiased transition between himself and Segretti, seemed to be a favorable trend bending in his direction. The quiet force that drives an alliance or a confrontation has a particular voice. Cummings had important access to the technology that set the tone to that voice. It was also one he found to be most welcoming.

Cummings folded the pages of the report and placed them in the envelope. He reached up and shut off the light in Freeling's car. Within the darkness, he hoped the vengeful glint in his eyes and sinister smile were not noticeable. When his business with Segretti became complete he could get back to all the regular things he could do in his life. No longer would he be defined by his fixation.

Freeling sat quietly expecting an answer from Cummings. He thought perhaps Cummings had not heard him. Nervously, Freeling tapped his fingers on the steering wheel.

"Andy," Freeling said. "How much longer?"

Cummings felt the twitching in his eye had stopped. His thoughts were no longer vague. He comprehended and appreciated the ease and simplicity associated to most things. A welcomed relief was gradually settling into his being. Cummings slowly turned and looked at Freeling. A strange pleasantness etched his face.

"Not much longer," Cummings whispered. "Not much longer at all."

PIETRO Segretti sat in his private Dassalt Mystere Falcon 100 jet as it was prepared to make an approach landing into Sky Harbor Airport. The flight from Leonardo da Vinci Airport had been long, but uneventful. Segretti tried to sleep most of the trip. Thinking about the potential danger awaiting him from Homeland Security, kept his mind troubled and uneasy. He knew entering the United States was dangerous. Using his private jet had the potential of drawing more attention. There was not much he could do to prevent the scrutiny from Homeland Security. Whatever may transpire eventuality would be subject to the command of his response. Instead, Segretti focused on applying his influence to an outcome he might be able to affect if he aligned himself with the prevailing fate.

Alberto LaTesta sat opposite Segretti. As a childhood friend, LaTesta was familiar with Segretti's expressions and moods. Observing his slight frown and his uneasy quietness, LaTesta knew Segretti was experiencing some sort of deep concern. He also knew to question Segretti would be a poor approach. Their familiarity allowed for enough of an informational range that made it unnecessary to probe further. LaTesta sat erect in the plush leather seat. Placing his hands on the armrests in a ruling gesture, it suggested a refinement of a man who cherished tradition and his heritage.

LaTesta was big-boned with thick, hairy forearms and legs. His facial hair was dark and coarse, appearing as if he was constantly in need of a shave. As a direct descendant of a Burgundian knight, who fought to reconquer Portugal from the Moors in the 11th century, LaTesta understood the origins of his inherent pride. After taking part in the Napoleonic Wars, his ancestors traveled east across Spain and settled in Calabria, Italy. The new beginnings of LaTesta's traditions soon became defined by fishing and wine making. The combined history of his ancestors was an evolution of contradictions. However, LaTesta felt more aligned with the warring temperament of the Burgundian knights. His strength and force were influenced by the line of warriors and nobles that blended his cultivated tolerance with his attachment to innate aggression.

As teenagers, he and Segretti had to confront the local Mafioso. His two body guards had disrespected Segretti's sister, beating her badly when she rejected the mobster's sexual advances. The gangster had misinterpreted the initial meeting by the two boys as a timid attempt at nobility. But in an instant, the young Segretti looped a wire around the gangster's throat and choked him. LaTesta appeared calm and dignified until the instant he attacked the two bodyguards. The sudden change in his demeanor became completely savage and uncontrollable. He stabbed each bodyguard with a silver pick that looked like a pen he had clipped to his jacket pocket. After they were stabbed, LaTesta pummeled them with a post he tore from a pig pen behind the gangster's house. He picked up their bloody, lifeless bodies and threw them into the muddy pen, where the pigs proceeded to defecate on them. LaTesta wondered if it was his tendency or his heritage that produced such rage. It was the one and only time he questioned his actions. In the end, it really didn't matter. It all came so naturally.

The small washroom door behind LaTesta opened. Gino Mafaldi emerged wiping his hands on a paper towel. Mafaldi sat next to Segretti and placed the rolled up paper towel on an ash tray. He looked at his watch and fastened his seat belt.

"We should be landing in twenty minutes," Mafaldi announced.

Mafaldi appeared restless. His large muscular body felt the constraints of the limited space in the jet. He was as tall and as broad as LaTesta, but distinguished by a nagging agitation acquired at birth. His dark, brooding eyes shifted constantly and appeared penetrating, and menacing.

Mafaldi reached for a travel magazine and discovered an article about grape farmers and sheep herders in Sardinia. The son of a chestnut and olive farmer, Mafaldi understood the affinity man had with the earth. He turned the page to a picture of farmers sitting under a grapevine eating bread and drinking wine. The cracked and weathered faces of the people celebrating a good harvest were similar to those Mafaldi knew from his youth. They were stand-ins for his family, who were content with their lives and their series of centuries-old customs and celebrations. They battled the elements and lived with rich and poor yields. They died without ever going beyond the length of their fields or the borders of their claustrophobic city. But as a boy, Mafaldi knew the earth was not his calling. On the day he met Segretti and LaTesta; all that changed for him. Everything he ever saw of the world from that day on was never in a magazine. As international arms dealers, they traveled the world negotiating with generals, revolutionaries and kings. They made deals in palaces and tents, yachts and windowless rooms. Mafaldi understood conflict was the nature of man and nations; a blood-birth doomed to duel. In some small way, he shared a complicity in that union. Along with Segretti and LaTesta, their ulterior mission was to fortify the meek. But Mafaldi instinctively knew the outcome to increased power was always deeper resentments and greater hostility.

All his travels gave him a better understanding of himself, the world and his relationship to it. Continents and oceans were no longer a mystery. Mountains and cathedrals shared a common reality. Kings and peasants were separated only by a thin sliver of fate, yet joined by the farce of assumptions. Holding to that insight made the gateway to his mortality tolerable. Mafaldi believed Segretti shared a similar philosophy. Consequently, he understood his frantic chase for the white, powdery relic on a core level. For both of them, it was an extension of their own longing, a relative quest for the collective deconstruction of limitations.

The jet made its final landing approach and glided with great ease onto the runway. The sleek plane, so natural in flight, taxied effortlessly to the appropriate gate. The twin Garrett turbo-fan engines reduced to a breathless whisper, and went silent. Segretti turned to LaTesta and Mafaldi as they stood beside him, expressing the kind of discipline and loyalty that builds trust and defeats threats.

The co-pilot emerged from the cockpit cabin and unlocked the door automatically lowering the stairs. Segretti's legs felt a bit unsteady from the long trip. As he walked along the tarmac, with LaTesta and Mafaldi, a terminal door opened. Two men, appearing official in dark, expensive looking suits, carrying briefcases, stood inside the terminal. Although he hadn't seen either man in over two years, Segretti recognized David MacMillian and Alan Dietz, partners in the law firm, MacMillian, MacMillian & Dietz.

The law firm of MacMillian & MacMillian had been founded by David's father, Jonah and his uncle Mortimer, who retired in 1963. David joined the firm twenty years later. Soon after, Alan Dietz became a member of the firm. They were made partners shortly thereafter. The young MacMillian and Dietz were board certified, criminal defense attorneys. MacMillian was also a former President of the National Association of Criminal Defense Lawyers. In addition, he was a long standing member of Arizona's Criminal Defense Attorney Association, where he earned a fierce international reputation as a protector of constitutional rights. MacMillian and Dietz were extremely successful in their representation in the defense of serious felony, misdemeanor as well as international criminal charges. Segretti kept the law firm on retainer. He thought it best they came personally to the airport in the event Agent Cummings or someone from Homeland Security would insist on undermining Segretti's constitutional rights.

Segretti approached MacMillian and shook his hand.

"Hello, David," Segretti said. "Nice to see you again. Thank you for coming. I know it was an inconvenience."

"Pietro, it was not an inconvenience at all. It's always nice to see you, too. How was your trip?" MacMillian responded.

"Very good."

"I'm glad. You remember my partner, Alan Dietz?"

"Of course I do. Hello," Segretti said and shook Alan's hand.

"Hello, Gino, Alberto," MacMillian said. "Good to see you both again. Please, come this way. I have a car waiting.

The group of men walked through the terminal thick with travelers. Segretti looked at the crowd, assessing it suspiciously. Once outside the terminal, MacMillian approached a long limousine. Both doors were opened. Segretti climbed into the back seat, along with LaTesta and Mafaldi. MacMillian and Dietz entered the second door and sat facing Segretti. There was a pronounced luxury within the interior of the vehicle. With mahogany and gold trim on the doors, it was more than a suggestion the vehicle was designed without restrictions.

Once inside the car and surrounded by the lawyers, Segretti felt protected and at ease with the similarity between himself and MacMillian. They both shared a comparable refinement and confidence that showed in the way they dressed and how they carried themselves. But, it was the bearing signs of ruthlessness and aggression, honed from a different set of circumstances that set them apart. MacMillian opened the panel in the door exposing imported bottles of cold water and handed them out. Placing his briefcase on the floor, MacMillian felt an odd legitimacy based upon his professional success. He openly balanced a type of power gained through judicial conflict, and his many legal triumphs.

"Obviously there was no security waiting for you at the airport, Pietro," MacMillian said.

"None that I saw. That doesn't mean they're not out there."

"Do you suspect a rogue element operating outside the official agency as a threat?"

"That's possible. The incident that occurred in the desert may have produced such a rogue threat; Agent Cummings."

"My office feels its best not to approach Agent Cummings. There's no extradition process filed with the Justice Department for you. So, it's best if we just let things be."

"That's good."

"There is also nothing filed with the Italian government. So, even though you may be watched, there is no apparent threat to you."

"So, I had you come here for no reason."

"Absolutely not. It's always better to be prepared. I'm your representation while you're here. Where can I take you now?"

"I have an appointment in Phoenix," Segretti said. "Not far from the university campus."

"Fine. Will you need me there with you?"

"No. That won't be necessary. I've made arrangements."

"Will you need me to accompany you when you prepare to leave?"

"It remains to be seen."

"If the situation changes and you need my services, don't hesitate to call."

MacMillian's proposal acted as a lever to help Segretti with his purpose. The attorney's presence offered a way to protect Segretti's conviction against the formidable alliances that could be gathering to prevent his objective. The culture of opposition was sometimes seeped in actual conspiracy. Segretti did not have the luxury of secrecy to conceal himself from any devoted rivalry. He was in the open, exposed to the whim of conformity the attorney could react to, but may be powerless to prevent.

Segretti was aware of most possibilities and remained open to those he was not. All he hoped for was an equal chance to indulge his efforts. He trusted his claim to some of the powder would be looked upon favorably and align with his sense of purpose.

AN unmarked, white van was parked up the street from Analisa Scotti's house. It was partially hidden behind a row of green, hop bush. From this vantage point, Agent Robert Heller could plainly see as the limousine stopped in front of Analisa's house. He watched, through binoculars, as Segretti emerged from the vehicle. Heller quickly jotted down the license plate and snapped pictures of Segretti, LaTesta and Mafaldi as they stood outside the house. Their presence appeared covert in nature to Heller's trained eye. They were surely linked to suspicion as they seemed to be preparing the stage for some sort of criminal activity. But Heller felt they were unaware they had entered a well-guarded premises. Their movements, phone conversations, as well as anything they discarded, would be minutely scrutinized and analyzed. They were now well entangled in a web of surveillance with nowhere to go, making Heller feel very confident.

Analisa emerged from the house and approached Segretti, greeting him with a warm hug. Segretti was glad to see Analisa. It had been years since he last saw her. He was amazed how much she had changed and how her beauty had developed. Segretti suddenly felt an odd sense of time, especially for the unseen things that transpired within it. In this instant, he could not measure the things lost in time. He only tried to gauge its effect.

"Analisa," Segretti said. "You look so different. Life has matured you."

"That's a polite way of saying I've grown older?" Analisa laughed.

"Not at all. More beautiful is closer to what I meant. You remember my friends, Alberto and Gino?" Segretti said.

"Of course I do. We met. I believe it was the last time I saw you. I'm trying to remember when it was."

"When you last came to Italy to visit Lucia," Segretti interrupted. "Seven years ago."

"Yes, that's right. I also met Gabriella. How is she?"

"She's fine, but unable to make this trip."

"I would have liked to have seen her. I understand through Lucia, Melia and Rosa are not doing well."

"That's why I'm here."

"Yes, I know. I spoke with Nicola. You're trying to help them. He told me you had been here sometime ago and were in the process of buying a product from a local miner."

"Yes, I was. You were away at the time of my visit."

"Unfortunately, I was on assignment in the Sinai."

"I know. Tell me, does this product have the capability of restoring health? Nicola seems to think it does."

"Come inside. I'll introduce you to Mitchell. He found the powder. It is capable of many things. Restoring health is just one."

Analisa escorted Segretti to the back of the house. Harrington and

Solis were sitting on the patio. When Segretti approached, Harrington stood and greeted him.

"Pietro," Harrington said. "I've heard a great deal about you. This is my friend, Hector Solis."

Segretti shook hands with Harrington and Solis and introduced LaTesta and Mafaldi.

"Make yourself comfortable, Pietro," Analisa said. "I'll bring out more iced tea. Or, would you like something else."

"No, ice tea is fine. Thank you."

"I've put something out for you to eat. I'm sure you are hungry from your long trip. Please help yourselves."

Segretti sat at the table with LaTesta and Mafaldi. Analisa had prepared an assortment of cheeses, fruits, a large platter of grilled vegetables and marinated, baked tofu. A basket of bread was on a separate table with a large bucket of ice.

LaTesta positioned his chair enabling him to see beyond the patio. Mafaldi, as if rehearsed, took up a position that gave him full view of the door behind Segretti. Segretti was intimately familiar with the edgy protocol that existed just before all negotiations. The list of unwritten specifications was a fine art, for which Segretti had full command.

He studied Harrington, weighing the equation of his authority with his own experience. There was an undeniable tension, but Segretti never questioned the outcome.

"I understand, Mister Harrington, you and Mister Solis were in Iraq."

"Yes, we were."

"I'm glad you returned safely. I'm sure it would be foolish to ask how it went, so I won't. I will just hope in time the experience is remembered without regret."

"It didn't get ta that point yet," Solis said.

"You will," Segretti responded. "The best thing about combat is a man can get to know those he can trust. Those are the kind of people a man keeps around for the rest of his life. That's what makes the battle secondary and soon something to be forgotten."

"You seem to understand the nature of combat, Mister Segretti."

"Let's just say, I appreciate trust. And please, call me Pietro."

"I also think you came to appreciate a by-product of the combat in Iraq," Harrington said.

"I'm sure you're referring to the white powder."

"Yes, I am."

"It's no secret. You know of my interest in the white powder. If not, I will be more than happy to openly discuss it with you now."

"Analisa has already told me why you're interested in the powder. I appreciate your reasons. How can I help you?"

"Let me be open about this. In my business, I know everything about the products I sell. In most cases, I bargain hard to make the right deal. I always come from a strong position. The people I sell products to desperately need my services. The products themselves serve man's most callous desires and have nothing to do with healing. But, I understand the powder you brought home from Iraq, can heal."

"Yes, it can. I'm not exactly certain about the application, but I certainly know the beneficial effect it can have. But, that's the least of its properties. The powder is the most unique element mankind has ever known."

"I know a little about it. I'm sure the powder is miraculous, but I'm only concerned about its ability to heal. It appears, you're confirming this powder does have that ability."

"It does. Testimonies go back to ancient times."

"I have family that can benefit from this ancient powder. Family is everything to me, Mitchell. I'll do whatever I can to help them."

"That's honorable of you."

"It's just what I do. I leave judgments to others. I will say this to you, my trade is negotiation, bargaining. When I'm dealing with a client, I never show vulnerability. I'm afraid I have broken from that with you. Because I'm pleading for my family, I'm bargaining from a weakened position. I'm at your mercy."

"Pietro, let me be honest with you. The powder is priceless. That's not meant to inflate the price or expose your position. I would never take advantage of you. Analisa tells me you're a man who appreciates honor. I can now see that for myself. That said, I wouldn't begin to know the powder's fair market value."

"I'm sure you didn't go through all the trouble to bring the powder home from Iraq and not want to make money for your efforts. You must have some idea what its worth."

"The powder is a product of history. Scientists will want it. So will governments and museums..."

"So will thieves," Segretti interrupted. "So will those who would want to destroy it, so they can manipulate truth."

"We already came across thieves in Germany," Solis blurted out.

"But it appears they didn't take anything from you this time."

"Not in the way of powder, they didn't," Solis assured.

"Yes, I understand how those things go," Segretti said with credible insight.

Analisa brought in the glasses of iced tea and handed them out. She tried to hide the concern in her eyes. Knowing what happened in Germany was manifesting in her mind. Harrington's avoidance of the issue didn't redeem her concern. It just let her know there were worlds he didn't want her to enter.

Segretti noticed how Analisa suddenly seemed isolated. She was unable to restrict the slight shift in her eyes from linking to Segretti's intuition. He suspected Analisa didn't know what happened in Germany, and believed the incident had been severe and threatening. But given his exposure to the nature of confrontation, his insights were more pragmatic than Analisa's. Segretti knew Harrington and Solis did not forfeit the powder, but they were robbed of a portion of their humanity. They were either struggling for a different kind of liberation, or were assessing their initiation into a world of contradiction that bore no kinship to their conduct in war.

"Thank you," Segretti said, taking the ice tea from Analisa.

"So tell me, Analisa," Segretti continued. What was it like after you did your scientific testing to confirm you had monoatomic gold? Nicola has given me a brief explanation of the substance. You must have been overwhelmed."

Analisa sat next to Harrington hoping to blend into the meeting. There was a slight shift to her demeanor. She had been cleverly misdirected by Segretti to abandon her concern for the incident in Germany and reconnected to something less frightening. As Analisa made the slow transition from the futility of worry to relevant astonishment, Segretti saw the curious part of her emerge. It was something he recalled seeing in Analisa when she was a young girl.

"Yes, I was overwhelmed," Analisa said. "I still am. The implications of the powder go beyond anything Nicola may have told you."

"How so?"

"Well, based on our communications, I believe there are aspects of the powder's origins he isn't aware of."

"He once told me the powder was used to build the pyramids of Giza and other temples."

"Well, that's speculation, but I believe it to be true. But, it's only part of the story. After all my testing, I concluded one aspect was truly amazing. The powder's optimum weight is actually fifty-six percent of the metal's weight from which it was transmuted. The forty-four percent must go somewhere. It does. It becomes pure light and translates into a dimension beyond the physical plane. My testing corroborates a finding in the

Alexandrian text which clearly states when the gold is converted to the white powder it outweighs any quantity of the gold. Not even a feather can tip a scale. Beyond that, the forty-four percent light can disappear."

"How can it disappear?" Segretti asked.

"It moves into another dimension...because it weighs less than nothing."

"If it disappears, can it reappear?"

"Yes."

"So, it stands to reason it's anti-gravitational?"

"Exactly."

"I'm impressed with your scientific abilities," Segretti said.

"I was trained well."

"I remember, as a child, you were always digging in your grandmother's garden looking for fossils," Segretti said, a slight melancholy smile etched on his face.

"Yes....Yes. I found an old tea cup once in her tomato patch," Analisa said, yielding to her own rising melancholy.

"I remember that," Segretti said. "I was there that day. It was an exciting discovery for a child."

"At the time, it was. Years later, I learned my grandfather had buried it for me to discover. I was disappointed when I found out."

"You shouldn't have been. It was his way of encouraging you to continue digging for discoveries. In the process, he hoped you would find your true passion."

"I never thought of it in those terms."

"Do you still have the tea cup?"

"No, I don't. Suddenly, that appears to be a pity."

"Not at all. You have something greater from your grandfather. All that he gave you will never leave you."

Analisa felt an ambivalence that was revitalizing. Whatever contradictions she thought existed between herself, and her past, suddenly became a single strain of consciousness. Like the white powder she tested, that had the ability to go in and out of dimensions; her past and present became one simultaneously.

"Mitchell, I understand you have a substantial amount of the powder," Segretti said, turning away from Analisa.

"Yes, that's correct," Harrington said. "Eighteen hundred pounds."

"Interesting. How much of an impact would it have to scientists, governments or museums if you sold off, say...two hundred pounds?"

"I don't know."

"I will offer you one million dollars for every hundred pounds. Does that seem like fair market value?"

Harrington paused, speechless in the wake of such an offer. He was shown a new example of loyalty and trust. In a way, the offer focused on kept promises and diminished his own accomplishments. Segretti's calm expression was kept within the confines of a small radius of concern, yet it encompassed the laurels of the whole world.

"You really want it that badly?" Harrington said, looking intently at Segretti.

"Yes, I do," Segretti answered. "In my case, and as you've confirmed, I know the value of its use."

"You also understand its dangers," Harrington observed.

"As you and Hector do," Segretti commented. "Tell me, Mitchell did you think it was by accident you discovered the powder?" Segretti continued.

Harrington suddenly became thoughtful, introspective. He had been asked to glimpse into his own fate and make an assessment of things he was unprepared to do.

"I don't know," Harrington responded. "I really didn't give it much thought. Is it important?"

"At the moment it is not, but that could change," Segretti said. "Can you at least show me this miraculous, ancient powder?"

Harrington reached under the bench and slid out the briefcase. He placed it on the table. Opening the case, he produced a single bag of the white powder and handed it to Segretti.

"That's ten pounds," Harrington informed.

Segretti opened the bag and looked at the powder. Mafaldi leaned forward as LaTesta looked over Segretti's shoulder. The powder captivated Segretti in a way that was mystical and seductive. It absorbed him through an unknown sacrament; one that went beyond the gospel of holy men. It seemed to pulse with an unusual connection between substance and spirit. It possessed a working knowledge of a second life and an alternate universe.

"It doesn't look like much, does it?" Harrington continued.

Segretti sensed the powder went back beyond ancient, with the capacity to extend well past the eternal. It seemed to have the power of transcendence and made a silent mockery of all doubt and disbelief.

"No. No it doesn't." Segretti said his voice unsteady. "But, then again it does. It looks like something special."

"I have more in the Sandretto Hills storage facility. I also have some buried in my backyard. I've buried about half of what we brought home from Iraq."

"You did?" Segretti questioned, like it was a sacrilege to bury the powder in dirt.

"There was an accident on the road to the storage facility. A chemical spill. The road was closed down. I just saw it on the news. The road has been reopened. We can drive there now. Along the way, I can think about your offer," Harrington said. "Hector is part of this. We also have three others who are equal partners. Unfortunately, they're all back in Iraq. They all helped get the powder out of Iraq. It almost cost Hector his life. So he may have the biggest say in all this."

Segretti's instincts about the confrontation were correct. So was his assessment about the personal toll of conflict. He also knew they were trying to justify the struggle. They needed the proper input from the powder to regain whatever they lost from it.

"Hector has the biggest say because of the incident in Germany?" Segretti said.

"Yes," Harrington said.

"It's still somethin' we all have ta decide on," Solis said.

"I understand," Segretti said, closing the bag and handing it back to Harrington. "Whatever you decide, I will agree to."

"Fine. But the final decisions will be up to Analisa," Harrington said.

Analisa looked at Harrington, then Solis and finally Segretti. She felt an uneasy grip as they all returned her glance. The perennial threat of responsibility came upon her, in an instant, with the weight of a thousand uncertainties. What words of accord or treaty could she manage to concoct. She was still weighing an unexplained incident in Germany with a discovery of white powder that, in the end, had proven to be as profound as the first tea cup she ever unearthed.

The question to Analisa became how far could something go until it surpasses its own limits? She was placed in a position where everything was changing rapidly. Boundaries and paradigms were shifting into uncertainty. She needed reassurance.

Analisa felt vulnerable until she saw Segretti nod his head and smile at her once again. He displayed a silent sensitivity and reassurance that was not much different than what were his tendencies during all his arms negotiations. Except, his gesture toward Analisa was genuine and fatherly, lacking all cunning and guile.

It was all the assurance she needed. Analisa felt a surge of comprehensive philosophy take hold of her. It spread within her and developed a rigor that grew commensurate with expectations. Suddenly, she was ready to move on with her own confidence. She trusted it would lead to the conclusions that would satisfy the ancient deities and their oracles. The result of her decision, she hoped, would help two aging family members, and forgive whatever transgressions occurred in Germany. Analisa felt in control of the bargaining and knew what decisions would be best for everyone. She knew this because she was convinced the powder had purposely linked them all through a fine intricate web.

"If that's the case," Analisa said. "Then, I think we should go to Sandretto Hills."

UMBERTO Nunarro stood on the balcony of the motel looking out into the dark night. He leaned over the railing watching as lights from an occasional vehicle sped along Commerce Drive. The sight of the recently opened road was a confirmation Nunarro saw as a cleared route to his personal destination. The world of complication had given way to a single directive that was nothing less than his potential coronation. His time had finally arrived. The short drive to Sandretto Hills would be the last part of his journey to eventuality.

Nunarro looked away from the road and saw the dark silhouette of a lone Harris Hawk circling above the motel. The hawk, which usually hunts in groups, gave out a distinctive, lonely cry. Nunarro let the bird's sound take shape. He listened to its full range, allowing it to coexist with his thoughts, but he did not permit it to intrude into his personal intent.

As he walked back into the room the cry of the hawk grew faint, as it climbed higher and deeper into the night. The sheer curtains billowed behind him as he approached the table. He picked up the bags containing the glass bottles filled with gasoline and sugar. Nunarro took a final look around the room. Then he handed one of the bags to Orisi; acknowledging the junctures of his devout mission.

"When we get downstairs, call Ubaid from the pay phone in the lobby," Nunarro said. "Tell him to be at the storage facility in one hour. He's to do nothing but show up."

Nunarro sat quietly in the passenger side of the car reviewing the plan in his mind. He closed his eyes and envisioned himself breaking the lock to the garage, knocking out the ignition housing of Harrington's truck, exposing the wires and crossing them so the truck would start. He would back out the truck while Orisi followed him to the export company in Phoenix. There he would deliver the white powder. Once the powder was delivered, he and Orisi would stay at another hotel under different names for several days. When he felt the time was right they would then fly home, hopefully arriving before the powder was delivered to the emir. At the completion of the successful journey, Nunarro hoped to enjoy a new high mark of honor to his business, and revise a stigma he could live with.

Nunarro watched as Orisi left the lobby of the motel, and placed the second bag of bottles on the back seat. Orisi's mood had changed noticeably. He appeared angry, clearly rattled by the phone call. He forcibly slammed the back door, a clear demonstration of his frustration.

"What went wrong with Ubaid?" Nunarro asked.

"He lives for conflict," Orisi responded. "He's mad because we didn't include him earlier in our plan. He looks for trouble even when it's not around."

"Put him out of your mind."

"I will. Especially after tonight. We'll never have to see him again."

"I don't need anything to go wrong tonight, Mario," Nunarro cautioned.

"It won't. Unless Ubaid continues to act like a fool."

"I don't care. Ubaid is important only for what we may need him to do if things go wrong. All that counts is getting the powder to the emir. If we know what Ubaid is like, I'm sure the emir does too. Getting the powder to him takes precedent over everything. So don't get distracted by that fool. He could undermine the mission. This mission is all that counts. But keep in mind; it will only be successful if we both get to see the powder delivered."

Nunarro removed his cell phone from his pocket, and the envelope the emir had given him with the name of the export company. In the envelope was a detailed map showing the exact roads leading to the export company. Nunarro had memorized the route, as well as the surrounding area. He tapped in the number and looked at the map one last time.

"Yes?" came a scratchy, terse response.

From the sound of one word, Nunarro suspected the man was possibly Egyptian.

"My name is Umberto Nunarro," he announced.

"Ah, yes. I was expecting your call," the man responded. "Actually, I expected you to call sooner."

Nunarro was certain the man was Egyptian. Listening carefully to his inflections, and the emphasis placed on short vowels, determined the dialect was Cairene. The most prominent in Egypt.

"Well, I called now," Nunarro countered. "I will be at your company tonight. Is that a problem?"

"No. I've pledged to our mutual friend, I would be available, anytime."

"Are you at your place of business now?" Nunarro asked.

"No. But, I could be there within the hour."

"You'll need to be. Do you have arrangements made?"

"Of course," the man responded curtly, a bit annoyed.

"Good. I'll call you again when I get closer," Nunarro said.

"Is there anything you need?" the Egyptian asked.

Nunarro thought for a moment. It was a perfect time to second guess himself. The offer was an opportunity to hedge against any potential trauma.

"Do you have a car I can use?" Nunarro finally asked.

"Yes. I will have one here for you. Or, would you prefer my personal car and driver?"

"Yes. Your personal car would serve me better."

"Our mutual friend also asked me to give you any assistance you need, including a private and safe place to stay. Is that something you need?"

Suddenly, some of the plans Nunarro had put in place, were no longer needed. He welcomed the help the Egyptian offered, and felt things were going in his favor. Yet, he still remained alert and attentive.

"That would be most helpful," Nunarro said.

"It's already been arranged. Based upon our mutual friend's request, I can arrange transportation for you out of the country. In fact, he insisted on it. You must be very important to him."

Nunarro felt a sense of worth beyond his expectation. It was something he hadn't felt in a long time. Taking the powder from Harrington was attached to a strange dichotomy, with uneven parallels and built-in pardons. Because his felonious actions would be condoned by the emir, that would become the one judgment needed for his vindication. Nunarro suddenly felt a sense of freedom, set loose from those things that had him bound to self doubt.

"I'll take your offer," Nunarro said. "I would need arrangements...for two."

"It's done," the Egyptian said. "Will there be anything else?"

"Just be ready for me."

"I'll await your call."

The Egyptian disconnected from the call. Nunarro put the phone back into his pocket.

"Things seem to be getting better for us," Orisi observed.

"We're not done yet," Nunarro cautioned.

"Are you going to call the emir?" Orisi asked.

"Not now," Nunarro responded. "Once we make the delivery, then I'll call. Let's go," he said. Orisi started the car and drove toward the Sandretto Hills storage facility.

AGENT Cummings had been in constant communication with the agents assigned to the surveillance plan to follow Analisa's SUV. Agent Heller began the surveillance. He continued to take pictures as Segretti, LaTesta and Mafaldi entered Analisa's vehicle with Harrington and Solis. Heller stayed at a safe distance as Analisa drove up the ramp to Interstate Ten. Traffic was sparse on the interstate, but Heller maneuvered behind a vehicle between himself and Analisa. She drove at a moderate speed, in one lane, making it easier for Heller to follow.

Agent Cummings had anticipated Analisa would be driving back to Prescott. He devised a tag team surveillance plan, involving multiple cars at different locations along the interstate. In addition to himself and Heller, Cummings assigned Agent Tyler as part of the team. Cummings wanted to keep the operation to a limited staff. By not drawing upon extensive agency resources, he was able to operate within the guidelines of his immediate directives and keep his ulterior motives from scrutiny.

When the targeted vehicle approached Marana, Agent Heller followed the surveillance plan and drove off the exit, where Agent Manning had been parked. Manning was in phone communication with Heller and entered the interstate, making a smooth transition to the surveillance. Agent Heller quickly got into another vehicle waiting for him, and continued on the interstate behind Agent Manning's vehicle.

As Analisa drove into Eloy, Agent Manning exited the interstate. Agent Heller resumed his surveillance. The pattern continued seamlessly through Eloy, past Casa Grande, Coolidge, Chandler and Cave Creek.

Based on constant coordinates from Agents Heller, Manning and Tyler, Cummings quickly positioned himself on the access road parallel to Pioneer Parkway. From the location Cummings had chosen, he could join the surveillance he anticipated would lead to Harrington's house. The sheriff's department also assisted in the surveillance. Sheriff St. Cloud had assigned two patrol cars to remain close to the house.

Cummings anxiously waited, intending to ensnare Pietro Segretti. His sinister anticipation revealed itself through a lurid sneer that contorted his face. His breathing became a bit deeper as he listened to the periodic reports relating to the progress of Analisa's van. As he anticipated, she drove straight for Prescott, bringing Segretti closer to his clutches.

Cummings enjoyed the flush of hatred blending into his vindictive nature. The impulse that ran concurrent with his vice would find the needed justification to his bruised vanity, and ultimately, would be dignified by time.

He withdrew an Italian Leverletto knife from the compartment in the armrest of his car. He would use the instrument as a backup; a prop to be planted, if he had to explain why he needed to kill Segretti. Before the night was over, Cummings knew his memory would align with his intentions and bring about a fulfilling reminiscence.

Cummings sat back in the dark car. He needed to be alone, cultivating the rumbling of his inner rant. It was such a bold calling it incited his feelings and increased his craving for his own worth. The culmination of his maddening quest was at hand. All he had to do was wait patiently a little while longer.

SHERIFF St. Cloud had been informed of the surveillance by Agent Cummings. He was positioned at Willow Creek Road, two miles north of Pioneer Parkway and south of Sandretto Hills. The briefing Cummings offered St. Cloud was limited. The omission of information was calculated. It was designed to inform St. Cloud of an in depth plan, but not the hidden intent. St. Cloud accepted the inclusion of his authority from the Homeland Security agent, but felt the protocol held an underlying danger. St. Cloud could not focus on anything specific causing him to remain doubtful and suspicious. Perhaps, it was because Cummings was vague and went beyond the concealment of certain information. Perhaps, it was because he knew of the simmering grudge Cummings held for Segretti, and how it spread beyond reason.

St. Cloud was accustomed to different levels of obscurity and danger. He sensed Cummings was propping him up as some sort of shield for his own purposes. Somewhere in the underground workings of repulsion, Cummings had poured a foundation of mire set to pull down anyone oblivious to the possibility of conspiracy.

St. Cloud felt attuned to some things while others fluttered nearby just within his reach. The premonitions of his Native America ancestors were a heritage that was always swirling around him. Spirits slipped through unknown dimensions whispering of caution in an unspecified language. It was a strange fascination that plagued St. Cloud as he sat in his car aimlessly waiting for Pietro Segretti, a potential terrorist, to arrive and to witness the actions of Andrew Cummings, a roguish Security Agent.

The quiet elements of the night made St. Cloud aware of a deep foreboding. Something else was brewing. He could feel a danger; a private cold war was heating up that had been secretly planned. St. Cloud sensed a deceptive narrative designed to include him into a coarse haplessness. The Sheriff knew he had to first identify the true danger. Knowing what that was, could prove to be his best protection.

ANALISA felt weary from the long drive. The ache in her back and her legs were feeling heavy and dull. Her shoulders automatically hunched.

She could feel the muscles tightening at the base of her neck. She shifted in the seat, trying to make herself more comfortable. Lights from the oncoming cars caused Analisa to squint and blink rapidly as her eyes felt dry. Analisa did not like driving at night, but she knew they were nearing Sandretto Hills.

Deciding to give Segretti the two hundred pounds of powder was a decision Analisa made with little reservation. However, all financial negotiations would be of no interest to her. She would not accept any part of the money. What she would like, although she had no rightful claim to it, was some of the powder. More importantly, Analisa hoped Harrington would tell her what occurred in Germany. It was more than curiosity that compelled her to know the mysteries of his life. Analisa understood her own life was about those things she discovered. Her discoveries where like giving birth. Those things that unfolded for her were hers by blood, entrusted to her nurturing. Her connection to Harrington was like an umbilical connection to the powder. It was ethereal, more than an urge to collect great art. Owning a portion of the powder was like possessing the past and having proof of its untainted existence. The powder was a real life, and one she could hold near. She felt its heartbeat...the heartbeat of the Universe.

"Turn right on Glassford Hill Road," Harrington said. "Then take the ramp to Eighty Nine to Pioneer Parkway. From there, it's a short drive on Pioneer to Willow Creek Road, then to Commerce Drive. You know where the storage facility is, right?"

"Yes," Analisa said. "I know where it is."

"We'll be there shortly, Pietro," Harrington announced. "It won't be long now."

MARIO Orisi looked in the rear view mirror. He saw Ubaid and his men in the car behind him. Although they were there for support, Orisi had a sense, not of danger but of trouble. The silent threats in Ubaid's eyes, the daring tilt of his head, the arrogant way he turned his back all concerned Orisi. Appalling traits of indifference, meant to threaten and offend, appeared to be Ubaid's sole expression. It was the only thing he had a relationship with.

Nunarro reached toward the back seat and retrieved the two painters' caps. He handed one to Orisi and put the other on his head. He lowered the flap covering his face. He adjusted it, so the holes allowed for an unobstructed vision. With his face completely covered, he had no concern for the four security cameras at the storage facility.

Orisi drove into the storage facility. He continued down the alleyway stopping in front of the storage bay that housed Harrington's truck. Nunarro quickly got out of the car, and retrieved the hammer and the nail punch from the back seat. He stood in front of the garage door and placed the nail punch directly on the lock. With one powerful swing of the hammer, the lock broke open allowing Nunarro to lift open the overhead door. Once the door was open, he reached for one of the bags filled with the bottles of gasoline and sugar, leaving the second one for Orisi. He closed the car door. Orisi drove out of the alleyway, continuing to a sandy buffer area behind the facility.

Ubaid's car entered the alley, passing Harrington's garage. He stopped at the far end. Ubaid opened the car door and stepped out. He looked up at the overhead security cameras with great distain, as he walked slowly toward Harrington's garage.

Inside the garage, Nunarro flipped on the overhead light. He could still smell the remnants of the chemical spill. The odor hung in the close confines of the garage. It was a noxious smell Nunarro could also taste. Nunarro quickly dismissed the smell. He walked to Harrington's truck and noticed the locked tool chest on the open flatbed. Jumping up on to the flatbed, he broke off the lock with three blows from the hammer. He quickly lifted the lid of the chest. Seeing the bags piled within it, he removing a knife from his pocket and sliced open one of the bags. Nunarro paused for a moment before touching the white powder. He blocked out his feelings and postponed any judgment for the powder. He deferred all needs, knowing there was much to do. The night could still hold contradictions, capable of nullifying any accomplishments.

After cutting open two more bags, he was certain he had found the intended treasure. The emir was sure to succumb to the purity of its whiteness; its rarity that had generated a desire and the commitment to all wishes. The powder was a force that could alter everything, including the need for the crime devised to bring its promise to fruition.

Nunarro quickly closed the lid of the chest and replaced the broken lock. Jumping down from the flatbed, he hammered out the lock to the door of the truck. It opened easily. He placed the bag of bottles on the passenger seat. Once inside the cab of the truck, he used the nail punch and hammer to dislodge the ignition housing. Once broken away, he reached in and touched the exposed ignition wires, causing the engine to start.

Ubaid approached the opened garage. He saw the red glow of the brake lights and heard the purr of the engine. Nunarro had started the truck and was about to drive it out, poised to revel in the glory of delivering the powder to the emir. Ubaid felt a twinge of jealousy, disappointment that Nunarro had taken the powder easily, and without complications. Being denied the simple victory, caused Ubaid to feel despondent being denied the privilege.

Suddenly, Ubaid heard the blaring of car horns. He turned quickly to see a car driving backwards toward him. Analisa's van moved forward in front of it. Three other cars turned abruptly into the alley behind Analisa's van. The lead car was driven by Agent Cummings. In the second vehicle were Agents Heller and Manning. Agent Tyler was driving the rear car.

Approaching from the opposite end of the alley was Sheriff St. Cloud. In an instant, all cars stopped, and the doors flew open. Shouts and confusion came from all directions. In an instant, the night became infused with insurgency and chaos. There was no time for calm reasoning, only anger, fear and aggression.

With his gun drawn, Agent Cummings ran toward Segretti. Grabbing him by the collar of his shirt, he forcibly put him against the garage. LaTesta quickly came out of the van and grabbed Cummings' arm. He yanked the gun, directing it away from Segretti. Cummings swung at LaTesta, hitting him on the side of the face. LaTesta retaliated twisting the gun from Cummings' hand and battering him against the wall. Mafaldi quickly joined LaTesta, punching Cummings, knocking him to the ground. Agent Manning fired a shot at Mafaldi, missing him by inches. LaTesta positioned his body in front of Segretti and reached for Manning who started toward them. He quickly grabbed Manning's hand, forcing his arm skyward. He then leaned his body into the agent's, battering him with his shoulder, while punching the agent in the face.

Heller and Tyler approached Ubaid's car. They crouched on either side of the car pointing their guns and shouting for no one to move. Shots came from within the car shattering the glass. The agents ducked and started shooting into the car. Gripping his gun, Ubaid walked toward the agents, comfortable with the challenge he craved. He fired a shot hitting the back of his car. From behind, he heard St. Cloud approaching and turned quickly to fire. St. Cloud leaned into the garage avoiding the bullet. He quickly fired his gun twice, hitting Ubaid in the shoulder. Ubaid spun around, tumbled backwards, hitting the floor.

From inside the garage, Nunarro heard the shouting and shooting. He quickly reached for one of the bottles of gasoline and threw it behind him at the opened door. The matches, extending from the bottom of the bottle, struck the pavement and ignited. The glass broke pouring the gasoline onto the match flames causing a fiery explosion. The saturated sugar formed an adhesive glob that stuck to the pavement and burned brightly. Nunarro threw two more bottles at the top of the open garage door. They too exploded. The blistering sugar dripped creating an impenetrable veil of fire.

Orisi had seen the other vehicles enter the storage facility. He heard the shouts, gun fire, and saw the smoke created by the gasoline filled bottles. Flashing lights and sirens from the sheriff's vehicles streaming down Commerce Drive toward the facility; distracted him momentarily. He wanted to drive back to Nunarro, but the plan was for him to wait on the opposite side of the garage. No matter what occurred, the plan was unchangeable. It was a tense moment, and Orisi fought his instinct to help Nunarro. His discipline kept him rigid within the parameters of the plan.

Over the sounds of shouts, gunshots and sirens, Orisi heard the roaring of the truck's engine. He heard it revving louder and louder. Then he heard the squeal of burning tires straining to catapult the truck through the closed wall of the garage. He watched as Nunarro crashed the truck through the wall. Chunks of wood, gusts of dusty plaster and streams of electrical wires and sparks spewed outward into the night. The truck broke through the wall and continued through the back lot of the facility. Momentarily, Nunarro had lost control as the truck fishtailed, dust kicking up around it. Nunarro spotted Orisi's blinking lights and drove toward them. They both continued out beyond the facility to Commerce Drive.

As they sped away, the two approaching sheriff's vehicle followed them with blaring sirens. Orisi quickly reached for one of the bottles. He threw it out the window. The bottle crashed to the pavement and exploded in a ball of fire. The first of the sheriff's vehicles swerved to avoid the fire. Orisi threw a second and then a third bottle. Fire rose up from the road causing the oncoming traffic to stop. The sheriff's vehicles reluctantly gave up their chase.

Shots continued to be fired from inside Ubaid's car at the agents as they ducked behind their own car. The back door of Ubaid's car suddenly burst opened. One of the men emerged firing an automatic weapon. The bullets echoed in the alleyway, crashing into the walls and doors of the garage. They struck the agents' vehicles and Analisa's van, perforating the doors and windows. Segretti grabbed LaTesta and threw him to the ground. He pushed Mafaldi down where they huddled, but Segretti tried to crawl to Analisa.

St. Cloud aimed at the man with the automatic, and fired one shot to the head. Blood and bone spewed from the man, as he lurched violently forward and fell to the ground. Manning and Heller continued firing at the car. Loud, painful screams emitted from inside it.

Harrington reached for Analisa and pulled her down on the seat. Throwing his body over her, he grabbed her head and buried it into his chest. He put his arms around her ears so she could not hear the carnage. Solis jumped over the seat and pushed Harrington and Analisa to the floor of the van trying to cover them both. Analisa remained quiet. Her eyes shut tightly.

"It'll be alright. It'll be alright," Solis shouted over the noise. "We're not gonna' die tonight. It just ain't gonna' happen."

There was no more shooting coming from Ubaid's car. A lifeless body slumped out from the open door. A mound of tangled bodies, riddled with bullets and saturated with blood, incorporated into the stillness of death. The alley rang with the echo of the gunshots and screams. Broken glass tumbled from the vehicles, as the distant sirens grew louder. Agent Manning turned quickly and aimed his weapon at Mafaldi, who was attempting to stand. He forced him against the wall as Agent Heller pinned LaTesta to another wall, his gun pointed directly at LaTesta's face. Agent Cummings slowly got to his feet and threw Segretti against Ubaid's car. He placed his gun firmly against his forehead ready to shoot. He managed to withdraw the Leverletto knife and clutched Segretti's hand with his.

"You son of a bitch," Cummings growled. "I knew I'd get you again. Get ready to die. Get ready to die."

Segretti freed his hand from Cummings' grip and the knife fell to the ground. Segretti reached for the agent's gun as it pressed against his head. They struggled and Cummings kicked Segretti, causing himself to fall to one knee. Cummings regained his balance and brought his gun to Segretti's face again.

"Enough! Enough!" Cummings shouted and finally gave into the seething urge to shoot Segretti.

LaTesta struggled with Heller trying to help Segretti. Mafaldi pushed Manning, defying his advantage and the gun. Ubaid regained his footing disregarding the blood and burning in his shoulder. He turned toward Cummings, raised his arm and fired one shot. The bullet entered Cumming's chest. At first, Cummings became rigid. He began to quiver and slowly went limp. His shoulders drooped, as the energy drained from him. He lost the strength in his hand, and the gun fell to the ground. He tried to retrieve it, but his hand would not respond to the command of his instincts. Cummings screamed from anger and the abject desperation born from being denied the gratification of killing Segretti. Ubaid fired twice more. Each bullet hit Cummings in the chest. He reared backwards, crashing to the floor.

Heller and Manning broke free of their struggles, turned quickly and fired at Ubaid. Six bullets tore into Ubaid's chest before he fell. LaTesta quickly dove for Segretti, once more trying to protect him.

"No," Segretti shouted. "Help Analisa."

St. Cloud ran forward, sweeping his gun side to side.

"Don't move!" he shouted. "Nobody move!"

Everyone knew stillness was their best protection. St. Cloud quickly approached Ubaid's car. He determined no one was alive. Agent Tyler jumped into Analisa's van, and held her gun to Solis' head.

"We're army vets and a lady scientist, don't shoot," Solis shouted.

"Just shut up and don't move," Tyler commanded.

As quickly as the shooting had started, was how abruptly it ended. The chaos began to subside. The lapse of danger had been recognized. LaTesta and Segretti stood together, defiant of the agents.

"Don't hurt those people in the van," Segretti commanded.

"Shut up," Agent Heller responded

"I said don't hurt those people," Segretti shouted. "Those people are no threat to you. They're my family. Hurt them, and you'll have to deal with me."

"You're in no position to give orders," Heller said.

"Hurt those people and that will change," Segretti said defiantly.

"Stand over there," Agent Manning ordered, and pushed Segretti and LaTesta against a wall, not far from where Cummings lay.

"Nobody's going to hurt anybody," Manning said. "Sheriff, get an ambulance here immediately," Manning continued.

"One will be here shortly," St. Cloud responded.

"Agent Tyler, get those people out of the van," Manning ordered.

Solis stumbled out of the van. Shards of glass and debris were lodged in his hair. Harrington followed, leading Analisa who was crying and shaking. Segretti started to approach Analisa.

"Don't move," Manning shouted to Segretti.

"Stop your shouting," Segretti said and proceeded to hug and comfort Analisa.

"It's okay. It's all over. It's all over, Analisa," Segretti whispered to Analisa.

The violence had subsided. Control had been reached. The disturbing tremors of aggression began to wane as a sense of restored humanity began to take hold. It was a complex victory, one ultimately measured in terms of restraint.

Segretti stepped back and looked down at Cummings. He saw blood seeping from the wounds, and the gripping agony that was the sum indictment of the waste of his revenge. The cross purposes that plagued Cummings ultimately yielded to a single dynamic. He was defiant in his choices, but the chain of attrition was formidable and offered no quarter.

Cummings meekly clenched his fist. He raised his arm slightly in a final act of defiance. He softly but angrily growled at Segretti. He parted his lips showing his clenched teeth. With his remaining strength, he feebly spit a tiny spray of blood that had gathered in his mouth. Slowly, everything began to grow quiet, dark and abstract for Cummings. Segretti appeared to be floating in the distance. He seemed to be going farther and farther away, disappearing behind a thick black cloud that eventually eclipsed him.

Cummings remained trapped by his unrequited anger. There was no escaping his personal failure that came in bitter rushes. The enormity of the night began to fold around him in uncompromising accusations. His unplanned desolation became acute as he felt abandoned even by the devil.

A guttural gurgle emitted from Cummings' throat. His face relaxed. His eyes became fixed, unblinking, seeing nothing. His chest stopped heaving. He became absolutely still, yet his fist remained clenched. Blood and saliva bubbled from his mouth, an inner spirit's final show of contempt. A final disconnect from a self-made delusion was witnessed by those standing around him. Segretti's glaring presence accentuated his humiliation and made his death more difficult. For Cummings, it was an unfulfilled passing. His own grumbling proved it was so.

A sorrowful mystery took hold of him with no regard for the possibility of a new life filled with forgiveness. The judgment of a coarse poetry rhymed only with dejection would be his epitaph. It would be insistent in its condemnation and have no meaning other than the hate died harder than the man.

UNITED ARAB EMIRATES

UMBERTO Nunarro walked among the crowd of Sheikh Rashid Terminal in Dubai International Airport. The terminal, like the entire airport, was elegant and refined. It had an order of civility that paid homage to the theater of dignity and taste. All around him was the unmistakable language of luxury. A thousand nuances glittered like polished silver, purposely conceived and placed to achieve a maximum reverence. Opulence on a grand scale, such as Nunarro saw all around him, was the art of preserving sovereignty.

The muted clamor of the crowd was a dignified mixture of cultures and geographies indulging in open privilege. The airport was just the entry point, opening to a land of exceptional prosperity. None of the human senses could possibly avoid the extraordinary order of enticement into a world of plenty. He saw the blatant abundance, and the state of acute luster, as a preoccupation and an offering of protection against anything.

As Nunarro continued his observation of the lavish surroundings, he began to believe it was only universal wealth that could settle wars. He walked under a row of lighted palm trees passing a kiosk where a woman was selling colorful silk scarves. The woman said something to a passing tourist in Arabic sing-song melody. She sang of the culture and tradition of marketplace sellers that had its roots in a nomadic antiquity. Another voice came over the public address system announcing the departure of a Royal Dutch Airlines flight from Gate 15. On his way to E-Gate, the designated area for passenger clearance, Umberto passed a prayer room. In the room, he saw several Muslim men kneeling and praying.

As he swiped the smart card given to him by the emir, the clearance system electronically scanned his data and allowed him to exit the terminal. Walking out of the terminal, a man dressed in a white thobe approached him.

"Excuse me, sir," the man said. "You are Mister Nunarro? Please come with me. I have a car waiting."

Nunarro followed the man to a black Mercedes Benz parked at the curb. Another man, also wearing a white thobe, stood by the back door, holding it open. Nunarro entered the car and the door closed behind him. The two men sat in the front. A dark glass petition rose slowly, separating them. On the side door was a silver tray containing bottles of cold water, a container of ice and a gold rimmed glass. Nunarro put several ice cubes into the glass and poured the water. He sat back in the seat and sipped it slowly, allowing himself to feel the reward and acceptance of his efforts. In the privacy of the car, he felt the soaring lyric of his deed. The well placed concerns and apprehensions, regarding the possibility of his failure, were rendered insignificant and dismissed by the cool feel of success. The plush leather of the seat and smooth, comforting hum of the car, were the reassurances that made Nunarro feel good about himself. It was no ordinary contentment, but rather an inner pronouncement of favored charm.

Nunarro looked out the window as the car passed in the shadow of the Jumeirah Mosque. The car continued on Jumeirah Road past the spice and gold markets, where people haggled for trinkets. Bargaining was a high art in the region, with a historical tradition in the selling of garments and pearls.

The emir was no stranger to the tradition. Consequently, Nunarro knew he had to be delicate with him. He would recommend a renegotiation to the original offer for the white powder. The emir was a man of enduring honor, and once an agreement had been struck, the slightest change would be seen as weakness and dishonor. Nonetheless, Nunarro knew he had no choice. He would risk his own disgrace for the nuance of a revised negotiation. He was certain the emir would not appreciate the renegotiation for the powder. He didn't know how much the slight alteration would affect him. There were times when foul air surrounds the best of intentions. His revised offer had the potential to be toxic. But, Nunarro knew nothing should wither his conviction.

The iron gate opened allowing the car to enter the rear of the palace. The yard was lush with palm trees, flowers and sculptures by Mohammad Hijjras, stating settlement and stability. Nunarro saw the emir standing under a shaded portico in front of a sculptured waterfall. The emir appeared slightly more relaxed, and a bit less preoccupied than the last time Nunarro had seen him. Perhaps, it was the delivery of the powder that gave him assurances and hope. The door to the car opened and Nunarro stepped out into the bright, hot day. He approached the emir who greeted him with extended arms.

"Good to see you, my friend" the emir said. "So very good to see you safe."

"It's good to see you, too," Nunarro said.

"How was your trip?"

"Your arrangements were precise. Thank you."

"I thought you already had too much to do. So, I took the liberty of making the travel plans for you."

"I'm glad you did. It took a great burden off me and made my plans easier."

"Come sit. Tell me how the operation went. I trust it was not difficult."

Nunarro sat in the chair next to the emir. A servant approached with a tray of water and fruit and placed them on the table. He poured the water and placed several pieces of sliced pears, dates and apricots on a dish. The servant added several pieces of thinly sliced ginger and a small group of seedless grapes.

"Thank you," the emir said.

Nunarro reached for the glass of water, and picked up a slice of pear with a fork.

"Are you hungry?" the emir asked.

"No, I ate on the plane. Thank you."

"You'll stay for dinner."

"Thank you."

"So, I understand not everything went well," the emir said.

"No, it didn't. But I trust you did get the delivery."

"Yes, I did. The shipment arrived yesterday. You did a fine job."

"Thank you. I trust the powder will suit your purposes," Nunarro said.

The emir suddenly became silent, nodding his head. He seemed to be trying to put together the simple elements needed to construct the words to explain a much needed reality.

"We'll see," he finally said. "Allah will show us what we need to see."

"It appears Allah has already been favorable by making it possible for the powder to be given to you."

"Yes, that may be so. I'm grateful I was chosen to receive the powder. There was formidable competition also vying for it."

"I was not aware."

"I monitored the incident. Present that night was Pietro Segretti. Have you ever heard of him or met him?" the emir asked.

"No."

"Well, I know Pietro Segretti. I know him well. For reasons only he knows, he also wanted the powder. He was denied. Hopefully, fate has lifted a hand for my needs. We'll see."

"As I said, I was there but somewhat removed from the others. When the situation got out of hand, I was fortunate to be in a position where I was bothered only by a limited struggle. Precise timing was favorable for me."

"Well, I'm glad for that. Pietro is not a man to confront. He's quite formidable."

"Then, I'm glad I avoided him."

"What brought about the difficulty with Ubaid?"

"I'm not clear as to what exactly happened. I was not directly involved in the situation. I was busy taking care of my affairs."

"Ubaid did not survive," the emir informed. "Neither did anyone who was with him. An agent of the U.S. Homeland Security was also killed."

"Your contact, the Egyptian, kept us very well secluded. I was not aware of the aftermath at the storage facility. I'm sorry about Ubaid. He was fearless."

"No man fears the guillotine, until the day his head is under it. At that time, there can be those who will still remain unfazed. For them, they are either fools or zealots. In either case…well…there is no either case. But enough of that. There's a matter between us. Our agreement is recompense for your efforts."

Nunarro felt a shaft of sunlight on his face as it cut through the overhead slats of the portico. He squinted but could not turn away from the glaring light or the blunt end of imminent negotiations. He sat there trying to prevent his body from going weak and slack. He felt the moisture in the palms of his hands. Rubbing them, he knew he could not alter the lines that traced his fate.

"Yes," he finally said. "The money."

"Twenty million dollars. You've earned it," the emir said.

"Well, perhaps I did. You agreed to pay me twenty million dollars for retrieval services."

"Correct."

"I'd like to part from our agreement," Nunarro said, his voice tentative, cracking slightly.

The emir became instantly enraged. His look became hard displaying disgust, sensing an undeserved betrayal. A true dimension of disbelief rose beyond the outrage and dishonor.

"I may be a fool and that may make me a zealot," Nunarro continued. "But in this case, there is a difference…."

"What is your demand?" the emir interrupted harshly.

"No. No demand…A request. A request that we forgo our original agreement. Our agreement was that you were to pay *me* twenty million dollars…"

"I know what our agreement was," the emir interrupted once again.

"Yes. The renegotiation is simple," Nunarro said. "With your indulgence, and permission, I would like the entire amount...all twenty million...deposited into this account," Nunarro concluded and put a folded piece of paper on the table.

The emir refused to look at the paper. He felt it was dirty and unholy.

"Please," Nunarro said.

"I refuse to touch that paper," the emir said defiantly.

"It can't hurt you. Not any more," Nunarro pleaded.

The emir remained defiant and stood up. His shadow fell across Nunarro's face. The emir's mind had already devised a punishment that would be totally appropriate to the level of dishonor.

"Please," Nunarro said again. "That paper contains bank information. Information that is the account of Mario Orisi. I want all the money to go to him. Our agreement was I would get the money. I want Mario to have it all."

The emir appeared confused and disbelieving.

"I don't understand," the emir said.

"I think you do. I'm not renegotiating our agreement in any way that would dishonor you. I would never do that. And, please don't look upon it as such."

The look on the emir's face changed to a strange, troubling delight. The redefined terms seemed implausible, in a way that was hopeful. Nunarro's reconstructed provisions defined pure nobility that was spoken by his blood.

"You had your reasons to obtain the powder, and I truly hope it can fulfill all its promise," Nunarro said. "I hope the application you choose for the powder can give you and Aaminah peace. I had my own reason for getting the powder. It had nothing to do with money. I want my own peace, and it has no price....Not twenty million...not any amount."

"You would give up that amount of money?"

"No, that's not the issue," Nunarro corrected. "How can I accept it?"

The emir looked at Nunarro and admired the way his power came by actualizing his emotions. Nunarro claimed a status for himself that had built-in encouragement. His truth and energy were overtaking things considered to be legends and myths. The emir realized Nunarro needed to be loyal to the future, even though he would carry with him many disappointments. But he had assigned conclusions for himself, made easier if the emir accepted his offer.

Nunarro stood up. There were no longer shadows crossing his face. He leaned close to the emir looking into his eyes searching for the slightest hint of acceptance. The emir reached down and picked up the folded piece of paper from the table. He opened it and saw the banking information for Mario Orisi. He nodded at Nunarro and smiled.

"Thank you," Nunarro said. "Thank you for everything."

The emir turned his head and looked up to the open doors of the second level of the palace. The breeze blew the curtains and billowed around Adilah. She was standing there projecting her own defiance and hope. Nunarro smiled and stepped around the emir. He climbed the white stone stairs to the upper level and walked through the garden. Adilah stepped out of the billowing curtains. She walked toward Nunarro and embraced him.

Nunarro suddenly felt joined to something greater than himself. Adilah had filled a void that had plagued him in the past. She offered him a key to his future, and the long held void faded away. There was a new life unfolding inside her embrace. A new textured set of experiences and mysteries had taken hold of him. Contradiction gave way to new possibilities. It all seemed to come from Adilah's embrace.

Nunarro was uncertain whether the powder could cure Aaminah, and provide the emir with some control over mortality. It remained to be seen if the powder had that capability. But, Nunarro was certain the powder had its own intentions, to bring him and Adilah together. Feeling her was all the proof he needed.

Any word would have been too much for Adilah to utter. The smallest syllable would have been a distraction. Silence was the power and secret needed to shelter her feelings. Just holding Nunarro was the only thing she could permit herself to express. Within her soft sighs, Adilah released all her apprehensions, and learned the most about herself. The willingness to allow for possibilities and surprise bolstered Adilah's trust in things she had formally resisted. A new set of motives that challenged traditions and superstitions suddenly shaped her future. There was something strong and personal about her conviction that was too deep to unravel.

Adilah's future was her own, spoken for by the pathology of renewed convictions. She felt a sense of safety that promised to bridge all human flaws. Adilah was certain her relationship with Nunarro would be the slightly imperfect antidote against the onslaught of time. It was her connection to Nunarro, planted on the very day he carried her off into a ditch protecting her from falling pipes; that developed according to a detailed plan. She was uncertain as to when it really all started. Her only conscious frame of reference was that day, in the ditch, announced loudly by the clanging of the pipes. The possible conjectures could come from many points of reference suggesting something different. She found it better to avoid the complexities of those possibilities. They no longer mattered. What she knew for certain was the demand placed on her that would require a new way for her to dream. Everything seemed to be fitting in the exact way she had prayed. Now, all she needed was to have the powder Nunarro had successfully retrieved to fulfill its legend, and restore Aaminah to good health.

ARIZONA

DAVID MacMillian and Alan Dietz sat with their client, Pietro Segretti, in Sheriff Joseph St. Cloud's office. Gino Mafaldi and Alberto LaTesta were also in the office, along with Henrietta Dell. When she heard of the shooting, Henrietta Dell abruptly left the County Supervisors Meeting she had been attending. Before she appeared at St. Cloud's office, she met with Agents Manning, Heller and Tyler. It was a detailed meeting, complete with horrific images taken from the security surveillance video at the site. Each agent briefed Henrietta individually and relayed an identical observation. They all admitted Cummings' actions incited the chaos by focusing on Segretti while ignoring the threat from Ubaid. He increased the level of confrontation and nullified any preventive responses. Henrietta listened intently to each of the agents' testimonies. She accepted what she had suspected. Cummings' motivations were revenge-based and self-serving. The reality left her with a high level of disappointment, and an increased disdain for human corruption.

The office was cramped with little room for anyone to move. The collective mood was sullen. It stayed thick and close. The residual energy of the violence had a pedigree Segretti was familiar with. In some cases, the consequences could be defensible.

He recalled his confrontation as a teenager with the local Mafioso who had dishonored his sister. In defending her honor, his response resulted in violence and death. The aftermath of the altercation had provided Segretti with an understanding and acceptance for the protocols needed for justice. He aligned his nature with the demands of reconciliation, especially because the mechanics involved for retribution, were thinly disguised as the laws of survival. It was through this philosophy for justice, Segretti was able to cope with the details of the incident at the Sandretto Hills facility. He was manhandled and threatened but emerged unscathed. His friends and Analisa were uninjured as well, allowing him to honor the delicate intricacies of fortune. Cummings' demise was the result of his own inner failings, and became insignificant. Segretti was acutely aware of the festering anger and remorse Henrietta felt over the killing of Cummings. But, he also knew she accepted the fact. It was Cummings' wanton indulgence and personal desire for revenge on Segretti, that summoned forces to ensure his own death.

Segretti looked at Henrietta. It was clear to him she knew there was little that was random about the slaughter at Sandretto Hills. She was aware the underlying paths to destruction had been drawn by the victims' own forces. Cummings' pettiness and spite were the dark catalysts that made him irrational, blinded by a fool's heart. The strain on Henrietta's face was a telling example of the fictions she needed to embrace that conflicted with the honor she needed to protect. It was personal to Henrietta because justifying the inconvenience of a misplaced authority, was an affront to her. Cummings' behavior went beyond the margins that framed the basis of her office and her nature. There was no way to exonerate Cummings for his misrepresentation of justice, other than to properly honor his assumed bravery and dedication with the usual distortions of specifics and details.

For Segretti, the matter was less problematic. Ubaid had unintentionally saved his life. That was a truth requiring no refinement. The reality allowed Segretti to sit in Sheriff St. Cloud's office with the confidence of marginal restraint.

"We all saw the videos from the surveillance cameras at the Sandretto Hills storage facility," Attorney MacMillian said. "It's very clear my clients did not perpetrate the incident. In fact, the images show conclusively my clients were victims."

"There are several other matters that need to be clarified before we can come to that conclusion," Henrietta retorted.

"Such as?" MacMillian said with a hint of annoyance.

"Let's first establish why Mister Segretti, LaTesta and Mafaldi were at the facility," Henrietta pressured.

"Mister Segretti was here visiting with a family member, Analisa Scotti, who he's known ever since she was a child. There's no disputing that, Miss Dell."

"Yes, we've already established the relationship, Mister MacMillian. But, we need to clarify why Mister Segretti, along with his associates, were at the facility with Analisa Scotti."

"Analisa was doing anthropological studies on a relic her fiancé, Mitchell Harrington, had found. She wanted to share with Mister Segretti certain details of her work. Perfectly innocent."

"Can you explain why the relic was hidden in a garage which Mister Harrington rented under an assumed name?"

"Stored, not hidden," MacMillian corrected. "Mister Harrington wanted anonymity before he found the proper time to present this relic to the scientific community."

"Can you go into detail regarding it now?"

"Without having met with Analisa to learn the particulars of the relic, I'd have to defer the question to her. But, I would assume she is being questioned about that very relic."

"Clearly, we will pursue the particulars of the relic," Henrietta said. "As for the identification of the men killed at the facility, only one of them is known to us. His name is Ubaid. However, we have reason to believe the two men shown in the surveillance footage, with their faces covered by masks, are Umberto Nunarro and Mario Orisi. Both are Italian nationals. Does your client or his associates know either of these men? Do they know Ubaid?"

"I'll defer to my clients on that question."

Segretti wanted to make the right impact with his response. He turned to Henrietta and looked directly into her eyes.

"No," Segretti said firmly and honestly. "I do not know any of these men."

"Given your varied business enterprises," Henrietta said. "You've never had any business associations or any other sort of dealings with them?"

"No, I have not," Segretti, said remaining firm and relaxed.

Henrietta turned to Mafaldi and LaTesta and asked the same question. She received the same response.

"Okay. Now, let's go back to the relic, Mister Segretti. Do you know of any reason why someone would want to steal it from Mitchell Harrington's truck?"

"I'm sorry, Miss Dell," MacMillian intervened. "We cannot establish for certain the theft concerns the relic and not Mister Harrington's truck. Unless we establish this beyond a doubt, it really becomes a non-issue."

"Fine, I won't argue the technical point no matter how obvious the theft. Mister Segretti, what is your real interest in the relic beyond your concern for your young cousin's work?" Henrietta asked pointedly.

Segretti took a deep breath knowing this was not a time for insincere pronouncements.

"I've been told the relic has properties that can heal; restore health. I have two ill and aging relatives back home. I came here to purchase a portion of the relic to administer to them in the hopes they could regain health."

"Is there no traditional medical assistance you could acquire for your family members? Why put all your efforts in a relic that may have none of the benefits beyond what a competent doctor can provide?"

"My relatives are beyond standard protocols."

"So, what is the benefit of the relic to their condition?"

"Once again, Miss Dell," MacMillian intervened. "Without specific information from Analisa Scotti, as to the potential benefit of the relic, I don't think Mister Segretti is qualified to make a medical assessment."

"Fine, let's leave it for now. Is there any portion of the relic left, Mister Segretti? Was it all on the truck?"

"I'm not certain. I need to discuss it with Analisa," Segretti said.

"Judging by the direction of this questioning," MacMillian interjected. "It's clear to me your focusing on the relic demonstrates clearly you recognize Mister Segretti and his associates, bear no responsibility for the incident at the Sandretto Hills facility. So with that established, and if there are no further questions, there's obviously no reason to detain my clients. Consequently, I'd like to recommend we conclude this preliminary meeting," MacMillian announced.

"Are your clients planning to return to Italy?" Henrietta asked.

"Yes, but certainly, my clients would avail themselves to any additional questions that can help unravel this unfortunate incident. They would remain in my recognizance and be more than happy to assist in any way possible in this investigation."

Henrietta reconciled with the fact, the incident at the facility had already been resolved. It became obvious there was no sub-text beyond what the images on the surveillance video described, and what her agents had reported. There was nothing more to suspect. For Henrietta, it was a matter of charged poles of human conflict between Cummings and Ubaid that subscribed to the rituals that brought about their collective demise.

Henrietta could not rationalize their destructive actions, nor did she even try. It was a prescription outside her authority, and distressing to her sense of concern. She rose from her chair and looked at Segretti. Instinctively, she knew Segretti's survival was based on something foretold and implemented by Ubaid's actions. There was an abstract proof Henrietta knew could not be argued rationally. Fatalism was governed by its own laws and patterns. She knew defying the laws was a fool's effort.

"No, Mister MacMillian," Henrietta said. "If Sheriff St. Cloud has no issues relating to his jurisdiction, and then I see no reason to detain your clients."

St. Cloud shook his head, indicating it was over. Except for Henrietta, the room suddenly became free of the choking atmosphere. Everyone was free to go, relieved of the potential for the violation of injustice. It was only Henrietta who still held on to the troubling thoughts that kept her burdened and disappointed. It would take all her effort to reconcile with the forces that pressed in on her to try and claim her perspective of trust. Ultimately, she knew she would regain her balance and spirit, but it would be a long time before she learned how to trust human nature.

ANALISA Scotti sat in the interrogation room down the hall from St. Cloud's office. Harrington and Solis sat separately in nearby rooms. Two Sheriff's deputies were assigned to each room and conducted the preliminary interrogations. The windowless rooms were identical in size. The bare walls were in need of paint. Each room contained a small table and three folding chairs. On each of the tables sat a tape recorder with a microphone. Strategically placed, in each room, was a video camera.

Analisa was still visibly shaken, and brushed the tiny shards of glass from her hair and clothing. Before being interrogated, Harrington had advised Analisa and Solis to be as truthful as possible. They were to reveal everything they knew about the incident, as well as the powder.

The interrogating deputies believed they would get most of the information from Analisa, as she appeared the most vulnerable. The deputies interrogating Analisa were professional, offering a gentle tone to gain her trust, so she would be more amenable to telling them what they needed to know. Consequently, the two deputies were female. Deputy Terri Blair was the lead interrogator. She was more experienced than Deputy Barbara Littleton. Before entering the interrogation room, Deputy Blair insisted she and Deputy Littleton wear feminine civilian clothing. Deputy Blair brought in a cup of hot water and a box of tea. She opened the box of tea and placed a tea bag into the cup for Analisa.

"Here. Drink some of this," Blair said. "It will help calm you."

"Thank you," Analisa said, and sipped the tea.

"Is there something else we can get you?" Deputy Littleton asked.

"No. This will do. Thank you."

"What occurred at the Sandretto Hills storage facility must have been a frightening ordeal," Blair commented.

"Yes, it was. It came on so suddenly. I've never seen such violence."

"You must have been shocked?"

"I was, yes."

"I'm glad you were not injured. Did any of the men there hurt you?"

"No. Actually, Mitchell and Hector went out of their way to protect me."

"Good. I'm glad. What's your relationship with Mitchell and Hector?"

"Mitchell and I are in a relationship."

"And Hector Solis is Mitchell's friend?"

"Yes. Hector and Mitchell met in Iraq. They are army buddies. I've only recently met Hector."

"How do you know Pietro Segretti?"

"He's family; a cousin to my sister's husband. I've known him since childhood."

"Did you live in Italy then?"

"Yes."

"Did you know the other men, Alberto LaTesta or Gino Mafaldi, friends and associates of Mister Segretti?"

"Yes, I knew them, too."

"Can you tell us why Mitchell's truck was stolen? Though, I don't think it was the truck the thief was interested in. I believe it was what was in the truck. Could you tell me what was in the truck?"

"I think you already know."

"Yes. It was a powder, I understand. But, I need some insight to the powder. Was it drugs, heroin?"

"Absolutely not. The powder was gold, pure gold."

"I thought gold was a solid, yellow, not a powder."

"It is. That's the gold most people are familiar with. This gold is different. It's pure gold, single-atom gold. In that state, it's white and a powder."

"I've never heard of such a thing."

"You have now."

"What can you tell us about the powder? The gold?"

"It's ancient, precedes biblical history."

"Mitchell and Hector brought it home from Iraq as what? A souvenir?"

"I wouldn't call it a souvenir."

"If they brought it home from Iraq, then could we call it contraband?"

"No, you should call it a relic. It belongs to science. That's why they brought it here. So scientists could study it."

"Is this powder illegal?"

"No more illegal than any gold ring you could buy in a jewelry store."

"But something tells me the powder is more precious. What makes it precious?"

"In the things it can do."

"Things that would interest Homeland Security? Why was Homeland Security involved?"

"You'll have to ask them. Other than instigating the problem, I can't think of any reason they would be involved."

The reminder of the results at the storage facility showed up on Analisa's face, causing her to frown. Her lips began to quiver. She needed to put some distance between herself and the night. Analisa felt mauled, physically and emotionally. There was an exaggerated slur to everything she felt and thought. The tiny shards of glass in her hair seemed to come alive and crawl under her skin, invading her like thousands of insects. Every word she spoke was a stand in for the tears she wanted to shed.

"Can I get you more tea?" Blair asked.

"No. But you can get me out of here, so I can go home and sleep. Mitchell, Hector, myself and Pietro and his friends were all victims tonight. We all just need to be left alone. Can you just finish up, so we can leave?"

Analisa's plea made the most sense of everything else that had occurred that night. Deputy Blair turned off the audio recorder and the video. She handed the box of chamomile to Analisa.

"Here," Deputy Blair said. "You may need to have more of this later."

Analisa walked out of the office feeling unsteady and chilled. She saw Mitchell standing at the far end of the hallway with Hector. Harrington was filling a cup from the water fountain, and Solis was leaning against the wall. Harrington turned to see Analisa. She appeared lost and fragile. He quickly drank the water and walked toward her. As she neared St. Cloud's office, Segretti stepped out. He, too, clearly saw the shock and dismayed look in Analisa's eyes. She temporarily guarded herself by crossing her arms around her body. But, it was the essentials of who she was that would navigate her back to her reliable core.

Segretti wanted to reach out to her, but he knew she would find her own way to put the night into perspective. Because she still had access to some of the gold, he knew it would guide her to a gentler reality. He smiled at her, and hoped it would start her in that direction.

"Analisa," Segretti said, putting his arms around her shoulders.

"I'm fine, Pietro."

"The worst is over We're all out of danger."

"I know. I just need some time to put this behind me. I'll be alright."

"I know you will."

Harrington approached and hugged Analisa. He kissed her cheek and pushed the strands of hair away from her eyes.

"I'm so sorry I got you involved in this, Analisa," he said.

"You had no way of knowing what was going to happen."

"I should have been more careful. You would think the army would have taught me to plan better."

"Don't be so hard on yourself. It's fine. Like Pietro said, the worst is over."

"I'm going to make sure it is."

"Mitchell, let's just go to your house, so I can shower and rest. That's all I really need right now."

"I understand," Harrington said, putting his arm around Analisa.

"Pietro, I have plenty of room at my house. You are all welcome to stay," Harrington continued.

"Thank you for the offer, Mitchell, but my attorney has made arrangements for us to stay with him. He wants us close in the event we need his legal services. He's also making arrangements so we can leave as soon as possible."

"Fine. I hope to see you before you leave."

"Please don't leave without seeing me," Analisa said.

"I won't. Trust me," Segretti assured.

Segretti hugged Analisa and shook hands with Harrington and Solis. A special trust had been forged between them.

Segretti left the office with Mafaldi and LaTesta. Once outside, Mafaldi took a deep breath of the cool early dawn air. He casually brushed the dust from his pants and the sleeve of his shirt. They got into MacMillian's car and drove away.

In the past, they had been involved in the type of violence that unfolded at the storage facility. It was something that disturbed them only to the extent they had to resort to skills and defer to a temperament they would rather avoid. Violence and destruction were never the aspect they liked about their work or their lives. It was just part of the warrior's art they accepted.

Analisa watched as MacMillian's car drove away. She stepped closer to Harrington and was glad when he put his arm around her. After Segretti's departure, she felt a little less safe. Harrington opened the door to the vehicle MacMillian had provided. Solis got into the rear of the car and spread out on the seat. He started to make a comment, but decided against it. There was nothing to say. At that moment nothing made sense.

Analisa moved closer to Harrington, resting her head on his shoulder. Several minutes into the drive, Analisa fell asleep as the silence in the car engulfed her.

IT was mid-morning when Segretti walked out to the cobblestone terrace of David MacMillian's house. The liquid pulse of the sun reflected off the beveled glass table on the terrace. The air was already oppressive. The only shade came from the two awnings that covered the sitting areas of the terrace. The soft sounds of the lawn sprinklers struck a melody at the heart of the lazy summer that Segretti recalled from his youth. Beyond the terrace was a large blue pool, surrounded by several lounge chairs. Mafaldi was sitting on one of the lounge chairs. LaTesta emerged from one of the colorfully striped cabanas. LaTesta wore a bathing suit and dark glasses that had been set out in the cabana. A towel was draped around his shoulders. He removed the towel and placed it on the lounge chair, then dove into the pool.

Adjacent to the pool was a clay-surfaced tennis court. Two grounds people were spraying the courts with water, and smoothing it with a mesh net.

MacMillian sat at the table, sipping water and focusing on an open laptop. Papers were piled on the table, an open briefcase by his feet. As Segretti approached, MacMillian looked up squinting against the sun.

"Pietro, how are you this morning?" MacMillian asked.

"Good. I see Gino and Alberto are taking advantage of your hospitality."

"That's what it's there for. Why don't you go for a swim and relax."

"No, thank you. Perhaps later. I'm thankful for what you've done for us," Segretti acknowledged.

"Any courtesy, I can extend, is my honor. I've been busy this morning gaining official clearance from Homeland Security. The difficulty I encountered, was freeing up your jet. But, you're cleared to leave whenever you like."

"Thank you. I'll arrange to leave after I say goodbye to Analisa. I want to see her before I leave. I'll go there later today."

"You're welcome to stay here as long as you like."

"That's generous of you. But, after I clear up some business with her, I will be going back home."

"Will you stay for lunch?"

"That would be nice. Can I impose upon you to arrange for a car to take me to Analisa's house after lunch?"

"I already have one at your disposal."

A slight breeze carried the smells of the clay dust from the tennis court, and the chlorine from the pool. They gathered on the air with a distilled sense of calm. Traces of a benign spirit swirled around the terrace and through the cedar slats of the porticos. It was a special alignment of nuance and remembrances Segretti yielded to. He sat back in his chair wondering if he should totally trust those things that bended in his favor. The cell phone rang, disturbing his thoughts. He reached for it and flipped it open.

"Excuse me," he said to MacMillian.

"Hello," he said into the phone.

"Hello, Pietro," he heard Gabriella say.

In an instant, Segretti recognized the trauma in Gabriella's voice. It was a level of distress he had never heard from her before. It was an offsetting rhythm that led him to suspect the worst of anything. "Gabriella, what's the matter?" he asked controlling his anticipation.

"Pietro, are you alright?" Gabriella asked

"Yes. I am. But, you're not. What is it?"

"I'm afraid I have bad news," Gabriella said. "It's Melia. I'm sorry."

Segretti understood the curtness. They were words used to convey the worst kind of tragedy. Segretti grew silent. Anger and remorse joined to form a cruel force. He closed his eyes and clenched his jaw. His whole body became rigid; a defense against all sights, sounds and his own rage. He no longer wanted to hear the lawn sprinkler with its melodic melancholy or feel the warm sun on his body. He wanted to ignore them, deny they existed. The sun, the sprinkler, his inner intensity, and Gabriella's words, all meshed, becoming elements of grief.

MacMillian watched Segretti and lowered the lid of his laptop.

"Pietro, are you alright," he whispered.

Segretti opened his eyes and relieved the pressure of the phone against his ear. He saw LaTesta emerge from the pool, and retrieve the towel, putting it around his shoulders. "Pietro?" he heard Gabriella say. "Are you there?"

Segretti took a deep breath, wanting to hide from anything else Gabriella had to say.

"Pietro?" she asked once more.

"Yes, I'm here," he responded. "I'm here."

"I'm terribly sorry about Melia."

"What happened?" he asked.

"She was late coming down from her nap. The nurse went into her room. That's when they discovered her."

"Was she in pain?"

"No. She had her lunch with Rosa; then went to take her nap. She was peaceful the entire day and in no pain."

Segretti felt a strong emotion gnaw at him, severing the connection that tethered him to Melia. He suddenly felt alone, adrift, almost like a helpless child.

"Pietro?" Gabriella whispered.

"I'm here," he responded. "How's Rosa" How is she taking this?"

"She hasn't stopped praying the rosary."

"Has she spoken to anyone?"

Gabriella did not respond. The scratchy tone of the long distance call implied something graver.

"Gabriella, why are you not answering me? Has she spoken to anyone?"

"Yes," Gabriella suddenly replied. "She has."

"Who has she spoken to? What did she say?"

"Everyone she speaks to is deceased. She speaks to her husband and Melia, asking them to take her with them. She was also singing."

"Singing? What was she singing?"

"An old local nursery rhyme, one from her childhood. She was singing it in a child's sing-song voice."

A deep sadness began to emerge within Segretti. He could remember Rosa singing the same nursery rhyme to him when he was a child. The past came back to him in bitter refrains. He recalled the children's rhyme was about magical birds carrying children over mountains, and to the stars, that remained bright at midday and never grew dim. The rhyme had themes of innocence, freedom and eternity. Suddenly, the meaning of the song for Segretti changed to reflect loss and regret.

Segretti felt the cold chill of guilt. He came to get the powder that might have helped Melia. But, it was too late. In addition, not being with her in the end and not being with Rosa was a braid work of torment that tightened around him. Regret and irony became linear and stretched out before him, giving every indication it would never end.

"Are you with Rosa, now?" Segretti asked, hoping for some type of reprieve.

"Yes," Gabriella said.

"Good. I'm leaving here as soon as possible. Can you stay with her until I arrive?"

"I had no intention of leaving her."

"Thank you."

"You know, Pietro, there's no reason for you to bring back the powder… Rosa has no use for it now."

"I know…I know she doesn't. I'm not going to purchase any. I'll just say goodbye to Analisa. Then leave. How are you handling all of this?"

"Call me when you're leaving," Gabriella said. "I'll feel better knowing you'll soon be here."

"I will. I'm sorry I came on this fool's journey.

"You did nothing wrong, Pietro. Time worked against you."

Segretti ended the call. He looked out into the distance. He felt emptiness, a loss of purpose and control. He desperately hoped for a signal to offer him meaningful direction.

"Pietro, what's the matter?" MacMillian asked.

"My aunt Melia died. I need to go back home immediately. You said I was cleared to leave anytime."

"Yes. I've already arranged it. What else do you need from me?"

"Have your driver take me back to Analisa's house. I'll have Alberto make the flight arrangements. When I return, I would appreciate if your driver could take us to the airport."

"Consider it done."

"You've been helpful, David, like a brother. I won't forget it. I just need you to do one other thing, if you don't mind?"

"Name it."

"Transfer two million dollars from my account, and put it into Analisa's bank account. Please get her banking information and complete the transfer for me. But I need you to do it after I leave. Not before."

"I understand. Anything else you need?"

Segretti knew there was a reason to distrust the flow of good fortune. Like all things that have opposites, luck was no exception. He looked down toward the pool and saw LaTesta and Mafaldi sitting comfortably on the lounge chairs, enjoying the calm and peace. They silently emitted a sense of reliability that Segretti found familiar. It was also a testament to accept the fluctuations of chance. Their presence, over the years, was a true example of kinship. They faced danger, such as the incident of the night before and proved their sense of connection transcended mortality. He thought the same of Melia and Rosa. Their collective spirits had evolved to a higher level. In some way, it offered Segretti the comfort he needed.

"No. That will be enough, David," Segretti responded. "I think I have everything I need."

ANALISA'S sleep was restless. She moaned, tossing and turning in sudden jolts. Harrington reached for her offering safety through his touch. At times, she opened her eyes to reassure herself he was there, watching and protecting her. Harrington resisted sleep, keeping a tight vigilance in the presence of any potential danger.

It was during those sleepless nights in Iraq, he taught himself to concentrate on the darkness. Surviving tense nights required a special kind of attention and familiarity. He would listen to the crackling sounds of wind blowing the sand, the in-and-out of his own breath and the blood rushing through his body. Now, he used his attention to comfort Analisa and measure her progress.

As the hours passed, he observed the dawn light had gradually yielded to the new day. Analisa twitched herself awake, turned from Harrington, and sat up in the bed. Her hair was stringy on her shoulders and covered her puffy eyes. She felt disoriented. There was an ache in her neck and jaw. Harrington noticed the bruises around her face.

"You okay, Analisa?" Harrington whispered, softly touching her face.

Analisa shook her head trying to untangle her hair. She combed her fingers through it, and gently massaged the back of her neck.

"I feel sore all over, but my neck and jaw feel worse."

Harrington knew it was because he held her head so tightly during the trouble at the storage facility. Analisa turned and saw the scrapes and tiny cuts on Harrington's hands and body.

"Are you alright?" she asked, running her fingertips along the angry looking cuts.

"They're nothing. I don't even feel them."

Harrington looked at Analisa's drowsy, swollen eyes. He saw in them a defiance that was disciplined and self-commanding. Analisa leaned forward and kissed his cuts and bruises. She stood and walked to the middle of the room and removed her shirt. She stood naked in front of the dresser mirror, and then walked into the bathroom with a sense of wounded victory. After a quick shower, Analisa emerged brushing her hair. When she was done, she put on a fresh pair of cotton shorts and a University of Arizona t-shirt. She walked over to Harrington and sat on the bed next to him.

"Why don't you stay in bed and rest," she suggested. "I'll go make something to eat. Do you still keep the coffee in the same cupboard?"

"Yes. Same place," he responded. "Nothing has changed since you were here last."

Analisa kissed his forehead and ran her fingers down his cheek and across the cuts on his chest. His muscles were just as hard as they had been several years ago. She suddenly noticed his skin was slightly rougher and weathered. She turned to the night table and saw a photo of herself standing with him. It had been taken sometime before he went to Iraq. She had not seen the picture last night nor had she seen it since the day it was taken. They were both leaning to one side, spontaneously reacting to something. His arm was around her. They were laughing. He wore a pirate's hat. She was theatrically fingering a plastic moustache. Her hair was shorter; his was longer. He was thinner. She was heavier. He was playful. So was she.

She turned from the photo and looked at Harrington. His eyes were fixed on her, more determined, somewhat frightened, and just a little less playful. Analisa gave him a small sardonic smile, and a reaffirming squeeze of the hand.

"Oh yes, it has," she responded as she left the room.

Analisa made a pot of coffee and toast. She put a bowl of fresh fruit on the table. Harrington came out of the bedroom wearing blue jeans, and a long-sleeved cotton shirt, refreshed by a warm shower. He poured a cup of coffee, and walked with Analisa into the living room. Solis emerged from his room and sat on a chair in front of the couch. The strains of the night were evident on Solis. He appeared to be a man who reached a point of abandon, but mostly he felt disappointed. He thought he had earned the right to leave violence behind him in Iraq.

"Good morning, Hector," Analisa said. "Would you like something to eat?"

"No, just coffee will do."

"I'll get it,"

"Stay there, I'll get it," he said and went into the kitchen.

"There's a mug on the counter next to the coffee maker. There's milk in the refrigerator. Fresh fruit and toast."

Solis poured himself the coffee, and returned to the living room.

"This is fine," he said and sat back in the chair. "Everybody doin' okay?" he continued.

"Yes," Harrington responded.

"Should we talk about it?" Solis said.

"I think we have to," Harrington confirmed.

"What in the name of anything, holy or scary, you think happened?" Solis questioned.

"I don't know. I was trying to figure it out all night. I came up with a lot of scenarios, but I can assure you none of them are probably what really happened."

"Do you think this is the same sort a thing that happened in Germany?"

A strange fright gripped Analisa at the mention of Germany. She looked at Harrington for a hint as to the vileness that occurred. She studied him for any clue to the incident.

"Possibly, but there's no way to know for sure," Harrington responded, remaining steady knowing Analisa was scrutinizing him.

"How did anybody know the powder was there? How did Homeland Security and the sheriff show up? Man, this was like a bad movie," Solis said.

"Well, we can be sure they were following us," Harrington responded, his breathing remained unstrained, his hands still.

"But, how were they on ta us? Who were the other guys that got killed? Where'd they fit inta all this?"

"They belonged to the guys that took the truck," Harrington reasoned.

"Yeah, but how did they know the truck was there? Did they follow us?"

"No, they were already there. They were in the garage when we pulled in. So they had to know the truck was there."

"Hey, Deuce, I hate ta bring this up, but do you think your friend, Tommy Bowles, had anything ta do with this?"

"Don't even think that, Hector," Harrington responded angrily.

"Just askin'. Don't get touchy. We were almost killed last night, so insultin' somebody ain't the worst thing."

"Questioning someone's honor is always the worst thing. Tommy would never turn on us. Don't even think or mention it again."

"Okay. Okay. I get it. So, the bottom line is we don't really know what's goin on."

"That's right."

"Do ya think this is all over? Ya think we're in the clear?"

"There's no way of knowing. But from now on, we'll act like we're being watched all the time."

"How much did they get?" Solis asked.

"About eight hundred pounds."

"That's not all of it, right? You had some stashed some place else, right?"

"It's a good thing I did. Something told me not to keep it all together. We also have what Heywood and Dobson mailed home to their families."

"Yeah, I still got what I mailed to my sister. That's another seventy-five pounds in all."

"So what happens now?" Analisa asked. "If you have more than eight hundred pounds left, what do we do with it?"

"Our plan remains the same. The scientific community becomes our focus now. We approach the proper channels with a great deal of caution."

"Do you think we should sell Pietro two hundred pounds?" Analisa asked.

"Losing half our inventory does make it a bit more difficult to sell," Harrington reasoned. "What do you say, Hector?"

"You said it was Analisa's call. That's the way it should stay. I don't think Black Eddie and Dobson would care. You know Bowles best, what do you think he'll say?"

"He'll leave it up to us."

"So it's done. What do ya say, Analisa, we sell ta Pietro?" Solis concluded.

"Yes. I say we sell him the two hundred pounds," Analisa responded.

"What we could have accomplished with more than eight hundred pounds, we can accomplish with six hundred plus. But, I want this to be very clear, I don't want a penny of Pietro's money," she reasoned.

"We'll talk about that when the time comes," Harrington responded.

"No," Analisa said adamantly. "We discuss it now. And, as far as I'm concerned, there's nothing to discuss. I do not want the money, nor will I accept it. That's final. You talk about honor. Well, I need you to honor my request. There's no negotiation here, Mitchell."

Harrington studied Analisa's face. Again he saw her fierce determination. She was on the edge of an offensive and offered no quarter. Harrington knew enough about the art of battle to know he was at a distinct disadvantage. He sipped his coffee and nodded his head.

"Right. Right." Solis said. "That's all resolved. Now, I need to know why all the fuss over the white powder. What ain't you tellin' me that I been askin' since the first day I fell inta the hole in the stinkin' desert and found this stuff. I ain't lettin' anybody outta here until I get my answers. Between Germany and now last night, I earned an explanation."

The mention of Germany once again sent a shiver through Analisa. She instinctively knew what occurred at the Sandretto storage facility was a mere extension of what singed the edges of every mention of Germany.

"Yes, you do, Hector," Harrington said.

"Glad you agree, Deuce. So, let's have it."

"What do you want to know?" Harrington asked.

"What do ya mean, what do I wanna know? I wanna know what you ain't been tellin' me. I wanna know about it all. Take me back ta the beginnin', the source," Solis demanded.

"The source is a good place to start," Analisa said. "Interesting you chose that expression."

"It just popped inta my head. So then, let's somebody start."

"I'll start," Analisa said. "But first, you need to clear your mind of anything you already know and believe," Analisa concluded, clearing her own mind and leaving the ghosts of Germany to remain a misty taunt.

" What I know about what?"

"You'll see as we go on."

"All I know is what I don't know. That's where you come in. Give it ta me from the beginnin'."

"The beginning is a perfect place to start," Analisa said. "The beginning I'm referring to is Genesis…"

"Genesis, like in the Bible?" Solis interrupted.

"What other Genesis is there, Hector?" Harrington said.

"Yes, Genesis like in the Bible," Analisa said. "Are you familiar with Genesis?"

"Just what I was told as a kid. You know Adam and Eve stuff."

"That's what I thought, years of misinformation to break down. Start opening your mind now. So let's go right to the heart of it," Analisa said. "Genesis, creation, the beginning. Genesis is where we're introduced to the Nephilim. Remember that term, it's very important…Nephilim."

Analisa rose from the chair and looked around the room.

"Mitchell, where's your Bible?" she asked.

"There," Mitchell pointed to the bookshelf next to the stone fireplace. "On the bottom shelf, where it's always been."

Analisa bent over and removed the red, canvas-bound Bible and handed it to Solis.

"What's this for?" Solis asked.

"To follow along. Turn to Genesis, Chapter Six," Analisa said.

Solis opened the book. He turned the flimsy pages, until he came upon Genesis and Chapter Six.

"Got it," Solis said.

"Good. Follow me. It says: 'That it came to pass when men began to multiple on earth…'"

"On the face of the earth," Solis interrupted. "It says 'men began to multiple on the face of the earth.' "

"Hector, you want to hear this or not?" Harrington intervened.

"Sorry."

"'Multiply on the *face* of the earth,' " Analisa said. 'Daughters were born unto them. The sons of God saw the daughters of men, and they were fair and they took them as wives. There were Nephilim on earth in those days.' "

"Great, I see it, Nephilim. That's what you're tryin' to show me, right?"

"Yes."

"Big deal. So, what I see here is, Nephilim married the fair women. So what? Who were the Nephilim?"

"Traditionally, Nephilim was interpreted as meaning giants…"

"Like Goliath?" Solis interrupted.

"Well, maybe and maybe not. In any event, that may be partially correct. In fact, Nephilim more accurately means: 'those who came down'. Or, 'those who descended.' In Sumerian, it means: 'those who from heaven to earth came.' "

"What do you mean those who came down like saints or angels?" Solis asked.

"No."

"No, No what? What are you tryin ta tell me, people came ta earth, like what, like extraterrestrial beings?"

"I'm not trying to tell you anything, Hector. I'm only relaying what ancient civilizations have observed. Their observations have been recorded on stone tables in caves…"

"Oh c'mon, I was only kiddin'," Solis protested.

"Hey, Hector," Harrington shouted. "You said you wanted to know, and here Analisa is trying to explain to you. So what is it? Do you want to know or do you want to remain uninformed?"

"I just didn't expect this."

"Truth can't be about what you would like it to be about," Harrington responded.

"I guess. But geez, don't rip off my head just because I'm findin' this hard ta believe."

"It's not your fault this is new to you, Hector," Analisa said. "You're not alone. Most of the world's population feels exactly as you do."

"That doesn't surprise me. We got every reason ta question this. So, these ancient cultures are sayin' what? Extraterrestrial beings came ta earth, right?"

"Yes."

"So, as just ta be clear, you're not puttin' me on. You're not lookin' ta have a good laugh at my expense?"

"Not at all. Why are you having difficulty dealing with this?"

"You're kiddin', right? It ain't right?" Solis protested. "It can't be."

"Why?" Harrington asked.

"Because I was never…I don't know…how can I believe that?"

"What do you believe, Hector?" Analisa asked.

"I don't know. Like I said, Adam and Eve stuff. I'll give ya the thing about the apple bein' a fairy tale. That was always hokey ta me, anyway. But, two people in a garden where they begot Cain and Abel, that bein' the way it all got started is somethin' my mind can deal with."

"So, I understand what you're saying. That scenario is easier for you to believe than what Analisa is explaining, right?"

"Yeah. What's wrong with that?"

"I don't know. You tell me."

"It's less complicated."

"Oh, is that right? How is it less complicated?"

"I don't know. Because it is, that's why."

"Only because that's what you've been told as a child," Analisa said.

That's what we've all been told for eons. Just because that's what we've been told, doesn't mean it's true."

"So, how do you know what you're sayin' is true?"

"The evidence is irrefutable..."

"Why? Because of what it says in Genesis?"

"That's not good enough for you?" Harrington responded.

"No, it's not good enough for me," Solis shot back. "It's just that I never heard it explained the way you're sayin'. That's all. Can you blame me?"

"No, I guess I can't."

"Good, because what you're sayin' runs contrary to everything established institutions have been sayin'."

"Keep in mind, Hector, the Bible is an institution," Analisa said. "It was written by men who had their own agendas. They wrote with an institutional arrogance thinking their conclusions would never be questioned or challenged. Genesis, as well as other parts of the Bible, is only small examples of truth with a heavy emphasis on myth and conjecture. There are other ancient texts, unearthed artifacts that express a different truth."

"So, wait a minute," Solis said. "So when you gave that lecture the other day about Darwin's missin' link, this is what you were sayin'?"

"Exactly."

"Now this time, you got my attention. I wasn't listenin' the other day. Go over it one more time for me. Real slow, so I can take it all in."

"Basically, what I was saying was Cro-Magnon or Homo sapiens did not descend from Neanderthal. They were different with different DNA. Enochian records suggest it was the Nephilim who spawned a new race prior to thirty-five thousand BC..."

"What are the Enochian records?" Solis interrupted.

"It refers to the first language of the Nephilim. It's considered to be the holy language used to name all things. It was the language last used by the prophet Enoch to directly interact with the Nephilim. The language is older than Sanskrit. After Enoch, the language morphed into a proto-Hebrew, which was a precursor to Biblical Hebrew. Enoch recorded the language in the Book of Loagaeth, which means speech of God, the speech of the Nephilim."

"Nephilim, those who came down from heaven?"

"Yes."

"Heaven bein' a better word for what? A star? A planet?"

"Exactly."

"I get it. I'll go along with that. What happened to the book of Enoch?"

"It was lost in the deluge. Certain modern linguists feel Enochian is not a consistent language. But, I guess that's the point. It's not a natural language as we know language…Anyway thirty-five thousand BC was the same era the advanced Cro-Magnons appeared and the Neanderthal faded out."

"Well, I'll be…They damn near hung Darwin for teachin' somethin' that went against the old beliefs. Now look what you're talkin' about. Makes Darwin look tame."

"We've come a long way since Darwin. But, we still have a long way to go."

"I don't know. I still can't get this concept inta my head," Solis confessed.

"Then go back a little bit in the Bible. Turn to Genesis, Chapter Three. I think it's twenty-one. Read what it says," Analisa said.

Solis flipped back through the pages until he came to Chapter Three.

"Here it is. Chapter Three. Twenty, what?" Solis asked.

"Try twenty-one, no twenty-two. Read it," Analisa said.

"Twenty-two 'Then the Lord God said See! The man has become like one of us, knowing what is good and what is bad! Therefore, he must not be allowed to put out his hand and take fruit from the tree of life, and thus eat and live forever.' "

"What do you think it means, Hector, when the gods say man has become like one of us? The word 'us' being the key here."

"Wow, one of us. That means multiple gods, right?"

"Yes, that's exactly what it means, and that's the Nephilim."

"Who were the multiple gods? I mean, did they have names?"

"There were many of them. Yes, they did have names. There are also stone reliefs of many of those gods."

"Gimme some of the big names," Solis said.

"The first would have to be Anu. He was Lord of the Sky. Then there are his two sons: Enlil who was called Lord of the Air, and his brother Enki, Lord of Earth and Water. Enlil and Enki were the original Cain and Abel. Then there's Lilith. Trust me, Hector, there's no shortage of Anunnaki gods."

"And there's like, what? Stone carvings of these gods?"

"Reliefs, yes. Anu is depicted with very large eyes, and what could be considered gold for hair and a beard. There are reliefs of both his sons. Unfortunately, compared to the writings and tables that have been discovered, much more has been lost to time, eroded by nature, bombed away by wars and just destroyed by organizations, because certain artifacts did not uphold the Biblical narrative."

Solis leaned back in his chair realizing he had been sitting on the edge of the seat, listening intently.

"Some of us have given this subject a great deal of thought," Harrington said.

"So, wait," Solis said. "You're basin' your argument on a coupla a chapters in Genesis."

"Don't be so naive, Hector," Harrington said. "Analisa and I have studied this for years. There's a whole scientific and linguistic community out there that has studied ancient tablets, read them and understood what they really mean."

"So where does this leave conventional religion?" Solis asked.

"The more progressive ones will hedge their bets. Some are doing so already by saying the Nephilim are the other children of God. The more moderate will deny, spin, ridicule. They'll do whatever they can to make it all go away. They've done a good job over the centuries to keep man in the Dark Ages. But, they're losing their hold. They know they can't keep the lie going forever. They know it, and they're afraid."

"Why would they be afraid?"

"Because they know the truth will always win out. And when it does, they lose all their power. Losing their power is their greatest fear," Harrington said.

"It's not power that corrupts. It's the fear of losing power that corrupts," Analisa said.

"Yeah, at least that much I know. Just hold up a little bit more," Solis said. "Let's get back to these Nephilim. Suppose, just for argument, I believe what you're sayin', or what the ancient texts are sayin'. What does that got ta do with the white powder?"

"The Nephilim set up a colony on earth approximately four hundred and fifty thousand years ago, to mine gold," Analisa said. "Things were going fine until the lower echelon of the Nephilim no longer wanted to do the work. So, the Nephilim combined their genes with Homo erectus. They created mankind so they would have someone to work the mines."

"So what you're sayin' is the Nephilim begot humans?" Solis said, feeling defeated.

"Yes. In their image and likeness."

"Yeah, and then what happened?"

"Well, the Nephilim also selected individuals, entrusting them with certain knowledge, like alchemy. Which I believe is converting the metal gold into the pure gold....The powder."

"Who were these people?"

"Who knows? A case can be made for many people throughout history."

"Who else knows about the Nephilim?"

"I would be confident in saying St. Germain knew of the Nephilim and the gold. He speaks of them. Read his work, you'll find it interesting. St. Germain refers to the time of the Nephilim as the Golden Age. He speaks of the Nephilim using airships for transportation. St. Germain talks a great deal about gold. He believed gold had its own inherent quality and energy to purify, vitalize and balance the atomic structure of the world. He knew gold contained an extremely high vibratory rate that could act on the expressions of life through absorption. He believed the energy within gold, was an electronic force that acted in a lower octave. The energy of gold acted as a transformer, passing the sun's force into the physical substance of our world, and the life evolving upon it."

"St. Germain is known to have created an elixir that could have made him bi-locational and gave him the ability to see into the future," Harrington said. "Not to mention a long life. In the middle of the eighteenth century, he was walking around Europe claiming to have attended the wedding at Cana. That was the catered affair where Jesus turned water into wine..."

"Is that true?" Solis interrupted.

"He says it was," Analisa responded. "And, if it was," she continued. "I believe the elixir responsible for his longevity was monoatomic gold. The people, who used the gold, as St. Germain explained, developed their spirituality. They become...well in a word, they become enlightened."

"Who else mentions the Nephilim?" Solis asked.

"There's a text called the Atra-Hasis Epic which chronicles the earth's history, and the need to create Homo sapiens to help mine gold so monoatomic gold could be produced. But, it was the Sumerians who were extremely familiar with it. There's so much evidence found from the Sumerian culture. Not as Nephilim, but as Anunnaki. That's how the Sumerians referred to them. Everything ever unearthed from the Sumerian culture indicates they knew about them. They saw the Anunnaki as gods fulfilling their earthly functions and communal duties. They were patrons, founders and teachers. They offered technologies, new ways of agriculture, and laws of justice. They were not idols of religious worship, nor were they ritualistic gods that subsequent cultures made them out to be. The Sumerians told us who the Anunnaki were. History and science can't disprove that."

"How did the Sumerians know so much about the Nephilim?"

"Because the Anunnaki led by Enki had their smelting and refining operation in Sumer."

"So, they went to Sumer. But where did they come from, these Nephilim, Anunnaki? What are they doin' now?"

"Hector, I think you heard enough for now. You need to let this all settle in. I don't think you're ready for the rest of it."

"You mean there's more?"

"More? Hector, there's a lot more," Analisa said.

"You know, Analisa, I don't feel any different knowing my origins. It's no big deal."

"The only thing that will make you feel differently is not being able to accept the truth about your origins. The origins of mankind. This is all about how we choose to deal with the things we discover. We can either accept the truth of those discoveries, or we can deny those truths."

Analisa saw from the look on Solis' face, he had gained a new insight into things he couldn't begin to imagine. Normally, she would ask for reciprocal knowledge, something he could impart to her that would also be informative. What he could offer, the thing he knew best, was the incident in Germany. He could explain the failings of human nature under the strains of conflict. After what she saw the night before, she would understand and not dismiss anything out of hand. It would be easy for her to understand. But because of her exposure to the violence of the night before, she knew she couldn't accept that knowledge. It was best if she didn't know what happened in Germany. Perhaps, when Harrington felt it was time to confess to her the particulars of the incident, she could be more able to open herself to the truth. But, the violence she witnessed was enough to last her a lifetime. There was nothing else she needed to know about the way a man screams and bleeds.

Analisa preferred to remain naïve about such matters. She needed to avoid the dark edges of a culture that can only bring destruction, damnation and despair. Avoidance was a form of protection Analisa needed. She had the ability to command it. It was her strength and her right. She would not yield. She found a comforting rationale through her choice of acceptance. From the look on Solis' face, he too found his own acceptance. He no longer struggled with things that were beyond his reach. Whatever existed, in the way of irrelevant theory and perpetuated fallacies that ran contrary to the texts of the ancients was of no concern to him. There was no reason for him to struggle with the enormous controlling forces in the world, when there was something as powerful as truth.

Solis knew Analisa was right about feeling good by accepting the truth. She seemed to be right about most things. All the concealed experiences throughout history had twisted themselves free and created a new kind of peace for Solis. There was no more reason for him to have nightmares over his days in Iraq. He knew why he was there, and why he fell into the deep hole to discover the powder. That became a new revelation for Solis. Not just a revelation, but the acceptance of a revelation that had given him an edge for the rest of his life. It was all a lesson, but Solis took the most comfort from Analisa's teachings, and he was glad for them. There was nothing else he needed to know. There was a new way for him to move through the world, knowing the greatest question he had about himself had been answered. He finally felt liberated.

Liberating the past, Solis reasoned, was the way to summon a new and proper future. A future where nothing was the same, only the way it was meant to be. Children of forgotten parents, left to find their own way. Wayward children struggling with their own journeys, until they found their way back home. Solis suspected that's what Analisa meant when she said: 'There's a lot more.' Maybe there was a lot more to know. More importantly, Solis knew there was a lot more to believe.

Solis wanted to ask her what that was. Then, he realized, there was no good reason to know how it would all end. Perhaps, somewhere in all the chapters of the book he held in his hands, contained all the answers. But, then again, he wondered what else the authors of the book would try to conceal or distort. What other inconsistencies or misinterpretations would they try to uphold, to protect the paradigms of control and convenience? Where in the book, or any place for that matter, was the fertile common ground best suited for the growth and maintenance of justice?

It all became too much for Solis to contend with. He deferred easily to accepting the path that led him to Analisa. She made it easy and plain for him. Once again, Analisa was right. Accepting the truth was all that mattered.

Solis remembered reading somewhere that "truth is beauty and beauty, truth." That might be so, but Solis felt that philosophy might be a bit overextended. Truth was truth. There was no other word for it. No other meaning was quite the same. Beauty could be debated, but not truth. Truth was absolute. It gave no quarter, no refinement, neither from history nor from itself. In the end, that's all he needed to know.

"You know what, Analisa...Deuce?" Solis said, feeling like he had suddenly become a new person, an orphan finally discovering his heritage.

Analisa smiled at Solis. Intuitively, she already knew what he was feeling and what he was going to say. For her, the matter of conclusion could be contained within his silence. Reconciliation had its own tone. It possessed its own language that resonated in just a passing glance or an ethereal expression. It was apparent through the spread of unimaginable fulfillment on Solis' face that convinced her she commanded the raw sprawl of his astonishment and his acceptance.

Solis was no longer an enigma to her. He broadened within a human dimension, where he allowed her to share the controversial knowledge. In the scope of that paradigm, and within the trust it generated, Solis became her friend.

Harrington did not share Analisa's intuition. He wanted to hear what Solis had to say. From the first day Solis was assigned to his command in Iraq, Harrington sensed the brash street-wise kid was a counter balance to his own judgments and experiences. He always seemed to belong just over his shoulder, and in his consciousness. Solis was a guide, a force that pointed to those things he needed to know and to breathe.

"What, Hector?" Harrington responded. "Tell me what you think."

"What I think is this, Deuce. Anybody not able ta deal with the truth about all this past lineage… the Nephilim…the monoatomic gold, all of it…well…they ain't got what ta eat."

END

Frank Prete is also the author of GORDIAN WEAVE and SECRETS TO NO ONE. He lives in Westchester County with his wife.